By Cynthia Keller

AN AMISH GIFT
A PLAIN & FANCY CHRISTMAS
AN AMISH CHRISTMAS

An Amish Holiday

An Amish Holiday

Two Heartwarming Tales

AN AMISH CHRISTMAS

A PLAIN & FANCY CHRISTMAS

Cynthia Keller

BALLANTINE BOOKS TRADE PAPERBACKS · NEW YORK

2012 Ballantine Books Trade Paperback Edition

Published in the United States by Ballantine Books,
an imprint of The Random House Publishing Group,
a division of Random House, Inc., New York.

BALLANTINE and colophon are trademarks of Random House, Inc.

An Amish Christmas and *A Plain & Fancy Christmas*
were originally published separately in hardcover in the United States by
Ballantine Books, an imprint of The Random House Publishing Group,
a division of Random House, Inc., in 2010 and 2011 respectively.

This book contains an excerpt from *An Amish Gift* by Cynthia Keller.
This excerpt has been set for this edition only and may not reflect
the final content of the forthcoming editon.

ISBN 978-0-345-52876-6

Printed in the United States of America

www.ballantinebooks.com

2 4 6 8 9 7 5 3 1

Book design by Liz Cosgrove

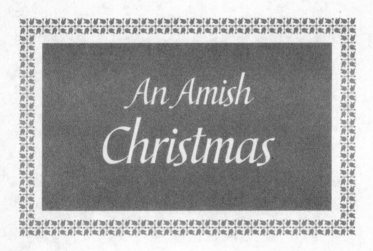

An Amish
Christmas

To Mark, Jenna,
and Carly

for whom I am grateful each and every day

And
for Jean Katz

we battle the darkness of sorrow
with the brilliant light of loving memory

Acknowledgments

It is a lucky writer who has the good fortune to have colleagues who are also friends. I have known and collaborated on many projects with my agent, Victoria Skurnick, for over two decades. She is supremely generous in deed and spirit, fantastically smart, and the most kindhearted person I know. She can also make me laugh until I cry, one of my favorite qualities in a person. In good times, she is the first to applaud me, and in bad, the first to extend a helping hand. It is a true privilege to call her my friend.

A special thank-you goes to Sharon Fantera, who is the godmother of this book and without whom it would not exist.

My editor, Linda Marrow, has been fantastic in every way, from her early support to her encouragement and wise suggestions. She is all you could want in an editor—plus, we had fun. I am thrilled and grateful that I had this opportunity to work with her.

I hope my husband and children know how touched I have been by their tireless cheerleading and their desire to help in whatever way I asked. Sharing this experience with you three has made it that much more meaningful. I love you with all my heart.

Chapter 1

✤

"You're looking a little pathetic there, Mom."

As her daughter, Lizzie, entered the kitchen, the words startled Meg from her reverie. Leaning on both elbows at the kitchen's butcher-block island, she'd been staring, unseeing, at the large tray of untouched cookies before her. She reached up to remove the tall witch's hat she'd been wearing for the past two hours, and set it down beside the tray.

"They're such cute cookies, aren't they?" Meg asked her daughter in a wistful voice. "Not one trick-or-treater this year. I can't believe it."

Lizzie, her laptop computer tucked under one arm, paused to stare at her mother's handiwork. "*Dude*, how long did it take you to make all these? They're insane."

"Don't call me 'dude,'" Meg responded automatically. "I thought it would be fun to try something different. It wasn't a big deal."

She had no intention of confessing to her fifteen-year-old how long the process had taken. After finally locating the correct chocolate cookies—the ones with the hollow centers—she had used icing to "glue" chocolate Kisses, points up, into the middles, then she'd painstakingly drawn hatbands and bows with a tiny tube of red icing. The result was rows and rows of miniature witch hats. Adorable. They would end up being tossed into the bottomless pits that were the stomachs of her thirteen-year-old son, Will, and his friends.

"Honestly, why do you bother?" Lizzie's muffled voice came from inside their walk-in pantry closet. Meg knew her daughter was grabbing her favorite evening snack, two Pop-Tarts that she would eat right out of the foil package. "No one cares. It's stupid."

Meg quietly sighed. Maybe it *was* stupid to hang the tissue ghosts from the trees in their front yard. To carve the jack-o'-lantern that was the centerpiece of the arrangement on the front steps, with hay, gourds, stuffed scarecrow, and all. Okay, so Lizzie and Will were too old for the giant figures of witches and goblins that she'd taped on the windows. Lizzie was at some in-between stage, too cool to trick-or-treat but probably looking forward to next year, when some of the kids would have driver's licenses. Meg anticipated there would be parties at different houses, no doubt with alcohol involved; she wasn't looking forward to that phase. Will had also declined going from house to house this year, preferring to goof around with his buddies on someone's driveway basketball court. But she'd thought Sam, her nine-year-old, might still have gotten a kick out of her decorations. Wrong. He never appeared to notice them, and he'd barely made it through a half hour of ringing doorbells before declaring he'd had enough of this holiday. What on earth had happened to Halloween being so much crazy fun, the way it was when she was a child? Didn't kids know how to enjoy a holiday anymore? Besides, she *was* cutting back on the fuss; in the past, she would have spent hours baking cookies for trick-or-treaters. This year she had simply combined premade ingredients.

Lizzie, armed with her snack, left the room as the jarring noise of the garage door opening announced that Meg's husband was home. She watched James enter and set down his briefcase in the mudroom before coming toward her. He looked exhausted. As the top in-house legal counsel to a large software corporation, he more than earned his salary. Somehow he managed to withstand endless pressure, maintain constant accessibility, and coolly handle one crisis after another. And those were only a few of his job requirements, it seemed to her.

Pulling off his suit jacket, he gave Meg a perfunctory kiss on the cheek.

"Happy Halloween," Meg said brightly.

"Ummm." His attention was already on the day's mail, which he retrieved from its customary spot on one of the counters. He was frowning as he flipped through the envelopes.

"Something wrong?"

"Too many bills, Meg." He sounded angry. "Too many bills. It's got to stop."

She didn't reply. In eighteen years of marriage, James had rarely complained about their bills. Sure, he wasn't thrilled with paying private school tuition for three children, but it was something he and Meg both wanted to do. Beyond that, it was understood between them and even among their friends that his wife was the saver and he was the spender.

Meg had always understood that *things* were important to her husband. It was he who purchased the designer suits, their fancy watches, her expensive jewelry. It was he who booked the first-class vacations. He was the one, in fact, who chose this enormous house. Even with three children, Meg had no idea why they needed five thousand square feet in one of the most expensive sections of Charlotte.

It was clear that growing up with very little had left a psychological scar on James that he tried to cover up with material trappings. She didn't like it, but she understood. That was what he needed to feel comfortable. He didn't brag or rub his success in anyone's face. Still, it was as if he had to have more of everything just to feel he was level with everyone else.

Recently, though, he seemed to have undergone a change in thinking. He had started complaining regularly about everything she and the children spent.

"Are you hungry?" Meg moved to open the refrigerator door.

He slapped the mail back down on the counter. "I mean it! The spending has to stop. We need to batten down the hatches."

She turned back to him. "You're right," she said soothingly. "We will—the hatches, I mean, and the battening. Now, can I get you something to eat?"

"I don't want anything," he snapped. "I'll be in my study."

Meg stared after him. Aside from his sudden financial prudence, he had been uncharacteristically irritable for a while now. And it had been getting worse, she realized, not better. She heard the door to his study slam shut. James was typically calm, even in a crisis. Especially in a crisis, she amended. That was one of the things she loved about him.

They met as sophomores at the University of Illinois in a nineteenth-century American history class. Meg happened to sit next to him one day early in the semester. When he began to juggle a pen, an assignment pad, and an empty soda can, it made her laugh. She grew more interested in him when he was the only one in class who was able to discuss all the major battles of the Civil War before the reading had even been assigned.

Their relationship had started out as more of a friendship. A little teasing back and forth led to some shared coffees, then pizza while studying for the final exam. Slowly, their connection grew and deepened. James proved to be a stabilizing influence on the flighty, directionless girl Meg had been. She had admired his strength, his solidness—not the physical kind but the kind that made her feel cared for and safe. Of course, she reflected with a smile, she hadn't minded that he was tall and broad-chested, with thick sandy-colored hair and large dark eyes whose intent gaze made her feel she was the most important person in the room.

By the end of junior year, it was clear to both of them that marriage would follow on the heels of graduation. While he went to law school, she set up their first apartment and helped support them by working in a boring but well-paying job as an administrative assistant. The plan had always been for Meg to go to law school once James had a job, but then she got pregnant with Lizzie, and that was that. Which was perfectly fine with Meg. She wouldn't trade one minute of time with her three children for anything in the world. Working would have been impractical for her, anyway, since they had moved to three different states over the years because of the series of job offers that came James's way. His drive and early success meant their lives were far more than comfortable. She and the children had everything they could ever need and more.

Maybe too much more.

She heard her older son coming downstairs—his feet, as usual, clomping rapidly rather than just walking. He was talking, his voice growing louder as he approached. "That is so *sick*, man!"

Meg rolled her eyes, understanding this to be high praise for whatever it was Will was discussing. She called out to him.

He stuck his head in the kitchen. He was slender and noticeably tall for an eighth-grader, with a face remarkably like his father's. Will wore a dark-gray sweatshirt, his face nearly hidden in its hood. "Hang on," he said to the room in general. "My mom, yeah."

Meg understood that he was using a hands-free phone. No doubt it was the newest, tiniest, most advanced gadget available. She swore that half the time she didn't know if her children were talking—or listening, for that matter—to her, to one another, or to someone else entirely on a cell phone or computer. Much to her chagrin, her husband aided and abetted the children's desire to be up on the latest electronic everything. It seemed as if he came home every other week with an updated version of some gizmo or other. The stuff just kept changing, rendering the previous purchases obsolete, but no one besides her seemed to mind. Though lately, she reflected, she hadn't seen the usual parade of new electronic toys, so perhaps James had heeded her protests.

"Will, what's the story with the science-fair project?" She tried to keep her tone light. Non-nagging. "And I'd like to see what you're wearing for the class photo tomorrow. No rock-band T-shirts, okay?"

He merely gave her a look as if annoyed by her interruption, then was gone. She heard him resume his conversation in the hall. "Two hundred? So what's the big deal?"

"Well, I certainly straightened *him* out," she muttered. She glanced at her watch. It was past the time she should have started hustling Sam into bed for the night; he invariably daw-dled, dragging out the process as long as he could. This evening there had been his minimal trick-or-treating, admiring and or-ganizing the candy he'd collected, and a full load of homework. He still hadn't taken a shower to wash off the remnants of green face makeup from his zombie costume. Rushing now, Meg transferred the cookies to a large plastic container. She frowned as she hurried upstairs; she would have to return to fin-ish cleaning up.

She found her nine-year-old seated at his desk, pencil in hand, hunched over a math book. He barely had enough space for the book, as his desk was nearly buried beneath the array of papers, random objects, and unidentifiable pieces of who-knew-what. Her younger son collected—anything. Meg didn't know why, but apparently Sam had never met a piece of paper, ticket stub, or souvenir he didn't love. Marbles, miniature cars and action figures, stickers, small plastic animals, and rubbery novelty toys—all were held in equally high esteem. His collection wasn't restricted to his desktop, however, or the desk drawers. Boxes and plastic containers of various sizes were scattered about his room, overflowing with the items Meg periodically gathered up from the floor. She didn't want to think about how many shopping bags full of his stuff were shoved into the back of his closet and on its highest shelves. She was just grateful he restricted himself to smaller treasures. If he'd amassed something like train sets or rocks, they would have been in big trouble.

"Sweetheart," she murmured, her hand on his shoulder. "It's late."

He looked at her and smiled. That grin always melted her heart. While Will looked like James, and Lizzie, with her chestnut-colored hair and hazel eyes, favored Meg, Sam was utterly unlike either one of them. His hair was shiny, almost black, and his brown eyes were so dark that they appeared black as well. Short for his age, with a slight build and pale complexion, he exhibited an inquisitiveness neither of his siblings did.

His nature was different as well. He was far more prone than the other two to feel anxious. He worried and fretted over what might or might not happen in his life, in the country, and in the world. He asked endless questions, which the family called "Sam's what-if questions," about how they would handle a wide range of disasters that might suddenly befall them. Hurricanes, fires, robbers, plagues, waterborne pathogens—Meg was often scrambling to explain how they would escape various calamities. Sam was her sensitive one. Even when the other two were younger, they hadn't seemed quite as fearful. For several years, starting when he was four, Sam often refused to go places that, for some reason or other, sounded frightening to him. It might be another child's birthday party or the beach or the zoo. No amount of reassurance could change his mind.

Thankfully, that phase had passed, but when he got under the covers at night, Meg still spent a few extra minutes sitting on the bed, just hugging him. She knew that, at those times at least, he felt utterly relaxed and safe.

Sam closed his math book and stood. Pale streaks of green makeup were smeared not just on his face but on his arms and T-shirt. There was an outburst of shouting downstairs as Lizzie and Will embarked on what Meg figured had to be their fiftieth argument of the day. Both Sam and Meg ignored the familiar sound.

"Do I have to shower?"

"Yes, sugar, and it has to be fast." Meg smiled as she put her arm around him and led him toward the bathroom.

It was nearly eleven-thirty before all three children were in bed and she had finished cleaning up downstairs. She was exhausted, but, as was her routine, she put on her nightgown and got into bed with her pink leather appointment book—a Mother's Day gift from James two years before—and five pens, each a different color. She had long ago determined that assigning each family member his or her own color made it easier to keep track of who had to be where and when.

She fluffed up two pillows against the headboard and leaned

back. She loved this room, with its soothing tones of pale green and beige, the soft cotton sheets and goose-down duvet on the bed, the muted lighting. It was so peaceful here. James still hadn't emerged from his study. Usually, by this hour, he was under the covers, reading a newspaper or business magazine, waiting for her to join him.

She opened her date book, enjoying, as always, the soft leather and thick cream-colored pages. Her own appointments were in red. Tomorrow started with a planning meeting for the high school's spring fund-raiser, after which she had to take in her BMW for a lube and oil. She made a note to bring her book club's choice for this month to read while she was waiting.

After that, food shopping for the small dinner party they were having on Saturday, so she could start preparing a few days in advance. She would pick up James's dry cleaning and the pearl necklace she was having restrung as a gift for Lizzie, a gift Meg knew would be unwanted now but which she hoped would be appreciated in later years. Then it would be time to drive to piano lessons (a protesting Lizzie—purple ink) and to the shoe store for new sneakers (Sam—blue ink). Swing back around to retrieve Lizzie, then get Will (green ink) from basketball practice at school, and home to make dinner. She scheduled an hour the next night to pay bills and catch up on paperwork.

She turned to her master to-do list, a veritable rainbow of color-coded tasks at the front of the book. Lizzie needed her dental checkup, and Meg jotted that down in purple below the forty-some other tasks on the list. No matter what she did, that list just kept getting longer. It seemed that for every item she completed, another two instantly took its place. Some of the less pressing obligations reappeared month after month, causing Meg guilt pangs over what she viewed as her negligence. Still, there were many days when she wondered what all of this was adding up to. Was there a prize for being the person who accomplished the most errands? Maybe the day you got to the end of your to-do list was the day you died. Just in case, she thought with a smile, it's a good thing I always leave some stuff undone.

She closed the book and was placing it on her bedside table when James came into the room. Having left him alone all evening, Meg had assumed that by now his bad mood would have dissipated, but she saw that she was mistaken. His mood was, if anything, darker.

"Honey," she began.

He threw her a hard look. "Not now." He began unbuttoning his shirt, his anger evident in his sharp movements.

"James, what on earth is the matter?" She refused to go along with this any further.

"I said not now," he snapped. Their eyes met, and he softened, his shoulders sagging. "I'm sorry, Meg, I shouldn't . . . I'm really sorry."

She leaned forward. "Why won't you tell me what's going on?"

"Nothing's going on." James exhaled slowly. "It's been a rotten day, that's all. I shouldn't take it out on you."

"You didn't even say hello to the kids tonight. Please tell me what's bothering you."

He sat down on the edge of the bed and kissed her on the

lips. "I'm sorry for being a jerk, but I swear, it's nothing." He smiled, shifting gears. "And a very happy Halloween to you, too. Sam better have saved me some of his candy."

"You know our Sam," Meg said lightly, her tone matching his change of mood. "He had a candy bar and some M&M's, then put the rest away to dole out to himself sensibly."

James shook his head. "I can't imagine doing that. My friends and I used to eat ourselves sick on Halloween."

"The simple pleasures of childhood."

He stood. "I'm going to brush my teeth and all that good stuff. Then we'll talk. You'll tell me about your day and the kids' day, and I promise you'll have my undivided attention."

"That's great." Meg smiled at him.

Bending over, he kissed the top of her head, then grinned and went into their bathroom. She heard the water running at his sink, her husband singing an old Bob Dylan song in an exaggerated scratchy voice. It would seem that he had put aside whatever unpleasantness was on his mind. She didn't believe it for a second.

Chapter 2

❈

Meg flipped through a rack of party dresses but made no attempt to pick out anything. She knew that any dress she selected for Lizzie would be met by an immediate veto. Meg understood that she wasn't exactly on top of what teenagers liked to wear, but she didn't think she deserved her daughter's inevitable look of disbelief whenever she held something up for consideration. As far as choosing something for Lizzie to wear to the high school's big Christmas Dance—Meg wasn't even going to try.

She looked over at her daughter, who was searching through racks across the Nordstrom dress department with great intensity. Her mind flashed on Lizzie's early years, when Meg had had the pleasure of outfitting her little girl however she wanted. She remembered the bunny-print pajamas, the white bathing suit with navy-blue bows, a yellow sundress. Little white summer sandals, a tiny jean jacket. That all ended around the time

Lizzie turned four, when she insisted that her rainbow T-shirt, flower-print stretch pants, and a white tutu were the perfect outfit for preschool. Every day. And, thought Meg with a smile, when she added the red glitter party shoes, it went so easily from day to evening wear.

"Okay." Lizzie appeared at Meg's side, her arms filled with dresses. "I'm going to try these on."

"Want me to come with you?"

"No." The girl bustled off before her mother could follow.

Meg had spotted a flash of dark purple satin and some black nylon material with big silver sequins among her daughter's choices. She reassured herself that the odds were against Lizzie actually choosing one of those. This was only their first attempt at finding a dress for the dance. No doubt they would have to endure several shopping trips before Lizzie, growing ever more tense and irritable, made the final decision. This was the reason Meg had allocated six weeks to navigate the minefield. All the hysteria had to unfold in, paradoxically, an orderly fashion. If past experience was any indication, Lizzie would question whether she had made the right decision until the moment she walked out the door to attend the actual event.

Sure enough, when Lizzie returned from the dressing room, she was holding only one dress, pale pink with simple beading details and cap sleeves. "What do you think of this one?"

"Very nice," Meg said, reaching for the dangling price tag. She froze. "Five hundred dollars? Are you joking?"

"Oh, Mom, come *on!*" Lizzie snapped. "These kinds of dresses are expensive."

Meg stared at her. "Did I somehow give you the impression

that I would spend five hundred dollars on a dress for a school dance? A dress you'll probably wear once?"

"What did you think it would cost? This is what a decent dress goes for. And it looked great on me." Lizzie sounded exasperated. "Excuse me, but what do *your* dresses cost?"

Meg drew herself up. "What my clothes cost is none of your business!"

"Well, how hypocritical is that?"

Meg was infuriated, but at the same time she felt a stab of guilt, knowing that she did have some obscenely expensive clothes hanging in her own closet. James liked her to dress a certain way when they went out. He even seemed to enjoy shopping with her every so often, encouraging her to buy the best suit, the good Italian shoes. Meg also had to admit that she was frequently inconsistent with her daughter, splurging on a ridiculously expensive sweater or skirt for Lizzie, then feeling she had gone too far and sharply drawing the line at another item.

Still, she didn't expect her daughter to take those treats for granted. And she deserved some respect from her child.

"Put the dress back." Her voice was cold. "We're going home."

"What are you talking about? We have to get something."

"No." Meg's eyes flashed. "No, we really don't."

"I can't believe this! All the good dresses will be gone by the time we can go shopping again." Lizzie shook her head. "Come on, Mom. You know you'll want to get me something nice in the end, so there's no point to this."

Meg didn't respond. She strode toward the exit, knowing

her daughter had no choice but to follow if she didn't want to walk home. When Lizzie caught up in the parking lot, she was empty-handed and silent. She spent the entire drive home texting on her cell phone. Meg's feelings vacillated between anger at her daughter for her sense of entitlement and annoyance at herself for the way she handled these issues. Sometimes being a parent was so hard, she thought, just so darn hard.

Back at the house, Lizzie slammed the car door and stomped upstairs to her room. Still upset, Meg went to the extra freezer in the garage, peering inside at her choices. She and James were going out that night with two couples, both of the husbands executives in James's department. She had left him a message that morning reminding him. She wasn't looking forward to it, but she understood that socializing was important to his success. Before leaving, she would put something together for the kids' dinner. Lizzie was responsible for watching Sam, something she did periodically and with surprising good nature. Will would be at home as well.

"Lamb chops it is."

Meg reached into the icy air to retrieve the shrink-wrapped package. She dropped the frozen meat into the kitchen sink and set her bag on the counter, hitting the play button on the message machine.

"I tried your cell, but it went right to the message," came her husband's voice. "Did you forget to charge it? I got your message about dinner tonight, but I'd forgotten all about it, and I can't do it anyway. There's an emergency meeting at work, so we have to cancel. I'll take care of it. Don't wait up for me."

An emergency meeting on a Saturday night? If I didn't

know better, Meg thought, I'd swear he was cheating on me. Fortunately, she knew he really would be at the office, because things there had been going from bad to worse over the past few weeks. That's where James was right now, spending a sunny Saturday behind his desk. Of course, he was hardly the only one whose company was in dire economic straits these days. He was closemouthed about the specifics of his firm's troubles, but she could see the stress in his distractedness and growing irritability, not to mention the new dark shadows beneath his eyes.

She had no idea what it all meant, but it frightened her. Was there a chance he might lose his job? He assured her that wouldn't happen, but she read the newspapers and, like everyone else, saw the layoffs going on across the country. In addition, Meg knew virtually nothing about where their savings were invested; James had always handled that end of their finances. She did—and didn't—want to know if they had lost anything substantial in the stock market over the past months. James made it clear he didn't wish to be questioned on these issues, and she knew better than to press him. She had resolved instead to stick her head in the sand because the only other option was to drive herself crazy with pointless speculation. Besides, she thought, it had to be more helpful for everybody if she remained upbeat.

Meg hoped that whatever was going on wouldn't get bad enough to interrupt their Thanksgiving plans. Every year for the five years they had lived in North Carolina, Meg had invited several families in the neighborhood for a huge feast, one she spent a solid week preparing. They were families who, like them, had no other relatives or lived far away from those they did have. Meg always put in a call to her parents, her only living relatives, but they weren't up to making the trip from Homer, New York. Not that they would have come anyway, she knew. Nor, to be honest, would she have wanted them if they did.

Meg had always had a strained relationship with her parents, both of whom were so controlled and controlling, so disapproving of everyone, including her, their only child. She could never understand their narrow-mindedness or why they felt entitled to pass judgment on everyone else's supposed shortcomings. One of the best moments of her life had been finding out she had received a full scholarship to college. The first day of freshman year couldn't come too soon for her. Her parents couldn't understand why she would go to a school so inconveniently far away, and she didn't bother explaining that was exactly why she had chosen it.

Before she was born, her parents had started what grew from a tiny general store to a small department store with a specialty in fishing equipment, selling everything from waders and rods to bait and tackle. They had never forgiven Meg and James for refusing to move back to her hometown and join the family business after they married. Without the couple's participation, the store, their lives' work, would disappear once they could no longer run it.

Their irrational demand had come as an unpleasant shock, and it was pretty much the last straw. Both Meg and James found this long-held grudge incomprehensible. It cast a pall over the few phone conversations she and her parents did have. But Meg tried to remain on decent terms with them for the sake of her children.

She often wished that the three of them had cousins, but James, too, had no siblings. His parents had died in a car accident when he was in his twenties. Sadly, there was no one else, other than James's elderly uncle, who was in a nursing home in California, in the advanced stages of Alzheimer's.

Meg loved Thanksgiving, so, despite the lack of extended family, she went all out. Up went all the construction-paper turkeys and pilgrim hats made by the children over the years in elementary school. She fussed over gourds, cranberries, and Indian corn to create painter-ready still-life arrangements. Berries and bright orange, red, and yellow leaves accented any surfaces that struck her fancy. Meg suspected that, as they had on Halloween, her efforts would go unnoticed at best or, at worst, be ridiculed. Nonetheless, she would do it for herself and for the younger neighborhood children who would be in attendance.

With an unexpected free evening, she could get a head start on her menu plan and to-do list. She went to get some paper, mentally reviewing what needed doing. Just for starters, polish the silver, wash and iron the linens, check the candle supply, bring up the largest serving platters from the basement closet. The list would be a long one. If she was lucky, she might get the kids to help with the platters, but that was about the only work she could expect to wrench out of them.

As she grabbed a pad from the kitchen desk drawer, she glanced up at the bulletin board that held the family's notes and schedules. She saw there was an addition to the Holiday

Posting. About a year ago, Will began tacking up a selection of each month's strangest yet real holidays, and it had become a regular feature on the board. Lizzie and Sam also weighed in—all this information culled, Meg supposed, from the Internet, apparently the source for everything in the universe. Or at least their universe. November, it turned out, was Peanut Butter Lovers' Month. Sam had written that it was also Diabetic Eye Disease Awareness Month. Today Meg saw two new contributions in Lizzie's handwriting: Start Your Own Country Day, following right on the heels of Absurdity Day.

Meg laughed. Now, *those* were holidays.

The front door slammed. That would be Will getting dropped off by Michael Connolly's parents. The two boys often went skateboarding in the park, with Meg and Emma Connolly sharing carpool duty.

Meg heard her son go upstairs. "Hi, honey!"

No response.

She walked out to the bottom of the stairs, spotting Will just before he disappeared from view on the second floor. "Hey, Will, how are you?"

He stopped and took a step back, holding on to his wildly colorful skateboard. "Oh, hi, Mom." He gave her a small smile.

Meg regarded him. Something didn't seem right. For two years, a full set of braces had slightly altered the appearance of his lower face, but in September they had been replaced by a smaller retainer. The facial change was minor, but it was visible to Meg. "Honey, why aren't you wearing your retainer?"

"You're fast, I gotta give you that." He shifted the skateboard in his arms. "Yeah, I was going to tell you."

Uh-oh. This was why he'd tried to bypass her downstairs: so she wouldn't get a good look at him.

"Will?"

"It broke. I left it on a bench, I swear, for, like, two seconds, and somebody must've sat on it or something."

"But the case should have protected it."

Will fiddled with a skateboard wheel.

"Oh. It wasn't in the case." She wrinkled her nose in disgust. "You took your retainer straight from your mouth and put it on a public bench?"

He shrugged. "It was bothering me, so I took it out, and when I came back, it was, like, all bent and busted up."

"Let me take a look. Maybe Dr. Russell can salvage it."

"Trust me, no way."

"Can I at least take a look at it?"

"I threw it out in the park. If you want, we could go get another one in an hour or so. I have some stuff I have to do first."

"Get another one?" Meg's voice rose. "Do you realize that makes three this fall? Three!"

"Mom, it's not my fault! I know I lost the first one, but that could happen to anybody. I can't help it that some jerk broke this one. Besides, that's only two."

"You need a new one. That would make three. At four hundred dollars apiece."

"Oh yeah, I guess you're right. Bummer." He scratched his head distractedly. "So, do you want to go later or what?"

"You can't just drop by the orthodontist's office. Besides, it's Saturday."

"Oh." He moved toward his room. "Okay. Whatever."

Meg gripped the banister in anger. "We invested so much time and money in braces, and now that they're off, you can't be bothered to hang on to a retainer for more than a month. But hey, it doesn't matter, right? We'll just keep replacing them. *Lizzie* has to have a five-hundred-dollar dress! You both *deserve* all these things, naturally. Nobody needs to be grateful or take any responsibility in any way, nobody needs to stop and consider that we are *not*—I know it's hard to believe—*made of money*."

"Whoa, Mom." Will held up a hand to calm her. "Chill."

"Don't you dare say that to me! You know what? I'm going to leave now before I lose myself. And I'm going to think about why my children are so incredibly spoiled."

There was a pause as Will took this in. "If we're not going to Dr. Russell, can I go over to Dan's house?"

Meg didn't bother to answer. She returned to the kitchen and sat down heavily at the table.

That makes the second time today that my children got me so angry, I literally removed myself from their presence, she thought. Was this normal? Maybe she was too impatient or not understanding enough. They'd always been great kids. Lizzie had been the child with the summer lemonade stand, donating her proceeds to Save the Children, and using her free time to make braided bracelets out of yarn, which she sold to her classmates, again for charity. In middle school, she had been the rare kid who invited every girl in her class to her birthday parties, not wanting anyone to feel left out. Will, too, had a generous side that, just a couple of years ago, led him to organize weekly softball games for the younger kids on their street. Yet lately it was as if some soul-stealing virus had infected them. It left them selfish and utterly full of themselves. Maybe it was just adolescence. But maybe not.

Meg wondered if she should take some action to teach them not to take everything for granted. Maybe she should call off this week's planned visit to the Festival of Lights in Winston-Salem. Every year they took the hayride through Tanglewood Park to marvel at what was reputed to be a million lights arranged in more than a hundred displays. It was an over-whelming sight that signified the start of the Christmas season to them. She sighed. Sam loved going so much; it wasn't fair to punish him because of the older ones.

The phone rang, startling her. She picked it up. "Hello?"

"It's me." James's voice was strained.

"Hi, sweetheart. You okay? Are you really staying at work late tonight?"

"Yes. I just remembered something. The trip in January— you need to cancel it."

Meg tried to hide her disappointment. "Oh. You're sure?"

"Of course I'm sure," he snapped. "I have to go."

She forced a cheerful good-bye and hung up. So much for their romantic getaway to the Cloister in Georgia. The four-day trip was James's anniversary present for her, already postponed once from their actual anniversary in September because of his work. Just the two of them, alone at the most gorgeous, lux-urious resort. Ever since the children were little, James had arranged a getaway for the two of them on their anniversary, even if they could manage it for only one night. This was the first time it had ever been put off—and, it occurred to her, he had said to cancel the trip. Not postpone or reschedule. She hoped that was all he was implying, but something told her "cancel" meant exactly what it said.

At any rate, she now had to make a slew of phone calls to deal with the various reservations and people booked for those four days to take care of the children and the house. With a sigh, she located the binder where she kept all her household-related notes and phone numbers. She would have to put off planning the big Thanksgiving gathering. Before she could stop herself, she wondered if she might wind up having to put it off until a different year altogether.

Chapter 3

✥

The spectators made their way from the narrow bleachers through the exit doors. It was quiet in the gym, the grim silence that typically followed a loss for one of Meadow Middle School's sports teams. The basketball team had a long-standing rivalry with Xavier Middle, but in the last several years, Xavier had won every game. That losing streak made Meadow's 49–27 loss today particularly humiliating.

Meg and Sam said nothing as they walked toward the car. They both knew what kind of mood Will would be in when he finished changing out of his uniform and came through the gym's side exit. Neither one of them was looking forward to it. Will wasn't a great basketball player by any measure, but his height and speed helped make him one of the best on the team. He treasured that position. It made up for the fact that he wasn't a good enough athlete to play football, which Meg knew was the sport that mattered most to the kids as they approached high school. It was the only sport that mattered to Will.

It had always been all about football for him. He and his father were rabid Carolina Panthers fans and owned a huge assortment of Panther paraphernalia. The football teams from Duke, UNC, or NC State provided additional hours of tension and jubilation. But Will had to make do with basketball, and he was determined to win at it. A victory made him happy for a week. A loss sent him spiraling into gloom. In most areas of his life, Will was a fairly easygoing child. When it came to this, he was irrational.

Sam got into the backseat and buckled the seat belt. Meg heard him sigh, no doubt anticipating the inevitable unpleasantness of the drive home. Will's innate competitiveness was completely alien to Sam, though he did his best to support his older brother by attending the games and cheering as if he cared. Victories brought rewards for such loyalty—Will might invite Sam into his bedroom to talk or to play video games. Losses brought his older brother's sulking.

Will was the first player to emerge from the locker room, throwing wide the heavy door. He yanked open the car door, slumped into the passenger seat, then reached out and slammed the door as hard as he could.

"Hi, honey," Meg tried.

"Don't even talk to me." He folded his arms across his chest and glared out the window. "Just don't."

Meg turned the car around and drove toward the exit. Most of the crowd had already left, a fair number of them before the game was even over.

"UNBELIEVABLE!" The word exploded from Will. "THOSE JERKS CAN SAY THEY'VE BEATEN US FIVE YEARS IN A ROW! DO YOU KNOW HOW BAD THAT IS? DO YOU?"

What Meg and Sam did know was that it was smarter not to answer. They remained quiet as Will continued his tirade. Meg could see Sam in the rearview mirror, fidgeting in his seat. Abruptly, he interrupted. "It's a *bunch of guys with a ball*. Not exactly worth dying over."

Uh-oh, Meg thought, even as she admired her younger son's willingness to put his head in the lion's mouth. Will whipped around in his seat to face Sam, only too glad to be able to target his wrath.

"What would you know about it, you little pus bag? You don't play anything. You're too scared—"

"STOP RIGHT THERE!"

Meg's voice was so loud, it startled even her. Will was about to escalate the personal insults to a point she wasn't going to allow.

"Oh yeah, of course, defend him, like you always do," Will spat out as he turned to face forward again.

No one said another word. Meg was glad when their house finally came into view. As soon as she had parked in the garage, both boys disappeared, headed to their rooms. Meg entered the kitchen to find Lizzie standing at the counter, her eyes red and puffy, sniffling as she spread peanut butter on a banana.

"Sweetheart, have you been crying?" Alarmed, Meg went over to her, putting a hand on Lizzie's arm.

"No!" Lizzie snatched her arm away.

"You want to tell me what's wrong?"

"Nothing. Nothing's wrong." Lizzie looked up at her mother's face, and her resolve crumbled. "It's Emily and Maya. I could just kill them!"

"What happened?"

"It's Facebook stuff. They're on some kind of campaign to get everyone to hate me."

Meg bristled. "Are you serious?"

Lizzie paused, jabbing the knife into the nearly full peanut butter jar so that it stood straight up. "Okay, not *hate* me, maybe, but they're saying a bunch of stuff that makes me look bad. I thought we were good friends, and now it seems like they never considered me a friend. It was all in my mind. I'm nothing to them."

Meg put her arms around Lizzie, and the girl rested her head against her mother's shoulder. She began to cry in earnest. "Why is everybody so mean?" she got out between sobs. "I used to have so many friends, but now it's like everyone's changed."

Meg rubbed Lizzie's back. "Oh, honey, the kids are going through their own stuff. It's not about you, it's about them."

Her daughter pulled away. "You always say stuff like that, Mom. It doesn't mean anything."

"It's really true, if you could just—"

Lizzie grabbed the peanut butter–covered banana and turned to go. "Never mind. I'm sorry I said anything."

"Sweetie—"

"Forget it."

She was gone.

Meg pulled the knife out of the peanut butter, shaking her head. The backbiting among Lizzie's friends had started around seventh grade and now seemed to be constant. Sometimes Lizzie was the target of the gossip, but by the time she got into high school, Meg suspected, her daughter sometimes did a bit of the gossiping herself. It drove Meg crazy, especially since computers and cell phones seemed to have brought the speed of gossip up to the speed of light. Like the news cycle on television, Meg reflected, the popularity cycle seemed to turn over every twenty-four hours.

Upstairs, Will must have emerged from his room as Lizzie was going down the hall, because Meg heard the two of them shouting, something about hogging a DVD. LizzieandWill-fighting, just one word, was how Meg thought of these frequent confrontations. She glanced at the clock on the microwave. Two-twelve. There was a lot more of this day to get through.

I will be cool and calm, she resolved, turning to look at the magnet on the refrigerator. It was a small one she had picked up years ago at a local fair, featuring North Carolina's state motto in Latin and English: *Esse quam videri*. To be, rather than to seem. Meg found it comforting, inspiring her not only to try and *appear* calm or wise or whatever she wished she could be at any given moment but actually to *feel* that way. She'd been looking at that magnet a lot lately.

She hurried upstairs to change into her workout clothes, then spent forty minutes on the treadmill in their basement gym. The room had been James's idea, a small area outfitted with the treadmill, a stationary bike, and some free weights, plus a large-screen television. He wound up using it only infrequently, on a Saturday or Sunday morning. Meg tried to put in four days a week, although she hated every minute of it. When she was finished with her workout, luxuriating under the cool stream of the shower, she was surprised to see James enter the bathroom. He didn't say anything but went directly to the sink to wash his hands.

"Hi," she said loudly over the noise of the water. "I thought you were playing golf all afternoon."

"We quit after nine holes."

"Oh, that's a shame—"

He left the room before she could complete her sentence. Meg dragged the washcloth up and down one arm. When it came to whatever it was that was troubling her husband, she was at a total loss. James was clearly going through some problem, but he refused to answer any of her questions. Initially, he had tried distracting her or jollying her along with humor, but he had given that up entirely; he had simply withdrawn. He came home early from the office, or ridiculously late, with no explanations. In the past few weeks, even the children commented on his irritability. She tried to gloss over it with meaningless phrases about how hard he was working.

Meg had repeatedly asked, cajoled, and demanded an explanation. Was he in love with someone else? Having problems at work? Was he sick or addicted to drugs or alcohol? She reminded him that he could tell her anything and she would do anything to help him. She got no response to her entreaties. In fact, he no longer turned to her in bed or showed her any affection at all. It was as if he wanted to be totally alone with his misery. At a loss by this point, Meg decided she would wait it out. Either he would manage whatever was bothering him, or, eventually, she would force him to confide in someone—if not her, then a professional of some kind. She was giving it until New Year's.

When Thanksgiving Day arrived, James's mood hadn't improved, but Meg had pushed ahead with her annual dinner for the neighbors. Eighteen people would be coming over at four o'clock to share in the feast. She had started cooking the previous Sunday, and today she was right on schedule. At noon she began setting the table, which consisted of their dining room table with all four leaves in it, plus two rented tables extending out from either side. Under duress, Lizzie and Will helped spread out the white tablecloths and napkins and carried in chairs from other parts of the house. Sam retrieved all the sterling silver flatware and ornate serving pieces from the basement closet.

Meg liked to do the final setting of the places herself. She enjoyed arranging the silver, china, and crystal, everything sparkling and gleaming. Next she had huge bouquets of flowers in water-filled buckets to arrange and two dozen candles to set out.

"Mom, no one does this anymore, you know." Lizzie paused on her way past the dining room, observing her mother adjusting the positions of multiple sets of salt and pepper shakers. "You don't have to make such a fuss."

Meg laughed. "C'mon, Lizzie, you know I do."

Her daughter smiled. "Yeah, I guess you do. Some people never learn."

Meg hastened back to the kitchen to baste the turkey, which had been roasting in the oven for hours. The juggling act would come later, when she was trying to heat up the enormous quantities of sweet potato pie, plus the peas and mushrooms, and extra stuffing beyond what the bird held. At the same time she needed to mash the cooked potatoes. She consulted her list for the meal. Hors d'oeuvres, spiked punch for adults, soda for children, cranberry sauce, whipped cream for the pies—all ready.

She decided she had earned a break. Pouring a glass of water, she moved to look out the window. The backyard always provided her with a feeling of serenity, its flat expanse of greenery surrounded by tall, shade-providing trees. The family had spent countless evenings grilling and eating dinner on the patio, and those times were among her favorites. She had also put many contented hours into nurturing the flower beds behind the house and along the lawn's perimeter. It gave her tremendous satisfaction to do something with her hands that created so much beauty virtually out of thin air. Try as she might, she couldn't interest any of her children in gardening, and James never had the time or inclination. It didn't bother her, though; she liked having something that was exclusively hers.

She took a long drink of water. Peering out more intently, she saw that the four Adirondack chairs on the far end of the lawn needed a fresh coat of white paint. She made a mental note to add that to the general to-do list.

Unbidden, the thought came to her that she was sick and tired of that list. Of all her lists. Truth be told, she never wanted to lay eyes on her stupid pink leather book with all those idiotic color-coded errands again.

Startled, she turned away from the window. Where had *that*

come from? she asked herself. Was she tired of doing what was required to keep the family running smoothly? No, that wasn't it. She had no intention of abandoning any of her family commitments. But she needed to do something different, something more. Her life might be busy, but it wasn't *full*. Maybe it was because the kids were getting older. They still required her time and attention, but it was a different kind of need than when they were little. Something was missing, though. Meg closed her eyes momentarily, willing her thoughts to take a different turn. She sensed that, just by having this conversation with herself, she was letting some kind of genie out of its bottle.

She brought her musings to an abrupt end by reminding herself that, given James's problems, this was hardly the time to be shaking things up. Anything having to do with her was going to have to wait. The color-coded calendar would remain.

At three o'clock, Meg went upstairs to change, trading the yoga stretch clothes she wore to clean and cook for black pants, black ballet flats, and a cream silk blouse. Quickly, she pinned up her hair and applied makeup.

It was already three-thirty when she came downstairs. It occurred to her that she hadn't seen James since she asked him to take care of the wine selection for dinner. That had to be nearly two hours ago, she thought, frowning. She hadn't expected any help from him on this dinner—although he hadn't insisted, his attitude had made it clear that he didn't want her to do it this year—but she figured he would handle this one small piece. By now he should have brought into the kitchen whatever wine he wanted her to serve.

No doubt he was in his study. She paused outside the door, listening. "James?"

There was no answer. She opened the door. "Are you in here?"

Her husband was seated at his desk with his arms and head down, like a child taking a nap in school. Papers surrounded him. He made no movement at the sound of her entrance.

"James, are you okay?"

Still nothing. Fear rose in Meg.

"*James!* Talk to me!" She started toward him, thinking she could grab the phone on the desk to call 911.

He raised his head.

"Oh, you nearly gave me—" Meg stopped short.

His face was red and wet with tears, and his expression was wild-eyed. Meg noticed a glass and a nearly empty bottle of Scotch on the desk beside him.

"It's all over." His voice was low but harsh.

"What's all over? Why are you getting drunk in here? You're not even dressed yet. We're having people—"

His voice rose. "Forget that. It's all gone, Meg. Our money. Everything."

Meg stared at him, uncomprehending. "What?"

His face crumpled. "I'm so sorry."

The slightest sensation of fear sneaked up Meg's spine. "What on earth are you talking about?"

He reached for the glass and gulped back its contents, then picked up the bottle of Scotch and refilled it. "I broke the cardinal rule. Let my emotions get the better of me. Of all people, I knew better."

Her fear growing stronger, Meg sat down in a chair near his desk. "Please tell me what you're saying."

"I didn't tell you. I *couldn't* tell you." He averted his eyes from hers. "I got fired." He gave a small, bitter laugh. "Well, that's not what they called it, but that's what it was."

"Fired? *You?*" Meg's mind was jumping from one thought to the next. How terrible this was for James. What it meant for the family short term. What he should do to find another job. She caught herself up short; it would do no good to panic. "Okay, let's wait a minute. It's not the end of the world. We'll be okay."

He only looked at her.

She frowned. "I can't believe they'd fire someone right before the holidays! When exactly did this happen?"

Another gulp from his glass. "August."

"*August?*" Meg sat up straighter in the chair. "You've been out of work since August, and you didn't tell me?"

He ran a hand across his forehead tiredly. "I thought I could find another job before I had to tell you. I thought I could fix things."

Questions were piling up in her mind. "But . . . what have you been doing every day when you tell us you're at the office?"

"Nothing. It doesn't matter. Going out, walking, hanging out at Starbucks."

"You've been pretending to go to the office." Meg was stunned, replaying in her mind's eye the months of his dressing for work, taking his briefcase, acting as if everything were the same as always.

"I didn't want the kids to know. Or you. It was humiliating."

Slowly, anger began to crowd Meg's fear. "You didn't tell your wife you were fired because you were *embarrassed*? Are you crazy? I could have helped. I could have done a million things." She was struck by another thought. "And instead of listening to your yelling about the bills, I could have put a halt to all spending. That's what needed to be done." She sank back in her chair. "This is unbelievable, James. In a million years, I never would have expected—"

His expression was pained. "Yeah, well, it was stupid, but you don't know what it feels like to get thrown out of a big job like that, do you?"

She was stunned by the jibe, but she let it pass. Her voice softened. "No, you're right. I don't. I'm just a bit horrified that you would put on such a charade. And that you didn't feel you could trust me enough to tell me." She took a deep breath. "Anyway, we have plenty of savings, and you'll get another job eventually."

He gave her a nasty smile, one she had never seen on him before. "But that wasn't the bad news."

She wasn't at all sure she wanted to hear what else he might say.

"In September I had a great opportunity to invest in a real estate deal. I jumped at it. It was a beautiful deal."

He stopped. Meg swallowed, waiting.

"A few weeks into it, one of the other big investors dropped out. The deal couldn't go forward, and I saw an opportunity to double my returns. I'd make enough so that I could retire, never even have to get another job. I took it. All in."

Meg's stomach clenched. "And . . . ?"

"The guy who put together the deal turned out to be a crook. He stole everything and disappeared."

There was a long silence in the room.

"How much did we lose?" Meg whispered.

"Everything."

Meg barely got the words out. "What's 'everything'?"

Anger at her slowness flashed in his eyes. "Everything means *everything*! All the money we had in the world. Whatever we had as collateral."

"You don't mean the house?" She silently begged him to answer no.

"Of course! The house, the savings, our investments."

"No, you didn't," Meg breathed. "You couldn't have."

Rage and pain flashed across his face as he smacked his hand on the desk. "I could, and I did. I was desperate, and that affected my judgment. That's what did it. McDowall knew I'd been let go, and he played on that, too."

"Is that who took our money? Are they going to find him?"

"They did, but it's not going to help us any. About an hour ago, I talked to another guy who was also an investor. They found McDowall last night in a hotel in Los Angeles. He shot himself. No money anywhere. Nobody knows what happened."

Meg's hand rose to her throat. "Maybe . . ."

He grimaced. "We're never going to see that money again. Like I said, it's over."

Meg sat paralyzed, trying to force her mind to make sense of what she had just heard. No, it wasn't possible. Things like this didn't happen to people like them.

The ongoing flood of emotions seemed to have exhausted

James. He spoke quietly. "We have to leave the house. Our cars go back because they're leased. I own the Mustang, so that stays with us. The kids can finish out the semester, since the school bill was paid long ago, but they're done there next month. The big things are obvious." He paused. "You need to understand that all we have is what's left in our checking account, which is about nineteen hundred dollars. And whatever you have in your wallet. I have a hundred and fifty bucks in mine."

He closed his eyes and slowly swung his desk chair around so that his back was to her.

Meg struggled to understand. They had nowhere to go and money that would last only a few weeks. They were homeless. Destitute. All because James had decided he could cover up getting fired. He had chosen to take every cent they had without even discussing it with her, then handed it over to a crook. No, she corrected herself, he had gone out of his way to *double* his investment.

She thought about the children. If they had no place to live, how would they go to school, private or otherwise? Forget about their having to say good-bye to everything they had ever known in life—their friends, the community in which they lived, their everyday activities. They would lose the very foundation of their lives, which was that they were safe and secure in the world, protected by their parents.

Meg stood, speaking through clenched teeth. "I could kill you right now, James. You've destroyed us. All by yourself. You were too smart, too important, to talk to me about anything you did. You never considered what that could do to your family. If you wanted to play roulette with your own life, that's one thing. But what about the children and me? You thought so little of us, you sacrificed us without a second thought."

James turned his chair to face her. Tears spilled from his eyes as she spoke. "I know," he whispered. "You're right. I don't know what to do to make it up to you."

"I can't imagine that you'll *ever* make this up to us!" She began to tremble, rage and terror threatening to overtake her. "We have *nothing*! James, *how could you?*"

They stared at each other, fury and confusion on her face, misery on his.

The doorbell rang.

"It's the Dobsons." They heard Sam's shout as he raced down the stairs. "I'll get it."

It was four o'clock. Their guests were starting to arrive.

Chapter 4

Bleary-eyed from exhaustion, Meg clasped a mug of steaming coffee with both hands as she made her way around the backyard. It was barely seven o'clock. Now, before the children got up and she had to face whatever this day might bring, she had some time to be alone in the garden. She reached out to touch the cyclamen's heart-shaped leaves, satisfied to see signs of its emerging white flowers. Looking over the remnants of her hydrangea and foxglove blooms, she recalled her small triumphs and disappointments with them over the seasons. Her crocuses would be in full bloom by Christmas, but she wouldn't be there to see them. Maybe it's silly, she thought, but I'll miss this more than the house itself.

She sat down on one of the Adirondack chairs. No need to worry about painting them now.

Yesterday's Thanksgiving meal was probably the hardest thing she ever had to endure. She could barely believe she had gotten through it. Smiling, making small talk, cooking, serving. All the while seeing her husband seated at the head of the table, downing Scotch after Scotch. His exaggerated cheerfulness, obviously fueled by the alcohol, made her wince. Worst of all was watching the children, all three in notably good moods at the same time, a remarkable occurrence. The things she was going to have to tell them—actually uttering the words "We've lost everything, and we have no idea what's to come"—were unimaginable. Meg set her coffee cup on the ground and tightened her robe against the chilly morning air.

After the meal, when everyone had finally left, Meg had the children help clear the table, then, to their apparent shock, dismissed them from further kitchen duty. She needed to be by herself, to let the corners of her mouth release her frozen smile, to fall silent. For the next two hours, she cleaned furiously, her mind blank as she gave herself over to the physical task. She loaded the dishwasher carelessly, dishes banging as she dropped them haphazardly into the slots. Hand-washing the crystal glasses, she squeezed a wineglass so hard the stem snapped, but she ignored the bleeding from her thumb, and after a while it stopped.

Later, when she could find nothing else to clean, she dragged herself upstairs, emotionally and physically drained. James was nowhere to be seen, which was fine with her.

"I'm going to sleep. G'night, kids," she called out from her bedroom doorway.

"Mom?" Sam's voice floated down the hall. It was unusual for her to go to bed without coming into their rooms to say good night.

"Go to bed, Sam," she replied, firmly shutting the door. She hated ignoring her son, but she couldn't face the children. Not tonight.

She peeled off her clothes, dropping them on the bathroom floor before grabbing a nightgown from the hook on the back of the door. What difference did it make what she did with the clothes now? she thought. All her compulsive housekeeping and keeping on top of things had only brought her to this point. Nowhere.

Sliding under the comforter, Meg was so exhausted that she knew, thankfully, she would find the oblivion of sleep quickly. She was wrong. Over and over, she replayed the conversation with James and his actions over the past months. Everything about their life since August was now recast in a completely new light.

It was not a light that reflected flatteringly on her husband. Despite her offering him a hundred openings, he had chosen to keep what was, in terms of a marriage, a monstrous secret. He had lied to her again and again through his silences, his pretense of going to work, his clandestine gambling of all they had.

This couldn't be her husband, her James, the man who had brought her a cup of coffee every morning since the day they married. Who always filled the house with peonies, her favorite flower, on her birthdays. Who, for years, had designated alone time with each child one Sunday a month to go to a museum or a ball game or wherever his son or daughter might want. He was a straight arrow and honest to a fault. Meg would have bet her life—the lives of her children—that he couldn't have done such a thing. Knowing she would have lost such a bet made her blood run cold.

The sound of the screen door opening brought her back to the moment. She watched James emerge into the morning air, holding his own mug of coffee. He wore the same clothes from the day before and was unshaved, his hair uncombed. It was obvious that he, too, had passed a sleepless night. She wondered if he was feeling hungover from all that Scotch. She hoped so. The sight of her handsome husband usually had a warming effect on her, a combination of love, attraction, and comfort. All that was over. Today she felt only anger and the stabbing pain of betrayal.

"I saw you through the window," he said as he drew closer. "What are you doing out here so early?"

She didn't reply. He sat down on the chair next to her. "Good coffee. Thanks for making it." He glanced down at her feet. "Aren't your slippers getting wet out here?"

She looked over at him in disbelief. "Are we *chatting*?"

His voice suddenly reflected his fatigue. "Look, it won't do us any good to go at each other. We'll have to work this all out, and we might as well do it as a team."

"James, we're not discussing where to go on vacation or whether the kids should take Spanish or French. We're discussing how you deceived me and what you've done to the whole family. We're talking about whether I'm leaving you."

He held up a hand and spoke soothingly. "I know you're angry now, Meg—"

"Don't patronize me." Her tone was icy. "I feel like such a fool, being all chipper to try and cheer you up, feeling sorry for you while you were busy nursing your wounded pride in coffee shops. You know, if we had worked as a 'team,' as you put it, when you lost your job, *that* might have been helpful. I never would have let you risk everything we had, no matter how fantastic the deal was." She stood. "True, you were the one with the high-powered job, the one who made all the money. You were the important one. Nothing I did mattered much. Raising the kids, running our lives—stupid stuff, I guess. Even so, couldn't you have thrown me a bone? Given me a hint what you were going to do?" She stooped to retrieve her coffee cup. "I'm sorry, but I really can't bear to look at you another minute. We'll have to sit down and go over some things later. Like when we have to get out of the house. And where on earth we're going to go."

James's tone was angry. "Don't twist everything around. I was only trying to spare you and the kids."

"If things had gone your way, that would have been fine. I'd never have been the wiser. It simply didn't occur to you that something might go wrong, did it?" She paused. "Maybe having such a high-powered job isn't always a good thing. The adrenaline of all that risk-taking, the thrill of so much money. It can lead to some pretty terrible consequences."

"You were perfectly happy to spend all that money, as I recall," he said.

She waited a moment to be sure she could sound calm. "Your nastiness aside, none of this is about money, don't you see that? It's about my never being able to trust you again. It's about the fact that our marriage is a big fraud because you're in one marriage, and I'm apparently in another. The person I thought you were would never put his family at risk."

Looking exhausted, he closed his eyes. "I'm the same person I always was."

"Well, James, that kind of makes it worse, you know? That means I never really understood what kind of person you were."

He looked at her, his gaze hard. "Could we stop all this, please? We have to make some decisions, and we don't have time for you to berate me for hours. What's done is done. We need to move forward."

Her eyes widened. "Wait—you get to do something this terrible, and then you get to dictate how much I can say about it? I'm *annoying* you?" Before he could reply, she turned and walked back to the house, trying to stifle her rage. She refilled her cup in the kitchen and sat down at her desk, her mind racing. There were phone calls to make and lists to compile, lists of awful and humiliating things to do. If only I could go back to my silly to-do lists in my pink leather book, she thought. I'd never complain about it again.

She rummaged through the filing cabinet beneath the desk to assemble an armload of files containing unpaid bills and legal documents. Setting them down, she grabbed a legal pad and a pen. She wrote "cancel" on the top left of the page and started adding whatever came to mind. Cable, newspapers, magazines, cleaning service. Credit cards. She had to find some way to pay off the balances, which were high, but to keep the cards in case they got desperate.

They also owed money at several local shops, many where

they knew the owners personally. It wasn't that they were in any great debt to these shops, but Meg typically waited to pay the bills until she had accumulated two or three months' worth. She recalled all the times Mr. Collins at the pharmacy had advised her when the children got sick. His many kindnesses were the reason she did her drugstore shopping at his tiny store instead of the less expensive chain. She must owe him a fair amount on the house account. He would never collect it. Alice, the lovely woman at the dry cleaner, would also go without getting paid on their open account. Glen Richards, their wonderful gardener with whom she had spent so much time discussing what plants worked best where. All these people would be cheated. The mental images made her cringe. She made a note to check on the balances and write IOUs. One day, somehow, she would make good on them.

So many ugly tasks. She jotted down their various insurance policies—medical, life, car. All paid for now, but when the next premiums came due, the policies would lapse, and if one of them got seriously ill or worse, the family would be completely unprotected.

She could see something of the lengths to which James had gone to hide his situation. For the past three months, he had been careful to maintain his usual system of transferring enough money into their checking account so she could pay the bills. What upset her even more was that if she had known the truth, she could have chosen which bills to pay. He had let her go on paying for cable television instead of putting aside funds for more important things.

Her mind drifted to the people they knew around town. She

wished with all her heart that she could disappear from Charlotte today, this very minute. She grimaced. To go where? She had several good friends here but no one she would ask to put up a family of five indefinitely. Besides, she could see herself telling her friends that James had lost his job, but sharing that he had lied to her and lost everything in a swindle was a different matter. She knew she could never bring herself to confide that to anyone. Realizing she had to live with this enormous secret made her feel completely alone in the world.

They could go to a motel until their remaining money ran out, but that wouldn't take long. And then what? To make matters worse, she didn't know if she could bear to go anywhere with James ever again. When had he become so obsessed with money and success that he'd given up all perspective? Losing everything, every last penny—it made no sense to Meg. He had no internal brakes, nothing to tell him that things should go so far and no farther. He had lost himself completely.

"Mommy, can you make me pancakes?" Sam stood in the kitchen doorway in his pajamas, his eyes puffy from sleep.

Meg put the pad facedown on the desk. She would give the children as long as possible to enjoy the life they knew before she yanked it out from under them. "Plain or blueberry, sweetie?"

As the day passed, Meg realized that James was avoiding her. Annoyed, she finally went to seek him out. She found him stretched out in the club chair in his office. He sat immobile, his head resting on the back of the chair, his eyes closed. "I'm awake," he said without moving.

The sight only irritated her more. "What are you doing,

holed up in here?" She stood in front of him. "We have about a thousand things that need to be dealt with, and I can't do it all by myself."

He opened his eyes. "What needs to be done?" he asked in a listless tone.

"Well, I made some notes and went over . . ." Meg trailed off as she saw that James was gazing somewhere over her shoulder, clearly not listening. "Is this how it's going to be? I do absolutely everything to clean up this mess? No, James. *No*." She crossed her arms. "Yes, I see you're sad, you're depressed, your heart is broken. But you and I don't have the luxury of those feelings. We have three children to take care of."

"Kids are resilient. They'll be okay."

Her voice rose. "Whether they'll be okay is another matter, but before that, they have to be *told*. Have you considered how to break this news to them?"

"I don't know." He rubbed his eyes tiredly. "What do you think?"

When had her husband become like this? Meg wondered. He had always been so strong emotionally. Now he seemed incapable of handling any part of the crisis he himself had brought upon them.

She took a breath. "I think we have to tell them the truth. Unfortunately, today. They need to know they can't spend any more money on anything. More important, they need to be told what's coming down the road. What happens to their everyday lives? To their activities, to their friends?"

"Simple enough," James replied. He snapped his fingers. "Poof. All gone." He abruptly leaned forward, grabbing the chair arms angrily. "You want me to be helpful, Meg? Fine! I will take the blame and tell them Daddy wrecked their lives. Will that be sufficient?"

Meg was unmoved by his words. "You *have* wrecked their lives. And yes, that will be sufficient for now. You do all the talking, and I'll be beside you like some philandering politician's wife. We'll present a united front. I'll keep up my end. Just be sure you keep up yours and tell them the truth."

It was nearly five in the afternoon when, seated side by side on the sofa, they called the children to the family room. Sam responded first, plopping down cross-legged on the floor. Lizzie and Will required another few shouts to get them to appear, then they slouched in armchairs, both looking somewhat put upon.

"Why the summit meeting?" Lizzie asked.

"We have some important things to tell you," Meg said. "So please, just listen to Dad until he's done."

She struggled to keep her face neutral as she listened to James lay out the situation. He omitted altogether the part about pretending to go to work for the past four months. His explanation relied on a bad economy and unlucky investments in a way that absolved him from any real responsibility. The children clearly didn't grasp the significance of what he was saying until he started explaining the immediate and painful consequences of not having any money at all. Tense, she watched her two older children's expressions shift from barely attentive to stunned to horrified. Sam's face remained impassive, but the growing intensity of his nail-biting said more than enough.

"*Please* tell me you're kidding, please, please, please!" Lizzie was perched on the edge of her chair, leaning forward, her hands gripping the chair arms. "You *have* to be!"

"Yeah, this is a joke, right?" Will's voice held anger and fear in equal measure.

By this point, Meg's stomach was clenched so tight, she was almost bent in half, her arms crossed over her abdomen. "No," she practically whispered. "No, it's not a joke."

Lizzie sounded frantic. "I don't understand. We don't have any money? *None?*"

James spoke firmly. "That's right. So there will not be one dime going out of this house from now on."

"But I need to pay Megan back for Ali's birthday present, and—"

"Lizzie, listen to me!" James said. "Not one dime. No paying back. No movies, no shopping, no nothing."

"We'll still have our cell phones and laptops, right?"

James shook his head. "Not after tomorrow."

Lizzie was wild-eyed. "You can't do this to us!"

"It'll be all right, honey," Meg soothed.

Her daughter turned to her in fury. "It will not! This is the worst thing that ever happened!"

"How are we going to live?" Will asked. "Will we be able to eat?"

"Your mother and I are taking care of all the details. Don't worry, you won't starve. But we'll be leaving the house in about two weeks, so you'll need to start getting ready. We'll only have my car, the Mustang. We can take just what we can fit into it and not one thing more."

"Are you crazy?" Lizzie shrieked. "That's impossible! We can't live like that!"

"Leaving the house for how long?" Will's face was white.

James paused. "For good. We're not coming back."

Meg tried to soften the blow of his reply. "We're not sure where we're going yet, but it'll be okay. It just won't be in Charlotte. But you have another couple of weeks in school here, which means you'll make it almost to the end of the term. I'm sure we can make arrangements with the school so you can finish your work and get final grades for the semester."

The children sat stock-still, trying to absorb what they were hearing.

"We're leaving school. We're not even staying in Charlotte." Will reviewed what he had just learned in wonderment. "We're poor, and we're literally homeless."

Sam finally spoke, his voice tremulous. "Are we going to die?"

Chapter 5

James sat on the edge of their bed, his head down and his hands clasped between his knees. Meg watched him brace himself for what he was about to do. She almost felt sorry for him. Almost.

She was no happier than he about this decision. There was no place on earth she wanted to go less than her parents' house in upstate New York. But it was the only solution to their problems that made any real sense. Their first priority was to find a place to stay. Only Meg's parents had the room to take them all in, and could be prevailed upon to let them stay indefinitely for free.

Of course, "free" was a relative term, Meg reflected. Payment might not be made in the form of money, but it would most definitely be made. And the cost would be extremely high.

She picked up the phone, punching in the numbers to her childhood home before handing it to James.

He took a deep breath, then stood as he brought the phone to his ear and waited for someone to answer. "Hello, Harlan?" James was trying to sound cheerful, Meg knew, but his voice came out sounding more strangled. "It's James . . . Hobart."

Meg turned away, fiddling with something on their dresser so he wouldn't feel her eyes upon him. She could hear him pace as he talked.

"How are you? Frances doing okay? Good, good."

The brief pauses required for her father's replies told Meg that he was being his usual terse self. James made small talk for a little while longer. Meg noted that her father did not inquire about her or the children.

"Harlan, I need to talk to you about something pretty serious." James was getting down to it but kept his tone casual. "We've had some setbacks here, you know, the economy and such. I'm sure you've been reading about all this. Well, we haven't been immune down here in Charlotte.

"So, what with my firm downsizing and such, turns out we're going to have to do some downsizing ourselves. We bit off a little more than we could chew, I guess, with the house. Foolish in retrospect."

With his last comment, James had purposely handed her father the opening to lecture him. The conversation was becoming increasingly painful for her to listen to, and she knew it was about to get worse.

"Yeah, you're right," James said contritely. Meg could imagine her father making some self-righteous remark about how this was to be expected when people overreached or didn't follow the tried and true.

"So, Meg and I have been talking. We think the best thing would be if we came to you and I started doing what I should have been doing all along: learning the business."

Meg looked up at her husband. Getting that out must have nearly killed him. While she was glad that he was finally dealing with some of the ugliness his mess had created, at the same time, his groveling was making her cringe in sympathy.

"That's right, Harlan, I am dead serious. It's time for us to get settled into a solid business that we can depend on. Those are the ones that last, no matter what. Like you always said. Heck, I'm definitely looking forward to doing something *real* instead of pushing papers all day. But we'd need to lean on your generosity a bit. You know, maybe staying with you until we get our feet on the ground up there."

James listened as his father-in-law responded.

"Unfortunately, in this market, we won't get anything out of the house. We put a lot of money into it, and I'm not hopeful we'll make it back. So, no, we don't have a whole lot of capital, as they say."

Meg wasn't surprised that her husband chose to finesse the issue of their losing the house. She couldn't really imagine him saying that they would be leaving with only the shirts on their backs. The conversation went on for another minute or so before he brought it to a close.

"Yes, you're absolutely right. Yes. Well, okay, then, that sounds fine. What time tonight? Good. Send my best to Frances in the meantime."

James pressed the off button and put down the phone. He turned to Meg. "You have to call back tonight at seven. He said your mother would handle any 'domestic arrangements,' as he so quaintly put it. She's out now."

"Will he give you a job?"

"Yes. He said it was about time I'd come to my senses."

"James, I know how hard that—"

"Oh, cut it out." His face contorted with fury. "You must have really enjoyed that. For the rest of your lives, you and your parents can hold it over my head, how I came crawling to them for help. *Begged* them to take in my family and give me some crummy job. Happy now?"

Meg took a step back in surprise. "You think that makes me happy?"

"I *know* it does." James left the bedroom, slamming the door behind him.

Whatever sympathy Meg had felt for him vanished. He viewed himself as a victim, she realized, and somehow she was going to be the villain. He was writing his own script about what had happened. Unfortunately, she could see that it wasn't going to have much to do with the truth.

Meg left the room only to be met by the sound of Lizzie crying. Ever since yesterday, when they told the children the news, Lizzie had been virtually holed up in her bedroom. She hadn't come down for dinner, and the dirty cereal bowl and spoon in the sink this morning were the only evidence that she had eaten anything between then and now. Periodically, Meg would knock on her daughter's door, but all she got in the way of a response was "Go away!"

She tried again with a gentle knock. "Lizzie? Please let me talk to you."

To Meg's surprise, she received silence in reply. She took that as an invitation and opened the door a few inches. "Can I come in?"

The only answer was Lizzie's sniffling. Meg entered to find her daughter stretched across the bed on her stomach, her face turned toward the wall.

"Oh, honey, I know this is so, so hard," Meg said.

Lizzie kept her face averted, and her voice was muffled by sobs. "No, you don't. You don't know anything. You may have grown up in some stupid little town, but nobody made you leave your house and everything you owned. Nobody destroyed everything you worked so hard to build—friends, your social life—everything." She turned her face toward Meg. It was red and tear-stained. "How could you do this to me?" Her voice grew louder. "Why did you let this happen? You have three children. Didn't you think about us at all?"

"Your father and I—"

"I can't understand how you and Daddy could be so stupid. And selfish. You didn't save anything or have any kind of plan. Boom, just like that, our lives are gone."

"There's a lot you don't understand about all this."

Lizzie regarded her mother dully. "I understand that I hate you. You've ruined my life, like, literally, *ruined* it." She turned her face to the wall again. "I wish I were dead. Leave me alone. I never want to see you again."

Meg stood there for a moment, trying to imagine what this all felt like to her daughter. Then she left the room.

As she made her way down the hallway, she saw the door to Sam's room was open. Peering in, she froze. Her nine-year-old sat on the floor in the center of the room, surrounded by a huge array of boxes and bags full of his collections. Meg watched silently as he lovingly examined some tiny rubber action figures.

His stuff. The stuff that made him the quirky, sweet kid he was. She hadn't thought about how he would have to abandon all the things he had collected. All the things that somehow represented to him security and control in a scary world. How could they ask him to do that? The other two children would have to part with clothes and gadgets and a range of things that were bound to be painful to them. But Sam would have to let go of a part of himself that he wasn't ready to give up. He shouldn't have to.

He saw her standing in the doorway and smiled. "Hi, Mom."

Of the three children, Sam was the only one who hadn't displayed anger toward Meg or James. After their gathering in the family room, Will had left the house yelling out angrily that he would be at Leo's as he slammed the door behind him. He wasn't supposed to leave home without a parental okay, but Leo lived within walking distance, and under the circumstances, no one was about to stop him. This morning he had sullenly allowed Meg to cook him scrambled eggs and toast, retreating with the plate to his room so he wouldn't have to sit with her in the kitchen. Apparently, he wasn't speaking to his parents any more than he had to.

Sam had been very quiet, but it was a different kind of quiet. He was clearly afraid, and he seemed to Meg more fragile. He had spent much of the morning in her presence, practically following her from room to room, trying to be helpful in any way he could. It was as if he needed to be with her but was trying not to add to the misery and disruption in the house.

Meg forced a smile to match his. "Hi, pumpkin."

He got up and went over to his desk, retrieving a crumpled pile of dollar bills there. "I saved this from my allowance and stuff. It's eighteen dollars. I thought maybe you and Daddy could use it."

"No, no, Sam." The words caught in her throat. "That's very nice. But you keep it."

She turned away before he could see her face. Hurrying down the stairs, tears burning her eyes, she went out to the backyard and got as far from the house as she could before bursting into long, loud sobs. It was the first time since all this had started, she realized, that she had cried. Now that she had started, she wasn't sure she would be able to stop. She cried for the children and for her marriage. She cried with fear, having no idea what the next months would bring. She cried at the realization that the security of her life had been such a flimsy illusion.

Much later, when she couldn't cry another tear, she stood, exhausted, and made some resolutions. She wouldn't let the children see her get down. No matter how furious she was at James, they would maintain the best possible relations in front of them. Last, she wouldn't rely on her husband to get them out of their financial straits because the likelihood that he could tolerate working for her father was pretty much zero.

At exactly seven o'clock that evening, Meg sat down at the kitchen table to call her mother. If Meg's mother had said to call at seven, she expected to receive the call at seven, not

7:01. Tardiness as a symptom of weak character had been a frequent topic of discussion between her parents during Meg's childhood. Whatever else tonight's conversation might bring, she wanted to eliminate that subject as a possibility.

The phone rang and rang. Meg could picture her mother in the kitchen, washing up after supper, unhurriedly drying her hands on a dish towel before reaching for the wall-mounted telephone.

"Hello." A flat statement without expectation.

That one word was enough to make Meg flinch. "Mother, hi, it's Meg."

"Hello, Margaret. Didn't hear from you yesterday on Thanksgiving, but I understand you've gotten yourself in a lot of trouble down there."

Double points, Meg thought grimly. The reprimand for the missed call and the put-down both in one sentence. The fact that her mother still insisted on calling her by her given—and hated—name of Margaret was just the usual icing on the cake.

"I'm very sorry we have to bother you like this. I really appreciate you and Dad letting us stay with you for a while."

"I'm hardly surprised it came to this, dear. That big-deal firm James worked for, all those fancy companies, you just knew they were going to come to no good. Dishonest cheats, all of them."

"I guess" was all Meg could get out.

Her mother's pinched tone couldn't disguise her satisfaction. "If you'd listened to your father and me when we told you to come back home after you two married—well, I don't have to tell you that you wouldn't be in this predicament now."

Meg forced a jovial tone. "But look how it's working out—James will be joining the family business after all."

"We'll see," her mother said primly. "Frankly, I wonder if he can handle going from those expensive suits and expense-account lunches to real life."

Meg wanted desperately to move the conversation in another direction. "This will be a chance for the kids to spend time with you. You can all get to know one another a lot better."

Her remark was met with silence.

Meg tried not to feel hurt. "They're nice kids, Mother."

"Just remember, Margaret, I brought up one child, and I'm not bringing up any more," her mother said. "Once was enough."

"Don't worry," Meg said sharply. "No one expects you to do anything at all for them." She caught herself. Getting into an argument wouldn't help matters. "You're doing plenty just letting us come. We really appreciate it, and we'll stay out of your hair."

"Fine. The three of them will sleep in the spare room, and you and James can have your old room."

"Of course. Thank you." Meg knew there wasn't any other choice, but the scenario filled her with dread.

"When are you coming?"

"It'll be a couple of weeks. Can I let you know when we get closer?"

"I can't have you calling me that morning to tell me you'll be showing up for lunch."

"No, no, Mother, I'll give you plenty of notice. How about if I call you next week and give you a firm date?"

"Fine. Call next Friday, at seven, like tonight."

"Yes, I will."

There was a pause. "I hope you two have learned a lesson. You were riding so high. And look at you now. To be your age and have to come home to live with your parents because you have no money . . ."

"Yes, well, these things happen," Meg said through clenched teeth. "So—good-bye. Talk to you next week."

She set down the telephone. Then she folded her arms on the table and buried her head in them. Today she and James had made only the first small installment of the many payments yet to come.

Over the next two weeks, Meg was grateful that the job of closing up the house kept her constantly busy. It made it easier for her to ignore any thoughts about how much she loved the landscape painting hanging in the living room, or the art deco perfume bottle James had given her one year for their anniversary. Early on in her marriage, she had done a lot of baking and, over the years, had amassed a large array of cooking and decorating tools. As she tossed the pans and pastry brushes into shopping bags, she fought to avoid recalling the birthday cakes and holiday pies she had made, the cupcakes for school events.

They weren't in a position to pay for storage, and her parents had little extra space, so she filled every old box and bag in the house with items to toss, attempt to sell, or donate to charity. Faced with the mountains of papers relating to the children's past schoolwork and art, she dedicated one plastic storage box to each of them and steeled herself to pare down the memories to fit. Vans pulled up to the house to haul away sofas, chairs, lamps, tables. Any money they made from whatever might be salable would go directly to the credit card companies—the most immediate problem—and the rest to the small-store owners with whom they had unpaid accounts. Although she and her family desperately needed money, it was critical to Meg to know she would take care of these local people after all. When she informed James of this, he nodded in agreement, a sign to her that at least some remnant of his basic decency had survived.

She boxed and shipped the family photo albums to her parents' house, plus some small items that held sentimental value for her. She told each child to pack two cartons of whatever they deemed important and sent those along as well. Despite the cost, some things were simply beyond her resolve.

They had under a week left until the day they would leave the house for good. Meg kept her eye on the deadline, forcing herself to remain numb to the sight of her life being dismantled. The children, on the other hand, made their feelings abundantly clear. Sam retreated further into himself, while the other two remained angry and sullen. Lizzie continued to do the most crying and yelling at Meg, while Will glowered, watching television alone in the basement playroom or disappearing into his bedroom, refusing to answer any questions. Meg told the children that they were responsible for clearing out their rooms, so they could choose what to keep. As she disposed of the things they'd left behind, she tried not to look at Lizzie's bags of favorite childhood dolls, and sadly emptied the cartons into which Will had carelessly tossed his basketball trophies and football memorabilia. At the last minute, she retrieved his favorite skateboard from a box; somehow they would make space for it in the car.

One of the few times she broke down was the afternoon she spent in the basement, sorting through Christmas ornaments. She had collected a few new ones each year and any time they traveled, ever since James and she had gotten married. Each one held a special memory. The lights, tinsel, angels, and decorations to adorn windows and doors—it was unbearable. Christmas was so soon, it killed her to think they would miss having it one last time in the house. Of all the holidays, it was by far her favorite and the one she made the biggest fuss over. Everything about it was exciting to her: wrapping presents, baking cookies, filling the house with the sound of carols and silly singing Santas. When she was growing up, her parents had little appreciation for a holiday they believed had degenerated into "nothing but an excuse to get people to spend their money." They would go to church and put up a small tree, the cheapest one they could find, which Meg would decorate with her handmade paper cutouts. On Christmas morning she would receive something useful, like socks or mittens. It was a joyless event all around. As an adult on her own, Meg did her best to create a virtual festival, with huge, lavish presents and mountains of food.

Now she was facing another holiday season back in her parents' house. They would approve of the fact that the kids would get little or nothing, but only because Meg and James could no longer afford big gifts. Or small ones, for that matter. Meg's tears were a mixture of sorrow and bitterness.

Whether James was thinking about any of this, only he could say. He spent most of the time in his study, even sleeping on the couch there at night. Meg asked him to handle the dismantling of that room and all the bookshelves' contents throughout the house, which he did without comment. Often he went out around dinnertime. It was obvious he wanted to avoid eating with the family. Meg would have liked to avoid those meals herself, with her two older children either sulking or complaining and Sam growing progressively more nervous and fearful. But she wasn't about to run out on them, and her resentment toward James grew deeper each time he failed to appear. She wasn't sure what to make of the hard set of his mouth when he did address her. Clearly, he was angry, but whether it was at her, himself, or the world, she couldn't quite say. Neither of them made any attempt to discuss it—or anything else beyond what was absolutely necessary.

The tension in the house only increased as all three children realized their ideas of what would fit in one suitcase were far off the mark. There were multiple sessions of Meg sitting on someone's bed as that child wept or raged over parting with ever more precious items. Even Sam yelled through his tears when he had to make the impossible choice between the large bags of tiny stuffed-animal key chains and assorted plastic aliens. "It's too much, Mommy," he cried. "Please don't make me do this."

Her heart ached for all three, and she suggested they each pack a second, smaller bag if they were willing to have it beneath their feet for the entire car trip. She hoped she was doing the right thing: It was roughly seven hundred miles to Homer, New York, with the kids cramped in the backseat. They gladly agreed with her idea to sit with their own pillows and blankets; that would keep them warm and comfortable without taking up trunk space. However, their pleasure dissipated when she pointed out that they also needed to wear their heaviest jackets and warmest clothes because the weather would be far colder going north. She didn't mention that they would nonetheless still be underdressed, as there had never been a need to outfit them for snow and ice. The blankets were necessities for the drive. When they got upstate, somehow she would have to provide them with warmer gear.

In some ways, it was a relief when the day they were to leave finally arrived. Meg didn't think she could stand much more. They were all exhausted and emotionally drained from disposing of their old lives. The children got out of bed as soon as she woke them, and they moved about quietly, speaking only when necessary. Everyone ate a quick breakfast, and, as planned, they were ready to go by ten o'clock. Meg knew there was no point, but she washed the breakfast dishes and sponged down the counters. She couldn't bring herself to leave the house looking abandoned and uncared for.

As she passed through the kitchen on her way out, she noticed that she had removed everything from the refrigerator door except the magnet with the state motto. Somehow she had overlooked it. *To be, rather than to seem.* She slipped it into her pants pocket.

James's 1969 white Mustang was his pride and joy, what Meg

called his favorite toy. He had bought it for himself as a reward when he had been hired for the job in Charlotte at a salary far higher than what he had been receiving at his previous company. Initially, he had driven the car a fair amount, but now he took it out only for an occasional spin, unwilling to forgo the conveniences of his BMW. Although the Mustang had two doors, it was designed to hold four people; the back had a bucket seat design, with a rise in the center of the seat and on the floor. Without a lot of interior room, it was barely comfortable for four, much less five. It had never been James's intention to drive the car anywhere with his entire family at one time, much less on an extended trip. No one was surprised when the backseat proved miserably tight for three people with small suitcases, pillows, and blankets.

It was also predictable that, as the youngest, Sam would be forced by his siblings to sit in the middle. "Why do I have to sit on the hump?" he asked unhappily.

"Because you *do*, that's why," Will said.

"Look, kids, you're packed in there like sardines," James said. "If you want to jettison some stuff, it might be a little better."

Unwilling to relinquish any of the little they had left, they immediately stopped complaining, while Meg and James grimly struggled to get everything in the trunk. Meg was keeping her fingers crossed that the car would be up to making the trip.

It was a sunny day, the blue sky streaked with patches of wispy clouds. There was total silence as they pulled out of the driveway. Meg noticed that neither James nor the children looked back at the house. She guessed that for them, as for her, it would have been too much to stand.

The leased BMWs had built-in navigation systems, but no such thing existed when the Mustang was manufactured. They would be using the driving directions Meg had printed out while they still had their computers, plus some old AAA maps. She removed the Southeastern States map from her handbag and unfolded it.

"Take the next left," she intoned, imitating the voice from her car's navigation system. "Drive twelve million miles. Then, destination is on the right."

No one smiled. All three children got out their iPods—with no monthly charges, they were among the few electronic gadgets they had been able to keep—and retreated into their music. Meg looked out the window at the streets of Charlotte flying by. If they had been leaving under different conditions, she and James would have been sharing memories and making comments on what they were passing. Instead, James stared straight ahead as he drove. No matter how things were resolved, she knew in her heart she wouldn't be coming back here. This life was finished.

Lizzie and Will started fighting before they got to Winston-Salem, and everyone was short-tempered by the time they pulled onto I-81, the highway on which they would be doing most of the driving. The route took them through Virginia. Thinking it would make for a pleasant interlude, Meg had planned a stop at Luray Caverns. If they had to make this trip, she figured, at least the kids could see a few interesting sights and learn something.

The one-hour tour of the underground caverns didn't go well. The two older children complained continually that they were cold and bored. Sam dragged his feet, saying he had a stomachache. James was either snapping at them to keep quiet while the guide was talking, or fruitlessly trying to interest them in the difference between stalactites and stalagmites. The less they listened to him, the more annoyed he became at their unwillingness to appreciate the beauty surrounding them.

It was a relief for all of them when they eventually checked into a motel for the night, the cheapest one they could find that seemed reasonably clean and safe. The children piled onto one of the beds and turned on the television. Meg took a shower so she could have ten minutes of peaceful solitude, the same reason, she guessed, that James went alone to fill the car with gas. She dried herself as best she could with the small, rough towel provided as she thought about what would be the least expensive dinner options.

The next morning the children were groggy, surprisingly unwilling to relinquish their scratchy blankets and get out of their uncomfortable bed. Meg and James dressed and split up so that one could get the free coffee and doughnuts from the motel's lobby while the other kept an eye on the children. It was nearly eleven before they checked out, and the amount of complaining and stops demanded from the backseat escalated considerably from the previous day. It was a slow, unpleasant ride under a cold and gray sky all the way to Pennsylvania.

When she had planned this drive back in Charlotte, Meg estimated that they would reach Lancaster County that afternoon. She knew it was an area with a big Amish population. Neither she nor the children knew much about the Amish, and this would be a wonderful chance to learn a little bit. It was Sunday, with few things open, but her research at home had turned up a film about the Amish with regular Sunday screenings. At least they could see that much.

Meg didn't recall what time the day's last showing of the film was, but when she saw it was four o'clock as they pulled off the highway, she knew they were probably too late. This detour had been a bad idea, she thought, but they might as well check on the movie and see whatever sights there were along the way. She directed James to an address in the town of Intercourse, the name of which provided Lizzie and Will with numerous snickers. It had snowed earlier in the week, evident in the graying snow and patches of ice on the sidewalks and roads. On the local Route 340, they passed closed shops that obviously catered to tourists the rest of the week. The town appeared deserted.

When they arrived at the theater, it was closed.

James exhaled in annoyance. "This was a waste of time."

"Turns out that's true," Meg said, maintaining a level tone. "So we'll go back to the highway and move on." She thought about how late it was. "Actually, we should probably find a motel around here for tonight."

James pulled the car back onto the road. It was completely dark now, and the evening brought with it the coldest weather they had encountered on their trip. Meg retrieved a penlight from her bag to consult her AAA guidebook. Busy flipping through the section on lodgings, she didn't notice when James somehow took a wrong turn and left the main road. It took her a while to notice that they were driving on unlit country roads, probably far from an area where they might find a motel.

"Where are we?" she asked James. "I can't see any street signs."

"How should I know? I'm retracing my steps back to 283."

"No, this isn't the way back. We definitely didn't come this way."

"Mom's right," Will offered. "There were stores."

"Are we lost?" Sam asked.

James's voice rose. "No, we are not lost! Would everybody just relax? Meg, can you see where we are on one of those maps?"

"No, I don't have anything with this much detail."

"If I had my navigation system—"

"Well, you don't," Lizzie interrupted. "Suck it up. *We* don't have anything we want, either."

"Watch it, Lizzie," James warned.

"It's really, really dark here," Sam whispered loudly to Will.

"It's called night, you idiot" was Will's retort.

"All three of you keep quiet!" James ordered. "Not another word." He braked at a stop sign. They could drive straight or take roads veering slightly right or left. There was also a tight hairpin turn to the extreme right, with the road sloping sharply down. He pointed in that direction to Meg. "Maybe that'll take us back."

She nodded. "Might as well try it."

James put his foot down on the gas and turned the wheel hard to the right.

"Ow, get off me!" Will yelled as the car leaned sharply to the side and Sam was pressed up against him.

Lizzie leaned forward to yell back at Will. "It's not his fault, stupid."

"Who asked you?" he snapped.

Between their raised voices and the closed car windows, none of them heard the horse-drawn buggy coming up the hill. Its flashing red lights were hidden from their view until it came around a curve in the road. In the brief moments it took for the car to make the turn and start downhill, the buggy was almost upon them. James braked hard, but ice on the road caused the car to swerve violently. Realizing that he was within split-seconds of hitting the horse head-on, James jerked the steering wheel to the right as hard as he could.

The Mustang responded, and its headlights illuminated the telephone pole on the side of the road just before they crashed into it.

Chapter 6

Lizzie and Sam both screamed. Will flung up his arms to protect his head. Meg felt the seat belt jerk her body back. The windshield shattered, spraying glass in all directions. The sickening noise of the collision and breaking glass were matched by the violent jolt of the impact, so jarring that it left Meg terrified.

She felt James's shoulder hit her hard as he leaned—or was thrown—toward her.

For a moment everyone was too stunned to speak. Through the open windshield, the cold night air rushed into the car.

"*Mommy!*" Sam's fearful cry broke the silence. "I got hurt. Will hurt me!"

"Mom, what happened?" Lizzie's tone was frantic.

Meg told herself to get control. She couldn't afford to panic. "What is it, Sam? Will, Lizzie, are you okay?"

"I'm fine," Will said.

"My head hurts," Sam whimpered. "Will hit me with his elbow really hard."

"It was an accident! There's nothing wrong with you!"

"Lizzie?"

Her daughter was beginning to cry. "I want to go home."

Meg turned to look at James. His face was white. Blood trickled down his temple from a cut on his head, and she saw several other slashes on his face and neck from the pieces of glass that seemed to be everywhere. "James?"

"I'm all right." He spoke quietly. "You?"

The door on Meg's side was yanked open from the outside, startling all of them. "You folks okay in there?"

A man in a black coat and black hat with a wide, flat brim peered in, an anxious expression on his face. He had a full brown beard but no mustache, and dark hair with bangs cut straight across his forehead. The man driving the buggy, Meg realized. An Amish man, of course.

"You need to get to a hospital?" He had an accent that Meg interpreted as something between German and Dutch.

James leaned forward to talk to him across Meg. "Just a little banged up. But thanks."

The children were staring at the man with mild fright. He looked them over, noting the heavy quilts surrounding the three. "You were lucky, wrapped up like that. Cushioned the blow, I'd guess."

"My brother hit me in the head," Sam volunteered.

"Shut up," Will shot back.

The man turned his attention back to James. "Do you have people nearby? You live here?"

"No, we're not from here," James said. "We were looking for a motel to spend the night. We got lost."

"Ah, well." The man nodded, thinking. "You best come home with me, then. In the morning you can decide what to do." He straightened up. "I'll bring the horse closer."

As soon as he moved away from the car, Will burst out, his cry urgent. "No way! We're not going to that freak's house!"

"He's totally creepy." Lizzie was just as vehement. "You just know their house is disgusting. You *can't* make us go there."

James closed his eyes and spoke slowly. "Our car is destroyed, and we have no place to sleep. So we're going to accept this very kind stranger's offer, and you are going to be perfect little angels. Do I make myself clear?"

Silence from the back.

"I understand, Daddy," Sam finally offered.

"Be quiet, you little suck-up," Lizzie hissed.

"Now, then, let's see if we can get you out of there." They heard the man's voice before they saw his face at the window again.

Meg shifted her body carefully among the jagged shards of glass scattered about. She realized that she, too, had a number of stinging cuts, some still bleeding.

But she was weak with relief to see that the children had escaped any real injury. Sam was already developing a lump on his forehead from Will's elbow, and it would doubtless be much bigger by the next day. Lizzie's left foot was bothering her; she must have smacked it on something, but it didn't seem serious. Thank goodness for those quilts and pillows, Meg thought.

Shivering in the icy night, the children clutching their quilts around them, the family surveyed the wreckage of their car. James had nearly managed to avoid the telephone pole, but his side of the car hadn't quite cleared it. The front left had smashed into the pole and was pushed in like an accordion. Thinking of their narrow escape, Meg felt faint.

"Let's get you out of the cold," the man said.

One at a time, he helped them up into the buggy, James and Will in the front seat, the others in back. A thick leather top kept the wind off them, but inside it was far from warm. Meg put an arm around Sam and Lizzie, who slumped miserably against her. James wrapped his arm around Will's shoulders, and, uncharacteristically, his son allowed it.

"My name is David Lutz." He got in next to James and picked up the leather reins. He made a slight clicking sound, and the horse began to trot. "I'll send my sons back for your bags. You need to get the car towed."

"We can't thank you enough, Mr. Lutz," James said loud enough to be heard over the horse's trotting.

"I don't know what we would have done," Meg added.

David Lutz turned his head so his words could be heard more easily. "No. I thank you. You put yourselves in danger so you wouldn't hit me. We just need to see you all get taken care of and get a good rest."

He faced front once again and said nothing else for the rest of the ride.

It was too dark to see much along the narrow roads. The

houses and farms were spread far from one another, with few lights on. My poor kids, Meg thought, still comforting Lizzie and Sam. On top of everything else, a car accident. Now this incredibly strange rescue.

Abruptly, the horse turned in to a long dirt road leading to a house, then came to a halt. The shades on the first floor were drawn, but faint light could be seen outlining the edges.

"Wait here," David Lutz said. "I'll be right back with some help."

He disappeared into the house. The children disembarked on their own. As Meg and James began to ease themselves down from the buggy, the front door to the house opened, and David Lutz emerged with two teenage boys, one taller than the other but both dressed identically. Despite the cold, they wore only long-sleeved dark blue shirts and black pants with suspenders. They hastened over to assist Meg and James.

"You are hurt?" The shorter boy, holding his hands out to Meg, had the same lilting accent as his father.

"Just a little shaken up," she said, grateful for his arm as she stepped down onto the icy ground.

"Come inside. My mother is making you something to eat."

All three of their children waited until Meg and James entered the house first, not out of politeness, Meg knew, but so they could hide behind them. They entered a large, dimly lit room that contained a kitchen on the far end and a huge wooden dining table surrounded by what might have been twenty chairs. The furniture was solid but simple. There were no decorations on the walls other than a calendar and a stitched sampler with words that Meg guessed to be German. She realized kerosene lamps were providing what little light there was. On the wall next to her, she saw a long, low bench and, above it, hooks mounted on a narrow piece of wood, each hook occupied by a black coat or cape. Some hooks also held either the same type of hat David was wearing or what appeared to be women's black bonnets. On the opposite side of the room, Meg saw wooden chairs and a sofa with padded blue cushions. Behind them were additional chairs next to several folding tables set up with crayons and paper, half-done puzzles, and a game of Monopoly still in progress. Everything in the room appeared old and worn from use but immaculately clean.

Behind her, Meg heard Will whisper. "Can you believe this place?"

Lizzie whispered back. "Kill me now."

Meg shot them a warning look.

A woman stood by the stove. Short and slender, she was dressed in a mauve-colored dress and a black apron. The dress came down to the middle of her calves, and below that she wore dark black stockings but no shoes. Her hair was all but hidden beneath a white cap whose strings hung down, untied.

At the sound of people entering the house, she turned. Her face was free of makeup, her features plain. It seemed to Meg that she could have been anywhere from thirty to fifty.

"Hello. Welcome to our house." The woman smiled warmly. "I'm Catherine. Would the children like tea or hot chocolate? I'm warming some stew, but that will take a little more time."

There was an enormous covered pot and a teakettle on the stove behind her.

"You're very kind," James said. "Thank you."

"Come." David Lutz ushered them over to the table, waving to the two boys to pull out chairs for their guests. Lizzie, Will, and Sam took seats, all three keeping their gazes down. Meg wondered if she looked as ill at ease as they did. She couldn't believe how nervous she felt, afraid she would say or do something inappropriate or even offensive to these people. She cast about to recall anything at all she might know about the Amish.

"These are two of my sons, Jonathan and Eli," David continued.

Both boys said a bright "hello."

"Oh, I'm so sorry. I feel ridiculous," Meg said. "We haven't even told you our names. I'm Meg Hobart."

"James Hobart." He reached out to shake David Lutz's hand.

They looked expectantly at their children, who mumbled their names, trying to avoid meeting anyone's eyes.

"I'll get some things for you to clean off this blood," Catherine said. She disappeared through a doorway.

Their host turned to James and Meg. "I sent my daughter to bring a doctor we know. He should look at all of you."

"Oh, no, you don't have to—" James protested.

David held up a hand. "While we wait, tell me if I can get you something."

"We have to make some calls about the car," James said. "We don't have cell phones on us, though. Do you have a phone I could use?"

"There is a telephone outside in the shed," David told him. "We don't keep one in the house."

The three Hobart children looked astonished.

James nodded. "Thank you. I appreciate it."

"Jonathan." David addressed his son. "You and Eli see what you can get out of their car. Their suitcases and such. Come. I'll tell you where."

He quickly strode out the front door as the boys grabbed black jackets from the hooks and followed. Able to see them a little better now, Meg judged Jonathan to be around eighteen, while Eli looked closer to fourteen. They both had blond hair in the same bowl-shaped haircut as their father.

It struck her that Eli was probably between Lizzie and Will in age. Somehow that didn't seem possible. It wasn't just the clothes and haircut. Maybe it was his demeanor or the open and direct way he spoke to them. She wasn't quite sure what the quality was that made him so different, but there was definitely something. She tried to imagine her children responding so quickly and respectfully to her. The mental image almost made her laugh aloud. Suddenly, she realized that the incongruity of her children and respectful behavior wasn't funny at all. Not even a little.

Meg rubbed her eyes, exhausted. When Lizzie was little, Meg would tuck her into bed at night and, trying to get her resistant child to go to sleep, say that it had been a big day and now it was time to rest. Lizzie would always shake her head and demand, "*More* big day!" The phrase had become something of a family joke.

"Too much big day," Meg said softly.

Lizzie overheard her mother's comment. "Darn right, too much big day," she muttered. "*Way* too much."

Meg looked over to see Catherine Lutz enter the room with several small towels and washcloths. She put them down on the table, then went back to the stove, pausing to stir the contents of the pot. "Almost ready," she said, peering in at what was no doubt the stew she had mentioned.

Meg had no desire to eat. All she wanted to do was crawl into a bed somewhere and sleep. She glanced at James. He looked as if he was struggling to keep his eyes open. Everything that had led up to this minute seemed to be catching up with them. Leaving the house, making this trip and dreading the day they reached their destination, everyone's bickering, and then this crash. Meg wanted to sleep for a hundred years so she didn't have to think about any of it. She would bet James felt the same way.

The children, on the other hand, were seated at the table looking bored but fully awake. Will was rhythmically kicking the rungs of his chair. Sam had folded his hands on the table in front of him and was turning them this way and that, intently examining them. Lizzie sat slouched over, an elbow on the table, her head resting on her hand. All this might catch up with them later, but for now Meg felt certain they would be fine sitting here, eating—or rudely turning up their noses at— whatever this lovely woman was nice enough to serve them.

Catherine came to the table with a large bowl of warm water. She dipped two worn but clean washcloths into the water, wrung them out, and handed them to Meg and James. For the first time, Meg looked closely at her own arms and saw the thin streaks of blood.

These are truly kind people, Meg thought as she dabbed at her cuts with the warm cloth. Imagine opening your house to help a bunch of strangers who had almost run you over. Taking a quick look at her sullen children, she hoped the Lutzes wouldn't come to regret it.

Chapter 7

✦

Meg opened her eyes to see an overcast day through the panes of an unfamiliar window. The gray sky gave no clue whether it was morning or afternoon. Trying to clear her head, she stared at the short beige curtains framing the window. As she shifted position on the bed, she let out an involuntary groan. Every inch of her body hurt.

It all came back to her at once. The accident, the buggy ride to the Lutz household, James going outside to the shed where the Lutzes kept a telephone so he could call a tow truck. His second call had been to the insurance company, and Meg had breathed a sigh of relief knowing that their policy was paid up until the first of the year.

When the doctor arrived, Meg had been surprised to see that he wasn't Amish, but he was a friend of the Lutz family. He examined them all to check for broken bones or signs of trauma and prescribed ice for the bump on Sam's head and the bruise on Lizzie's foot. As the doctor removed slivers of glass from the cuts on James and Meg, he warned them that they might feel a bit battered in the morning. Reassured that they had ibuprofen in their possession, he left, refusing James's offer of payment.

After that, Catherine Lutz had served bowls of steaming beef stew with warm home-baked bread and butter, tall glasses of water, and hot tea. Meg hadn't realized she was hungry until she caught the aroma of the food put in front of her. Although she and James quickly finished their portions, she saw that her children ate only the bread, making disgusted faces at one another behind Catherine's back as soon as they tasted the thick stew.

After she finished eating, Meg picked up her bowl and glass and came around to Will, who was about to step away from the table. "Clear your dishes and push in your chair," she whispered.

His startled expression confirmed that he hadn't thought of doing either, but he carried his plates to the kitchen counter. Lizzie and Sam followed suit.

Catherine told Lizzie she could share a room with her daughter, Amanda, who was sixteen. She had gone to a friend's house nearby, but she would be back later. Will and Sam would be given the bedroom of the Lutzes' seventeen-year-old son, who was away. They all grabbed their bags, which had been retrieved and neatly lined up near the door, and trooped upstairs, Lizzie limping and complaining about the pain in her foot. Only a few kerosene lamps lit the steps and hallways. It was a large upstairs with numerous doors, Meg noted, but without having seen the outside very well in the dark, she found it difficult to make out just how big the house might be. She wondered how many people lived there.

Catherine directed them to the room at one end of the hall where Lizzie would be sleeping. As her daughter went in and dropped her bags on one of the twin beds, Meg took a quick look around. Plain wooden furniture, a dresser and a night table with a Bible on it. The curtains, doubtlessly hand-sewn, were yellow-and-white-checked, and the beds had yellow sheets and unadorned white dust ruffles. There were no computer photos, posters, or decorations like Lizzie or her friends would have displayed. Instead, Meg saw that the room's inhabitant had hung up rows of notes, cards, and letters she must have received over the years.

The room where Will and Sam were to spend the night was very different. Meg saw free weights in one corner, an archery bow propped nearby, and posters of various athletes hung up on the walls. On the high chest of drawers, she spotted a framed photograph of several smiling Amish teenagers, buddies having a good time.

Sam reached for a quick good-night hug from his mother, the fearful look in his eyes causing her to kneel down and put a hand on his cheek. She smiled at him. "We're right here," she murmured into his hair as she held him close, "and you'll be with your brother."

"Yeah, come on," Will said as he dropped his bags on the floor. "I'll tell you ghost stories."

Sam shot his mother a look of panic.

"Just kidding, Sam." Will laughed.

Meg hugged and reassured Sam for another minute before he was willing to let her go.

Catherine led Meg and James to the far end of the hall. The bedroom was spare, with two small windows framed by beige curtains, and furnished much like the others with a heavy wooden dresser and a night table in between twin beds. The beds looked freshly made.

"This is Annie's old room," Catherine explained. "She's married now and living next door. Amanda put clean sheets on while we were downstairs."

Meg and James tried to express their gratitude once again, but Catherine waved away their words. "We eat breakfast at six, but you don't need to get up that early. Is eight o'clock all right for you?"

"That would be wonderful."

Catherine nodded and headed toward the stairs. Meg closed the door.

"This is quite the situation," James said, dropping down onto one of the beds to take off his shoes.

There was a tap on the door.

"I know we've gone back to 1742," Lizzie said with sarcastic sweetness, "but could you please wake me when it's the present again?"

Meg yanked open the door. "Not funny, Lizzie." She looked past her daughter to scan the hallway. "And please shush. They might hear you."

The girl rolled her eyes. "Relax, there's no one up here but us. I looked. But come on, Mom, we're in some kind of time warp. We're in *Little House on the Prairie*! Which, by the way, was on the bookcase downstairs! Are you kidding me? Please just get us out of here tomorrow first thing."

James looked up at her. "How should I do that, Liz?" he asked in annoyance. "Build a car with paper-towel tubes and duct tape?"

Lizzie's expression turned dark. "I don't care what we have to do, but I'm not staying here a minute more than I have to."

Meg kept her annoyance in check. "Go on back to your room. We should all get some rest."

"It's *nine-thirty*! Who goes to bed at nine-thirty?"

"Tonight," Meg replied, "we do. And remember to make your bed in the morning and clean up after yourself in the bathroom. We're guests, so let's behave like guests."

"It's weird up here, all deserted. Everything's so ugly."

"Good night, sweetheart." Meg gently closed the door.

"Sure, what do you care?" Lizzie's complaints grew fainter as she moved down the hall. "You're not sharing a room with someone who thinks this is the eighteenth century."

Meg felt she couldn't move another muscle. She found one of her nightgowns in her suitcase, slipped it on, and crawled under the covers, falling instantly into a deep sleep.

Waking up now, she was amazed that her body, which had felt tired but fine the night before, could be so stiff and sore.

She looked at James, asleep in the other bed, then reached for her watch on the night table. The slight movement made her feel as if every single muscle in her body were screaming in protest. It was seven-forty.

"James," she called out, slightly panicked, "wake up! We're supposed to be downstairs at eight. That's in twenty minutes!"

He mumbled something and rolled away from her voice. With a long groan, Meg forced herself to sit up.

"You have to get up," she said with more force as she made her way to her purse for the small bottle of ibuprofen she always kept there. She was particularly sore on her side, where James had collided with her at the moment of impact.

"Oh, wow, everything aches." James stared at the ceiling, tentatively stretching out his arms.

"Here, you want two of these?" She held out the bottle. Whatever their problems were, for now she would have to put aside her resentment toward James to get through the situation. "We have to wake the kids up. I'm sure they're dead asleep, and we're supposed to have breakfast now."

Grumbling, the children threw on their clothes and headed downstairs, Lizzie still limping slightly. By the time they had all assembled in the kitchen, it was nearly eight-thirty. Meg saw that Sam had a huge, angry-looking lump on his forehead, but he didn't say anything about it, so she didn't bring it up.

They found five places set for them at the table, including glasses filled with orange juice. There were several boxes of cereal, a plate with chocolate-chip cookies, doughnuts, and what appeared to be homemade zucchini bread, plus a bowl of strawberry preserves. Next to all of that were pitchers with milk and water. The room was dim, and Meg realized that the windows were the only source of light. Of course, she thought. No electricity, but it was daytime, so it wouldn't be necessary to light lamps or candles.

Meg looked around. "I have to say, this house is so clean, you could perform brain surgery on the floor of any room."

The Hobart children sat down at the table and glowered. Lizzie touched the flowered plastic place mat with distaste. "Gross."

"These aren't normal cereals," Will complained. "What is this, all generic?"

"They're the same as cornflakes and Cheerios," James answered.

"My bed was so hard, I might as well have slept on the floor. And if I hadn't had my own blanket, I would have frozen to death under that thin thing they had on the bed." Lizzie reached for a cookie.

Meg ignored her remarks. "Did you see their daughter?"

"I saw her at some point, but she woke me up by accident, and it was dark, so I don't know if it was when she came in or got up to leave." Lizzie grinned. "Maybe she was out until all hours. These people are party animals."

Will laughed and high-fived his sister.

The door opened, and Catherine Lutz came inside, her face flushed with the cold. Will and Lizzie immediately fell silent. Sam poured himself a bowl of cereal.

Catherine removed her black cape, talking cheerfully as she hung it on a hook. "Good morning. I thought you might need some more sleep, so I just put this out. I can make you some hot food now. Eggs and ham? Coffee?"

"No, thank you," James answered. "This is plenty. But coffee would be great."

David Lutz appeared behind his wife, wiping his feet on the

doormat before he came in. "Ah, I'm in time to sit with you. How are you folks feeling today?"

"Like the doctor warned us," Meg said. "We're stiff, but it'll pass."

David sat down at the head of the table. "Would one of you like to say grace?"

Sam, who had been reaching for the milk pitcher, froze, then dropped his arm into his lap. Will's and Lizzie's eyes widened.

Meg had no idea what constituted grace for these people. She doubted James did, either, which he confirmed with the note of doubt in his voice. "Uh, thank you, but no. It's your house, so please, you go ahead."

David nodded. "Our Father, who art in Heaven . . ."

Oh, thought Meg with relief, it's the Lord's Prayer. What had she been expecting? She and James joined in, their children sitting silently, the two elder ones doing a poor job of hiding their pained expressions. The Lutzes, Meg saw, either didn't notice or were gracious enough to pretend they didn't.

"Where is everybody?" Will asked when they had finished. He took a bite of a doughnut. "Are you the only people here?"

David smiled. "Oh, there are lots of people here. The younger children are at school. The older ones are doing chores. Some of our children are married and don't live here, but they'll be by at some point. They live in the houses nearby, so the grandchildren run in and out a lot, too. Be careful you don't trip on them."

"Whoa," said Lizzie in surprise before she caught herself.

Meg realized that her daughter had never been exposed to

an extended family living so close to one another. They barely had relatives, much less ones that might run in and out a lot.

"You didn't get to meet Amanda yesterday," Catherine said to Lizzie, "but she's breaking up the ice in front of the barn, and she'll be in a little later."

Lizzie's forced smile matched the tone of her words. "That's great."

Catherine brought over a pot of coffee and poured cups for Meg and James. "It snowed a little during the night, but mostly there is ice now."

"When you're done with your coffee," David said to James, "we can find out the situation with your car. I'll take you over to the repair shop."

James looked grim. "We'd better find out what we're dealing with. Thanks."

Meg saw that her children had finished eating. "Kids, why don't you clear your plates, then run upstairs and make your beds?"

"Sure, you bet." Will jumped up with false cheerfulness.

Meg happened to catch James's eye. She saw he was no more pleased with their older children's behavior than she was.

Finally, David and James left, and Meg was alone with Catherine, helping to clean up.

"How many children do you have?" Meg asked, stacking dirty dishes in the sink. She tried to ignore the soreness that accompanied her every move.

"Nine," Catherine said.

"Nine children," Meg echoed in amazement.

"Two are married. You met Jonathan and Eli. There's

Amanda, who's sixteen, and Benjamin, who's seventeen. The youngest are Aaron and Rachel. They're eleven and eight. They were visiting at my sister's house last night. And then there's my daughter Barbara. She's getting married next week." Catherine began washing the dishes.

"Really?" Meg asked in surprise. "Next week?"

"Yes. We're having family and friends from all over to cele-brate." She gave a little grin. "And do lots and lots of eating. The lunch and evening supper will be across the road at Joseph's house. He is one of the married children I told you about. About three hundred people are coming."

Meg reached for the small towel that was resting near the dish rack. She tried to picture herself being as calm as this woman if she were having three hundred guests at her house in a week.

"How will you manage . . ." Meg hesitated, wanting to ask more, but fearful she would say something foolish.

"Everyone helps," Catherine said. "Lots of people cooking, serving food, cleaning up."

Meg dried a pitcher, feeling ignorant and nosy at the same time. She didn't ask any further questions, and Catherine fin-ished the rest of the dishes without volunteering anything else. When she was done, she excused herself. "It's laundry day. I know you're not feeling well, so you rest."

"You know, Catherine, I really don't know what will happen with the car," Meg said. She paused, unsure what she wanted to say or ask.

It was obvious the car wasn't going to be ready to go any-where today, but they had no place else to go. Maybe the Lutzes would take them to a motel or something. Meg dreaded the idea of the five of them cooped up in a motel room for an indefinite period. Not to mention the cost. Yet they couldn't impose on these people any further. For all Meg knew, they hated having non-Amish people in their house.

Catherine looked at her. Her eyes, Meg realized, were a pale blue. They crinkled at the edges as she gave Meg a warm smile. "You're welcome to stay here as long as you wish."

"I . . . We can't . . ."

"You can if you want," Catherine said simply, heading out through another door leading from the room.

Chapter 8

❁

Having persuaded Catherine that she was indeed up to performing some sort of work, Meg sat on the couch next to a veritable mountain of towels. Catherine had brought them to her from an outside clothesline, and they were cold and rigid from the December air. Meg shook them out as best she could with her sore shoulders, then folded them into thirds and in half. She paid close attention to the task, wanting this minimal contribution to be done properly. These people clearly had very high standards, at least in housekeeping, and she didn't want anybody to have to redo her job, small as it might be.

Meg found it was a relief to become totally engrossed in the task. She didn't have to think about the fact that she and her family were stranded with virtually no money, or that their only form of transportation was a twisted wreck that might not even be fixable. Nor did she have to think about how furious she was at her husband, who had lied to her, basically stolen all the family's money only to throw it away, and brought them to this point. She could also block out the vague but horrible image of what their immediate future would look like when they figured out how to get from here to her parents' house.

Shake, fold, smooth, put to the side. The graying, scratchy linens made her recall the white towels in the bathrooms of their house in Charlotte. Lots of detergent, bleach, fabric softener, and a hot dryer kept those enormous Egyptian-cotton bath towels fluffy and blindingly white. They held a sweet, lightly performed scent, noticeable only when she wrapped herself up in one, an especially cozy feeling after it had been resting on the electric towel rack, warming on a winter's morning. Meg picked up a towel from the pile and held it to her nose. No perfume, but she found that she liked its absence, the smell of fresh air somehow infused into the rough fabric, making her want to take a deep breath.

Bracing, she thought, but probably not so inspiring when you're dripping wet on a freezing morning.

The door opened, and Meg tensed as she saw the expression on James's face. His mouth was set in a way that told her the news was not going to be good.

"What happened?" she asked. "You've been gone for hours."

He unzipped his jacket. "The place they towed it to suggested we might want to get to a shop that specializes in vintage cars. So we did that. But the guy there can't even do anything until the insurance guys take a look. Someone will come by today or tomorrow, hopefully. They'll call us at the phone outside here, or I'll have to keep calling them."

"Is it a big deal to fix?"

"The guy gave it a quick look while I was there. He said there's extensive damage from the front fender all the way to the rear quarter panel. In other words, lots of bodywork needed on the driver's side."

"How long will that take?"

James scowled. "That's the thing. He said a week or two."

"A week or two?" Meg repeated. "We can't stay here for that long."

James gave her an exasperated look. "What would you have me do, Meg? You sound like Lizzie. I can't snap my fingers and get us out of here. If you have any ideas, please feel free to share them with me."

They were interrupted by Sam, who had been outside with his sister and brother. Meg had told them all to go for a walk earlier when their whining about how bored they were had become too much for her.

"Hey, sport, what are you up to?" James asked Sam.

"They were fighting too much. Besides, I'm freezing."

"Come over here." Meg moved the folded towels away and patted the couch beside her. "I'll warm you up."

Sam sat down, and she put her arms around him, vigorously rubbing his back through his fleece jacket. She kissed the top of his head as he leaned in to her. James went over to the sink to get himself a glass of water. Meg guessed he felt as uncomfortable as she did prying into their hosts' cupboards or refrigerator.

One of the doors opened, and the three of them looked up at the sound. An elderly man, slightly stooped, stood in the doorway. His hair was nearly white, and he had bangs falling across his forehead, plus a long, full beard. He was dressed just like all the other men they had seen in the house, in black pants with suspenders and a dark blue shirt. He wore a black vest as well.

"Ah," he said, smiling. "Our visitors." He came forward, moving to take a seat at the big table. "I am Samuel Lutz. David is my son." He jerked a thumb in the direction of the door from which he had emerged. "We live there."

James went over to introduce himself and Meg and shake Samuel's hand. Then Samuel turned his attention to Sam. "And who is this young man?"

Shyly, Sam identified himself.

Samuel Lutz's eyes lit up. "Ahh, another Samuel! Very good!"

Sam obviously hadn't put his name together with the name of this odd-looking man. "Oh. Yeah."

The older man smiled. "We will be good friends, then. I will call you Young Samuel."

Sam looked uncomfortable but said nothing.

"I heard we had visitors. I wanted to meet you before the crowd comes in for lunch. My daughter-in-law will be here soon, I think, to put it out."

As if on cue, Catherine joined them from outside. She was in conversation with a young girl dressed much like she was, down to the white head covering with the untied strings.

"Hello," said Catherine. "This is my daughter Amanda. She and your daughter are in one bedroom."

"Oh, yes." Meg looked at the girl with interest. "Lizzie said she didn't get a chance to meet you last night."

"I was out," Amanda answered with the family's accent, "but I got up early, so we never talked."

"But now it is lunch, so you'll meet her." Catherine moved to the kitchen area and opened the oven door to check on what she had inside. "Everyone will meet everyone."

Amanda pulled open a kitchen drawer.

"Thirteen," Catherine said. "Plus some little ones. Maybe three."

Amanda nodded and reached into the drawer to pull out flatware.

Meg whispered to Sam, "Run outside and get your sister and brother. We all need to help."

By the time the table had been set and everyone was assembled, there were seventeen people. They all seemed to be speaking in a language that sounded like German, although Meg couldn't be sure. As soon as they saw the Hobarts, they switched to English.

The Lutz family said grace silently, and Meg realized the spoken grace when they first arrived probably had been done for their benefit. Introductions were swift, and she didn't remember all of the names. A few stood out. The older man, Samuel Lutz, was married to Leah. Somewhat stout, with a full face and lips, she was polite but no more than that, lacking her husband's genuine warmth. Two men arrived with small children in tow, and Catherine explained that their wives were baking. Meg had no idea why that meant they had to miss lunch, but it didn't seem like the right moment to ask. She knew she would remember Barbara, a bubbly young woman who was introduced as the daughter getting married the following week. Jonathan, the older of the two sons who had helped them the night before, also joined them at the last minute.

Meg's children, silent with the strangeness of it all, seemed taken aback by the size of this lunchtime gathering, which apparently was a daily occurrence. Catherine indicated that the two teenage roommates should sit next to each other, and Amanda greeted Lizzie with a smile and obvious interest. Lizzie barely returned her greeting and said nothing more to her. The men and women took their places on opposite sides of the table.

With Meg and a stone-faced Lizzie joining them, the women helped serve what seemed like an endless succession of overflowing bowls and platters. The main meal consisted of bean soup, chicken in gravy, meat loaf, buttered noodles, brussels sprouts, peas and carrots, creamed corn, and hot biscuits with butter. The Hobart children ate little, pushing the food around on their plates, until they got to the desserts, which included pound cake, apple dumplings, rice pudding, and mixed fruit.

There was little conversation at the table. Meg observed the line of men across from her, all with the same haircut. The older ones had beards and no mustaches. Their clothing was virtually identical. The women kept their hair tucked under bonnets, and all had on the same simple dresses, some with black coverings like full aprons, the top half of which resembled an upside-down triangle. The dresses differed only in color: muted, dark tones of blue or purple or gray. Meg wondered at the fact that even by this point in the day their clothes remained perfectly pressed. She noted that the garments were held closed with straight pins rather than buttons or zippers. There was not a single piece of jewelry or a hint of makeup on any of them.

The men reported to one another on the progress of whatever they had been working on that morning. David had missed much of his morning work by taking James to see about the car, but he managed to get to the barn, where they were shoveling out manure, bringing it to an area where they stored it to be used as fertilizer. One of the men updated the others on repairs he was making on their horses' harnesses. James asked if he might help with that job, saying he didn't think he could manage a shovel just yet, but he could try to make himself useful until he could put his back into something. David nodded.

Lunch was over quickly. The men left, and the women cleaned up before dispersing. The smaller children were left behind, giving Meg an idea for something to occupy her own children's time. Catherine said it wasn't necessary for anyone to watch her grandchildren, that they would be fine playing near her, but Meg insisted that her children babysit. All three of them shot daggers at her with their eyes, but Meg was delighted to see that it wasn't long before they actually seemed to be enjoying interacting with the toddlers.

Amanda said a smiling good-bye to all of them and ran out to where her brother Jonathan waited in a buggy.

"She's off to deliver to the store, and I'm going to prepare for supper," Catherine explained, setting out a large knife and chopping board. "I have to get back out to hang up the rest of the laundry."

She hadn't even sat down after serving lunch, Meg observed, and now she was on to the next meal and more chores. Did she ever rest?

"Do you mind if I ask you what store you mean?" As she spoke, Meg saw an opportunity to repeat her earlier job of drying dishes and reached for the dish towel.

Catherine had begun cutting up potatoes to put into a large pot of water. "It is a store in town. King's is the name. We make them things to sell. Bread, cakes, jams. Different things, depending on the season. That's why my daughter Annie and my daughter-in-law Sue weren't at lunch. Today was their day to do the baking. They brought fresh bread and rolls in the morning, and now Amanda will take over the pies with Jonathan."

"You make everything here?"

Catherine nodded. "Oh, yes."

"Jams?"

"Jams, jelly, all kinds of preserves. We pickle things. Make vinegars, too."

Meg was fascinated. "I'd love to see how you do that."

Catherine heaved the large pot onto the stove and covered it. "We make a lot of it in the warmer months. I will take you downstairs, and you can see it. After I finish cutting up some vegetables, I'll show you."

"Thank you." Meg's admiration for this busy woman was growing. "I've always loved the idea of making jams and preserves, but I never had time to learn." She regretted the words the second they had left her mouth. To say she didn't have enough time to someone who worked as hard as Catherine was ludicrous. "I guess," she amended, "I didn't make the time."

Catherine was immersed in cutting up carrots and celery

and didn't reply. When she finished, she set down her knife. "I will take you downstairs."

Meg followed her to a door that led to the basement steps. As she reached the bottom of the staircase, she caught her breath at the sight before her. Although the room was primarily below ground level, windows had been installed high up enough to let outside daylight in. Like everything else in the house, the basement was spotless. What surprised Meg were the rows upon rows of open wooden shelving, set up like library stacks. The shelves sagged under the weight of hundreds of glass bottles and jars containing a vast array of different foods. Nearby, Meg saw a table with what appeared to be a setup for the final packaging, with squares of fabrics, rubber bands, labels, colored markers, and scissors.

"You do all this yourself?" she asked in disbelief.

"Oh, no. All the women in the family do it. The women and the girls. We have much more in my daughter's and son's houses."

Catherine waited patiently while Meg walked up and down a few of the rows. She marveled at the intricacy of this business, at the fact that it was tucked into such a tiny space. The shelves had handwritten labels identifying the containers' contents. Onion Relish, Apple Jam, Apricot Chutney, Chowchow, Strawberry Preserves, Chili Oil, Sweet Pickled Peppers, Bread-and-Butter Pickles, Corn Relish, Rosemary Vinegar. Meg was struck by the beauty of all the bottle shapes and the colors and textures of the foods within them. "Amazing. Such variety, too. What a job all this must be," she exclaimed.

"It's not hard once you learn how," Catherine replied. "Now I must get back to cooking."

Turning to go, Meg caught sight of a large area at the far side of the basement devoted to storing what she saw were root vegetables. She could identify onions, carrots, parsnips, potatoes, and something she guessed was horseradish in large crocks lined up in neat rows.

When they rejoined the children in the living room, they found that Samuel Lutz had returned, this time with a puppy in his arms. The elderly man was seated on the couch, talking to his great-grandchildren as he stroked the puppy's head. They must have been used to the dog, Meg thought, because they weren't exclaiming over it the way children typically did at such a sight. Now that she thought about it, she realized she had passed a number of dog bowls set out near the back entrance to the house. Some of the barking she had heard coming from outside must have come from dogs belonging to the Lutzes.

Will didn't seem interested in the scene before him. He sat at one of the folding tables, flipping through the pages of a book. Lizzie, however, was scratching the puppy under its chin, making cooing sounds, and Sam was sitting next to the older man, staring at the light brown ball of fur.

Samuel Lutz must have noticed the boy's interest. He held the puppy out to him. "Young Samuel?"

Sam's face lit up as he reached for the dog and nestled him in his lap. He looked happier than Meg had seen him in weeks. She watched him rub his cheek against the dog's soft head, the widest smile on his face. Of course, Meg thought. I can't believe I didn't I think of it before. Sam should have a dog. It was a simple and wonderful idea.

Her heart sank as she remembered that they were heading to her parents', who had never wanted anything to do with a pet in their house. As a child, Meg had begged them to let her have a dog or a cat, anything at all, but they always said no. Pets were messy. There were cages and bowls to clean and expensive food to buy. Meg felt pretty certain they were unlikely to have softened on the topic as they had gotten older.

She sighed, watching the puppy lick Sam's face, her son giggling with pleasure. Samuel Lutz leaned over and spoke quietly to him about the dog, lifting a paw and showing him the pads underneath, gently opening the dog's mouth to explain about the teeth.

Meg went over to a window and looked out. She wished she were in a position to do something so good for Sam. She looked at the clothesline where Catherine had hung out the wet clothes. The different-colored dresses and the men's shirts, black pants, and jackets were attached with clothespins in neat lines, each type of garment grouped, each garment attached at the same points. It looked to her like a line of people—flat people, to be sure, but a big family, ordered and serene.

With a start, she realized she had been so preoccupied, she hadn't yet gone outside to look around. "I'm going to take a walk unless anyone needs me," she announced to the room in general.

"Can I come?" Will asked, reaching for his jacket, which he had thrown on a chair.

Meg was surprised. "Of course, honey. Let me grab my coat." She hurried upstairs, feeling the soreness in her back. As she passed the room Will and Sam were occupying, she paused long enough to notice that, while their beds could technically be considered made, it would have been easy to think otherwise. She hurried to get her jacket, anxious to get out.

With her son beside her, Meg stepped out into the cold daylight to see that the house was set amid enormous open fields. The ground sloped beneath the gray sky, providing a panoramic view of other farms, their neat houses and barns nestled close to tall pairs of silos and pens. Straight paved roads crisscrossed the landscape. The bare tree branches and frozen ground gave the scene a stark silence. Off in the distance, she saw a horse and buggy on the road, the horse trotting at a brisk clip.

"Like a painting," Meg murmured.

"This place is *so* weird" was Will's response.

She turned to him. "You know, you guys are being pretty horrible to the kids here."

"Oh, please." He gave a little snort of disgust. "These kids are the biggest bunch of losers I've ever seen."

"Why? Because they're different from you?"

"Because they're different from *humans*. The stuff they wear! And the way they talk. It's like we're in some bad museum exhibit or something."

Meg shook her head. "I guess I'm surprised at you. I would have expected you to be a little more curious about something so different from what you've always known. Not so judgmental."

"Don't try to guilt me with that 'I'm disappointed in you' stuff," Will said. "This is just plain wacko."

Meg frowned. She tried to remember if she and James had ever actively tried to instill any curiosity in Will about the way other people lived. Over the years, the family had vacationed at Disney World and the Grand Canyon, in the Caribbean and the Outer Banks. Fun places, and beautiful, but hardly educational when it came to learning about the rest of the world. Their dinner-table conversation had focused on the kids' daily activities and who needed to get what or go where.

She shoved her hands in her coat pockets. "Let's walk."

Meg saw now that the Lutzes' house was quite large, with a fresh-looking coat of white paint and dark-green shades at all the first-floor windows. Two rocking chairs and small outdoor tables sat to one side of the front porch. On a side porch, she noted used children's toys, a dented tricycle, and an assortment of mismatched chairs, one of which held a sleeping gray cat. Empty terra-cotta and hanging pots suggested the display of numerous plants and flowers in the warmer weather. Meg noticed several birdhouses filled with birdseed. She was surprised to discover that what she assumed was a portion of the house was a second, attached house, slightly smaller but similar in design. That, she realized, must be where Samuel and Leah Lutz lived, and the doorway through which he had emerged when they first met must be the connection.

Meg came upon a patch of land that was clearly a garden, now put to bed for the winter. With her son behind her, she walked along its borders.

"Mom? What's going to happen to us?"

She stopped, startled by her son's unexpected question, by

the fear in his tone. She had been wondering when the children would start to ask more pointed questions about their situation. Apparently the moment was now. She decided to see how far into it Will really wished to go.

"What'll happen is we'll get the car repaired, and we'll head up to Grandma and Grandpa's."

She waited to see if that explanation would hold him. No such luck.

"That's not what I mean, and you know it. Stop treating me like a little kid," he said.

She turned to face him. "Okay, Will. Here's the truth: We're kinda starting over. We'll be okay. But for now we're pretty much broke, and that's for real. I'm not sure if you guys really get that, but if you don't, you will soon."

"Yeah, in a way, I still don't believe it."

"I know," Meg said. "Sometimes I don't, either. But we have to stay with your grandparents because we need to find work and save money. Then we'll take it from there."

He closed his eyes and made a pained face. "It's gonna be so *awful* to live with them. They don't even like us."

Meg wanted to agree with him but knew she shouldn't. "It'll be okay, Will. We'll work it out."

"How do you work out people not wanting you around?"

"You don't know they feel that way—"

"*Mom.*" Will gave her a look that told her to stop placating him.

Meg reached out to straighten the collar of his fleece jacket, automatically registering that he needed a haircut. "Here's the story. I'm going to work as hard and as fast as I can to figure out something that will allow us to be independent again. That I promise."

"What about you and Dad? You guys seem really angry at each other. Like, more angry than I've ever seen you. Are you getting divorced?"

She gazed into Will's eyes and saw he was not going to let her get away with anything less than the truth. He might be her little boy, but he was growing up fast. She took a breath. "I don't know," she said. "I just don't know."

He looked away.

"I'm sorry, honey," she said.

He nodded, then walked off without another word. She watched him go. The wind picked up, whipping his sandy hair in every direction.

She pulled her collar more tightly around her neck and was still staring after him when she heard James come up behind her. "Everything okay?" he asked.

"As okay as possible, I suppose," she replied without turning around.

He rested his hands on her shoulders. Startled, she slipped out of his grasp. "What are you doing?"

He shrugged. "Just trying to be nice. I mean, here we are, so we might as well make the best of things. No point in being angry, is there?"

"There is a point, yes, there is. Being here doesn't mean you get a free pass. Nothing has changed."

"Come on, Meg," he said, annoyed. "You can't keep rehashing the past. We have to move forward."

"We haven't exactly 'rehashed the past.' We haven't even

talked about it. Besides, you may not be happy with what happens when we move forward. Let me put it this way: I don't know if there *is* a forward for us."

"You're not still thinking of breaking up the family, are you? That would be crazy."

"Wow." Meg shook her head in disbelief. "You actually think that letting a little time go by should be enough to wipe the slate clean. I should just forgive and forget. That would be the most convenient thing for everybody."

"What's wrong with forgiving?"

"Can you even forgive a person who's not sorry?"

"I *am* sorry. Don't you think I feel—"

David Lutz came around the corner of the house, wearing muddied black rubber boots and holding a bucket in one hand. At the sight of him, James stopped talking.

"I'm going to the barn. Want to come?" David asked.

Relieved to have this argument interrupted, Meg nodded and strode toward him, James right behind her. The barn was a huge building set away from the main house. The smell of horses grew stronger as they approached. Inside, they saw shovels, pitchforks, rakes, an ax, and other tools hanging from hooks on the walls. The roof extended up two stories, with ladders and steps leading to haylofts and other perches. The wooden floor was swept completely clean.

"Horses are this way," David said, going down a passageway to the left. He pointed to a large cobweb in a corner. "My website."

Startled by the unexpected joke, Meg and James both laughed. Meg knew that their hosts were people like everyone else, but David's comment made her realize that she hadn't quite believed it until now. They weren't saints or judges. They knew what was going on in the world, they could joke about it, they had a sense of humor. And they weren't going to be offended by questions or mistakes. For the first time since they had arrived, Meg felt herself relax.

Coming around a corner, she saw two large stalls with five horses, several of them munching on hay. David walked up to the nearest horse and stroked his neck. "Most are for farming, but we keep two just for pulling the buggies."

James put out an open palm under another horse's muzzle. "Beautiful animals."

"They're like family to us, you know." David moved past the horses. "Over here, you can see where we keep the buggies."

They followed him into a partitioned area housing two buggies, with space for a third. They were identical from the back, gray with gray coverings and high, narrow wheels, plus a variety of red triangles and lights on the back to render them more visible at night. Meg looked into the front seat of one, surprised to see the woodwork on what was the equivalent of a dashboard. The rich dark wood was intricately carved and polished until it gleamed. It had been too dark the night before to notice.

David indicated the empty space. "The one that goes there belongs to my son Jonathan. He got his own when he turned sixteen."

"No heating, I guess. Cold in the winter, riding in these," James observed.

David smiled. "We use armstrong heaters. You know those?"

James shook his head. "No, I don't."

David threw an arm around James's shoulders and pulled him tight. "This is an armstrong heater."

James grinned. "Oh. Got it."

Laughing, David led them outside. He pointed to the fields stretching out before them. "We grow lots of crops. Tomatoes and peas, which we sell. Hay for feeding. Catherine has a garden with herbs and about, oh, twenty vegetables. We pickle and can them, some for us and some to sell."

Meg nodded. "Catherine showed me."

"In the spring, we have a road stand. Tourists buy vegetables into the early fall. Also, we have chickens, so we sell their eggs." David pointed to a white house across the road, then to another one some fifty yards away. "That is where my son and daughter live, those two houses. They have the cows. For dairy."

The tour was interrupted by the appearance of a boy and a girl running up to where the trio of adults stood, only to come to a stop before them. They were both blond, with pale-blue eyes, and they regarded Meg and James with open curiosity. The little boy had on the same type of wide-brim hat the men wore, while the little girl was bareheaded, her fine blond hair neatly pulled away from her face.

"These are my children, home from school," David said. "My son Aaron and my daughter Rachel."

"Hello," James said, smiling at them.

Meg took a step closer. "Hi. I guess you were at school this morning when we got up, so we didn't get to see you then."

They both nodded and continued gazing at her, their expressions friendly and direct.

"How old are you?" James asked.

"I am eleven," Aaron answered. "My sister is eight years."

"It's very nice to meet you," Meg said. Rachel gave her a wide grin. "Did you meet our children? They're inside," Meg went on.

The idea of other children clearly sounded exciting to them.

"May we go? Please?" Rachel asked her father.

"Yes, but after you say hello, you do your chores. Fun is later."

They ran off, smiling.

Dinner that night was served at five o'clock to an even larger crowd than at lunch. With the exception of Benjamin, the son who was away, all the Lutz children were at the table. Meg was able to straighten out who were the two married ones: Joseph, the son who lived across the road with his wife, Sue, and their two children, and Annie, the daughter who lived in the house immediately next door with her husband, Nicholas, and their three children. All their children were under the age of five, and they were quiet throughout the meal, other than a few requests for assistance. The few who were old enough to comprehend that the Hobarts were outsiders stared at them with fascination.

After grace, all of them worked their way through fried chicken, ham with pineapple rings, rice, butternut squash, beets, and sauerkraut. Taking a bite of corn bread, Meg reminded herself that, unlike her, these people performed physical labor all day long, so they could handle the calories they were consuming at meals. It also dawned on her that James must be unhappy with what they were being served. He had always been far stricter than she when it came to his diet. Just looking at the fat and cholesterol on his plate was probably enough to give him a heart attack. Normally, she thought, she would have been trying to figure out how she could find him something he would prefer to eat without hurting her hostess's feelings. At the moment, however, she wasn't concerned with his preferences.

What she was concerned with were her older children. Yet again, their behavior was making her want to wring their necks. Will refused to make eye contact with anyone at the table despite the obvious desire of Eli Lutz, the fourteen-year-old son who had helped them the previous night, to talk to him. Eli kept glancing over at him but seemed to know better than to initiate anything. Lizzie appeared to be barely enduring Amanda's efforts to converse with her. Meg was surprised by Amanda's persistent attempts to be friendly despite Lizzie's continued rudeness.

With relief, Meg saw that Sam was deep in conversation with Aaron, the eleven-year-old Meg had met outside the barn. From across the table, where she sat with the women, eight-year-old Rachel watched the two boys with unwavering intensity.

Here's what's wrong with this picture, Meg said to herself: As a child gets older, his or her manners should get better, not worse. It was only her youngest child who displayed any manners at all. The older ones were clearly on the decline when it came to even minimal politeness. What I thought of as typical teenage behavior, Meg rebuked herself, may have been typical or not—but that didn't make it right.

As they were finishing dessert, Amanda, Eli, Aaron, and Rachel stood up in a row facing the table, joined by Annie Lutz's five-year-old. Hands at their sides, with no musical accompaniment, they began to sing. Meg didn't catch all the words, but she understood that it was a song primarily about gratitude. All the diners were silent, watching and listening, smiles on their faces. Old Samuel nodded in time. Even his wife, the unsmiling Leah, seemed pleased.

Meg was mesmerized by their sweet, pure voices. More startling to her was that they showed no signs of embarrassment or resentment at being forced to perform. Their faces registered only concentration on their task. Meg saw that her own children could hardly bear to listen to the performance. They looked as if they would give years of their life to be anywhere else. Even Sam squirmed uncomfortably.

When the children were finished singing, the two eldest sat down and the other three remained standing to sing a second song. Meg noticed that the five-year-old didn't know all the words, but that didn't stop him from participating as best he could. Next, David and Catherine Lutz sang together. Afterward, no one applauded. Almost everyone seemed to have enjoyed it all, but no comments were made. Meg's children rolled their eyes at one another. Dinner was concluded.

Meg tried to imagine the children of anyone she knew getting up and singing so gracefully and willingly. Impossible. Why, she wondered, was it so outlandish to think that children could get up and sing without imitating rock stars or rappers, without trying to appear cool or amused by the irony of their own performance? Some kids would play the piano for their parents' friends, and she could recall seeing girls perform a dance they had made up or planned to do for something at school. That kind of thing, yes, she thought; and always followed by extravagant praise. This was entirely different. It was a simple and somehow *vulnerable* performance. Traditional. Something that spoke of beliefs and prayers passed down from one generation to another. And so very beautiful.

Serving the evening meal, Meg saw, was far from the end of the day's work for the women in the house. When the kitchen area was spotless, Catherine and her daughters began sewing. They had a pile of men's black pants and jackets on the table and were repairing torn seams, replacing hooks and eyes, letting down hems. Amanda was stitching together pieces of black cloth.

"Amanda, are you making an apron?" Meg asked, taking a sip of coffee.

The girl looked up at her. "Yes."

"We make our clothes," Catherine explained. "Everything for the women and the children. Some families make their men's summer hats as well, the straw ones, but we don't do that. We buy those."

Meg tried to tally up what it would mean to make or repair the wardrobe for a family of eleven. A wardrobe limited in style, to be sure, but a huge number of garments that required skill and precision, since they had to look a very specific way.

"I use a sewing machine, mostly," Amanda added, "but I will not have time to do much tonight, so I am just working on it a little bit."

Catherine could see the question forming in Meg's mind. "It's not electric. A treadle sewing machine. It was my mother's."

"Mom, look!"

Meg turned to see Sam coming toward her, the puppy trotting along behind him.

"He's following me," Sam cried happily. "He knows me!"

Catherine stood up and went to a kitchen cabinet. "Maybe you want to give him a treat."

Sam took the piece of cracker Catherine handed him. "Here, Rufus. Here, boy."

As Sam held the puppy close and fed it the small treat, the dog licked his face. Meg had never seen Sam look so blissful.

Which made her think of her other two children.

"Would you please excuse me?" Meg rose from the table. She found Lizzie and Will upstairs, sprawled out on the beds in Amanda's room. Will was lying on his back, tossing a ball up in the air and catching it.

Her daughter sat up as soon as Meg entered the room. "Mom, thank goodness. Can you tell us what's going on? When are we getting out of here?"

"I don't know any more now than I did before. We have to see what happens with the car."

"We could take a plane. Why do we have to wait for the stupid car? It's horrible, anyway. Driving in that little car is, like, the worst thing in the world."

"Is that so?" Meg made no effort to hide her lack of sympathy. "'The worst thing in the world.' That's really saying something."

Will raised himself up on one arm. "Come on, Mom. This place is a loony bin. You gotta do something."

Meg looked from one to the other. "How about we do this: You two stop behaving like spoiled brats. For however long we're here, you smile and act grateful for any little thing anyone does for you. I don't care if you *are* grateful, but *act* grateful. Ask how you can help anytime you're not occupied. And then actually help."

"That's not fair! We cleared the dishes when you—" Lizzie burst out.

"No, now you don't speak. You only listen," Meg interrupted sharply. "I don't think you two understand how upset I am with you. I can't believe how awful you're being to the kids here. They want to talk to you. Talk to them!"

Will groaned. "They're so lame."

"It's you and your sister who are 'so lame,' Will." Meg didn't raise her voice, but her anger was escalating. "I don't see why these people are willing to put up with two sulky, self-absorbed teenagers when they don't have to. But that's going to stop." Meg paused, then pointed to the bed Lizzie was on, the covers carelessly yanked up. "Whatever you do, please do it properly. These people keep their house a certain way. I won't have you creating any additional work for them. They work hard enough." She looked at her son. "That goes for you, too."

"Take it easy, already," Lizzie said. "We get it. You want us to become Amish."

Meg's eyes flared. "It would be a massive improvement over what you seem to have become. I don't want you to become Amish. I want you to become people. Nice people."

"Okay, Mom." Will sounded a conciliatory note. "I'll try."

"Good," Meg said sharply. "Lizzie?"

"All right, all right. We're stuck here, so fine." Lizzie's voice turned exaggeratedly sweet. "I'll be a perfect lady."

Meg matched her tone to her daughter's. "That would be lovely, dear."

The three of them looked at one another in a tense detente. Then, with a quick sigh, Meg leaned down to kiss them good night. "I understand this isn't easy, kids," she said, smoothing back Lizzie's hair. "But I'd like to see you rise to the occasion. I know you can do it."

Wan smiles followed her as she turned to leave the room. She headed down the dark hall to the bedroom she shared with James, not eager to get into another argument.

She felt as if she had been dropped into a different world, one in which everything was inside out—especially her family. Overall, she decided, this had been one of the longest and strangest days she could ever remember.

Chapter 9

❖

Aside from the buggy's constant bouncing, it was remarkably cozy in the back, Meg thought, adjusting the blanket on her lap. The temperature may have been low, but the sun poked through the clouds, making the day feel warmer. Plastic windows acted as a windshield and gave some protection from the elements. While David Lutz and James rode up front, Meg was content to sit behind them, looking out onto the passing farms. There were still patches of ice and snow glistening in the fields and along the road. She could hear bits and pieces of the men's conversation, which seemed to be about crop rotation, but made no effort to follow it.

As much as she liked the Lutzes, Meg hoped that when they reached the garage, the car would be miraculously fixed and ready to go. Staying a couple of nights was one thing; freeloading for an extended period was another. She was too embarrassed to admit to their hosts that they couldn't afford to stay anywhere else. If luck was with them, they could pack up the kids, say thank you to the Lutzes, and leave the farm without burdening them further.

The buggy left the quiet country roads and traveled on bigger, busier routes. Meg was amazed that the cars and trucks passing within what seemed like inches didn't hit them. Just as she was beginning to feel her stomach had been jogged up and down past the point of discomfort, they turned in to the repair shop, its sign announcing that it specialized in vintage cars. Let's hope so, she thought, tossing aside the blanket and getting out. James joined her, but David stayed behind, saying he would wait for them.

A middle-aged man in stained gray work clothes emerged from the back of the shop, recognizing James at once from their earlier meeting.

"Ah, the '69 Mustang," he said, extending his hand. "I've been expecting you." He turned to Meg. "We had a long talk, your husband and I. Beautiful car."

"Okay, Ray," said James. "Lay it on me."

"It's not as bad as it could be, but it's definitely not good. Driver's side is a mess. So you're talking about all new metal, headlight, front fender, paint job—I'm going to do my best to blend the paint so we don't have to repaint the whole car."

"How long will all this take?" Meg asked.

He shrugged. "Like I told your husband, I think you're probably looking at a week or two."

"Oh, no," she breathed.

"Listen," James said, "we're really in a bind here. Isn't there any way we can make this happen in less time?"

"I'll do the best I can for you, but I wouldn't bet on it. This is pretty time-consuming, and what with the paint and all . . ."

"Yeah, I understand." James was visibly frustrated, but it was clear there was no one to blame.

"You still at that phone number you gave me?"

James nodded. "I'll call you tomorrow anyway. We're at an Amish house, so there's no phone inside. It's easy to miss a call."

"Right." Ray held out his hand again. "Sorry the news isn't better. Look on the bright side. The car will be fine in the end. And at least insurance is willing to pay to fix it. I'll go get you the paperwork." He disappeared into the recesses of the shop.

"A week!" Meg repeated. "How can we stay here for that long?"

James cursed under his breath. "I told David that we wanted to pay him if we had to stay any longer. He said in no uncertain terms they wouldn't take any money from us."

"It isn't right for us to use them like some kind of hotel."

"I know, I know. I feel awful about it."

Taking the computer printout from Ray, they thanked him and left. As they approached the buggy, James leaned over to whisper to Meg. "We're going to have to get them to take us to a motel or something."

"Which we can't afford," she replied.

David was sitting in the buggy. He looked up at James. "How is your car?"

"Not great. It's going to be awhile. At least a week."

"A week?" David readied the reins. "Excellent. We shall have the pleasure of your company for a little bit longer."

James began to protest. "No, David, please listen—"

David grinned. "We still have so much to learn from you English. Your ways are so interesting and unusual."

Meg laughed as she replaced the blanket on her lap. "We're just a tourist attraction to you, eh?"

He turned to face her, more serious. "We were both on that road the other night. This is how it should be. No need to talk about it more."

He made a clicking sound, and the horse began to trot. At Meg's request, he stopped at a supermarket so she could run inside. She was out of ibuprofen, which she and James still needed, and she wanted to get some cleaning supplies. If her family was going to be staying in the house, she decided, she could at least take responsibility for the quarters upstairs. It occurred to her that she would have to call her parents to inform them of the delay, but she pushed it out of her head. She didn't feel like dealing with it at the moment.

Carrying her grocery bags back to the house, she saw Barbara, the soon-to-be-married daughter, sweeping off the front porch. A brown-and-black dog kept watch by her side. Meg smiled. "Good morning."

"Good morning to you." Barbara returned the smile.

Meg glanced down at the dog, who was eyeing her warily. "I don't believe I've seen him. Or is it a her?"

"Oh, this is Racer."

"Because he's fast?"

"He used to be, but that was a long time ago."

Meg knelt, setting down a bag, and let him sniff her hand.

Barbara went on, "Your son Samuel really likes him. Racer spent a lot of time with him this morning."

Meg looked up at her. "He does love your dogs here. Do you happen to know where Sam is now?"

"He and your other son went with Eli to work in the barn."

"Really?" Meg was happy, if surprised, to hear that her boys were out of the house, doing something useful.

"If you are looking for your daughter, she went with my mother to Annie's." Barbara nodded in the direction of the house next door. "They're baking. For the store."

Lizzie was baking with the women? Wonders never cease, Meg thought. She grabbed her grocery bag and stood up. "Thank you, Barbara. Do you think it would be all right if I went to Annie's?"

"Oh, yes." The young woman resumed her sweeping. "I will go there soon, too."

Meg went inside to unpack the grocery bags before walking over to Annie's house. Like the Lutzes', it was painted white and had dark-green window shades behind all the first-floor windows. Meg had noticed those same green shades in a number of the houses during her buggy ride, so she guessed it wasn't a coincidence.

When she was almost there, a side door opened, and Lizzie emerged. As soon as she saw her mother approaching, she hurried over, still limping slightly on her bruised foot. "I thought I'd never get out of there!" she burst out in greeting. "Catherine said I should go with her, and I couldn't find a way to say no." She gave Meg a look. "Because now I'm such a perfect lady."

"Ahh, yes," Meg said.

"Yeah, well, they have some kind of insane assembly line going on in there." She shuddered. "These people give me the willies."

Meg sighed. She should have known it was too good to be true. "Okay, listen. If you're going back, please clean up in the bathroom we've been using. I have a sponge and stuff in the cabinet beneath the sink. Straighten the towels, wipe down the sink and toilet, all that stuff."

"Oh, ew—*no*."

Meg regarded her with impatience. "I'm not asking you, Lizzie. I'm telling you." She moved past her daughter.

"Wait," Lizzie yelled after a moment. "What about the car?"

"It could be another week," Meg replied over her shoulder. She was glad she was already a few yards away so she didn't have to respond to her daughter's wail.

"WHAT? A *week*? No WAY!"

Meg knocked on the door, glancing back to see Lizzie frozen to the same spot, staring at her. "Ice your foot, honey," she called out, flashing her daughter a bright smile before a voice hastened her inside.

The first thing to strike Meg was the warmth of the kitchen and the incredible aroma of apples and cinnamon. The room was a scene of vivid color and motion, the women in their bonnets, dressed in deep-hued tones of teal, green, purple, and blue, all moving smoothly and efficiently from one task to another. They were quiet, immersed in their jobs, although they looked up to murmur a greeting to their visitor.

"Hello, Meg." Catherine welcomed her with a smile. "You are doing well today so far?"

"Thank you, I'm fine."

Meg watched in fascination, noting row upon row of un-cooked pie crusts in aluminum pie plates set up along an enor-mous table. She saw that the kitchen had a huge kitchen island and two large double ovens, all four of which were already pressed into service baking batches of the fragrant pies. Cather-ine and her mother-in-law, Leah, were rolling out additional pie dough on large floured wooden boards. Sue, who was mar-ried to Joseph, the eldest Lutz son, and lived across the street, and Amanda held large ceramic bowls and used wooden spoons to pour the apple filling into the crusts. Catherine and Leah moved behind them quickly to put the covering layers of dough on the fruit filling. Annie, whose house it was, followed right behind them, expertly pinching the edges to form perfectly scalloped ridges. Amanda then made X-shaped slits in the cen-ters.

Meg hesitated but decided to jump in. "Is there some way I could help?"

Leah gave her a quizzical look, but Catherine replied at once. "You need oven mitts. We will take the finished pies out in a minute."

With that, Meg was drawn into the whirlwind of the group, removing the golden-crusted pies from the hot oven and care-fully handing them off to be whisked into a nearby room to cool before being wrapped for sale. When the ovens were empty, they refilled every rack and began preparing a third batch.

Meg marveled at the efficiency of the operation but even more so at the pleasure the women seemed to take in what they were doing. They obviously enjoyed one another's company, and rather than trudging through a task they must have done hundreds of times, they seemed to find it completely engaging. At one point Leah started to sing something that Meg guessed to be a hymn, and the others joined in. Meg found their voices soothing.

"Will you stop after the apple pies today?" she asked during a momentary lull in the activity.

"Barbara will come later, and we will make other pies," Annie answered. She adjusted her wire-rimmed glasses and smoothed her apron front. "Each week is different. Later this week, shoofly pie and whoopee pies. Every morning there is bread and muffins. Tomorrow, I think, we will make carrot cake, peanut butter cookies, and some pastries."

"Yum," Meg said.

Annie laughed. "Yes, but maybe not if you see them every day for years."

"Annie can resist them," Catherine said, smiling. "But we always make enough to have here as well."

"I'm sure." Meg grinned.

"We also bake for some restaurants and bakeries. We don't make so much now. In the warm months, there are many more tourists." Catherine washed her hands at the sink. "Now

Amanda and I must go to make lunch. Jonathan will take her to the store with these pies later today."

"Would you mind if I went with them, just to see the store?" Meg asked.

"That would be fine." Putting on her wrap, Catherine turned to Amanda. "You finish up here and then come."

It was only a short distance back to the Lutz house, but Meg used the opportunity of being alone with Catherine to tell her about the delay with the car repairs. Catherine only nodded calmly. Somehow Meg felt she couldn't leave it at that; she owed this woman more of an explanation.

Meg stopped walking and put a hand on the other woman's arm to get her to stop as well. "Please understand. We don't want to take advantage of your generosity."

Catherine's blue eyes held her usual direct gaze. "You do not."

"We—my husband—he lost his job," Meg managed to get out. "We're going to my parents in upstate New York because we pretty much have nothing. We have to stay there until we get back on our feet."

Catherine took this in, nodding, her expression unchanged.

"That's why we can't leave our car. If we weren't in this financial situation, we never would have stayed in your house like this. I mean, we're strangers. Five strangers, no less, and not even Amish. We know this is a huge imposition on your family."

Catherine smiled gently and put a hand over Meg's. "You are here, that's all there is to know. If there is anything we can do to help you, we want to do that."

Tears of relief stung Meg's eyes. She hadn't realized what a burden it had been, keeping the secret of why they were traveling and why they hadn't made plans to leave the Lutz household. She also couldn't remember the last time she had met such generous, good-hearted people. "Thank you," she whispered.

"Now," Catherine said, starting to move forward again, "we will have lunch. Today is a good day to take a little rest after."

Meg shook off her melancholy thoughts. "Ah, you *do* sometimes rest."

"Of course I do. But I meant *you* should take a rest today. I will be doing the ironing."

Meg hurried to keep up with the other woman's brisk pace. She imagined her old pink leather appointment book in Catherine's hands. Do everything in the whole world, it would say on each day's page. The image brought a smile to Meg's face.

It occurred to her that she had gone forty-eight hours without a scheduled appointment. I knew there was something really amiss, Meg thought wryly. The upheaval wasn't in her marriage or their financial ruin or being in a place that was unfamiliar in the truest sense of the word. It was that she didn't have her entire day scheduled down to the minute. No rushing around doing errands, no sense of juggling everyone's schedule.

It was, she decided, pretty great.

When they got into the house, Sam came running to greet her, hugging her around the waist. The bump on his head was turning dark shades of blue and purple, but he didn't seem to know it was even there.

"Mommy, where have you been?" He rushed on excitedly without waiting for an answer. "Aaron took me to collect eggs from the chickens before he left for school. It was so fun!" He took a step back, sharing his newfound expertise. "They don't lay as much in the cold weather, you know, but they do lay some eggs. I got two all by myself. At first I was scared, but then I wasn't!"

Meg grinned. "That is extremely cool, Sam."

"Aaron was really nice. He let me put out their feed and everything. They kind of smelled, but that was okay. And you know what? He said if you and Dad and his parents said it was okay, I could go to school with him one day. He goes to a special Amish school. All the grades in one room, first grade up to eighth grade. I hafta see this."

"It's fine with me if it's okay with everyone else."

Sam gave her another squeeze. "Thanks, Mom. You're the best." He turned to go. "I left Rufus in my bedroom, so I better get back."

Well, Meg thought, Sam was looking more relaxed than he had in ages, and he was obviously having the most fun of anyone in their family. Who would have guessed?

She caught a glimpse of Will and Eli walking past the window and went over to watch them. Her thirteen-year-old had his fleece jacket zipped up under his chin, his hands deep in his pockets. Eli wore the customary black brimmed hat and simple black jacket. He was talking and gesturing. Will nodded, his face neutral. Meg knew that face; it indicated he was participating in the conversation but didn't want anyone to think he actually cared about it. At least he was participating, she told herself. That was an improvement over yesterday.

Lunch was another huge meal, with fourteen people at the table. James had spent the morning out in the field with some of the men, and he sat on the men's side of the table, away from where Meg sat with the women. He didn't exactly blend in, she thought, with his expensive jeans and running shoes, now covered with mud, but he was enjoying himself.

The two of them had exchanged barely ten words since the day before. Apparently exhausted from whatever farmwork he had done, he had uncharacteristically gotten into bed at nine P.M. and fallen asleep almost instantly. The truth was, Meg had nothing to say to James at the moment, and he seemed to be taking advantage of the situation to stay away from her as well.

Several family members were taking a break after lunch, and Will, Eli, and Sam started a game of Monopoly. After helping clean up in the kitchen, Meg decided she would take Catherine's suggestion and lie down for a half hour to rest her back. Upstairs, she saw Lizzie, who had ducked out of the lunch cleanup, stretched out on her bed, arms crossed behind her head. She was staring at the ceiling.

Meg leaned against the doorjamb. "What's up?"

"Oh, if only there was something—anything—up," Lizzie answered, not bothering to look at her. "I'm so bored I want to scream."

"Where's your iPod?"

"Needs to be charged." Her voice grew more petulant. "But that would require an outlet, which would mean having electricity—which these freaks don't believe in."

Meg crossed her arms. "Hey, did you ever read *Tom Sawyer?* For school, maybe?"

Lizzie gave her mother a disdainful look. "Uh-uh."

"I saw it downstairs on the bookshelf. Definitely worth reading. It's a classic."

"Oh, a *classic*," Lizzie said with exaggerated awe. "Well, in that case . . ."

Meg ignored the crack. "That means it's good. Pick it up. I think you might enjoy it."

"This is what I've been reduced to: scrounging for old, boring books. Please just shoot me now. Really, I'm not kidding."

Meg turned around so Lizzie wouldn't see her smile. Her daughter was having to fend for herself without a cell phone, iPod, computer, or television. She might actually be driven to pick up a good book. Imagine. There were some unanticipated benefits to having a car accident, Meg thought as she shut her bedroom door behind her.

The day grew warm enough to melt whatever snow was left on the ground. By late afternoon, when the children had returned home from school, they congregated outside, where they were joined by a growing number of friends. Watching from the porch, Meg observed Amish children arriving on foot, roller skates, or scooters. One teenage girl came on a large scooter with a basket in front and oversize wheels; she brought along a little girl and boy in a small low cart with wheels attached to the back.

All the children seemed to be bursting with energy, delighted to have this unusually warm, sunny day in the middle of winter. Most threw off their jackets or capes. The younger ones ran about, playing games, shouting and laughing. Meg spotted Rachel, the youngest Lutz child, talking and giggling with three other girls.

The teenagers, both boys and girls, assembled at the side of the house to play volleyball. It was quite a sight, Meg thought, all the girls in their richly colored dresses, their hair so neatly coiled into pinned-up braids. The boys, too, with their black pants and suspenders and similar haircuts.

She reflected that her children's friends also wore matching clothes, the same jeans, sneakers, and T-shirts. When she was a kid, she, too, had wanted to fit in by wearing the same clothes as the other kids. Not that her parents would pay for the stylish brands.

There had been rules then, even though unspoken, and there were rules now. It was different here, in that the clothing rules were dictated. They never changed. But at least everybody fit in, and no one had to struggle to do so. In that way, it was a lot easier for an Amish teenager, at least when it came to getting dressed in the morning.

Sam was out there with Aaron and another boy who appeared to be around their age. The boy was on in-line skates, making rapid circles around Sam and Aaron. Aaron held a long stick and kept tossing up small rocks, attempting to hit them as if they were baseballs. The boy spoke to Sam and pointed to a scooter leaning against the house. Sam raced over to grab it and was gone from sight.

"Mrs. Hobart?"

Meg turned around to see Amanda and Lizzie, zipping up her jacket, standing behind her.

"You said you want to go to the store. It is late, but we are going now. Do you want to go with us?"

"Oh, yes, thank you." Meg grabbed her coat. "Lizzie, you're coming?"

Her daughter shrugged. "It's something to do."

They followed Amanda to where Jonathan waited in what Meg now knew to be his buggy. He jumped out and extended a hand to help her up onto the front seat beside him. Amanda and Lizzie got in back.

They set out. Meg studied the young man next to her. Beneath his black hat, he had Catherine's blue eyes and brown hair. No doubt, Meg thought, he'd had the same light-blond hair as his younger siblings when he was a boy. Initially, she had found the bangs and bowl haircuts on the men incongruous, like children's hairstyles on grown-ups. She was getting used to them; they no longer seemed odd in the least.

"Do you do these deliveries every day?" Meg asked him.

"No, ma'am," he replied, his eyes on the road. "Depends on the season, how much we need to bring. A lot of things."

There was so much Meg wanted to ask him. She was dying to know how an eighteen-year-old Amish boy experienced the world.

"Please forgive me if I'm being rude, but I was wondering if you only work on your family farm or if you go to school, or anything like that."

He flicked the reins, and the horse picked up the pace.

"We go to the school until eighth grade. Then we have a class one time every week. Like Eli. When we turn fifteen, we are done."

Meg realized her daughter was leaning forward in the back, trying to hear what Jonathan was saying.

"Sounds good to me," Lizzie interjected.

He turned his face a little to the side so she could hear him better. "It's necessary for us. We have to work. The American government gave permission so we can do it our way."

"All anybody talks about here is work. Don't you do anything for fun?"

"Lizzie," Meg admonished her, "that's so rude."

He smiled. "It's okay. Teenagers do a lot of things. After church, on Sunday nights, they have sings, and we have many ways to have a good time."

"What are 'sings'?" Lizzie asked.

"The girls and the boys go to someone's house, and they sing songs. It's a big social event. That's where many people find someone they like. Then they go out."

"Go out?" Lizzie echoed. "Like on dates?"

He smiled slightly. "Not like you would think, I guess. They spend time together."

"Do you mind if I ask whether you're dating someone?" Meg inquired.

"Oh my God, Mom!" yelled Lizzie as Jonathan turned beet red. "You did *not* just ask that!"

"I'm so sorry," Meg said. "That really was wrong of me. I'm very sorry."

For the first time, Amanda spoke up from the back. "It is

okay, Mrs. Hobart. We never like to tell about those things to the grown-ups. When people are ready to be married, then they tell."

Lizzie faced Amanda. "So you never meet anybody besides the other kids who live here?"

Amanda hesitated. After a moment, Jonathan answered. "When we're sixteen, we can spend some time seeing the world if we want. We're allowed to visit new places and do different things. If we want to meet new people, we can. That way we know when we are ready to join the church."

Meg was confused. "Wait—aren't you members of the church already?"

He looked at her with the same gaze as that of the younger children of the house: direct, guileless, and open. "No. That's one of the things about the Amish people. We believe you should be baptized when you decide to be a church member, as an adult. So you have time to go out and think it over. See what you're missing in the outside world."

"Did you do this, leave for a while?" Lizzie asked him. She turned to Amanda. "Wait—you're sixteen. Are you doing this?"

Jonathan answered again. "I tried some things, yes. But I knew what I wanted, and I was baptized."

Amanda's answer was firm. "I don't need to do anything different. I am happy as I am, and I will be baptized, too."

Lizzie spoke slowly. "I think I've heard about this someplace. There's a word for it, right?"

Amanda sighed. "The word you are thinking about is *rum-*

springa. Many tourists ask about it. So, some kids maybe get their own apartment. They drive a car and wear the English clothes. We do things we are not allowed to do at home, and we see how we wish to live. Amish or not."

"Your parents are okay with this?" Meg asked.

Neither said anything. Finally, Jonathan answered. "Some kids decide fast, or they are like Amanda and they already know. Sometimes they take a long time to decide, and it causes a great deal of trouble. Like with our brother Benjamin. He's been gone now almost four months. My parents are very un-happy about him. They worry he'll be one of the ones who don't come back."

"Jonathan," Amanda reprimanded him, "you should not tell about this!"

That explained why they had the empty bedroom, Meg real-ized, the one that belonged to the son with all the sports equip-ment and posters. He was off somewhere, deciding about his future. Catherine had described him as being "away," with no further explanation.

So, Meg thought, even Amish parents sometimes had their guts taken out by their teenagers.

Jonathan looked annoyed at his sister's efforts to silence him but said nothing more. The horse trotted over the hilly roads, its hooves making their own music in the otherwise total quiet. The sun was setting, orange and pink streaking the sky. Meg guessed that by the time they got back to the farm, dinner would be ready, and everyone would gather for a silent prayer and the evening meal. She leaned back, relaxing into the jostling of the carriage, not thinking about anything at all, and watched the sky transform into breathtaking purples and reds.

When they returned to the house, however, Meg had to acknowledge to herself that she had put off far too long making the call she had been dreading. Her parents were expecting her to arrive the day after tomorrow. That was out of the question. Still in her coat, she asked Catherine if she might use their telephone.

"It's in the shed around the back. Walk past the gazebo."

Meg thanked her and took a lantern outside. She pulled open the shed door and raised the lantern high enough to reveal a wealth of gardening tools and empty pots, all neatly arranged and well used but clean, ready be retrieved in the spring. Behind a wheelbarrow, she saw a small table with a telephone and answering machine, plus a white pad and several pencils. Meg almost laughed out loud, realizing she had somehow been expecting an antique phone, something tall and black, with an earpiece that she would hold up to her ear while shouting *"Operator, operator!"* This wasn't a cordless phone, and the answering machine looked fairly old, but they were both perfectly serviceable.

She stood the lantern on the table, where it cast an eerie glow on the shed's low ceiling, and dialed. Her mother picked up on the sixth ring. "Hello." As usual, the same flat tone.

"Hi, Mother, it's me," Meg said.

"What's wrong?"

Resisting the urge to scream at the assumption behind the question, Meg answered, "Nothing's wrong. I wanted to let you know we've had a little delay. We won't make it to you quite when I thought."

"Why?"

"It's not a big deal, really. The car needs some work, and we have to wait for it to be done."

"What do you mean 'needs some work'?" Her mother's suspicions were raised. "You had an accident, didn't you?"

Congratulations, Meg wanted to say. You got it in one. "Just a small mishap" was what she said instead. "The car ran off the road. Everyone's fine, and it'll be fixed. But they have to order a part or something, and it could take a few days. Maybe even a week."

"A week? That's not some small mishap."

Meg closed her eyes and rested her head in one hand.

"Will insurance pay for it?" her mother wanted to know.

Nothing about the well-being of her grandchildren, Meg noticed. "Yes, the money's not a problem."

Her mother let out a short snort of derision. "It's hardly surprising. That old car wasn't in any shape to make this trip. You knew that."

"We didn't have much choice, if you recall," Meg retorted, knowing she was perilously close to inviting an argument.

Her mother chose to ignore the invitation. "Where are you?"

"We're in Pennsylvania."

"What on earth are you doing there?"

"This is where it happened. I can give you the phone number where we're staying in case you need to reach us."

"You're in a hotel? How can you afford that?"

Oh, boy, here it comes, thought Meg. This is going to be a moment to remember. "No. We're staying with an Amish family. They're lovely people. And they refuse to let us pay them for anything."

There was dead silence on the phone.

"Mother? Did you hear me?"

"I heard you, but I don't believe you."

Meg only sighed.

"*Amish* people?" her mother asked. "You mean the ones without electricity and the weird clothes? The ones who refuse to live in the real world? I didn't even think those people still exist."

"They do. And they're very nice."

"Well, Margaret, that's a new one on me." Her mother made no attempt to minimize her monumental disapproval. "What are you doing, mixing with people like that? And you have the *children* with you? You let them be exposed to this cult?"

Meg bristled. "You have no right to say that. They are most certainly not a cult. You don't know anything about them!"

"I know that people don't let strangers stay in their house for free, I can tell you that! They want something from you. Are they talking religious things to you? Don't you let them try to convert you."

Meg thought that if she had the proper medical instruments, she would be able to see her blood pressure skyrocketing. "Stop it, Mother, stop it right now!" She had promised herself she wouldn't yell, but she couldn't help it. "You have no right to talk like that. These people are just nice, period. Can't you imagine such a thing, people being nice?"

A deafening silence.

"If they're so nice," her mother said, "perhaps they'd like to take you in permanently."

Checkmate. If Meg didn't capitulate, and fast, she would have no place to go once the car got fixed. Deep breaths, she told herself, deep breaths.

She didn't bother taking any deep breaths but rushed out the words before any further damage could be done. "Okay, Mother, why don't we just figure the car will be fixed in a couple of days, and we'll be on our way to you. I'll make sure the children aren't exposed to anything radical or dangerous." She lightened her tone, certain the strain of doing so would take five years off her life. "We're looking forward to getting back to the original plan. We'll be there in time to celebrate Christmas together."

That seemed to throw off her mother, who apparently hadn't given any thought to the approach of the holiday. "Your father and I stopped buying Christmas trees a long time ago. And I know you can't afford to waste whatever money you have left on a bunch of useless presents. So I'm not sure what celebrating you're planning on."

"Maybe I'll make a cake . . ." Meg trailed off, unable to keep up this conversation for another minute. "Well, we'll all be together. So I'll call you when I know more."

"Yes, I think you had better."

"Thanks, Mother."

"Margaret, you be careful of these people. You understand?"

"I understand."

"Fine. Good-bye."

Grabbing the lantern, Meg opened the door and stepped outside. I'll count until ten, she said to herself, and if my head doesn't explode by then, I'll know I'm okay.

Chapter 10

✤

Lizzie grimaced at the tall laminated menu. "Why aren't all these people dead of heart attacks? I can't even believe what they eat."

James smiled. "Not exactly like the restaurants back home, is it? No arugula salad, say, or grilled fish."

Lizzie wrinkled her nose in distaste. "Ick. It's not like I eat that stuff, either."

"They really love their ham here, you gotta give them that," Will added as he scanned the offerings.

The restaurant was a sea of empty tables. It was lunchtime on a Wednesday afternoon in December, so Meg was hardly surprised that the cavernous restaurant was practically deserted. Other than a young couple with twin toddlers and an elderly couple lingering over coffee, she didn't see any other customers. This place must serve a billion tourists in the summer, she thought. Which was probably a good thing.

Delivering the pies the day before, she had come to understand what a strange relationship the Amish had with tourists. Or at least it seemed strange to her. While the tourists invaded the peaceful existence, they also brought in money to sustain it. During the ride, Jonathan had explained that the increasing price of land made it difficult for the younger generations to buy property near their families. As much as the Amish valued farming, they'd turned to other professions to support themselves, and many had taken jobs outside their community. Selling food, crafts, furniture, and the like to tourists had become an important source of income.

Meg didn't know how all the Amish felt about it, but some had obviously made their peace with it. If tourism brought in critical dollars, then Meg supposed they had to work with it, not against it.

The Lutzes' solution combined farming with making food and other things to sell. They didn't sell directly to the public but to shops and bakeries. The store where they dropped off the apple pies clearly catered to tourists. When they'd arrived, the owner was locking the front door, closing for the night. Jonathan, Amanda, and Lizzie brought the pies in through a back door while Meg roamed the store aisles, perusing an array of crafts. Amid a seeming ocean of goods, she paused to examine colorful place mats and napkins, candles, dried-flower arrangements, the summer straw hats worn by Amish men, and small, soft faceless dolls in Amish dress. She grew hungry just reading the labels on the endless packages of homemade food, everything from apple butter and pickles to candy and chutneys.

By the time they got back to the Lutz farm, everyone was assembling in the kitchen for supper. Meg let herself be carried away on the gentle wave of quiet goodwill at the supper table and the sight of all the activity in the room afterward. While she cleaned up with the other women, the young cousins from next door and several children she hadn't seen joined the Lutz children for the evening. Lizzie and Will even sat in on some board games, while Sam made Christmas cards with Aaron and Rachel near a crackling fire. Curious, Meg observed them using glitter, rubber stamps, and markers to make their own cards, none of which featured Santa or presents but, rather, simple religious words or themes. Yes, Barbara confirmed when Meg asked her as they wiped down the kitchen counters, they did send Christmas cards to their faraway relatives and some English friends. Sam, Meg noted with a touch of sadness, made several cards but didn't personalize them or take any to send; apparently, he wasn't interested in keeping up with the kids back in Charlotte.

It had been a peaceful, happy evening, ending with pretzels and ice cream for everyone. Meg was still full from the night before when she came down in the morning to find a table laden with oatmeal, cold cereal, eggs, bacon, hash browns, muffins, warm bread, and butter.

After breakfast, James and she agreed that they had to give the Lutzes a break from including the five of them in the household meals, even if it meant dipping into their meager funds. Not to mention that her children were still complaining about how few things they could stand to eat at the meals. When Meg informed Catherine that they would be going out for lunch, Catherine protested but eventually gave in. She suggested that Jonathan drop them off at the restaurant and retrieve them later. Meg was glad they had come, even if it looked as though this wasn't going to be quite the success she'd hoped in terms of her family finding something to eat.

"I have to tell you," James said, peering over his menu, "I've been doing some work with the men—not even anything big, mind you—and I've been starved when we get in for dinner. These people don't need gyms or treadmills, and they don't need diets." He grimaced. "Although the cholesterol is going to kill me."

"Their cooking comes from another time and place, before anybody cared about that stuff," Meg remarked.

Sam, seated at Meg's left, hadn't said anything since they sat down. "They come from Germany," he offered. "In the beginning, I mean."

They all looked at him in surprise.

"How would *you* know?" Will asked.

He shrugged. "I talk to Aaron and Eli. Don't you talk to anybody?"

"I guess I'm not as popular as you, big shot" was Will's snide reply.

Sam went on, "People call them Pennsylvania Dutch, but they don't even speak Dutch. They talk in a German dialogue."

"'Dialogue'?" asked James. "You mean 'dialect'?"

Sam nodded. "Yeah, I guess so. In church, they talk in real German. Plus, they learn English. So that's, like, three languages. Pretty cool."

"Definitely," said Meg, impressed with her son's fact-finding.

"A long time ago, back in Germany, people wanted to kill them. That's how they wound up here."

Lizzie muttered under her breath, "Probably wanted to kill them 'cause their clothes are so ugly."

Will let out a guffaw.

James's eyes flared with anger. "You kids are the most obnoxious, ungrateful— What is *with* you?"

"Oh, come on, Dad," Will said. "Seriously, you think you would have liked being here when you were our age?"

"Okay, that's a fair question." James was quiet for a few seconds, considering. "I might not have liked it," he said finally, "but I know I would have kept my opinions to myself. I would never make fun of people right under their noses, or act like it was all too much to be born, the way you and Lizzie are acting."

"I think these people are great," Sam said. "They're so nice."

"What do you know?" Lizzie snapped. "You're just running around with a puppy and your new fake grandpa, so you think the world is suddenly a beautiful place."

Meg stared at her. "When did you get so cynical?"

The waitress appeared at James's elbow. She was a teenager, with enormous hoop earrings and dark hair pulled back into a tight, high ponytail. "Hey, there, you folks ready?" she asked.

James looked apologetic. "Can you give us another minute?"

"Sure thing. Just sing out if you have any questions." She left, her ponytail bouncing behind her.

Lizzie mimicked her in disgust. " *'Just sing out if you have any questions.'* Is anybody in this place for real? I feel like we're among the pod people or something."

"They're not pod people!" Sam's voice rose with emotion.

"Aaron and Eli are, like, the best guys I ever met. And they're so lucky to be in that family."

There was a moment of quiet, then, without another word, Lizzie burst into tears. Everyone sat, stunned, as she buried her face in her hands, sobbing. Meg jumped up and came around the table, kneeling to wrap her arms around her daughter. "Lizzie, what on earth is it? What's going on?"

Lizzie raised her face, flushed and wet. "Yeah, they're lucky because they're actually *in* a family. We used to be a family, too." She looked briefly at Meg, her voice cracking with the effort of holding back tears. "You and Dad used to love each other. Now you hate each other. We're nothing but a bunch of homeless people, and nobody loves anybody anymore. We're just sponging off of these people until we can go to our horrible new lives with more people who don't love us and who we don't love." She covered her face again as she sobbed.

"Dear God," James breathed.

Meg felt her throat close up, as if she couldn't take a breath. She wrapped her arms more closely around Lizzie, feeling her shake with the force of her sobs.

I can't believe I could be so stupid, Meg berated herself. How could I have thought the kids would just get in line and do whatever we said. No problems, no worries, as long as we patted them on the head and told them how we expected them to behave. As if, by following a few simple rules, they could overlook the fact that their world had exploded.

She met James's pained eyes across the table. It wasn't the house that was the problem, nor the money, nor the moving. That stuff the kids could deal with—not easily, maybe, but eventually. It was the fact that they could plainly see the rift between their parents. That was the worst thing of all. She knew that she and James had done a terrible job of pretending to get along, but the children understood that their parents' marriage was hanging by a thread.

She turned to Will, who looked miserable as he continued making believe he was absorbed in running his finger around the rim of his water glass. Sam was watching her, clutching his napkin in both hands, his eyes brimming with tears.

What could she tell them? That she and James weren't splitting up? She couldn't make that promise. That everything would be great when they got to her parents'? Not likely, and they wouldn't believe her anyway.

She rubbed Lizzie's back. "Don't worry, sweetie. It'll all work out," she murmured.

"Will it?" James asked.

She gave him a murderous look. He stared right back at her. No one spoke. No one moved.

This, she realized, this very moment, was the lowest point of her marriage, her family, and, quite possibly, her life.

Chapter 11

Sam paused on the front porch to give his mother a hug. She stopped sweeping, bending to kiss him on the cheek. "Have fun, pumpkin," she told him. "And put on your gloves."

He ignored her advice, running after Aaron and Rachel to get into Old Samuel's buggy. Today Sam was going to be a guest at the school. He'd been thrilled to be treated like the other two children that morning. Catherine had handed him a silver lunch box and a glass bottle full of soup. Then she sent him off with a pat on the head. Once Sam was safely ensconced in the rig, Old Samuel nodded at a waving Meg, then snapped the reins. The horse set out at a slow trot.

Meg resumed sweeping the front steps. As the week had passed, she had been assuming additional chores around the house. Typically, Barbara Lutz cleaned up the porch and front yard, making sure the grounds remained neat. When Meg's soreness from the accident had almost completely dissipated, she insisted on taking over that job. She hadn't expected to enjoy the early-morning quiet as much as she did, punctuated only by a dog's bark or a brief commotion in the chicken house. The broom's rhythmic noise against the porch was soothing. She pictured the ornate front door at their house back in Charlotte, knowing full well she never would have enjoyed sweeping those steps. Was it only in this environment that such satisfaction could be found? she wondered. Was there any way to hold on to the simple pleasure of a job well done? Maybe a person needed to have more simple jobs to do, until they crowded out the ridiculous things that typically took up so much time.

Moving toward the side of the house, she saw Racer stretched out on his side on a brown patch of ground. "Hey, boy," she called.

He stayed exactly as he was, but she was absurdly gratified by the two thumps of his tail she received in reply.

She finished up and put the broom away inside before heading over to Annie's house. Today the women planned to bake two hundred muffins, an assortment of blueberry, cranberry, and corn. Meg would do whatever they assigned her. Being around the daily baking was making her itch to do some of her own, but so far she had refrained from asking. She did not want to interfere with their schedules or, worse yet, cause any additional work.

As she walked, she wondered what kind of morning James was experiencing. Things between them had become even more tense since their lunch in the restaurant, and all five of them seemed unable to deal with it. Each of them acted as if it had never happened. She and her husband were at a complete impasse. She wondered what on earth it would take to change things.

James had gone off early this morning with David, Jonathan, and Eli to help butcher meat in a neighbor's barn. Meg admired the perfect logic of the activities here. Anything having to do with planting and harvesting took top priority; whatever else had to get done was scheduled around those months. That explained everything, down to why most of their weddings were held in November and December, when obligations in the field were at a minimum.

Meg didn't care to know too many specific details about the butchering, but she had been surprised by how enthusiastic James was about pitching in. Amazing that the man who once fussed over wine in a restaurant was now hefting a pitchfork, wielding a cleaver, and slogging around in manure wearing borrowed boots. She wasn't sure if he had embraced all this farm labor or if he was using it as a distraction from their troubles. At the very least, she thought, it was a welcome delay in reaching his in-laws' house, and she couldn't blame him for feeling that way. He seemed to have become awfully comfortable, though, with their being the houseguests who wouldn't leave.

Of course, she didn't know what James was thinking because they were barely talking. All this division of labor between the sexes, all the hours spent apart, made an argument with your spouse unlikely, she thought. But once you'd gotten into one, it was also a good way to avoid dealing with it any further.

Entering Annie's house, Meg spotted Lizzie and Barbara in a

corner of the living room. Without electricity, all the Hobart children had been going to sleep a lot earlier than they were used to. As a result, they were wide awake in the mornings. Even Lizzie, queen of the late sleepers, had adjusted her internal clock.

Barbara held a hand-painted plate, removed from a display of dishes in an enormous oak breakfront, and was pointing out the fine details of its pattern to Lizzie. Meg went over to them. "Good morning, Barbara, Lizzie."

Lizzie glanced up at her mother without much interest, but Barbara flashed her usual big smile. "Good morning, Meg. I'm showing Lizzie what I hope to get after the wedding. As gifts. I have some dishes such as these that I have gotten over the years, but I hope to get the rest."

"Mostly, they get stuff for the kitchen and the house," Lizzie added. "They don't ask for any fun things. Fancy dishes are, like, the biggest deal when it comes to something special."

Barbara laughed. "Lizzie is having trouble with this idea. She says a bride could ask for anything, but we are happy to get mops and pitchers."

Lizzie shrugged. "I mean, I never heard of getting a shovel as a wedding gift."

"The English maybe like different things, that's all," Barbara said.

"You know," Meg said to her daughter, "we have wedding showers, and that's often all about things for the house. And people get lots of appliances for wedding gifts. You're just thinking of all the extra, unnecessary things." She laughed.

"Like the million vases and candlesticks people gave Dad and me when we got married. How often do I use those?" She corrected herself. "How often *did* I use those? Or all those crystal glasses, which were almost too fragile to handle."

"I don't mean to sound greedy or anything," Lizzie said. "It's just that this is the one time you can flat out ask for cool things and nobody minds."

Barbara put an arm around Lizzie. "When you get married, you will decide what is important to you. But this is how we do it here. It makes sense for us."

"I should join the others now," Meg said. "Want to come, Lizzie?"

"Nope."

Meg turned to leave. "See you later."

Midmorning, everybody congregated back in Catherine's house. The families sat down for lunch, their usual silent prayer followed by yet another enormous meal starting with meat loaf, lima beans with molasses and ketchup, and the ever-present bread and butter. After lunch, work began in earnest to transform the barn across the street at Joseph's house for the wedding. The enormous space was better suited to a large event than David and Catherine's barn, but the Lutz men, James, and a crowd of men from the community got to work framing an extension to make space for all the tables and benches that would arrive on Monday. Will and Lizzie disappeared, but Meg and the women went back to Annie's home to sort a steady stream of arriving dishes, glasses, silverware, and pots and pans, all lent and delivered by neighbors and friends.

"You know," Catherine said to Meg as they sorted platters by size, "we would like to ask you and James to be among the people who cook and serve at the wedding."

Meg smiled at her. "You know you can count on us."

Catherine picked up several pitchers, cradling them in her arms, and moved to put them in a different spot. Joseph's wife, Sue, had come into the kitchen with a box of coffee cups and was unpacking them near Meg. She moved closer to speak to her.

"We love to celebrate happy times like a wedding," she explained to Meg. "Everybody wants to be part of it, to help make the food, but only about thirty people can. It is good for you to have this big honor, to be asked to cook?"

Meg turned to her. She'd had no idea. "Yes, of course," she said. "We're very honored."

Sue's smile was gentle as she moved away. Thank you, Meg thought. Without that little tip-off, she never would have appreciated the significance of Catherine's request. She made a mental note to tell James.

When Catherine returned, Meg smiled at her with genuine warmth. "You have been so good to us," she said. "I can never repay you."

Catherine frowned. "Repay me? What a bad idea. That makes it sound like business."

Barbara walked by them, carrying a bucket and some clean rags.

"She starts washing today." Catherine's eyes followed her daughter. "Our house, Joseph's house. Wherever the guests will come." She sighed.

"What is it?" asked Meg.

"No, nothing. I am just—you know, a mother can't help it. It is a little sad that she is moving to her husband's family farm."

"Oh, yes," Meg said sympathetically.

"It is the right thing, and I want her to do it. It is not so far away, just about ten miles, so I am very grateful. But it is a big change, your daughter leaving your house for always."

Meg nodded, trying to imagine how she would feel when her children left to be on their own. She could guess that, as much as she wanted to see them grow up to be independent, it would be devastating.

"If only my son Benjamin would decide. I don't even know if he will come home for the wedding or . . ." Catherine stopped.

It took Meg a moment to recall that Benjamin was the son who was out in the world, finding out if he wanted to remain a member of the Amish community. How painful this must be for Catherine and her husband. Meg lightly put a comforting hand on her shoulder, and Catherine put her own hand over it.

"Surely he'll want to—" Meg was interrupted by Leah, who appeared behind her. Where had she been standing?

"Catherine, please to come with me." Leah's accent was heavy and her words generally difficult for Meg to understand. She understood these, though, and the disapproval behind them.

Meg tried to pretend she wasn't watching as the two women retreated to the farthest point in the room. She didn't have to hear them to interpret Leah's stern expression and rapid speaking—no doubt in their own language—as criticism of Catherine. When Leah, seemingly unconsciously, briefly pointed in Meg's direction, Meg knew she was the cause of this tongue-lashing.

Abashed, Meg kept her face down as Catherine returned, slightly pink in the cheeks but otherwise composed.

"I'm so sorry," Meg whispered. "I got you in trouble with your mother-in-law, didn't I?"

Catherine came very close to her, reaching her arm across Meg to pick up a large bowl. She turned her head so no one could see her answering. "We don't speak of our problems to outsiders," she whispered back. "For a minute I forgot to think of you as an outsider. As my little Rachel would say, silly me."

Meg paused in what she was doing, so surprised she forgot to pretend they weren't having a conversation. Catherine grabbed some more bowls and hastened away as someone called her name. Before Meg could think about how wonderful Catherine's words had made her feel, she was distracted by Lizzie's appearance at the door, Amanda trailing behind her.

Meg's eyes met her daughter's, and she raised a questioning eyebrow. Lizzie shrugged as she approached.

"I'm here to help," Lizzie said. "Amanda said we had to. She said we'd all be in trouble if we didn't."

Meg sighed. "You wouldn't have thought of helping on your own?"

"Mo-om! I'm here, aren't I? What do I have to do?"

"Well, Barbara has a bucket. I think she's washing furniture. You like her, so maybe you want to help with that."

Lizzie made a face. "I don't like anybody *that* much."

Meg was growing impatient. "Why don't you go over there and ask Sue what needs to be done."

Lizzie was assigned to count the forks, knives, and spoons, separating them into piles. Meg was pleased to see someone had put Will to work as well. He came through the door struggling under the weight of split logs. She watched him unload the wood near the fireplace. Something was stirring in her memory, although she wasn't sure what.

It came to her. This past Thanksgiving in Charlotte. It was only last month, but it felt like another life. She had set the table, and the children had helped bring in chairs. She remembered the hours she'd spent orchestrating the placement of her sterling silver salt and pepper dishes. As if it mattered in the least, she couldn't help thinking now.

Someone set another box of serving platters beside her, and she began to unpack them. That had been their last holiday, she recalled, the last huge feast they had shared as a family. It was the day she had found out what James had done with the family's money. It was the last day of their old lives.

"Watch it, stupid!"

At the sound of Will's voice, Meg turned around to see what was going on. Lizzie, carrying a large basket piled high with serving utensils, had apparently tripped over Will's foot as he knelt to stack wood near the fireplace. Her daughter had recovered her balance just in time to avoid falling.

"*I* should watch it? You're the one whose foot is sticking out," Lizzie snapped. Her tone was disgusted. "Jerk."

All the faces in the room turned toward the two teenagers. Mortified, Meg practically ran across the room.

Will had risen to confront his sister more directly. "We can't all be worrying about staying out of Your Majesty's way."

Meg reached them and took each one by an arm firmly enough to communicate that she meant business. "Why don't we discuss this outside?" she said as calmly as she could manage. She hustled them the mercifully few feet to the front door. The instant they were outside, each one started yelling to Meg about the other.

"Both of you be quiet this instant!" she hissed.

They stopped talking.

"Do you see the kids here treating one another like you two do?" she demanded. "No. They are nice. They are kind. They are even, believe it or not, respectful."

Two sets of shoulders sagged as they realized they were going to get a long lecture.

"I'm so sick of your behavior, I don't even know how to describe the way I feel," Meg said. "You embarrass me. Worse, you embarrass yourselves." She surprised them by turning away. "I wonder if you can even understand that."

She opened the door and went inside without looking back. Had she been alone, she realized, she probably would have given in to the self-recriminations that were flooding her mind. She wanted to weep with disappointment over her children's ongoing bad behavior and for whatever hand she may have had in it. But the women here didn't seem to know the meaning of self-pity, and she knew not one of them would stop working to feel sorry for herself. They put one foot in front of the other no matter what.

She might not be Amish, but she could learn a lesson from them. She smoothed her hair and composed her face. She didn't try to adopt a cheerful smile but quietly returned to her task. From the other women's behavior, it was impossible to tell that anyone had noticed her children's bickering. Meg was immediately absorbed back into the conversation.

The sun was beginning to set when she went outside to take a break, a steaming mug of coffee in hand. The kitchen had been growing progressively hotter, but the extreme cold instantly made her appreciate the coffee's warmth. Not having put on her coat, she held one arm tightly across her midsection, shivering a bit while she sipped on the hot drink.

Out on the main road, she spotted Will and Eli, both on skateboards. Will, she noticed, was using his own, the one she had salvaged. She was glad she had. A number of the children here had skateboards, so it had been useful for Will to have his. At the moment he and Eli were clearly racing, both speeding from some unknown starting point. Meg stifled her natural impulse to yell out at Will to slow down, knowing he would never do it, especially considering he was in the middle of an actual race. She just held the mug's handle a bit more tightly. They were really flying, she thought. When they passed the designated finish line, they both slowed down and then stopped sharply. Eli held up his fist in a momentary gesture of victory.

Meg watched Will skate over to talk animatedly to Eli, who nodded. She could guess that her son wasn't willing to concede defeat so easily; he would be making sure he got another crack at winning. Reversing direction, the boys aligned themselves side by side, and she could hear Will's voice as he shouted "Go!"

This time Meg could almost feel her son's determination as he increased his speed, his head slightly lowered, his body locked into position. Eli was going fast, too, but his body didn't communicate the same frantic desire to win. Sure enough, Will sailed over the finish line well ahead of Eli. Will jumped off his skateboard, repeatedly pumping his fists in the air. Eli came to a full stop, one foot on the ground. He appeared to be patiently waiting for Will to finish his strutting. Then, with a wave of his arm, Will challenged Eli to two out of three. They took off down the street once more.

Eli got there first, just barely. He simply bent over, picked up his skateboard, and stood there. Will brought his skateboard to a screeching halt, jumped off, and gave it a good kick. Meg watched her son, his arm's jerky gesticulations indicating his displeasure as he undoubtedly ranted about whatever he believed had caused him to lose. Eli shrugged. Will went on for a bit more until the other boy nodded toward his parents' house and started walking. Will stared after him. Eli stopped, turned back, and put out a hand as if to ask whether Will was coming. Meg observed Will take a moment, then grab his skateboard and drag himself after the other boy. As soon as he caught up, Eli leaned in to him and said something that made Will laugh.

Meg sighed. All boys may like to win, she reflected, but not all boys need to rub their opponents' faces in it when they do. Will had been treated to an example of a gracious winner. She hoped with all her heart that he had taken note.

The screen door opened, and Catherine stuck her head out. "We are done here," she said to Meg. "It is time to go back to my house now."

Meg nodded and stopped inside to wash her coffee mug. It was almost dark and growing still colder as the two of them walked toward the house. Talking along the way, Meg learned Barbara's soon-to-be-in-laws ran a dairy farm, but Moses, the man Barbara was marrying, was their youngest son, and they were elderly, ready to retire. They were handing over the main responsibilities for the farm to Moses and Barbara, who would move into the main house. His parents had built an attached house for themselves, which Meg learned was called a *Grossdaadi Haus*, just like the one in which Leah and Old Samuel lived.

"This is how it happened with David and me," Catherine finished as they came into her house and hung up their outer clothes on the wall pegs. "His parents lived in this part before we were married. We built the house across the road for our son Joseph when he married Sue, and that is the biggest one of all of them."

Meg tried to imagine having in-laws living in an attachment to her house in Charlotte. Thinking of Leah, she gazed at Catherine with new admiration.

Almost as if she had read Meg's mind, Catherine said, "We respect the elders of the community very much. It is a good thing when you grow old here—no one is alone, we are all together."

Ashamed of her uncharitable thoughts, Meg nodded.

"Mommy!" Sam came bounding into the room. "I thought you would never get home! I want to tell you about my day at school."

"I can't wait to hear." Meg hugged him tightly. "Let's sit down, and you'll tell me everything."

"It was great!" he announced as they settled themselves on the couch.

"Doesn't Daddy want to hear this? We should get him," Meg said.

"I already told him in the barn. I'm sorry, but I couldn't wait anymore, and you just weren't anywhere."

She smiled. "Okay, go ahead."

"It was soooo different from at home," Sam gushed. "The teacher's name is Sarah, and they call her that, her first name. There was a fire in this old-fashioned stove to warm up the room, and she put some of the lunch stuff on it so it would be hot later. Like my soup."

"Clever," Meg said.

"Yeah, one kid had a baked potato wrapped in foil stuff, and it cooked right there by lunch!"

Meg nodded. "I like that idea. Neat trick."

"Sarah was super nice. So, all these kids are together, all different ages, up to the eighth grade." Sam's voice dropped to an awed whisper. "They're really well behaved, you wouldn't believe it. I mean, it was crazy. I know Mrs. Whitford wouldn't believe it."

Meg smiled. Mrs. Whitford had been Sam's teacher in Charlotte.

"They said prayers and sang songs. Some of them were in German. I didn't know any of them, so I just sat there next to Aaron, trying to look like I knew what was going on. As if!"

"I'm sure they didn't expect you to," Meg pointed out.

"They were so nice to me." The words came rushing out. "Everybody did different things, 'cause of what age they were. Big kids helped littler kids. They did math and reading, all stuff like I do. We had recess and played games. I got to play darts. It was awesome." Sam stood up. "I could see it—going to school just till eighth grade, working on the farm." He looked thoughtful, then shrugged. "But I'm not Amish, and we don't have a farm, so there you go," he finished. "I gotta find Old Samuel. Y'know, he actually *whittles*. I've never seen anybody whittle in real life. He's going to show me how. And I have to find Rufus."

"See you later, then."

"It was a super-cool day, Mom. Bye." He ran off.

A super-cool day indeed, she thought.

Dinner was delayed that evening as they waited for Jonathan and James to get back. They had gone to check on the progress of the Mustang after David told them a message from the repair shop had been left on the answering machine for James. When they finally arrived and everyone sat down for the meal, James announced that he had been summoned to the repair shop only to okay the paint job. The car wouldn't be ready for another week.

Meg watched the reactions on her children's faces. Predictably, Sam looked delighted, while Will and Lizzie were horrified. Meg herself had mixed feelings. They should be getting back to their own lives, yet she knew how wrenching it would be to leave the Lutz family. She had to admit she did not feel as bad about the delay as perhaps she should.

Later on, when she and James found themselves alone in their bedroom, she questioned him further about the car.

"The guy wanted to make sure I was okay about his just repainting the damaged part of the car instead of painting the whole thing," he said. "It looked great, but we're still stuck. What would happen if we weren't here with these people?"

"They've been amazing," Meg said. "Feeding us, lending us everything we need."

"I know, I know," James retorted. "You don't have to remind me that we have no money. That we're charity cases because of me."

"That's not what I meant," Meg said, stiffening. "Not everything is an indictment of you."

"Well, that's how it feels."

"Maybe that's because it should be," she snapped. "You have yet to say or do anything to show that you even get it. That you have a clue about what you did."

"I know what I did."

"I mean what you did *to us*. Me and the kids. You don't seem to get that at all."

"What do you want me to do, Meg? I'm sorry, but I can't replace the money."

She glared at him. "It's not about the money, I keep trying to tell you that. It's that I can't trust you. On any level. So where does that leave us?"

His reply was angry and abrupt. "Damned if I know." He left the room, and she listened to his footsteps go down the stairs.

Meg didn't want to sit alone in the bedroom, thinking about how angry she was. She decided to go downstairs and see if anyone might be around. What she found were six children she didn't recognize playing with the younger Lutz children and her son Sam, all of them illuminated by the fire and the glow of kerosene lamps. They were spread out around the room snacking on bowls of popcorn.

Meg saw four Amish women she hadn't encountered seated at the kitchen table with Catherine, Leah, and Amanda, most of them working on a quilt.

"Oh, excuse me," Meg said, pausing in the doorway. "I didn't mean to interrupt."

Catherine gestured to a chair. "Come in, Meg."

Meg sat at a little distance from the group so she wouldn't be in their way. Introductions were made. It appeared they were fairly far along with the quilt, which had numerous pieces of fabric sewn into intricate patterns on a black background. She craned her neck to study it. "That is absolutely beautiful," she exclaimed.

One of the women, who appeared to be in her seventies, looked up to peer at Meg. Her English was heavily accented, but Meg could make it out. "It is for the schoolteacher. A Christmas present from the families."

"Sarah," Meg recalled aloud.

The woman smiled. "Yes. You know of her?"

"My son spent today at the school. He enjoyed it very much."

One of the other women looked up at her. "My daughter told me about the little English boy with Aaron."

Meg nodded. "Yes, Sam is my son."

The second woman said something to the others in their own language. They all smiled as they continued to work.

Catherine turned to Meg. "She is explaining how my father-in-law calls him Young Samuel." She was sewing the hem of a white apron.

"No quilting for you?" Meg asked.

"Not tonight," Catherine answered. "This is for Barbara to wear at her wedding. After this, I will finish work on her cape. She wears special white clothes. They look like our other clothes, but new ones, for this use only."

"Almost only . . ." Leah put in, without taking her eyes off her work.

"True." Catherine nodded. "After the wedding they are put away, and she will be buried in them."

Meg hoped her face didn't betray her surprise at this piece of information. She turned the idea over in her mind. She supposed it all fit, the tight linking of family traditions.

"Do you also make these quilts to sell, or only for yourselves?" Meg asked.

"Both." The older woman answered again for all of them. "We maybe do some different patterns for the tourists, things they like. They are often on white backgrounds."

Catherine went on, "We sew many different designs. Like Wedding Ring, which is circles that are locking together. We have many kinds."

Another woman glanced up at Meg. "Can you sew?"

"No, not really." Meg tried not to feel abashed by her ignorance of what was a most basic skill to these people. "I can knit a little," she added with a laugh, "but just enough to make a scarf, I'm afraid."

Leah, who was sitting next to Amanda, leaned over to her and whispered something into her granddaughter's ear. Amanda nodded, excused herself, and left the room. She returned a few minutes later with a skein of dark-blue wool and two knitting needles.

"Maybe you would like to make scarves for your children," Leah said. "I see they do not have."

Meg didn't know what made her feel more taken aback—the fact that Leah would do such a kind thing for her, or that she had bothered to notice Meg's children weren't dressed properly and cared enough to do something to rectify the situation.

"Thank you very, very much," Meg said to her. "It's a lot warmer in our home state, and the children don't have the proper clothes here. This means a great deal to me."

Leah gave a little nod. "I have more of this blue wool" was all she said.

Now, thought Meg, let's hope I can remember how to do it.

Happily, her fingers seemed to begin casting on by themselves, and she became engrossed in knitting. The women worked mainly in silence, but occasionally they shared an observation. When the subject turned to Barbara's wedding on Tuesday, they became more animated, discussing what had yet to be done.

"Soon it will be finished, a wonderful memory," one of the women said to Catherine. "You will go back to visiting."

Meg looked at her inquiringly.

"In the cold months," Catherine explained, "we do much visiting with family and our friends. The wedding keeps us busy now, but after, we will go to people's houses, and they will come to ours."

"Especially Barbara and Moses," Amanda added. "They go on so many visits after. That is when many people give them the wedding presents, and it's time to see a lot of the people who came."

Everyone resumed their tasks in silence. In the background, the children moved about, most of them in their socks, their conversation punctuated by loud bursts of laughter. Every so often a young child would approach the table and look at Meg before whispering a question. Sam, she saw, was fully absorbed in a game of Sorry with two boys she didn't recognize.

"Do you do a lot of visiting with relatives?" the woman who had just spoken asked Meg.

She shook her head. "We don't have many. My parents are the only ones, really." She hesitated. "Unfortunately, we don't get along well with them."

Catherine raised her face, concern in her eyes. "This is true?"

"No, no, I shouldn't have said that," Meg answered. Why had she felt the need to air her personal problems?

Sensing her reluctance to discuss it further, the women changed the subject. The evening slipped by in what seemed like minutes. Meg had made substantial progress on her scarf when it dawned on her that she should really give these women time to themselves. I've been enjoying myself far too much, she thought, wrapping up her knitting. The women must have things they want to discuss that they can't, or won't, talk about in front of me.

"It has been lovely to meet all of you," Meg said. "Please excuse me now. I must go to bed."

They nodded, but no one stopped what they were doing.

"Sam," she called out to her son, "finish up and come upstairs."

"Okay, okay," he called back. "In a minute."

Meg headed to the staircase, holding her knitting. As she climbed the steps, she wondered if she was intentionally getting too involved in these people's lives. She was allowing herself to be lulled into ignoring her situation, had even complained about her problems.

This was not her world, and it never would be. Sooner or later she would have to face the mess that was her real life.

Chapter 12

✤

On Saturday morning Meg looked out her bedroom window to see the countryside completely covered with a soft, thick quilt of snow. Everything—houses, barns, trees—stood partially hidden beneath at least half a foot of snow, all sounds muffled by its weight. Tree branches sagged beneath the heavy snowfall. The temperature must have dropped further in the hours before dawn, and many of the trees were decorated by glistening ice that sparkled when the pale sunlight managed to break through the clouds. The magnificent serenity nearly took her breath away.

She tore herself from the view to wash her face and brush her hair. Getting dressed in the mornings was considerably faster here than it had been at home, primarily because the Amish didn't keep mirrors in the house. The only time Meg looked at herself was when she picked up the tiny makeup mirror she had in her own purse. There was no way of fussing over how her clothing looked. After a day or two, she had abandoned the idea of putting on makeup altogether, not only because she couldn't see well enough in her mirror to do it properly, but because it made her uncomfortable around all the other women with their fresh-scrubbed faces. By this point, the notion of wearing a face full of makeup struck her as faintly ridiculous, as if she were slathering dirt on herself.

She didn't know how to do the hairstyle favored by the women here—what she thought of as a version of French braids tied back—but she had taken to gathering her hair into a neat ponytail. That kept it off her face while she was working and, more important, while she was cooking or baking.

Buttoning her sweater against the morning chill, she came down for breakfast to find the main room of the Lutz house a scene of controlled chaos. The great-grandchildren were there with their mothers, selecting from a long row of ice skates that had been set out this morning. Meg noted every type of skate, from beginners' runners that attached directly to shoes to adult heavy black skates for hockey and racing, most of them well worn from years of being used and, no doubt, handed down. The younger Lutz children rushed in and out, balancing the completion of their chores with locating appropriately fitting skates for themselves. Meg noticed about a dozen hockey sticks stacked against the wall and a pile of thick black gloves on the bench.

James and the children were sitting off to one corner, also trying on skates.

"Hey, guys," Meg said as she came over.

"They invited us to skate with them," Sam said. "There's a pond that'll be ice! I've never done that before."

Lizzie was lacing up a pair of old but serviceable white skates. "You want to come, Mom?"

Meg hesitated. "Is Catherine going? Or any of the other women?"

"No," James answered. "They said they had too much to do. It's just dads and kids, I guess. We may get to play some hockey with them, too."

Meg already knew there would be a lot of work going on that day. Saturday was the regular cleaning day in the house, and the big event was on Tuesday. If the other women were staying behind, she would do the same.

"I'll stay here this morning," she said. "Maybe later I'll have a chance to get out and mess around with everybody."

James had moved to kneel in front of Sam and help tighten his laces. "Okay, these are good." He gave a couple of solid pats to the black skates before turning to Will. "How is it going?"

Will shook his head as he yanked off a skate. "Kinda tight." Clutching the skate in question, he got up to check out his other options. Seeing they didn't need her, Meg went back toward the kitchen area. Barbara stood at the table, a group of kerosene lamps gathered from around the house spread out before her. She was carefully cleaning them with a rag. Meg greeted her and, reaching into a cabinet for a mug, asked if she could assist.

"No, thank you. But my mother is at the root cellar, getting some food to cook for today and tomorrow. Maybe she needs help. The front walk is shoveled, but I don't know about the back . . ."

Meg, nodding, filled her cup with coffee. Practically hidden from view, she observed Jonathan and Eli hurry into the room, yanking on jackets and gloves before grabbing skates, hockey sticks, and hats. Several teenage boys in coats and black mufflers came to the front door, entering the house just long enough to pick out hockey sticks.

"Later," Barbara said to Meg, "we can go for a sleigh ride or be outside with the children, if you like."

Sam came running up to Meg to say good-bye. "It's so cool the way people come into each other's houses, isn't it? Everything's just right there, all together." He gave her a hug. "Bye. See you later."

"Have fun," she called out to her family.

James gave her a wave and a smile. Her older son and daughter also called out their good-byes, Lizzie applying the lip balm she always kept in her jacket pocket as she left.

A sliced loaf of banana bread had been set out on a plate on the counter, although most of it was already gone. Meg reached for a piece and took a bite. On a Saturday at home in Charlotte, she reflected, James would have been at the office or in his study working. If the kids had a free day, she would be the one taking them skating at an indoor rink, assuming she could have gotten them to agree to go in the first place, which was unlikely. Even so, she would have to drag Lizzie and Will practically by force. And it wouldn't have been happening until well after noon, when they might be willing to get out of their pajamas and into clothes.

"Are David and Samuel going skating, too?" she asked Barbara.

"No, they're cleaning out the barn now. Aaron already cleaned the chicken coop, so he left, but they have a lot of work. And tomorrow is a church Sunday. They want to finish things."

Meg was confused. "Don't you go to church every Sunday?"

Barbara shook her head. "No, every other Sunday."

"Oh." Surprised, Meg finished her coffee and rinsed out the cup. "Well, I'm going downstairs to see if I can help your mother. Then I'll shovel in the back."

Barbara nodded, her attention on a spot on one of the lamps that was giving her difficulty. She rubbed at it furiously.

Meg rotated her shoulders in small circles as she walked, wanting to loosen them up a bit as she went to help Catherine lift the enormous sacks in the cellar. Who needs free weights when you have beets and potatoes, she thought with a smile.

Everyone returned in time for lunch, the children ruddy-cheeked and in high spirits. James came over to kiss Meg hello on the cheek, cheerfully complaining that he had used muscles he didn't remember he even had, and would pay for it the next day. While she wasn't sure how friendly she wanted her response to him to be, she was genuinely pleased to see that the four of them had had a wonderful time together. James and Will discussed the fine points of their hockey game with the other participants during the entire first course of hot beef barley soup and bread. Lizzie, seated next to Meg, ate her entire bowl of soup without complaint as she told her mother how much she enjoyed the skating, even though so many kids had appeared throughout the course of the morning, she wouldn't have been surprised if the ice had opened up and they'd all fallen into the pond.

After lunch almost everyone headed back outside to play in the snow. This time Meg and the Lutz women bundled up and joined in. Snowball fights broke out everywhere, and children screamed with delight as they ducked. When sleighs began pulling up, the horses whinnying in the frosty air, the Hobarts were thrilled to find places amid the Lutz children and the neighbors offering the rides. Cuddling under blankets, her children and husband laughing beside her as they bounced along behind the trotting horses, Meg wondered why everyone in the world didn't want to take a sleigh ride every time it snowed. Rapt, she drank in the sights of the passing farms in their picture-perfect state, the deserted animal pens, their usual inhabitants inside the warm barns, and the gently rolling farmland, an endless narrow strip against the overwhelming expanse of the afternoon sky.

She glanced over to see James and Lizzie, their heads close together, looking out at something far away, James's arm outstretched as he pointed. The two of them engaged in conversation: That was something she couldn't recall seeing in ages.

"Is this not the greatest treat in the world?" she asked Will, who was sitting next to her.

"It's pretty awesome, I gotta admit," he answered, his eyes wide open and clear, his expression one of pure happiness.

She put an arm around him. He didn't pull away.

By the time evening rolled around, everyone was exhausted. After dinner most of the children settled down to board games, accompanied by snacks of pretzels and roasted marshmallows. Meg found herself seated at the table with Catherine and Barbara, who explained that they were going over seating details for the unmarried teenagers at the evening supper. Meg wanted to know more but refrained from interrupting them with what she guessed seemed like her endless questions.

During a momentary lull, she decided to jump in with a request she had been pondering for the past few hours. "I truly don't want to add to the things you have to deal with," she started, "but I wonder if you would do me a favor."

Both women looked at her as she chose her words.

"Every Christmas I bake my special brownies and oatmeal cookies. I've been doing it forever, and it kind of makes it Christmas for us. Would you do me the favor of letting me bake them for your wedding, Barbara? I promise I won't disappoint you—I really think your guests will like them."

Barbara smiled. "That's a wonderful thing you're offering to do."

"It would mean so much to me, for so many reasons," Meg said. "But it would be my little contribution to wishing you a happy marriage."

"Thank you. I would be honored."

Meg laughed. "I'm not sure you should be honored. I don't know if they're *that* good."

"We'll see, won't we?" Catherine grinned. "On Monday we will add them with other baking that is still to do."

"Thank you. Thank you so much."

The two women had no idea of the significance it had for her, Meg thought. She hadn't missed a year since Lizzie was born. All three of her children adored the very fudgy brownies and the oatmeal cookies shot through with cranberries. It would have been unbearably sad for her to see the holiday come and go without them. Of course, Meg expected that they would be at her parents' house when the actual holiday rolled around. That was exactly why she needed to bake them before they left here. She knew perfectly well her parents weren't going to be excited about the cost, the mess, or the idea of letting their grandchildren run amok by eating all the brownies and cookies they wanted until they had run out.

That was the whole point, though, in Meg's view. What made it fun was the seemingly inexhaustible supply of sweets without—just this one time in the year—limits applied. Breakfast, lunch, or dinner, if you wanted brownies or cookies, you could have them. It wasn't such a big deal, considering they were gone in about three days, everyone satiated to the point of nausea, wanting nothing more to do with them until the next year.

Meg went to bed that night feeling that she had done her best to salvage a little bit of home for her family.

The next morning she got up to see the Lutzes leaving for worship, dressed in what must have literally been their Sunday best, black clothes that were basically the same style but not the same garments they wore during the workweek. They hadn't invited the Hobarts to go with them, and Meg and James sensed that it wasn't appropriate to ask.

Once all five of them had made it to the kitchen, they took seats around the table in the dim morning light to eat the breakfast Catherine had left for them. The dogs settled beneath the table, Racer snoring lightly, Rufus sitting at attention in case someone should drop a piece of food. Sam scratched the puppy's head.

Suddenly the five of them felt awkward in the silent house. Sam broke the silence first. "Old Samuel told me about their church service," he offered as he poured himself a bowl of cereal.

"You are so weird, spending all your time with that old man," Will said, although he was still too sleepy to put much energy into the insult. He took a long gulp from his glass of orange juice.

"I don't spend all my time with him," Sam answered in annoyance. "But at least I know stuff, and you don't, stupid."

"Oh, big expert over there," Will said with disdain.

"Let me guess," Lizzie broke in. "Their church service is twelve hours. Then there's a five-minute break, and they go back for another twelve hours."

Sam made a face at her. "No. I just know that it's always in somebody's house or barn, a different place all the time. They have, like, these benches they take around. The men and women sit separate. There's this book with all their songs and stuff that they've been using for, like, four hundred years."

"Sam, that's really interesting," James said, helping himself to some buttermilk pancakes, golden but, by now, cold. "Thanks for telling us."

"You're very welcome," Sam said primly before sticking out his tongue at Will. "Some of us prefer not to be ignorant."

"Some of us prefer not to be obnoxious little freaks," Will retorted, reaching for the pitcher of maple syrup.

"I wonder what time they'll get back," Meg said.

"They eat and hang around after," Sam informed her.

At the unexpected sound of the door opening, all five of them turned. Racer jumped to his feet and tore over to the door, barking wildly, startling them with his ability to run, much less move that fast. The puppy took off after him, loudly yapping.

A tall young man stepped inside. He was wearing blue jeans, work boots, and a plaid flannel shirt beneath an open quilted down jacket and a navy-blue knitted cap. In one hand he held a knapsack that he let drop to the floor. The two dogs were jumping and barking for his attention.

Clearly shocked, he stared at the people sitting around the table. "Who the heck are you?" he demanded.

James drew himself up in his chair as if positioning himself in case he had to confront this intruder. Meg's gaze was drawn to the boy's blue eyes.

"Excuse me, but we're guests here—" James started. As James spoke, the boy tugged off his cap, revealing a thatch of blond hair.

Of course, Meg realized. She put a hand on James's arm. "Wait."

Her husband stopped and looked at her.

Meg stood up and smiled at the boy. "You must be Benjamin. I'm *so* glad to meet you."

Chapter 13

❖

By eleven o'clock on Monday morning, Meg couldn't decide which was more impressive: the amount of work being done by the dozen or so couples who had appeared at the Lutz house early that morning, or the calm and organized way in which they went about it. One couple, relatives of David Lutz, had been designated to oversee the entire operation, but, once assigned a task, everyone seemed to know exactly what to do. The members of the community had done this many times before, Meg reflected, but their efficiency was nonetheless startling.

The men had their own list of chores, and Meg couldn't resist sneaking out of the baking in Catherine's kitchen for a few moments to see the activity going on in Joseph's barn. She paused just inside the doorway to watch a small group assemble temporary long tables, rigging benches to table height and covering them with white cloths. Several men gathered around what appeared to be a floor plan of the seating, consulting on the arrangement of tables.

At that moment, Catherine's daughter Annie passed by and stopped to tap Meg on the shoulder. Guiltily, Meg jumped and turned around. "I know, I'm slacking off," she said, surprised to feel her face turning pink. "I'm sorry."

"It's okay." Annie laughed. "You are curious." She peered inside. "Okay. Over there, see where the tables meet to make like a letter L? That's the *Eck*, the corner place where you can see them best, where Barbara and Moses sit with the people in the wedding party." Annie pointed to a group of men in a different area, assembling and sorting huge quantities of food. "That is to make the bread stuffing that goes with the chickens. A *lot* of chickens."

"Where is all this cooking being done?" Meg asked. "There's not enough room in our three kitchens."

"Many houses. My father is now at a neighbor's barn to kill the chickens and prepare them for roasting, and my grandparents are chopping celery at a different house. I'm going back to my house, where we are peeling potatoes." Annie laughed. "It is quite a job, making mashed potatoes for three hundred people. Be glad you are not doing the mashing part."

Meg's eyes widened. "I hadn't thought about that. Wow."

"We have many other people making gravy and tapioca pudding, things like that. As much as possible, we cooked all this week, too. We rented propane stoves to set up in a tent here. We spread the work out tomorrow, too, so everybody has some time to enjoy themselves, right? First, most important, are the church service and the wedding vows. Then the celebration. It's the beginning of a new family, so it's a very happy day. And we have always done it exactly the same way."

Annie smiled and walked off. Meg watched her, thinking about what the young woman had just said. This marriage was truly about celebrating a union. They followed their traditions to bring a new Amish family into being. Anything else was outside the realm of what was important. Nobody had to compete with anybody. She had to laugh, thinking of the vast sums of money spent on some of the weddings she and James had attended over the years, most of it for the sole purpose of impressing.

As she headed back toward the Lutz house, she briefly pondered if it was truly possible to eliminate all desire to show off, even the tiniest bit. Several times she had heard the Lutzes talk disapprovingly about something or other being prideful or vain. They worked hard to avoid that.

Meg looked down as she crossed the road to make sure she didn't slip on the ice. When she happened to glance up, she saw the figures of her sons following behind Aaron, Eli, and Jonathan with their newly returned brother, Benjamin. All six carried what obviously were heavy buckets, the older boys straining under the weightiest loads. They deposited them by the back door at Annie's house, closest to her kitchen, and set off back to Catherine's. Will and Sam lagged behind, talking; Meg could see the younger Lutz boys engaged in animated conversation with Benjamin, practically jumping to get his attention. She smiled. The two boys reminded her of Racer and Rufus when Benjamin had appeared at the house yesterday morning. Jonathan, the elder brother, seemed to be keeping his distance. Benjamin was wearing Amish clothes today, but his haircut, trimmed relatively short and without the ubiquitous bangs sported by the other Amish men, made him stand out. Meg guessed the change in clothes was a sign of respect for his family, although the tension between Benjamin and his parents bubbled painfully close to the surface.

Meg had noticed that, as warm and friendly as they were, the adults of the Lutz clan were not particularly affectionate, at least not in front of her, with the one definite exception of how they treated the young children. Babies and toddlers got plenty of hugs and kisses. But she couldn't recall seeing the adults exchange a hug or a kiss or even an unnecessary touch. Perhaps they considered that private, not something for public display, or it just wasn't their way. Meg had no idea and was hardly going to ask. Even so, she was taken aback to see the cool greeting Benjamin received from his father and grandparents when they returned from their church service and found him at home. Maybe it had something to do with his indecision about his future. While warmer, Catherine had refrained from any big display of emotion, although Meg could see both joy and anguish on her face at the sight of her long-absent son.

Initially, the adults hadn't asked Benjamin where he had been or what he had been up to. The younger children, however, couldn't wait to hear about his escapades and hustled him off to another part of the house where they could have him all to themselves. He seemed only too glad to leave the room. Walking along now, watching the group of boys, Meg pondered the difficulty of Benjamin's choices. All she knew for sure, she reflected, was that the lives of these people were infinitely more complex than she understood.

By late afternoon, Meg was exhausted from the day's labors, but she never would have admitted it. Everyone around her was still going at full steam. One of the older women came over to inform her that she could start on her brownies and cookies. Meg was gratified that they had in fact set aside time for her. She had begun to think she would have to get up in the dead of night if she wanted a chance at her own baking.

James had purchased the supplies, only too glad they could contribute something to the celebration, however small. After sending little Rachel to find Lizzie, Meg began to assemble her ingredients. The goal was four hundred brownies and three hundred cookies. Just a tad more than the usual Christmas batch, she laughed to herself, but hey, this is the land of the Amish. They can do everything, and maybe, as long as I'm here, I can, too.

When Lizzie came running into the house behind Rachel, she was red-faced and out of breath. "What's wrong, Mom? Rachel said . . ." Lizzie trailed off as she saw the familiar baking ingredients. Her face broke into a wide grin. "Oh, Mom." She sighed with pleasure. "The brownies. And the oatmeal cookies, too? You're awesome."

Meg smiled at her. "Only if I can get some help. We need to make enough to feed a small city. So wash your hands and tie your hair back."

Lizzie didn't have to be told twice. "One sec, I'll be right there," she called out as she dashed toward the sink.

Meg was happy to see her daughter so excited. Her daughter's obvious longing for something familiar didn't escape her. Even when they left here, though, they weren't going back home, only on to another unfamiliar world. It would be soon, too. Just another few days, according to the mechanic.

Meg smoothed down the front of her borrowed apron. Then she moved forward, assessing what it would take to lift the enormous sack of flour before her.

When she and Lizzie finished arranging the last platter of brownies, both of them breathed sighs of vast relief. The desserts had come out just right, though they had never before attempted to bake them in such huge quantities. Catherine tasted a brownie and a cookie, giving a brisk nod and pronouncing them good in a definite tone of voice. This, Meg knew, was high praise. After the last pan was washed and put away, she and her daughter shared a high five and a long, tight hug.

By the time she got ready to head upstairs for the night, Meg felt that if she couldn't partake in any other part of the wedding celebration, she would be grateful for what she had already been allowed to see and do on this day. Just the time spent baking with Lizzie had been a supreme treat. She tried not to compare the obviously tight bonds of these people with the ephemeral connections of her own past. It made for a very sorry assessment of what passed for relationships. To be fair, she reminded herself, most of these people were related in some way. They spent all their lives together. And they had their own problems with one another. Yet Meg could see that the bonds of their religion and community overrode all other considerations.

After an incredibly long day, the huge but relaxed crowd of workers sat down to a supper infused with goodwill and laughter. They truly lived by the adage that work was its own reward, Meg reflected. Seated at the table, looking at the open, kind faces around her, she knew she would remember this day for a long time to come.

By the time she said her good nights, Meg was so tired, she wanted nothing more than to feel the pillow beneath her head. On her way down the hall, she passed the door to Benjamin's room, which was slightly open. When the boy had returned home, he'd kindly allowed Will to continue to stay in the room with him, while Sam moved in with Aaron. As Meg went by, she heard Benjamin say something and Lizzie and Will laugh in response. Guiltily, she paused to find out what they were discussing. She had no idea what her children talked about with the Lutz children, and the opportunity to find out was irresistible.

"No Christmas tree or lights or anything?" Will was asking in disbelief.

"No Santa Claus, none of that," Benjamin said. "We just hang out, have a big family meal, a couple of small presents. Nothing big, and mostly stuff you can use. The next day we go to worship."

"The next day?" Will asked. "The day *after* Christmas?"

"Yup."

"Can't get much different from that back where we live—I mean lived," Lizzie said. "People have huge trees. Tons of presents. A lot of kids in my class would be away on vacation this week in Europe or, like, on a safari in Africa or something."

"Hart Jenkins was going to Cabo," Will said. "He goes every year with his parents and his grandparents."

"I've never heard of Cabo. Where is it?" Benjamin asked.

There was a momentary silence. "I don't totally know where it *is*," Will said as offhandedly as he could manage to cover his ignorance. "But it's hot, and tons of people go there."

"The people who stay home go to a lot of parties," Lizzie put in. "That's what I'd be doing if we were home. Will, remember last year, when Patricia Woods had to get her stomach pumped?"

"Oh, man, that was nuts." Will sounded gleeful. His tone changed as he explained the situation to Benjamin. "She was a senior, but everybody heard about it, even in my school."

Lizzie picked up the story. "The assistant principal's son had a New Year's Eve party because his parents were away. She got so drunk, she hurled all over their white couch. Then she said she felt better, so she drank some more. She totally passed out, and they had to take her to the hospital to get her stomach pumped. She almost *died*, no kidding. They said, like, another twenty minutes and that would have been it.

"People at the party were so freaked." Lizzie's voice rose slightly in her excitement to share the icing on the cake. "Her friends who drove her to the hospital actually left her outside the emergency room and took off. Left her right there on the ground."

There was a pause as if they all were considering this display of concern for the unconscious girl.

"Whatever," said Lizzie, sounding a bit chastised. "But don't you want to get out and see more of the world?"

"I've seen some of it, at least some of this country," Benjamin replied. "I traveled around."

"Oh, man," Will said, "why would you come back here if you didn't have to? You don't have anything here. It's been so long since I've been on my computer, I'll never catch up with what's going on."

"Yeah," Lizzie sneered. "Like what pathetic girl hooked up with your buddy Harry because he played her that insanely bad song." Again an explanation for Benjamin's sake. "This kid is in ninth grade, and he wrote this one pitiful song. He picks a girl and tells her he wrote it just for her. He can't even, like, play the guitar, but he does this little serenade thing, and the girls fall for it every time. It's so disgusting!"

"Come on," said Will. "It's pretty brilliant, you gotta admit. Or it was until enough girls found out about it. They really ganged up on him. None of them will even talk to him anymore."

"Serves him right. I mean, they're stupid, but at least they're not *that* stupid," Lizzie retorted. "But yeah, about not talking, I wonder what happened with Suki and Michelle."

"You mean those skanky girls you hang out with, with the insanely straight hair? The ones with all those jangly bracelets and crap?" Will asked.

"They're not skanky, and they have their hair straightened with this process that everybody does. It looks great, for your information."

Will snorted. "If you say so."

Lizzie deigned to continue. "The point is, they went on this hike together, and when they came back they weren't speaking. They won't tell anybody what happened." She paused. "I'm kind of happy I don't have to deal with that anymore. Everybody had to take sides. It was hard, because we didn't even know what they were so mad about. But it was getting really ugly."

Meg leaned against the hallway wall. This was the first time she had heard any of these stories. It appears I know absolutely nothing about the lives my children have been leading, she thought.

Lizzie went on, her tone more reflective. "I have to admit, it's been pretty great to be away from all that. It was totally getting to me. You guys here definitely don't have the stress of the social stuff."

"One thing is," Will said, "it was kind of boring at home. I mean, everybody's on the computer or their phone all the time, and you have to do that or you're just out of things. I didn't used to think that, but now I kinda do. At first I thought it was insanely boring here, but there's really something to do all the time. I miss basketball, but you do lots of other sports and outside stuff. There's nothing to do at home, ever."

"Yeah, and I like the feeling of having done something you can see and touch, you know?" Lizzie added. "Maybe that sounds stupid. I mean, there's way too much work here. It's ridiculous. But it's nice to *do* something. Does that make any sense?"

"It's kind of like there's nothing to do here *but* work and then get a little break," Will reflected. "But when you get to play, it's like you earned it."

Meg was practically holding her breath, hanging on every word.

"So when do you decide what you're going to do about leaving or not?" Lizzie asked.

As Benjamin spoke, Meg realized he had virtually no trace of the family accent—perhaps, she thought, because he had spent the most time living among outsiders.

"I liked a lot of what I saw while I was traveling. I had a bunch of jobs, met a lot of people. It was all really interesting. I love music, and I'm going to miss that. I also really liked driving a car, and TV and movies. And the computer, of course."

His bed squeaked; Meg could tell he had stood up and was moving around the room.

"But it's all the stuff you're talking about. I met really nice people, but I saw that people can also be rotten. And lonely. And a lot of things I don't like and don't want to be. Besides, it would be really hard on my parents if I left. There's also a girl here that I missed." His tone turned severe. "You tell anybody about her, and you'll be in big trouble."

"Okay, okay," Will said. "No problem."

Benjamin went on. "So I've already decided that I'm coming back. After Christmas, I'll go finish up some things, and then I'm moving back for good."

Meg inhaled sharply. He had made up his mind. He was returning for good. She wanted to jump up and down with happiness for Catherine and David.

"Did you tell anybody yet?" Lizzie wanted to know.

"I'm waiting until after the wedding. It's not a time to draw attention to myself."

No, no, no, Meg implored him silently, it's okay to draw attention to yourself this time. Don't torture your parents anymore. Don't torture *me* by making me keep that from them.

Will spoke with exaggerated seriousness. "Your secret's safe with us."

"Thank you, my man," Benjamin said, laughing.

The three of them continued to talk, but Meg hurried down the hall to her own room. She was grateful for all she had learned from her eavesdropping. Thinking back on the many times she had told her children that it was absolutely wrong to eavesdrop, she fervently hoped they would never find out about it.

On the morning of the wedding itself, the atmosphere in the house turned more serious. Everyone left for a worship service at nine. It was expected to last about three hours, with the actual wedding vows taking place near the end. Meg felt an almost maternal thrill at seeing Barbara go off in her new white cape and apron over a dark-blue dress, the same color worn by the girls who were her attendants. Having been told that the bride and groom wore new clothes, Meg knew there were other differences from their regular Sunday clothes, but she wasn't knowledgeable enough to discern the subtleties.

Other non-Amish friends of the families were among the invited guests; they had been asked to arrive at eleven o'clock, closer to when the wedding vows began. Much to the surprise of Meg and James, David and Catherine stayed at the house for most of the morning as well. The Hobarts remained behind the entire time, helping others get ready to serve the luncheon meal. Just before guests were due to appear, they retreated to their rooms to change into whatever clothing they had with them that might be appropriate. None of them had packed anything resembling party clothes, but the casual clothes they did have, washed and neatly pressed, felt better suited to the occasion of cooking and serving.

All at once, it seemed, dozens of buggies pulled up to Joseph's house, guests spilling out into the cold. As she retied her hair into a neat ponytail, Meg watched from her bedroom window. It was such an incredible sight, she thought, all those buggies pulled by horses, truly like stepping back in time. She noted a line of cars parked nearby as well, no doubt transporting the English guests.

"Okay," James said, coming up behind her to glance out the window. "This is really going to be something. Let's go."

Meg turned to look at him. Gone was the furrowed brow she had seen for months, the pursed lips and angry expression. He appeared healthy and relaxed. She followed him out of the room.

"C'mon, everybody, let's get going," she called out to her children as she hurried down the stairs. They, too, had assignments for the day, from keeping water glasses filled to collecting dirty dishes. Grabbing their coats from the wall of hooks, she and James practically ran across to Joseph's barn to reach the tented-off workspace containing the propane stoves.

Meg and James watched from what felt like backstage as Barbara and Moses took their places at the central location of the *Eck,* the bride to the left of the groom, attendants and young relatives seated nearby. Girls and boys filed in, sitting apart. Today, Catherine had explained to Meg, the new couple's aunts and uncles had the honor of tending to the needs of all those in this area of the reception.

Meg soaked up the sights and sounds. She was intrigued by the numerous vases and jars containing celery that ran down the length of the tables like floral centerpieces, apparently a long-standing tradition. Most guests hadn't brought gifts to the wedding, but many of the English guests, or relatives from far away, had, and the presents were set aside in a small display; she noted the assortment of useful items ranging from roasting pans to a chain saw. Those working in the kitchens somehow knew the correct order in which a seemingly endless parade of food was to be presented, and Meg heaped hot food onto platter after platter, not just the chicken and bread stuffing dish but hams, ducks, the infamous mashed potatoes, creamed celery, noodles, salads, casseroles, pickled beets with eggs, coleslaw, bread and butter, fruit, pudding, and ice cream. She was stunned by the sheer number of cakes and sweets set out.

Toward the end of the meal, she couldn't resist going to check on how her brownies and cookies were faring with the crowd—and was relieved to see that the guests had found room for them. Judging by the rate at which they disappeared, Meg noted, they must have met with everyone's satisfaction. Abashed, she reminded herself that she was experiencing a decidedly un-Amish moment of pride.

The closest relatives, including David and Catherine, took their meal at a table in the kitchen. Teenagers and younger guests were done first and then left the dining area. When all the guests had finished, it was two-thirty, time for an afternoon sing. Meg was pleased to recognize the doctor who had treated her and James the night they had arrived at the Lutzes', and she went over to thank him again for his help. They talked while some of the adults attempted to round up the teenage guests from wherever they had scattered, although Meg could see many of them remained elusive, including her own. She noticed Sam standing with Aaron and another boy, but there was no sign of Lizzie or Will. In the back of her mind, she wondered if she should check on them, but first one and then another distraction drew her attention. When the singing got under way, she was glad for the opportunity to sit down. She knew she would be helping to serve another meal later in the day. Annie had explained that the younger guests would stay for supper and the celebration would continue until very late.

The day was progressing like a lovely, slow-moving dream. The sensation was shattered when she saw Will run into the barn, crying, blood smeared around a large cut on his chin. Wild-eyed, he looked around.

Meg jumped up and ran over, the people seated close to her turning to see what was wrong.

"Will, what is it?" Meg wrapped an arm around his shoulder, hustling him outside the barn, away from the guests, as she smoothed back his hair so she could get a better look at his injuries. "What happened? Where are you hurt?"

"It's not me." Will was crying harder, having difficulty getting out his words. "Amanda. I think she broke something."

"What? What are you talking about? Where is she?" Meg

200 _ Cynthia Keller

took his chin in her hand, forcing him to look her directly in the eyes. "Tell me."

"It's— It was stupid, and I'm really sorry." Will wiped his running nose with his jacket sleeve, his face growing redder as the tears came in full force.

Meg's voice rose. "Where is Amanda? Is she okay?"

"Lizzie's with her back there, on the road." He pointed in some general direction as he tried to catch his breath. "The buggy turned over. Going t-too fast. She can't walk now."

"*What?* Oh, Will, oh no!" Meg turned, grabbing his hand. "We have to get Catherine."

"No, don't tell her," Will wailed. "She'll be mad."

Meg had already started running toward the tent where she had last seen Catherine. "Hurry."

They found her talking with a group of women, but she broke away when she saw a frantic Meg approaching with her son in tow.

"Tell her," Meg commanded Will as they got closer.

"I'm so, so sorry," Will began, words tumbling out of his mouth. "The buggy fell over. Amanda got hurt, maybe broke her leg. Lizzie's with her. They're on the side of the road, it's not far. But Amanda can't walk at all."

Catherine's expression didn't change. She nodded and quickly moved past them. "Come with me. You will show us."

Meg kept Will off to the side, hoping they would be less disruptive, and watched Catherine make a beeline for a gray-haired non-Amish woman in a pale-green silk dress at one of the tables. Catherine bent over, whispered in her ear, and the woman rose to her feet, smiling and saying a few quick words to the guests she had been seated with. The woman grabbed her coat and headed toward the exit with Catherine. Meg and Will hurried to catch up, and the four of them headed to a parked car.

Catherine looked around to make sure Will was coming and got in on the passenger side. Meg realized that Catherine might not be allowed to drive a car, but she was allowed to be a passenger in one, and it was a lot faster to get to her daughter in a car than a buggy. Meg and Will practically dove into the backseat as the woman pulled onto the road.

"Will," Catherine said calmly, "say where."

"Just up there, you make a left turn." His voice was shaky. "It was when we went around that corner, the whole thing fell over."

"Is Amanda awake? Can she talk?"

"Oh yes, yes, it's nothing like that," Will rushed to reassure Catherine.

She expelled a small breath and turned to face them in the back. "This is my friend Nina Moore. She can take Amanda to the hospital if we need, so that is good."

Will let out a small, tremulous sob. "I'm really sorry. It was my fault. I know I shouldn't have touched the reins."

Meg stared at him. "Touched the reins? What do you mean?"

"We, we . . . Lizzie and me, we were gonna deliver stuff with Amanda and Jonathan," he started miserably.

"The pies," Catherine said. "Jonathan and Amanda had to take pies to King's. The regular delivery."

Meg was startled to think the two would leave their sister's wedding to make a delivery. Then it occurred to her that it was a Tuesday, so businesses would be operating as usual. The Lutz family had a delivery to make, so they would make it, wedding or not.

"Go on," she said brusquely to her son.

He seemed to shrink in his seat. "Amanda and Lizzie were in back, and I was sitting in the front. Jonathan was gonna drive, but then he had to go back inside to talk to somebody for a second. So Lizzie was teasing me. You know how she can be." He looked for sympathy in his mother's eyes but found none. "She was daring me to drive the buggy, saying, like, even Aaron could do it, stuff like that." He paused to wipe his face with his jacket sleeve. "All I did was pick up the reins a little, and the horse just started going. I didn't do *anything*, I swear. We were having fun, really, it was okay. Amanda said to stop, but you know, for a minute I was really driving. Then the horse started going too fast, and I couldn't get him to stop. It was scary." Fresh tears filled his eyes.

"What happened next?" Catherine asked.

"When we came to this corner, I didn't tell it to, but the horse just turned really fast. The whole thing tipped over. Everybody screamed, but Amanda couldn't get up." His voice got very small. "So I ran back. That's it."

For the first time, Meg heard Nina speak: "Here they are." She pulled over, and all of them got out. Meg caught her breath at the sight before her. The horse stood upright, still partially connected to the rig, which Meg recognized at once as Jonathan's buggy. It lay on its side, badly damaged, the rear wheel shattered. Smashed pies and boxes were strewn everywhere, the snow smeared with pieces of crust, apple filling, and chocolate. Just past the mess, sitting on a blanket, Lizzie had a protective arm around Amanda, who was rocking back and forth, her leg extended in front of her. Lizzie's terrified expression turned to naked relief when she saw the women emerge from the car.

In an instant, Catherine was kneeling beside her daughter, softly asking questions. Amanda winced as Catherine lightly touched her leg, trying to determine the extent of the injury. When Lizzie and Catherine moved to help her up, Amanda cried out in pain before even attempting to put any weight on her foot.

Nina Moore was standing next to Meg and Will, watching. "That leg very well may be fractured. We'll go straight to the hospital."

Meg was amazed by Amanda's stoicism. Although pale, she stood uncomplaining, leaning against Lizzie and Catherine, while Nina brought the car as close as she could and they helped her maneuver into the back. Then Lizzie came over to join her mother and brother.

Meg made a quick decision. She turned to her children. "I'm going to the hospital. One of you stay here with the horse, and one of you run and find Jonathan. Tell him about his buggy. Ask him how you should clean up the mess and who can help you. When I get back, there shouldn't be any trace of this food left."

She headed back to the car. Catherine had climbed in the back beside her daughter, whose silence belied the pain in her eyes.

"Mom—" Lizzie called after her own mother, but Meg yanked open the car door.

"Just go," she said.

At the hospital, Nina and Meg took a seat in the waiting area while Catherine followed her daughter through the inner double doors to the emergency room for an X-ray.

"Well," Nina said, "this has turned out to be an even busier day than anyone could have guessed."

Meg shook her head. "I don't know if I'm more angry or embarrassed. My kids have done a lot of things I'm not too proud of since we've been staying here, but this . . ."

"I heard about you being here. You and David almost crashing into each other. The Lutzes are a wonderful family, aren't they? You got very lucky when you wound up in their house."

Meg smiled. "Yes, but we only wound up there because we nearly killed David Lutz. Not so lucky for him."

Nina smiled back at her. "But you didn't kill him. Instead, you made friends with him."

"That's a very nice way to put it." Meg felt grateful to her.

"Happily, it all worked out."

Meg grew serious. "I'd like to know how this is going to work out. Let's see: My kids have injured Amanda, destroyed Jonathan's buggy, and disrupted Barbara's wedding. Oh, and wait—last but not least, they ruined the entire restaurant order, which means the family lost that money altogether. All because of their completely thoughtless behavior. It's not as if they don't know better."

"Take it easy," Nina said. "It'll be okay."

"You don't know how incredible these people have been to

us," Meg said. "They're the last people on earth I'd want to cause trouble for. And to hurt one of their children—I can't bear it."

The other woman put a comforting hand on Meg's. "Look, if you know them, you know they're very understanding. Nobody was seriously hurt. That's what matters."

Meg sighed.

Catherine pushed open one of the double doors and walked over to them. "Her leg is broken, but it's not such a bad break. They have to put on a cast. We'll be here for a while. You two go back and enjoy the rest of the wedding."

"No, Catherine, don't be silly," Nina said. "We'll wait."

"Of course," said Meg.

"There is no reason for you to sit here. Go back."

Meg shook her head firmly. "Absolutely not."

Catherine looked at her and saw she would not be dissuaded. "If you wish." She turned to go back to her daughter.

Meg and Nina spent the next hour talking about what it had been like for the Hobarts to experience life on the Lutz farm. Meg was thrilled to be able to discuss some of what she had observed with another non-Amish person who knew about their way of life. They talked about the wedding and all the traditions associated with it. Meg learned from Nina that Barbara and Moses would not go on a honeymoon. As Amanda had partly explained on the night all the women were quilting, they would do what was typical of newlyweds, spending weeks visiting their wedding guests, sometimes making multiple visits in one weekend or traveling far afield. That way they would be ready to get back to work in time for the spring planting.

Nina was so easy to talk to that Meg felt as if they were old friends. She found herself describing how she had loved baking with the women, the soothing rhythms of the work and the camaraderie. She explained what a privilege it was to be allowed to bake for the wedding meal. Laughing, she recalled her immense relief that multiplying the recipes for her brownies and cookies to feed hundreds of people had worked out.

At the mention of Meg's desserts, Nina's eyes lit up. "You made those? They were fantastic."

"Thank you so much."

"I was wondering where they came from. I assumed it was some distant relative because I've never had them at any of the local Amish functions. Well, the ones I've been invited to."

"I make them every year. My family likes them."

Nina leaned in closer to Meg. "You know, I run a small inn about twenty-five miles from here. Every afternoon we serve tea with some kind of biscuit or sweet. Would you consider baking me some brownies and some of those cookies? Or other cookies, if you've got any recipes you really love. Give me a price, and if it's reasonable, I'll get a few dozen of each, and we'll try it out. I love to serve things that people can't get anywhere else."

"Really?" Meg was so flattered, she didn't know what to say. "Are you serious?"

Nina regarded her with mild surprise. "Well, of course. Why not?"

Meg smiled. "Yes. Why not?"

Chapter 14

Meg approached Annie's house with dread. After yesterday's fiasco, she was as embarrassed as she could remember ever having been in her life. Her children, for whom she was responsible, had wreaked havoc on one of the Lutz family's most important occasions. She was also exhausted, which made her feel even less able to cope with her mortification. Too upset to sleep, when she finally did fall asleep, she was awakened in the middle of the night by what she assumed was a dream in which she heard people moving around downstairs. She kept dozing off only to wake again, thinking she'd heard voices.

In the morning she learned that she hadn't been dreaming at all. She had been hearing Barbara and Moses downstairs in the still-dark early morning, following another Amish tradition in which the bride and groom spend their wedding night at the bride's parents' house and get up especially early to clean the house. The idea intrigued Meg. So unlike the usual concept of a wedding night. Again, the tradition was about helping the community and each other, not just the individual.

All the early-dawn cleaning by Barbara and her new husband meant that the downstairs was spotless, but Meg had circles under her eyes and wanted only to crawl back into bed and hide. Amanda was stuck in the house with her leg in a cast, dependent on crutches to get anywhere. The buggy sat in pieces in the barn. And now the Lutz women had to congregate at Annie's to replace yesterday's entire order of pies. Miserable, Meg had dragged her feet for as long as she dared before coming over this morning.

"Mom, wait up."

Meg turned to see Lizzie running after her, sliding a bit on the icy ground. Meg had said little to her daughter or to Will since returning from the hospital yesterday.

Late last night, after they had all gotten back to the house, she had heard James yelling at them for a very long time. She decided that adding her own screaming recriminations wouldn't help matters. Whatever James had said, it must have gotten through to them, because when the children emerged from the room, they were pale and practically shaking with guilt.

Now Lizzie caught up to her mother, breathing hard. "I want to come with you. To help. I know you have to make the food all over again."

"Okay." Meg looked at her for a moment. "It's strange, but I didn't even think to ask you to help." She shrugged.

Lizzie didn't reply, pursing her lips and looking down.

When they got to Annie's house, Meg hesitated before

reaching for the doorknob. She was trying to prepare for the silent stares they would receive.

Inside the kitchen, it was a day like every other, the room fragrant and warm. Leah, Catherine, Annie, and Sue were combining the ingredients for apple and shoofly pies. They all glanced up at the appearance of Meg and her daughter, but their greetings were indistinguishable from those of any other time.

"Good, you are here," said Catherine, in the process of stirring batter in a large wooden bowl, "so you can measure the flour for the next batch."

Perhaps noticing Lizzie's fearful expression, Sue took the unusual step of handing her an apron instead of letting her retrieve one herself. "After you wash your hands, you can help me slice more apples," she told Lizzie. Her voice held only friendly politeness.

Leah offered Lizzie a knife. "Here, you use this one."

Meg almost sagged with relief. *I could kiss these women,* she thought. *Even Leah is acting as if nothing has happened.*

She stood next to Annie, who was taking a measuring cup to a large tub of butter.

"Can you replace everything from yesterday?" Meg asked.

Annie nodded. "We will make extra pies, but we talked to the store owner." She smiled. "He will take some of the cookies and pastries we have left from the wedding instead of twice as many pies today. He can't sell so many pies, but maybe he can sell pies and cookies. So everybody is happy."

That's one problem solved, Meg thought, thanks to the resourcefulness of these women.

When she found herself next to Catherine later, she tried to think what words might possibly help to make things right. She was unable to come up with any. Nonetheless, she couldn't pretend nothing had happened. "I'm so very sorry about—"

Catherine interrupted her. "Thank you. But you think I don't know how you are feeling about this? I see it on your face. Please don't be unhappy. You should not be. It was an accident, and nothing so terrible happened. Amanda's leg will be fine. Everything else can be fixed. It is not important."

"Oh, but it is important," Meg cried. "There's Amanda, and the wedding and the damage to the buggy—how can you ever forgive us?"

Catherine stopped what she was doing and turned to look directly at Meg. "It is already forgiven. We believe in this very, very strongly. If we ourselves are to be forgiven, how could we not forgive someone else?"

Meg felt tears fill her eyes. "You're an amazing person," she said.

"No," Catherine said, "no more amazing than anyone else. I just follow what I believe, and it always leads me down the right path."

Meg felt an enormous weight being lifted from her shoulders. She resisted the impulse to hug Catherine.

Back at the Lutz house, Meg told James about the conversation. He shook his head. "These people are something else, aren't they?" he agreed. "Will came out to the barn to help repair the rig, and they were as nice to him as if he'd just stopped by to give them a hand instead of being the one who'd broken the darn thing. Frankly, I think their kindness has made him feel worse."

"I guess, in a weird way, it would probably be easier for the kids to deal with everyone being angry at them," Meg said thoughtfully. "They could shrug it off. They could whine about how they hadn't *meant* for anything to happen. You know"—in an exaggerated tone, she mimicked their indignant protests—"'It was an *accident*. I'm *sorry*, okay?'"

James smiled at her impression.

"But no one's even asking for an apology," she went on, "so their usual ways of dealing with being in trouble won't work."

"Fiendishly clever," James said with a laugh. "The worst punishment of all."

"But it's not like the Lutzes even want to punish them," Meg protested.

"Among their own people, it's a whole different thing. But for our kids, it's like they're being killed with kindness."

"Well," said Meg, crossing her arms, "we certainly let them get out of control. I feel pretty responsible."

"Hey, I agree they've been pretty bratty here. But it's not so shocking that they would act up, given what they're going through."

"Does that justify what they pulled yesterday?"

He shook his head. "No, not at all. But let's watch what happens now that they're dealing with some real consequences for their behavior."

They watched what happened almost in disbelief. For the rest of the day, Lizzie was either doing Amanda's regular chores or sitting beside the younger girl, talking to her, fetching whatever she needed. Will was also busy all day, attempting to help on the rig repairs, then assisting the men who had come to dismantle the extension to the barn. The materials were going straight to the home where the next wedding was to be held.

Meg suspected the children's goodwill might wear off by the next day, but on Thursday there was more of the same. Both children served, cleared, and cleaned up after breakfast without a word. Lizzie helped Amanda get to the table and waited on her, making conversation as if they were old friends. Will divided his attention equally among Eli, Aaron, and Sam, a shock in itself to his younger brother. Sam had heard the whole story, but he instinctively understood that it was not a subject he should bring up, much less tease his older siblings about. He acted as if it were nothing new for his brother and sister to be solicitous of him, an extremely wise move on his part, Meg thought.

Neither Lizzie nor Will showed the slightest sign that they were anything but sincere. Even better for them, no one in the Lutz households appeared to notice—or, in their usual kind way, chose not to notice—that anything was different. Meg and James were careful to follow their lead. They refrained from making any comment that might make Lizzie and Will retreat into a defensive posture.

To Meg, it was as if some invisible wall around her children had been knocked down, allowing them to drop their air of superiority and get on with the business of being themselves. Or rather, she corrected herself, their best selves. In fact, she realized, they weren't even arguing with each other anymore.

At one point, she passed the open door to Benjamin's bedroom and stopped to stare in amazement. Even though Benjamin was a little better than Will at cleaning up, there hadn't been much change in the condition of the room. Today Meg saw that, for the first time, Will had made his bed as if he were an army recruit, neat and tight. Everything on his side of the room had been put away, every surface was clean. When she went to look into Amanda's bedroom, she found more of the same, but the entire room had been gone over thoroughly. This could only have been done by Lizzie that morning, given Amanda's condition.

Every time Meg saw her daughter that day and the next, she was either working or attending to Amanda. At one point, Meg found the two girls relaxing on their beds, each with a book in her hand. She stuck her head in the room to ask if they wanted anything. Lizzie looked up over the top of her book to say thanks, they were fine. It was then that Meg saw that her daughter was three quarters of the way through *Tom Sawyer*. Meg had to turn away in a hurry so Lizzie wouldn't catch the smile on her face.

It was more of the same with Will: If he wasn't hard at work with his father or David, he was outside with Eli and his friends, walking through the snow-covered fields or running off to skate or play ice hockey.

Both her children initially steered clear of Jonathan, whose buggy they had wrecked, but quickly they saw that even he bore them no ill will.

When Meg decided it was time to take Nina up on her offer to buy some brownies, Lizzie was right there to help get them ready. Meg decided to bake a few different kinds of cookies along with the oatmeal-cranberry ones. She and Lizzie debated the merits of chocolate versus fruit fillings, and peanut butter flavoring versus coconut. Meg struggled to remember recipes she had made years and years before. They measured and mixed for hours, then watched over their creations, teasing each other about how often the other one wanted to open the oven doors to check. When the cookies came out golden brown, they celebrated with war whoops. As far as Meg was concerned, if that had been the end of the entire endeavor, it would have been well worth it just to have spent that afternoon laughing with her daughter again.

As it turned out, Nina picked up the food in person. She had wanted to stop by and see how Amanda's leg was faring. While she was there, she sampled one of everything and pronounced it all wonderful. Before she left, she requested a second, larger batch for the following week.

Catherine was delighted for Meg. "Now you will have your own business," she teased Meg as they cleared the table. "I will tell everyone that the master cookie baker got started here."

Meg laughed, but she was uncomfortable. Catherine had spoken the thought Meg herself had been too afraid even to voice. Day after day, watching these women turn out the endless pies, cakes, and breads, Meg saw that baking for a business was backbreaking work. Yet it could be done. The business required loving care and constant tending, but it was possible to maintain a small-scale operation. Somewhere in the back of her mind, it had occurred to her that perhaps she could do something like it on her own. But it was a thought she had refused to let herself develop.

Now, as Catherine voiced the idea, Meg's spirit lifted hearing her words. But almost as quickly she came up against the same obstacle that was in the way of everything else: She wouldn't be going back to her own home. She was going to be a guest in her parents' home, and they would never support such an endeavor.

Without support, both financial and personal, it would be unmanageable. Her parents didn't have the equipment, and they would never invest in any—that Meg knew without having to ask. What they *would* have was an endless list of reasons why the idea was doomed to fail. Now that she thought about it, she wondered what kind of customers she could come up with in a town like theirs, where specialized baked goods were not exactly in high demand.

No, she quickly realized, it was a pointless idea. She had no kitchen equipment, no money to pay for the initial supplies, no customers beyond Nina, and no prospects for any others.

She would have to figure out something else.

Chapter 15

✦

The buggy approached the house, David Lutz and James barely visible inside. It was late afternoon, and they were returning from a trip to buy some farming supplies. In addition, they had checked on the progress of the Hobarts' car. Meg and Catherine sat on rocking chairs on the front porch, bundled up against the cold, enjoying a few minutes of quiet conversation before heading inside to start preparing supper.

The horse came to a stop just outside the barn. The men jumped out on opposite sides of the rig and hurried over to the two women.

"Wait until you hear this," James said.

Meg and Catherine looked up at him expectantly.

"The car will be ready in the morning."

David nodded in agreement. "Ready for the road and like new, the man said. You can pick it up tomorrow."

Meg sat up straight. "No! Are you serious?" She was so startled by the news, she realized she had actually stopped thinking this day would ever really come. Feeling her stomach drop, she also realized that she had come to hope it never would. Which made no sense. *It's not as if we can stay with these people forever*, she reprimanded herself. *Sooner or later, we have to go back to reality—our reality, at least.*

"They did a fantastic job, I saw that much," James went on. "It really does look like new."

Meg could only nod. The thought of the five of them piling back into that car and heading for the highway made her want to shudder.

James was watching her obvious distress. "We should get to your parents' house before Christmas Eve," he said, his tone hopeful.

It was a weak attempt to sound encouraging. They both knew the truth. Spending Christmas there was not an inducement to get going but, rather, something they would both prefer to avoid.

Catherine listened as she rocked in her chair. Meg glanced up in time to see Catherine lock eyes with her husband as something unspoken passed between them. David nodded almost imperceptibly.

"It is a very busy time on the roads now, right before Christmas," Catherine said as if she were mulling over travel conditions. "That is not so good." She paused. "Would you maybe stay with us a little longer? Then the roads will be safer."

"Wow. That's a wonderful offer," said James. "But we can't put you out any more than we already have. The roads will be okay. Remember, we'll be in a car."

"We all know your car is not safe," David said. "It tried to kill me."

"And it would be nice for all the children to have Christmas Day together," Catherine went on, as if no one had spoken. "I believe they would enjoy that, yes?"

Meg knew she should protest, say they had already stayed too long as it was. Yet those were not the words that came out of her mouth. "The children would enjoy it, and we would enjoy it, too." She looked at James. "I would like to stay. Wouldn't you?"

James smiled. "Of course I would." He turned to David. "If you're sure about this . . ."

"Yes, we are sure," David replied.

Catherine stood. "That is settled. Come, Meg, we will get some peaches from the basement for supper, and some beets."

Meg got up. She loved Catherine and David even more for the way they had handled the invitation. They were far too thoughtful to come out and flatly offer to rescue the Hobart family from what promised to be a dreary holiday. And Meg was touched beyond words that they wanted her family to share this holiday with theirs.

"James, you and I have to go see the chickens," David said, turning toward the coop. "Aaron tells me we have some wire to fix."

A little later, when Sam asked Meg permission to go to the store with Old Samuel and Leah, she saw an opportunity. She handed Sam some money and gave him instructions, then swore him to secrecy. Proud of the trust she was putting in him, and a little anxious about the responsibility, he told her she could count on him and went off to carry out his assignment.

After supper that night, the house was buzzing with activity. Lamplight cast a glow throughout the main room. The littlest Lutz children from next door and friends of varying ages made ornaments, simple stars and words that celebrated the religious meaning of the holiday. These, along with some pieces of greenery and pinecones, were the only decorations to be hung up.

Leah and Catherine sat at the table putting the final touches on the quilt that would be a holiday gift for Sarah, the schoolteacher. In the kitchen, Lizzie and eight-year-old Rachel made chocolate-dipped pretzels under the direction of Amanda, who sat nearby with her leg propped up on a chair. The enticing smell of melted chocolate permeated the air. Will and Sam played Monopoly with Eli and Aaron. Sam held Rufus the entire time, scratching the contented dog behind the ears. Annie dropped by to pick up all the youngest children and was delayed when her presence drew David and Old Samuel into the main room. Somehow, the greetings of the adults evolved into a session of storytelling for the children.

Meg and James found themselves at loose ends. Everyone around them was occupied. "Want to go get some air?" he asked her.

She nodded. Grabbing jackets, they headed out. It was bitingly cold.

"Freezing," James remarked. "Feels like it'll snow tonight."

Meg laughed. "You're beginning to sound like a farmer, speculating about the weather. Boy, that was something I don't think I ever heard you do in Charlotte."

At the mention of the city, they both fell silent. They stood on the porch, surveying the stars in the night sky.

"Charlotte feels very far away," James finally said. "Everything feels very far away." He moved off the porch, then turned to her. "The moon is pretty bright. Want to walk a bit?"

"Okay."

They set off toward the road.

When James spoke again, it was so hushed, Meg wasn't sure she heard him correctly. "I've never really apologized for what I did. I know that."

She didn't say anything, just kept walking, her eyes on the ground ahead of her.

"I guess," he went on, "I didn't know how to. But that's not an excuse."

"No, it isn't."

"I was so angry at myself. There was just no way a guy as smart as I am could be as stupid as that. I couldn't handle it."

There was another silence before James spoke again.

"The first problem was getting fired. It isn't the end of the world, I know that, but it was for me. In a million years—I was just *not* a guy who got fired. Impossible. Yeah, there were financial problems at the firm, things that had nothing to do with me, but we were in a bad position. Still, the ones who were getting laid off weren't gonna be me."

He didn't say anything for another few minutes. They walked along, ice and snow crunching beneath their boots.

He sighed. "It's hard to be the kind of jerk who can't handle life when he isn't the alpha dog anymore. That's what led to the next step and the next, until the whole thing exploded in my face."

"Not just in *your* face," Meg pointed out. "All of our faces."

"Yeah, that's the part I didn't get until it was too late." He shook his head. "But by then I couldn't admit what I'd done. Not even to myself."

"And now?"

"If we had gone straight to your parents' house, I really have to wonder if you and I would have made it. The tension between us was too much. I don't think we could have survived. But here, we've been removed from everything that defined us, good *and* bad. To tell you the truth, this feels like the first time I've been able to breathe in months—hell, in years."

Able to breathe, Meg thought. Exactly. Here, she was able to breathe again.

He stopped and turned to her. "I don't know if you'll forgive me or not. But I am sorry from the bottom of my heart. You have every right to leave me and every right to hate my guts. I understand that you don't trust me anymore. I wouldn't trust me, either. Frankly, I have no idea what it would take for me to win your trust back." He took a deep breath. "But I do want to win it back. I want us to go on together."

"I'm not sure I know what to say. I can't tell you, 'Okay, thanks for saying sorry, everything's fine again.'"

"I know."

"I'm not sure I *can* ever trust you again, or how you could make that happen. Right now I'm more worried about how we're going to survive, *literally* survive, once we leave here.

And going to live with my parents is a sorry answer to our problems. It's not an answer at all. The more I think about it, the worse I know it's going to be. It's not like we're nineteen and have to put up with staying in the basement for a few months. This is going to be a nightmare for all of us."

There was no need for him to comment. She knew he agreed with her.

"We'll be at each other's throats again in no time," she added.

"I wish I could come up with another solution." He kicked at a small rock in the road.

"For a minute there, I thought I had one," she said. "Remember the woman who drove us to the hospital when Amanda hurt her leg? She runs an inn, and she bought some of my brownies and cookies to serve to her customers. She really liked them."

James looked at her in surprise. "You're kidding! That's great. You didn't tell me that."

Her tone was wry. "Well, it's not like we're sharing a whole lot lately, is it? Anyway, Catherine got me thinking about starting my own little business. You know, like they sell their homemade pies and breads to stores and restaurants here? I could sell the things I do best—the sweets."

"Really? I wouldn't have guessed you'd have an interest in something like that."

"I didn't," Meg admitted, "until I started baking here every day. I used to do it a lot more when the kids were little, remember? I forgot how much I liked it."

"Wow. I have to admit, this is all news to me. But I guess it makes sense."

She shrugged. "It doesn't matter. It's a ridiculous idea. You need a kitchen with decent equipment, more than one oven. You need money to invest. Most important, you need customers. I'm not going to find any of those things in Homer."

"Hmm. Unfortunately, I see what you mean," he said.

"Worse, what I *am* going to find there are Harlan and Frances. Killers of dreams. Destroyers of spirits."

He picked up the theme. "Experts at extinguishing the fires of hope. Stompers-on of hearts."

They looked at each other and burst out laughing.

When they had quieted down, he looked at her seriously. "Meg, I promise we'll come up with something. I don't know what it'll be, but something."

"There's a promise to hang my hat on," she said.

He smiled. "You mean your bonnet?"

"My bonnet, yeah." Her tone turned wistful. "If only we could just stay here. You think we'd make good Amish farmers?"

He sighed briefly. "No, we wouldn't. We'd make terrible Amish farmers. And we can't stay here."

"I know." She straightened up. "We'd better be getting back."

As she started walking toward the house, she heard his voice behind her.

"I love you, Meg."

She stopped, not turning around. She wasn't sure what to say. In the end, she said nothing but just kept going.

Chapter 16

James's prediction turned out to be correct, and several inches of fresh snow covered the ground by the next day. Everyone gathered around the breakfast table to eat before setting out together for the school's annual Christmas pageant. Meg knew that Rachel and Aaron had been working hard on learning their parts. They were practically bursting with excitement and anticipation, especially since they were rarely allowed to perform in front of people this way.

They all piled into buggies and set out for the small schoolhouse. Leaving their outerwear on the porch, parents filed into the classroom to sit on desks and benches around the room. The Hobarts split up, and Meg and Sam found a spot for themselves in a corner. She was charmed by the children's colorful drawings of farm and winter scenes she saw hung up around the room. She studied the handwritten program, enjoying the whispers and rustling of the children preparing to start.

Meg sat entranced throughout the pageant. The children studied English in school and spoke mostly in English during the program, welcoming their guests, performing religious poems, skits, and songs, all from memory. Their parents smiled and laughed where appropriate, but Meg noticed they did not applaud. Sam had helped Aaron practice his poem and was so thrilled to see his friend get through it flawlessly, he started to clap at the end. When he realized he was the only one doing so, his face turned beet red. Meg put an arm around him. "No big deal," she whispered in his ear. "I'm sure Aaron appreciated that you were glad for him."

Afterward the parents presented the finished quilt to Sarah, the teacher, who accepted it with warm thanks. She, in turn, handed out gifts of a pencil and small notepad to each student.

Back at the house the children were in high spirits. They had lunch, and most of the household took advantage of the snow to go back outside for hours of play. Catherine and David even joined Meg and James for some snowball tossing.

Later, when Jonathan brought a sleigh around front, James, Meg, and Sam hopped in with Aaron and Rachel. As she settled in, Meg spotted a car pull up and park some thirty feet away. Two heavyset strangers, a man and a woman, got out and stood there, staring at the Lutz family. The man began taking pictures of them. Meg watched in annoyance. She believed most tourists were aware that photography was not welcomed by the Amish, although they may not have known the reason was that pictures represented a forbidden graven image. Even if they didn't know, she thought, frowning, what kind of people felt it was all right to park in a family's front yard—*any* family's front yard—and shoot pictures of them?

She wondered how the Amish could bear being gawked at this way. With a guilty start, she recalled that she and her family had originally come here to learn something about these supposedly quaint people.

We were only going to see a film about them, she halfheartedly reassured herself, not park outside their houses as if they were animals in a zoo. Still, she could envision her own family on the road, driving by Catherine and David in their buggy as she or James pointed out to the children the novelty of the clothing and transportation. She was embarrassed by the memory of her own ignorance.

Meg saw the woman tilt her head as if puzzled, then lean toward the man and say something as she pointed in Meg's direction. Meg tapped James, who sat beside her, on the shoulder.

"Look," she said. "Those tourists over there. They're watching the show, the Amish-at-Play. But now they see these crazy English people in the middle of all of them. They're wondering what the heck we're doing here."

James looked over to see. He grinned and gave the people a huge wave. "We're the real Amish," he shouted to them. "The rest of these people are just phonies in costumes. They've kidnapped us. Please help!"

"James!" Meg's reprimand dissolved into laughter.

Her husband laughed, too. They could hear David chuckling up front. The onlookers appeared disgusted before they got in their car and drove away.

Meg and James continued to laugh a few seconds past the

point when their amusement wore off—only because they were both enjoying the now-rare sound of their laughter together.

After everyone had come back in for hot chocolate and cookies, Meg and Lizzie found themselves cleaning up alone in the kitchen. Meg washed the dishes while Lizzie filled a small bucket with water and fetched a mop for the floor.

"Why is it," Lizzie asked her mother, wringing out the mop, "that the men and women here have such incredibly stereotypical roles? I mean, talk about so-called women's work and men's work—they've got it covered."

Meg didn't answer immediately. "That's a tough one," she said finally, "because you and I are looking at it from our perspective. We can't really understand their perspective."

"What difference does that make?" Lizzie said, pulling chairs away from the table so she could clean underneath it. "Don't the women ever want to do anything else?"

"Well, wait. Some of them run businesses, right? Like restaurants and stores. The women in this house have a business with the food they sell. You're just looking at the housework part."

"Okay, I'll give you that."

"When you think about it, didn't we have a traditional arrangement in our house? Dad went to the office and I ran the house."

"Yeah, but this seems way more intense."

"I think it's more complicated than that. But I guess I prefer to admire how many skills the women have. Also, they have this calm approach to whatever they do, you know, this steadiness about things. It's as if they have this special strength in their body and their spirit."

Lizzie mulled this over. "That's a good way to put it." She stood up and stretched out her back. "And they do know how to do a ton of things."

They worked in silence for a few minutes more.

"You know," Lizzie said, "what's cool is that they can make things they need. They know how to work stuff. It's like they do *real* things. I hope when I'm older, I'll be good at doing real things."

Amazed by these words, Meg stared at her daughter, but Lizzie was too engrossed in pushing the mop back and forth across the floor to notice.

Meg hadn't wanted the day to end, knowing that the next day was Christmas—the day they would be leaving for good. Later that night, after taking a shower, she put on a robe and sat on the side of the bed, rubbing her wet hair with a towel. Idly, she wondered if she would bother going back to using a hair dryer when they left.

James entered the room. "Ah, you're here."

"Hi. What've you been up to? Did you say good night to the kids?"

"Yes, I just stopped by their rooms. I was downstairs talking to Catherine."

Feeling the chill of the night air in the room, Meg rubbed her hair more briskly. "Oh?"

"We were on the phone outside with Nina."

Meg stopped what she was doing. "Nina? My Nina, with the inn?"

"The very one."

"Whatever for?"

He sat down next to her and removed the towel from her hands. Then he placed one of her hands in his. "Last night, after you and I talked, I discussed some things with Catherine. She talked to Nina, and we figured it out."

"Figured out what?" Meg was hard-pressed to imagine James and the two women conferring.

"First of all, Nina left this morning for Philadelphia to spend Christmas with some relatives. That's where she's from originally. Anyway, she has an old friend there, this really successful guy who owns six or seven restaurants and a few specialty food stores. She took along some of the stuff you'd given her and drove it right to his house for him to taste. The guy really liked it. He wants to place an order for the restaurants, plus some to sell at the food stores. A huge order, Meg. Really huge. "

Meg stared at him in disbelief. "Are you joking?"

He held up one hand as if taking an oath. "I swear I am not joking."

"That's incredible. That can happen just like that?"

He shrugged. "I guess so. Nina knows the guy, he liked what he tried, he ordered a bunch."

"But wait." Meg seemed to deflate. "I can't deliver that order. I have no place to bake or anything else."

"Now comes the best part," James said, smiling. "Catherine and Nina have lived here an awfully long time, and they know everything and everyone. It didn't take them long to come up with an answer to that. Seems there's a little restaurant about twenty miles from here that's only open for breakfast and lunch. It caters to the businesses in the area, but there's no night life there. The man who owns it is willing to rent you the kitchen from five P.M. to three in the morning. You'd get in there at night, do your baking, and be out before they open. It's pretty cheap, because it's found money for him—obviously the kitchen isn't generating any income in the middle of the night. So everybody's happy."

"But James," she protested, "where are we living? How is this possibly going to work?"

He stood up and started pacing. "Look, Meg, we both know going to your parents' house is a move of total desperation. We can't go there. We shouldn't. And now we don't have to." He stopped in front of her. "If we have income from this Philadelphia thing and Nina's orders, and we use whatever we have left in the bank, we can stay in this area. There are some efficiency apartments that we can rent by the month. We'll work like dogs to see if we can build something. By the spring we'll know one way or the other. If we fail, we're no worse off than we are now, right?"

Meg stared at him. "You've really thought this through, haven't you? I can't believe it."

He sat back down beside her. "This is truly the least I could do—to try and help you achieve something that you want."

"But what about the kids?"

"The kids'll be fine. They'll start at a local school after New Year's, so their days are already set. With your night hours and whatever else—they'll just put up with what they have to put up with." He smiled. "I think they probably would have flipped out if this had come about a few months ago. But they can do it now."

"You feel certain?"

He nodded. "More than that. I talked to them about it just before supper. They're game."

"You're joking! And nobody said anything to me?"

"I asked them not to. I wanted to hear what happened with the Philadelphia guy first."

Meg ran a hand through her damp hair. "I am— I'm dumbstruck." She paused. "What are *you* going to do? This can't work if you have nothing to do."

"Where'd you get the idea that I'd have nothing to do? To begin with, I'll be your business manager. Your job is to bake. I need to do the paperwork, order your supplies, do shipping, handle everything other than making the food. The biggest thing I need to do is get you new clients. Somebody's got to be selling."

"I guess that makes sense . . ." she said slowly.

"And I've come up with a second job to do at the same time."

"Really?"

"You've seen the furniture they make here? One day I was helping Joseph Lutz move some things out of his basement, and I saw he had about half a dozen bureaus down there, these incredible handmade chests of drawers. We got to talking about all the carpentry work the Amish men do to supplement their incomes. Some of them do it at home, and sometimes they work directly for factories."

"You're going to become a carpenter?" Meg sounded exactly as skeptical as she felt.

He laughed. "No, I'm not good enough for that. But hey, we come from North Carolina, the furniture capital of the country, and I know people who can connect me to the right places.

"I want to help with this stuff, to sell it to people who are dying for it even if they don't know it right now. I know the carpenters we've met have some distribution already, but I'm hoping I can expand that." He paused. "I want all of us to maintain our connection to these people. And in a small way it could encourage their financial independence. It could make money for us and for them."

"Wow," Meg breathed. "This is a lot to take in."

"From talking to Joseph and David, I understand now how much work goes into the furniture. It's rare to get something of this quality at such decent prices." James laughed again. "I should know, considering all the overpriced junk I insisted we buy for our house. But I also like the idea of supporting their work. It's kind of the least I can do for the community. They saved us—in more ways than one."

"So I guess you'll have plenty to keep you busy."

"Yes. Although the focus has to be on your new business." James looked her directly in the eyes. "Please let me help make this happen for you. You deserve it. And I owe it to you. We both know that. Please, Meg, give it a chance."

Meg sat in silence. He had covered every angle and every possible objection. He truly wanted her to allow him to do this for her. When he asked her to give it a chance, he wasn't just talking about the business. For the first time since Thanksgiving she saw genuine remorse in his eyes. She also saw fear that she would say no.

She considered the extraordinary generosity behind the offer. Here was a guy who, until a few months ago, was a powerful executive. Now he was encouraging her to follow her own small dream. And he was willing to give it everything he had to make it work for her. It reminded her of why she had fallen in love with him in the first place.

She looked at him and nodded. Relief flooded his face. He put his arms around her and brought her close. She rested her head against his shoulder, inhaling his familiar smell, feeling his hand stroking her hair. It had been a very long time since they had sat like this.

She couldn't say she was going to forgive and forget all he had done, all he had put them through, but she was willing to try. And up until now that had been something she hadn't even dared to hope she would ever feel again.

Chapter 17

✦

Christmas Day was overcast, the air outside frigid. Gusting wind created swirls of powdered snow lifted from the ground. Inside the house the Lutz and Hobart children were sitting near the fire, listening to Old Samuel reading from the Bible. Lizzie occasionally wandered over to stir the contents of the large pot on the stove, a thick pea soup. Despite their having recently consumed lunch, the soup would remain there, warming all day, for anyone who cared to take a bowl. Lunch had been even more crowded than usual, with nearly thirty adults and children feasting on turkey and ham, German potato salad, carrot-and-raisin salad, green beans, noodles, potatoes, cheese, bread, chocolate cake, and carrot cake.

The sky grew dark enough for Catherine and Meg to set out candles to add to the light of the kerosene lamps. As she moved about the house, Meg kept glancing out the window at the Mustang parked at the far end of the dirt drive. James had driven it back to the farm yesterday. He had told her the repair shop had done an excellent job. It did indeed look like a new car, every surface polished and gleaming—almost like a crouching animal, she thought, lying in wait.

David explained to Meg and James that the family celebrated Christmas for two days and normally would exchange gifts on the second day. However, since the Hobarts were leaving the following morning, they would share gifts today. When Old Samuel finished his reading, adults and children alike sang a hymn. Then everyone scurried to retrieve the presents they planned to give and reassembled several minutes later, the children bright-eyed with anticipation.

The gifts for the Lutz children were in bags or plain paper wrapping. Rachel received a book and a new dress made by her mother. All the boys got socks. For Amanda, there was a quilt made by Catherine and several china plates to add to her collection for when she got married. Aaron was thrilled to receive a much-begged-for skateboard of his own, and Jonathan got a pair of binoculars for his new hobby of bird-watching. Eli and Benjamin got shovels and trowels. The children had made special cards and ornaments for one another. Meg and James were touched to see they had included Lizzie, Will, and Sam, providing each of them with angels and stars.

Watching Aaron examine his new socks, Meg remembered the years her parents had given her socks or something equally practical for Christmas. Why had that felt so empty and disappointing when this felt so loving?

"For you," Catherine said, handing a large, flat package to Meg. "From all of us."

Meg pulled away the brown paper to reveal four large cookie sheets.

"To get started," David said. "Proper tools are important."

Meg fought the tears that threatened to fill her eyes. She hugged the pans to her. "I'll think of you with everything I bake. Which I would have done anyway." She smiled. "This is the most wonderful present. I'll treasure them. Thank you."

"And for James," David said, handing him a bag.

James reached in to pull out a can of WD-40, pliers, and a screwdriver.

"You need to keep things running smoothly," David said with a smile. "This will help."

James laughed. "You're right, as usual. Thank you."

Meg had knitted mufflers for David, Catherine, and all their children. Knowing they would not wish to draw undue attention to themselves, Meg had chosen black wool for the adults and dark gray for the rest. Sam had done an excellent job in buying the wool, the assignment she had given him when he made the trip to the store with Leah and Old Samuel. The yarn was so perfect, so sturdy yet soft, that Meg was certain Leah had been the one to make the selection. Meg had made the scarves in her room to keep the gifts secret. All of the recipients seemed genuinely pleased.

She and her family had agreed that they wouldn't exchange gifts among themselves. The children had accepted the news without a word of complaint.

Which was why Meg was so surprised when James handed her a small brown cardboard box tied with a red ribbon. "I know we said we wouldn't," he told her, "but this is different."

Puzzled, Meg untied the ribbon and opened the box. She reached inside to lift out the object within. Her eyes widened as she realized what it was. "Oh my . . ." she breathed. "Did you make this?"

"Joseph helped me," James said. "Okay, he helped me a *lot*."

Meg turned it around in her hands to look at it from all angles. It was an almost perfect replica of a telephone table, an old-fashioned combination of a wooden chair attached to a table designed to hold a phone, and beneath it, a space for a phone book to rest. Back when Meg and James were still college students, before they started dating, Meg had come upon the full-size version of this telephone table in the street, abandoned by a curb. It wasn't particularly well made or of good wood, but Meg was intrigued by its art deco design and the fact that the need for such an item had long ago passed into oblivion. She dragged it back to her college dorm to keep. Although the bulky piece served little purpose, mostly taking up precious space in her small room, she loved it for its charm and impracticality. The idea of sitting in one spot for no other purpose than talking on the phone, and the idea that telephoning had once been a major activity requiring your full attention—she was taken by the romance of the entire notion.

When she and James married, the telephone table came to their apartment. James thought it was ugly and useless. From the day they moved in, he had asked Meg to get rid of it. She adamantly refused. It was both a reminder of her life as a student and a beloved orphan she had saved from destruction. But eventually, she'd allowed James to shove it into an out-of-the-way spot. When they moved to their first house, he protested that it was an eyesore, and it was relegated to the basement. By the next move, Meg realized the table would never see the light of day again. When James asked if she would please donate it to Goodwill, she gave in, hoping someone else would love it as she had.

Here it was now, a five-inch replica, every detail exact. James had carved it out of plywood, then sanded and shellacked it until it shone.

"You loved that table. It meant something to you," he said. "I had no right to ask you to get rid of it. Heck, you should have put it dead center in the house if you wanted to. I'm really sorry about that." He smiled. "Along with a lot of other things."

Meg looked at him. "Thank you, James," she said.

The rest of the day passed quickly, with Christmas storytelling and more singing of hymns. Supper was only somewhat lighter than lunch. Meg and James joked about how lucky they were to be getting away from all this fattening food, while the Lutzes teased that the two of them would be too weak to work hard enough to be of any use.

After supper, the older boys went to visit some friends, and the rest of the children spent one last night playing games together. They went to bed earlier than usual, because the Lutz family was leaving at six A.M. to spend the day with relatives who lived a three-hour ride away. When it came time to say good night, the children all exchanged hugs. The Lutz children, Meg noticed, were affectionate and composed. It was clear that they were sorry to see their new friends go, but they remained cheerful. Will, Lizzie, and Sam were more visibly upset, Lizzie and Sam in particular getting teary-eyed over their farewells. James reminded them that they would be living under fifty miles away. The Hobarts would be driving back often to visit.

When the children were settled in for the night, Catherine and Meg sat at the kitchen table to share a final cup of tea. As soon as Meg started to look for the words to express her appreciation, Catherine cut her off. "Please do not say these things." Despite the firmness in her tone, she looked pleased. "Instead, I will tell you something. Benjamin is coming home for good. He told us today."

"Oh, that's wonderful," said Meg, thrilled that it had been brought out in the open in time for her to share the good news with Catherine. "It's beyond wonderful." Meg reached across the table to take the other woman's hand. "I can only guess at what you've been going through. I'm so happy for you."

Catherine smiled at her. "Thank you, my friend."

They drank their tea in an easy silence. When they had finished, Catherine took their cups and washed them out, standing them upside down in the dish drain. She turned to face Meg. "So you are leaving, but we will see you again, yes?"

"Yes."

"You won't forget us?"

Meg smiled. "Not likely."

Catherine nodded. "When you come to visit, you will bring us some brownies. One thing less for me to bake."

"It's a deal."

"And when summer comes, I will show you how we make

the jams and preserves like you see downstairs." Catherine grinned. "I think you will find time for it."

Meg laughed, astonished that Catherine remembered her earlier comment about always being too busy to learn. She came around to Meg and gave her a hug. "I believe you will all be fine. This will be a good thing for you."

Meg was startled. It was the first personal comment Catherine had made about the Hobarts' situation.

Catherine looked at Meg with her customary directness. "You will be all right. And you come see us soon." With a nod, she turned and left the room.

In the morning the Hobarts were subdued as they made their final preparations to go. Quietly, they gathered whatever last belongings had migrated around the house and finished packing their small bags.

Meg shivered in the cold morning air as she dressed. Tucking in her shirt, she felt something in one of her pants pockets. She reached in to discover the refrigerator magnet she had taken from the house as she walked out the door in Charlotte.

Esse quam videri. To be, rather than to seem.

She stared at it. The motto had been her inspiration for so long, as she tried to *feel* the way she thought she should be, rather than just to *seem* to feel it. Now she saw it in a completely different way. These people, Catherine and David and even their young children, had shown her what it meant to *be* rather than to *seem*. They didn't talk about what they did, how they felt about it, or what it meant. They knew how to just *be*.

They knew what they valued: religion, community, work. They followed those values, and as a result they were completely genuine in everything they did. To be, rather than to seem. A far, far harder ideal than Meg had ever imagined.

When James and Meg went downstairs with their bags for the last time, they found Sam with Old Samuel. Sam was clutching Rufus, tearfully burying his face in the puppy's neck.

"I go to get my wife, and we will leave now, Young Samuel. So we must say good-bye," Old Samuel said.

Tears wetting his face, Sam rushed into the older man's arms. "Good-bye, Old Samuel," he managed to get out.

Samuel patted him on the head and stepped back. Sorrowfully Sam extended Rufus to him. "What is this?" Old Samuel asked.

"We're leaving, too, so could you take him now?"

Samuel shook his head. "Everyone knows this dog belongs to you. He must go with you, wherever you go."

Sam looked stunned. "You want me to take him?"

"The two of you are always together. He is your dog."

"I can't just take him."

"Why not? We have many dogs here. We will have more dogs again. I know you will take good care of Rufus."

Sam looked at his parents.

Meg turned to James. "Will they let us have a dog at this place?"

"I'm not sure." He thought for a moment. "Wait, I think I saw a dog near the front door there. Somebody has one, even if it's just the owner."

"Then it's fine with me," Meg said. "What do you say?"

James looked at Sam. "Congratulations, sport. You are now a dog owner."

Shock and joy lit up Sam's face as he turned back to Old Samuel. "This is the best thing that's ever happened to me. Thank you."

Old Samuel rested his hand on Sam's head once more. "Many more best things will happen to you, Young Samuel." The old man turned to go but paused. He addressed himself to Meg and James. "Take good care of my young friend."

Then the three of them were alone.

"Wait until I tell Lizzie and Will," Sam burst out, rushing toward the stairs.

James brought the Mustang up the roadway, close to the front of the house. This time the children helped pass bags to their parents as they packed the trunk, and all five of the Hobarts walked around the house one last time to make sure nothing was left behind.

No one had to give voice to what they were all thinking: how strange it felt to be getting into a car instead of a horse-drawn buggy. When James slammed the trunk shut, the children took their pillows and blankets into the car and shoved their small extra bags beneath their feet. Sam was still relegated to the least comfortable spot, the middle of the backseat, but now he had Rufus on his lap.

The sun had risen to shine brightly in a crisp blue sky. When they were all settled into the car, James turned the ignition key, and they heard the familiar sound of the engine coming to life. Slowly, they drove the length of the roadway. Every one of them turned for a last look at the big white house, at the barn, at the attachment where Old Samuel and Leah lived, at the houses next door and across the road.

James braked at the end of the dirt road, then made a right turn and picked up speed on the main road. Through the swells and dips of the hills they saw the farms and homes extending in all directions. Here and there they observed gray buggies, singly or in pairs, moving along the snowy roads.

From the backseat, Will's voice was jarring. "Can you believe this place?"

Meg and James turned to look at him, aghast at the all-too-familiar snide tone.

"Kill me now," Lizzie answered.

It took but a moment for everyone to recognize the words. They were what the two had said when they first set eyes on the Lutz farm.

The family's laughter echoed as the car turned onto the highway.

A Plain & Fancy
Christmas

To Kristin and Meghan Fox
With love and appreciation

and

To Jean Buchalter
Music, light, and love personified

Acknowledgments

�֎

I am very grateful to the people of Lancaster County who were so helpful to me in the course of researching this book. Their willingness to answer my endless questions and their generosity of spirit made this a wonderful writing experience.

Thank you as well to my editor, Linda Marrow, and my agent, Victoria Skurnick, for—once again—their professional expertise and wisdom. It is a supreme pleasure to work with them both. I am also most appreciative of Junessa Viloria, who does an amazing job and is always ready with a helping hand or the answer.

A big hug to Monica Chusid, who went above and beyond. As always, the busiest person I know has all the time in the world when I need her for any reason, big or small. Thank you to the greatest friend anyone could wish to have.

For their help and support during the writing of this book, I am also supremely grateful to Sheryl Suib Cohen, Jennifer Crowne, Stacy Higgins, Jurijs Petunovs, and Linda Meyer Russ.

Lastly, to my husband, Mark, and my children, Jenna and Carly—I love you. It's funny that I, who never stops talking, can't begin to express all the joy you've brought to my life.

Chapter 1

�֎

"You forgot the raisins, didn't you?"

Rachel Yoder made a pained face. "I did, and I'm so sorry."

Annie King allowed herself the smallest of sighs as she considered the shredded carrots and mayonnaise in the wooden bowl before her. She glanced over at her sister-in-law, and made sure to keep her tone even. "Well, we have a lot more supper to cook, so let's not waste time. Maybe we can use the carrots some other way."

"No, no, I'll go home and get them." Rachel turned away from the kitchen counter where the two women had been working. "It will only take a minute."

She was out the door before Annie could protest. Supper that night was to be at her brother's and Annie's house, and the two women needed to work efficiently to have food for twenty-four people ready in time. Rachel started down the long path from the front door toward her house across the street, appreciating the unusually warm April afternoon. She saw a neighbor's horse and buggy approaching, and she reached the road just in time to wave and call out hello. Once across the street, she headed toward the kitchen door, but looked over at the sound of her name being shouted from the barn. Her father stood in the wide doorway, a cloth in one hand as he polished some shining object.

·"I need more rags here," he called out. "Can you bring some?"

She nodded, picking up her pace. "I'll be right back."

Perspiring by this point under her long, dark blue dress beneath a black apron, she went inside the house, grateful for the relative cool in the dim kitchen. Her mother stood near the sink with Rachel's daughter, eleven-year-old Katie. Rachel's mother was grating and bottling horseradish with Katie. The women in the family preserved large quantities of fruits and vegetables, much of which they sold, and Katie shared the responsibility for this job with them. For now, she was still learning, but she would be expert at it by the time her grandmother could no longer do it herself. That day was still a long way off, however; Rachel's mother was of less-than-average height but strong and sturdily built, and behind her silver wire-rimmed glasses, her light blue eyes seemed to take in everything. She and her granddaughter spent many hours together, especially in the summer, making all different types of preserves, jellies, and pickled vegetables.

Katie turned at the sound of the door opening.

"Hi, Mama."

Rachel couldn't resist going over and putting an arm around

her daughter's slender shoulders, leaning down to give her a quick kiss on the cheek. "You smell like peaches. And sunshine," she said to her. "No, wait—like summer, if summer were a little girl."

Katie laughed and hugged her back. "Silly."

Leah King watched, frowning. "Something wrong? Aren't you making supper at Annie's?"

"I came back for raisins. And Papa needs some rags."

"Take the rags in the hall closet, bottom shelf," Leah said. "Katie, mind that you don't hit anything with those tongs."

"Sorry, Grandma." The eleven-year-old snapped back to attention, anxious to avoid her grandmother's disapproval, which was quick to appear and slow to fade.

Rachel opened a cabinet and took down a large glass jar of raisins, measuring out the three cups she needed into a clean bowl. Leaving the bowl on the counter, she went to a closet full of cleaning supplies and took four rags from a neatly folded stack, remnants from old sheets that could no longer be used or salvaged.

She paused on her way out, thinking she might persuade her father to take a break if she brought him a glass of water; it would be good for him on a hot day.

Stopping at the sink just long enough to fill a glass, Rachel grabbed the rags and stepped out onto the side porch. She was unable to resist pausing to kneel down and scratch Buster behind the ears, the old dog snoozing in the bit of shade behind a rocking chair. Humming, she made her way to the stables, where she found her father forking hay. When he saw her, he stopped, lifting his straw hat and wiping his arm across his forehead. He wore a dark blue shirt, black suspenders, and black pants. His beard was full, but, as was traditional for married Amish men, he had no mustache and his brown hair was long around the sides, with bangs across his forehead.

"Are these enough?" She held up the fabric squares.

"Just right." He took the water with a nod of thanks and drank the contents in one long gulp.

The barn housed four horses, two of which were used only to drive the buggies, the other to work in the fields. Rachel walked over to the stall where Driver, her favorite horse, stood swatting flies with his tail, regarding her with soft brown eyes. She stroked the narrow patch of white between his eyes. "How are you, my friend?" she asked him in a soothing voice.

"He's fine," her father answered, "but I would be a lot better if he could use a pitchfork."

"You wouldn't like that. You'd have to sit around doing nothing."

Rachel grinned. Her father would sit down at worship or for meals, or to talk with visitors or his many grandchildren, but doing nothing—that was inconceivable. The farm was a round-the-clock job for him, his wife, and everyone else in the family.

He laughed. "I imagine I could find something to occupy myself, don't you worry."

He came over to stand next to his daughter, and ran his hand along the horse's neck. "Katie inside with your mother?"

She nodded.

"She's okay? Seems to me she looks a little sad lately."

Rachel didn't answer right away, reviewing her daughter's

recent actions. Despite how busy he was, she knew her father stayed attuned to her and Katie's moods, somehow always aware if they were having a hard time or a particularly bad day. It had been that way ever since her husband, Jacob Yoder, died three years ago. Actually, Rachel knew her father had always been unusually aware of her moods, even when she was a child. She had been closer to him than she had ever been to her mother, closer than she'd been to any of her four siblings. They just seemed to have a special connection, for which she would always be grateful. When Jacob died, she knew her father felt the weight of her pain in a way no one else did.

As much as her husband's death had devastated Rachel, it was equally terrible for Katie. His humor and spirit, the boundless energy for life that had made Rachel love him so, also made him a wonderful father. It had been only six months from the diagnosis of cancer until his death, and there was no time to prepare physically or emotionally for what was to come as Jacob quickly wasted and weakened. She and Katie spent the first months after he died in a dreamlike state of shock, going through the motions, while their relatives and the community sustained them with food and support. When Rachel was finally able to look around and take stock of where she was, she recognized what everyone already knew, that she couldn't manage the farm alone. One of Jacob's older brothers took it over, and she brought her child back to live with her parents, in the house where she had grown up. At least here she could contribute, helping with the chores and earning money from the quilts she was so good at making. They brought in an income that had been a useful supplement during her marriage, but was not enough to support her and a child now that she was on her own.

Rachel was grateful that she had the blessing of a family to take her back in. It was only at night when she lay alone in her narrow, childhood bed that she permitted herself a few moments of wishing she could have found another option. She had lived away from her parents for the nine years of her marriage, ten years counting the year when she actually lived outside the community in an apartment she rented with another Amish teenager.

Her time away occurred during her *rumspringa*, which for Rachel, had lasted nearly two years. At sixteen, Amish girls and boys had the chance to go out and experience the world beyond their communities, to be sure they wished to be baptized into the Amish faith. Few went as far as Rachel had in moving off the farm completely, but it wasn't that much of a shock to the family when she'd left. She had always been the one who had trouble staying on the straight and narrow, the one with the most questions about the way they lived, their faith, their place in the world. Rachel knew she was the child who caused her mother to frown the most often. It was to Rachel that her mother directed most of her lectures and warnings. Rachel's sisters and brothers all seemed perfectly suited to Amish life on a farm; three of them had experienced their own *rumspringa* adventures, but no one had any serious doubts about whether they would be baptized into the faith. The youngest sibling, her nineteen-year-old brother, Daniel, was still in the process of deciding his future, but they all believed that he, too, would come around.

Rachel knew she had caused her parents genuine pain, as they worried that she might be lost to them forever. When she actually moved out during the second year, their worrying increased exponentially. In the end, however, she returned. She never told them about all she had done during her time away, and they never asked. Nor had she told them that the reason she came back was not so much that she had made a clear-cut choice, but that she simply couldn't imagine a life without Jacob, who had, in fact, decided to be baptized. Whatever her hesitations about the demands of Amish life, nothing could override her need to be with him. She loved him to distraction, maybe, she had sometimes worried, too much. Besides, she had come to see that her entire support system was here, and nothing in the outside world could ever come close to the peace and security of being part of her Amish community. When she returned, she and Jacob had married as soon as possible after their baptisms.

She never told anyone, not even Jacob, how unworthy she continued to feel, harboring so many doubts about her ability to live up to the ideal of a good Amish woman. She tried, always, doing her best to keep her home clean, to keep her appearance tidy and modest. Every day, she resolved to exemplify the virtue of humility. Somehow, she always fell short. She carried her shame in secret, knowing that secrecy added yet another layer of failure in her efforts to be the woman she wished she could be.

The years of her marriage had been far and away her happiest. The two of them moved onto the farm, which they rented from Jacob's parents. Rachel worked harder than she had ever worked before, but with the joy of knowing they were building their own family together. Was it allowed for a woman to love a man as much she loved Jacob? Were married couples supposed to laugh as much as they did? She did not know and did not care.

With Katie's birth, Rachel felt her heart overflow with gratitude for everything she had been given. That they had never been able to have another child was their only sorrow. Rachel had suffered two miscarriages, both of them when she was nearly halfway through the pregnancy. And then, nothing. She had always assumed they would have a large family, and they had looked forward to creating their own loving brood. Nonetheless, they knew that whatever happened was the way things were meant to be.

Rachel had sincerely believed that, until Jacob's death. After, she wondered how it was meant to be that she should lose, first, their two babies, and then, her great love. She understood life was hard, and people suffered in many different ways. But why give her that kind of love and passion, only to snatch it away? On top of her anger and doubts, she felt guilt about having such emotions. Two of the most important tenets of Amish life were obedience and submission. She struggled to maintain her footing, and remain true to the values in her life.

By now, three years after losing her husband, she had recovered her smile. Every day, she said a prayer of thanks for Katie, Jacob's wonderful legacy. Their precious child looked exactly like her father, with sandy hair and hazel eyes, so Rachel was able to glimpse him whenever she looked into Katie's face.

Still, there was sadness behind her eyes that disappeared only when she was around her daughter.

Katie was all that mattered now, making sure that she grew up with the best guidance and the least possible amount of disruption in her life. The Amish community would make sure that Katie knew she was loved and cared for, no matter what happened. That was a great relief to Rachel. They were safe here in every possible way.

Thinking about what her father had just said, she tried to recall if she had seen any signs of Katie slipping back into the sorrow that had dominated the little girl's life for so long after losing her father.

"I haven't noticed anything," Rachel said, "but I'll keep an eye on her."

Her father waved a hand. "My imagination, probably. I'm sure she'll be just fine. In fact, I promise to have her laughing by supper."

Rachel froze. "Supper!"

"What about it?"

She shut her eyes tightly and let out a groan. "The *raisins!*"

"What? What rai—"

But Rachel was already gone.

Chapter 2

Ellie Lawrence kicked off her shoes as she sank down onto her desk chair. The shoes were new and the heels even higher than those she usually wore—too high, she thought, to wear anyplace except going from her apartment straight into a taxi. By the time she got out of the subway and walked the three blocks to her office on Fifty-sixth Street, she was practically hobbling. She massaged her inflamed toes, annoyed at herself for being so impractical.

"The price of being fabulous," she muttered.

Wheeling her chair closer to the desk, she tucked her shoulder-length, blond hair behind her ears, then reached for the computer mouse, and clicked twice. She nearly groaned aloud. Seventy-eight new emails. Her chronic stomachache, the one that kept her company during most of her working day, made its presence felt more acutely. Hurriedly, she scanned the emails to see what could be put off or ignored altogether. In her years of working at Swan and Clark Public Relations, Ellie had found that making a list of priorities and sticking to it was the only way to get through the day. Without priorities, distractions ate up the hours. She had a lot of work to get through; she had to leave the office by eleven-thirty to get to a luncheon for a new magazine's launch, and then there was a reception at the SoHo showroom of a new but extremely hot handbag designer.

As usual, her iPhone had started chiming to notify her of texts and calls around seven that morning, and it continued to do so. She scanned it to see if there were any new fires to be put out. Satisfied that everything could wait, she got comfortable in front of her computer and started outlining a press release.

Almost immediately, she was interrupted by the phone sounding the first notes of "Bad to the Bone." She had given this ring tone to Jason Phillips, the man she had been dating for the past year, a lawyer in one of New York's bigger firms. She picked up the phone.

"Hey."

"Hi. You busy?" He didn't wait for her reply. "Some depositions missing. Long story and boring. Want to come over, say, like nine? We'll order in Chinese."

"Jason, did you forget? I'm going to dinner at my parents'," she answered. "Remember, they asked if you would come, too? They would really like to meet you. If you can get out by seven, I could swing by in a cab and pick you up—"

"Honey, I'm having a crazy day. I can't leave at seven," he said, not sounding too disappointed. "Do you want to come by after your family's shindig? If you can make it by nine-thirty, I'll wait for you to eat."

"Maybe—" Ellie stopped herself. "No, it'll have to be another night. Sorry."

"Have it your way. Send my best to your folks." He ended the call.

She put down the phone. Their relationship wasn't supposed to be serious, as they had both agreed. Still, she thought, after all this time, he should want to meet her parents.

She forced herself to return her attention to her computer. By the end of the day, she had accomplished everything on her list and a lot more. She had made inroads into the discussions with a major cosmetics company about using one of the firm's clients as their "face" for the following year, and gotten a commitment for a young singer to be featured on a major magazine cover. Successes like these were so satisfying; being good at what she did gave her a thrill. With each task completed, she felt as if she were one step further away from failing at her job, one step closer to believing that she deserved her position at the firm. Those feelings drove her relentlessly. She often hated to go home at the end of the day when there was so much more she could be doing, double-checking, confirming. She would force herself to leave, reminding herself over and over that things could indeed wait until the next day, that the world wouldn't fall apart if she didn't make that one call or send that last email until the morning.

Now, though, it was already seven-thirty, and she still had the cab ride to her parents' apartment on the Upper West Side. She would be late, but not more than usual. She struggled back into the now-hated shoes, and left.

Luckily, she found a taxi almost at once, and traffic was

light, so she was riding up the elevator to the eleventh floor by eight o'clock. Pausing outside the door to the apartment, she could hear the muffled voices of guests inside, punctuated by laughter and ice clinking in glasses. Friday night family dinners were a tradition over the years, although Ellie's attendance had dropped to once a month, sometimes less. A.J., her younger sister, lived with her husband in Rhode Island, so she made it only infrequently. The youngest of the three siblings, Nick, lived and worked downtown, only a subway ride away, but his attendance had also grown sporadic. The number of diners on any given Friday ranged from her parents by themselves to twenty or so relatives crowded into the dining room.

Ellie rang the doorbell. Her father's familiar footsteps approached as he loudly inquired of no one in particular, "Who could that be?" Whenever someone rang the bell, he always asked the same question in exactly the same tone.

"It's me," she called out.

Gil Lawrence threw open the door, a big smile on his face, his eyes crinkling with pleasure at the sight of her. She stepped across the threshold into his warm hug.

"Hi, sweetheart." He noted her beige silk suit and the leather briefcase she carried. "You came straight from work?"

She nodded as she put her briefcase on a small table in the foyer. "Long day, Dad."

"What mayhem did your clients cause today?"

She shook her head. "You don't even want to know."

"You're right, I probably don't." Gilbert Lawrence was a thoracic surgeon whose interest in his daughter's professional life extended only as far as it affected her well-being. They walked down the apartment hall, its walls lined with framed photos of Ellie, A.J., and Nick at various points throughout their childhoods. "It's time to forget all that and relax. Everybody's here. We were just waiting for you."

"I'm sorry I'm late, it's just—"

He waved her excuse away. "I didn't mean it like that. Uncle Jack has his Scotch, Aunt Leslie is getting lots of compliments on her hors d'oeuvres; believe me, everybody's happy. But now we'll move on to the main business of eating until we can't move."

They came to the three wide steps leading down into the living room, large by New York City standards, but crowded now with the Lawrence relatives. Built-in bookcases across two full walls sagged under the weight of books and mementos from her parents' travels, while another side of the room was lined with windows overlooking Central Park West. Ellie had always loved that view of Central Park, and, growing up, spent hours staring out those windows. She knew the four-bedroom apartment in a prewar building was now worth a small fortune, although her parents had bought it long ago at a fortuitous moment when the real estate market was in a slump. At this point, Ellie couldn't imagine them living anywhere else in the world, so entrenched was her image of the two of them in the long, narrow kitchen, sitting beneath the large chandelier in the dining room, or moving about their bedroom, always so quiet with its thick carpeting and heavy drapes.

Setting down a tray of cheese and grapes on the coffee table, Ellie's mother caught sight of her. Her face lit up. As usual,

Nina Lawrence was wearing black, which set off her chin-length salt-and-pepper hair and silver jewelry.

"There's my girl!" Nina hurried over to give her a big hug as Ellie came down the steps.

She kissed her mother's cheek in return. "Hey, Mom."

Nina looked past her daughter. "Did you bring Jason?"

"No, he couldn't make it tonight. Prior work commitments."

Nina searched her daughter's eyes, but said nothing.

She changed the subject. "Do you need any help?" Ellie glanced through the doorway to the dining room, where all six leaves had been inserted in the table to extend it as far as it could go. The table nearly filled the large room, with barely enough space for the guests to file in and take their seats. Atop the white embroidered tablecloth, her mother had put out the full spread of good china and sterling.

"No, we're all set. You go ahead and say hello to everyone."

Ellie made her way around the living room, leaning in for kisses, answering the usual questions about what was new and how her job was going. Most of her aunts and uncles from both sides of the family were in attendance with their spouses and a few of their grown children, Ellie's cousins.

She spotted her grandparents off to one corner and hurried over. Louis Lawrence was in his eighties and still a handsome man with silver hair, his posture straight beneath his suit jacket.

"Hi, Gramp."

"Rachel." He looked at her with pleasure as she put her arms around him. Her grandparents were the only people who still called her by her given name. Her nickname had come about when her younger sister A.J. was a baby and couldn't pronounce Rachel. She had started out with something that sounded like Ull, which became Ell and finally the one that stuck, Ellie. Most people had no idea she even had another name.

"How's my favorite grandchild?"

"I'm good, thanks." She smiled. Everyone knew he called all his grandchildren his favorite. She bent down to kiss the frail woman seated in an armchair by the window. "Gram, you're looking great."

Blaine Lawrence reached up to smooth back Ellie's fine blond hair, which always swung down in a sleek curtain when she leaned forward. Before the elderly woman could reply, her daughter, Ellie's Aunt Lillian, appeared beside them. Lillian was a tall, fashionably thin woman in her sixties, her hair dyed black and swept up into a bun, her wrists jangling with bracelets. As usual, she was wearing what Ellie's sister A.J. laughingly called her signature look, a tight, too-short, brightly printed dress.

"Where's the boyfriend?" she asked Ellie by way of greeting. "I heard we were going to get a look at him."

Ellie forced a thin smile. "Not tonight, Aunt Lillian."

Lillian ran an appraising eye over Ellie's outfit. "That's a very nice suit, honey. You look very professional in it, which I guess is what you want. Not like a young girl would typically dress, but professional."

Ellie forced herself to maintain a smile, as if she hadn't understood the underlying barb. The backhanded compliment was Aunt Lillian's specialty.

"It's a hard balance for you girls, once you're out of your early twenties," Lillian reflected. "You need to look businesslike, but you don't want to look *too* frumpy. Especially if you're single."

The smiled faded from Ellie's face.

"But you're divinely skinny. You must have sworn off food altogether." Her aunt turned to Blaine Lawrence. "Mother, can I get you something? Are you thirsty?"

The elderly woman nodded. "Some water would be nice."

As Lillian went to fetch the water, Blaine met her granddaughter's gaze. "I think you look both young and professional, and as beautiful as always."

Ellie laughed. "Thanks, Gram."

Her grandfather took Ellie's hand in both of his. "Try not to take Lillian's remarks personally, dear."

Ellie didn't say anything. She could understood how these two lovely people had produced her father, but how did they wind up with such a sharp-tongued second child? The fact that Lillian was so different from her brother Gil never failed to mystify Ellie. Still, as she well knew, siblings could be as different as night and day.

She hadn't heard the doorbell ring again, so she was startled to see her father return to the living room engaged in conversation with Jason. So he had changed his mind. When he caught her eye, he grinned and looked back at Gil, gesturing toward Ellie. Gil nodded and smiled as the two shook hands. Apparently, Ellie thought, Jason's first introduction to her father had gone well. Watching him cross the room to join her, she couldn't help but think that he looked as handsome and well-dressed as one could ever hope a date would be.

"Hi, honey," Jason said, slipping an arm around her waist and kissing her on the cheek. "There was a change in plans, so I was able to make it." He turned to her grandparents. "Forgive me if I'm interrupting you."

"Not in the least," Blaine said.

Ellie made the introductions, still pleased and surprised that he had gone to the trouble of coming.

Her mother emerged from the kitchen, calling out in a loud voice. "Dinner, everyone! Let's all move into the dining room!"

Louis Lawrence helped his wife stand. Ellie started toward her grandmother's other side to assist as well. Her grandparents were really the best, she thought, with a rush of affection.

"Please let me, Ellie," Jason said, stepping in to offer his arm to her grandmother.

"We shall escort the two most beautiful women into the dining room," her grandfather said to Jason with bravado. He tucked his wife's arm into his and offered his other arm to Ellie.

"You flatter me, Gramp," she said, matching his grand tone as she linked her arm through his. "Let's make our grand entrance and chow down. I'm starving."

Chapter 3

�֍

The teakettle began to whistle. Violet Thornton got up from the Formica-covered kitchen table, where she had been waiting for the water to heat up, trying not to think about what she was about to do. Heavy with dread, she poured hot water over a tea bag in an old porcelain cup.

She set down the kettle and tightened the sash around her robe. Carrying the cup and saucer, she took slow, careful steps into the house's living room. Her powder blue terry-cloth slippers flopped noisily as she went to sit at the desk, an antique her husband had prized. From the top drawer she removed several sheets of pink stationery. Then she opened the bottom side drawer and reached under a pile of papers to remove a large white envelope, ragged with age. She extracted its contents, spreading everything out before her. To whom would she write first?

It didn't matter one bit, she realized. Two women in two different states would receive the same letter. Then she could breathe freely at last, knowing she had done what she should have done so long ago.

Still, until today, her love for her husband had stayed her hand every time she contemplated writing these letters. When she had met Paul Thornton, she had fallen instantly, totally in love with him. He was new to the staff at Griffith Hospital, a handsome, fifty-year-old pediatrician who had the sick children smiling and laughing even as he soothed the fears of their parents. He had moved to Pennsylvania from a town in the Midwest, recovering from a divorce, as he told her, and glad to be there. She loved his graying hair and strong hands. Violet was a nurse in the newborn nursery, and she swore she could actually understand the concept of swooning every time he came in to examine the new babies. She had had several boyfriends over the years, but no one she cared about enough to marry. Certainly, no man ever came close to making her feel the way Paul Thornton did, and, at forty-four, she had resigned herself to remaining single.

The miracle was that he took an interest in her. From sharing coffee breaks, they progressed to dinners, a weekend getaway, and, finally, marriage. From the day they said their vows at City Hall, Violet woke up every morning astonished to find it hadn't all been a dream. She really was married to the incredible Dr. Thornton.

Her new husband had neglected to tell her one important fact, however. He was an alcoholic who had managed to stay sober only since he moved to Pennsylvania. It was barely six months into their marriage when he went into a bar on his way home from the hospital one evening, and didn't come home until the morning, incoherent and reeking of alcohol. From that point on, Violet could only watch as he balanced his duties as a doctor with his need to drink. He consumed drink after drink every night, sometimes working himself into a smoldering rage, other times becoming maudlin and weepy, more often falling into a stupor in his chair, then passing out until morning. Yet there he would be at work the next day, examining children, prescribing medicines, laughing and charming everyone around him—the model of professional dedication.

As horrified as she was, Violet never loved him any less. He might get angry when he was drunk, but he never turned his anger on her, and, later, when he sobered up, he was as regretful as a child, sometimes crying with his head in her lap, her hand stroking his head. He begged her to forgive him for his weakness. She did her best to convince him to go for help, but he refused. Word would get out, he said, and his career would be ruined.

Eventually, inevitably, the two sides of his life began to bleed into one another. He'd show up to work bleary-eyed, a bit short-tempered, forgetting what this or that nurse had just told him. He started making medical mistakes, small ones, but people began to notice. Violet was afraid for him, knowing he would fall completely to pieces if he were stripped of his identity as a physician. He had told her countless times that medicine was what saved him, kept him going. Being a doctor was all he'd ever wanted to do. She couldn't guess what might happen if he couldn't do that anymore.

The mistakes at work grew worse. His prescription for amoxicillin for a child whose chart clearly indicated he was allergic led to a first reprimand. Misdiagnosing a case of Kawasaki disease resulted in a near fatality for a seven-year-old, and brought a slew of questions and a serious warning. After he was caught sleeping in the doctors' lounge when he was supposed to be in the operating room attending a difficult delivery, he was put on probation and told that one more infraction would result in dismissal. They would be watching him.

At the time, Violet and Paul had been married nearly three years. Working the four-to-midnight shift one week, she arrived to start work long after Paul had begun his day at the hospital. There were six babies in the nursery that week, a relatively high number. As she glanced over the paperwork before making her rounds to look over her tiny charges, Violet saw that one of them had been discharged that morning.

As she came to the closest bassinet, she glanced at the name on the card, then peered at the infant inside. She stopped, puzzled. She looked at the card again. *King, Rachel.*

Violet spent eight hours a day with the babies for as long as they remained in the hospital. She prided herself on getting to know and recognize each one. She had been finishing her shift yesterday at midnight when Rachel King was delivered.

This was not that same baby. Violet recognized the baby in this bassinet as one she had spent time with for the past two days. The parents weren't local, but had been driving through the area when the mother had gone into labor. There had been some difficulties, which led to an emergency C-section.

Violet felt her throat constrict with fear. She went back to the nurses' desk to look once more at the discharge papers. The baby discharged by her husband that morning was listed as Rachel Lawrence, who'd left with her parents, Gilbert and Nina Lawrence, official residence New York, New York.

No, no, thought Violet, this is all wrong. The baby here in the hospital was Rachel Lawrence. This was the three-day-old C-section who should have gone home to New York with her parents.

Violet's heart was pounding as she went back to stand over the infant in the King bassinet. The baby girl slept, long dark eyelashes against her cheeks. Careful not to wake her, Violet lifted the tiny hand to look at the hospital I.D. bracelet on her wrist. *Lawrence, Rachel.*

It was exactly as she feared. Rachel King, the Amish baby born yesterday, was gone. The Lawrence family had taken that baby home. Their daughter was still here, mistakenly put in the bassinet for the Amish child, Rachel King.

Afraid she might be sick, Violet made her way back to the desk and sat down. Think, she commanded herself. Switched babies were every maternity hospital's worst nightmare. Once this became known, no one would ever again come to Griffith to deliver a baby—or maybe for any other reason, either. She had to be careful about how she handled this.

But there was her husband to consider. Violet took a ragged breath. She knew he had been drunk the previous night, but was off to work on time as usual in the morning. This, of course, would be the end of the line for him. He would be fired, maybe lose his license to practice. Even if he kept his license, no other hospital or practice would hire him when the story got around about all the mistakes he made, culminating with this one. She had no trouble envisioning him taking his own life over the shame and public humiliation. Whatever happened, he would never recover from this. Any hope of curing his drinking problem would be gone.

Almost without thinking, she retrieved a small scissors from the desk and went back to the King bassinet. She reached in once more for the baby's wrist and snipped off the identification bracelet, dropping it into her uniform pocket. Next, she made copies of both babies' birth certificates and wrote down what she knew about the circumstances of their births. She didn't know what she would do with all of it, but she sensed it was important to keep track of exactly what had taken place that day. She put the materials in a large white envelope, which she folded and stuffed into her purse. Then, as if in a dream, she went back to changing diapers and preparing to give the babies their bottles of formula.

An odd thought struck her. Why hadn't the Lawrence mother recognized that the baby wasn't her own? Violet searched her memory for the sequence of events. That first day, the mother would have been woozy from anesthesia from her C-section, so it was easy to imagine that she might not have imprinted the baby's face clearly in her mind. After that, she now recalled, there had been some complications with the mother. Loss of blood, infection—she wasn't sure, but the mother had barely seen the baby over the past two days. The two babies were quite similar—the same size, delicate features, little hair to speak of—so a change could easily have gone unnoticed by a woman still on medication and in pain.

Which left the Amish parents, Leah and Isaac King, according to the birth certificate Violet had just copied. She remembered that there had been some concerns about the delivery that brought the couple to the hospital instead of having a home birth, which she knew the Amish preferred. Based on the hospital's schedule, the babies would have been brought around to the mothers earlier this afternoon, so that mother had seen and probably held this baby today. Yet, apparently, no one said a word about anything being amiss.

Violet recalled the mother had come in very early yesterday morning, already having contractions, and endured at least twenty-four hours of labor. An exhausted mother holds her newborn, takes a loving look, counts fingers and toes, then relinquishes it to a waiting nurse and falls asleep. Violet had no problem understanding how the woman might not have noticed any difference between that baby she'd seen for a few moments and the one she saw today.

The magnitude of the mistake was too much for Violet to contemplate any further. She went about the business of her shift, and left the nursery when her husband came in to sign discharge papers for the King baby. She wasn't there to witness the Amish couple take home Rachel Lawrence, believing her to be their child. Later, without indicating anything was wrong, Violet updated the nurse who came to relieve her at midnight and went home.

Paul was asleep in their bed when she arrived. She smelled alcohol on his breath, but shook him, calling his name until he awoke, his legs thrashing as he was yanked from dark oblivion.

"What is it? What?" His words were slurred.

"Paul, get up! It's important. Listen to me—the babies you discharged today . . ."

"Babies?" His voice faded as he closed his eyes again. "Always dis . . ."

"Do you know what you did?"

He struggled to open his eyes, staring at her uncomprehendingly.

"Get out of bed," she commanded.

Violet made a pot of coffee as he roused himself and came into the kitchen. She didn't say anything until they were seated at the table, cups of hot coffee in front of them, her husband more alert.

"What's the emergency?" Paul asked, taking a gulp of coffee. "I'm listening."

Violet paused, wondering how to begin. "In the morning, you sent home a family from New York named Lawrence with their baby, Rachel."

"Okay," Paul nodded, "makes sense. I don't remember their name, but okay. Why is that a problem?"

"Because the baby they took home *wasn't their baby.* They took Rachel King, the Amish baby that was delivered near midnight yesterday."

The color drained from his face. "No, no. That can't be."

"This afternoon," she continued, "you sent the New York baby, Rachel Lawrence, home with the other set of parents, an Amish family from here named King. *You mixed up the babies and sent them off with the wrong families.*"

Her husband shook his head in frantic disbelief. "Oh, no,

that's impossible. I would never . . . I would have double-checked . . . I always do."

Violet said nothing.

He leaned his head against one hand, going over what he could remember of the two discharges. "I followed procedures, checked the mother's ID, the baby's . . ." He paused. "Didn't I check them both?" he muttered. "I know I did for the baby in the morning."

"The babies were both named Rachel. Do you remember that?"

He continued to think, then raised his eyes, which were filled with fear. "That must have been it, the first names. I must have glanced at the first name and not really taken in the last name. And I was rushing, I remember now. But, still . . ."

Neither one of them spoke for a few moments.

"Violet, what am I going to do? We have to make this right." His words came pouring out. "I have to call the hospital." He got up from the table.

"Paul, stop. Listen to me for a minute. Please."

"What? Yes, you're right, it's too late. It'll have to wait until the morning." He sat down again.

She reached over to take his hand in hers. "You understand this will be the last straw at the hospital. And the end of your practicing medicine."

He stared at her.

"I just want to make sure you understand," she said as gently as she could.

"But if we make it right, and everybody is okay with it . . ."

She shook her head. "Come on, Paul. Be realistic."

He nodded, biting his lip, thinking. Finally, he gave her a sad smile. "I don't think I could stand that, Violet, you know?"

"Yes. I do know."

"So where does that leave us?"

She paused, steeling herself to say it all aloud. "There are only two choices that I can think of. You can tell the hospital and sort it out, which means you will be finished as a doctor. Actually, we'd probably have to move away from here altogether. I can't see either of us staying with everyone knowing."

"And the other choice?" he whispered.

Her eyes filled with pain. "We say nothing. We let the mistake stand, and hope no one ever figures it out. The families don't know they have the wrong babies, and they'll just raise them as their own."

"We couldn't. No. We couldn't do that."

They sat there, the kitchen clock's ticking suddenly unbearably loud.

Paul was first to break the silence. He spoke slowly. "If I had a second chance, I can tell you one thing. I would never, *never* touch another drop of alcohol for the rest of my life."

She closed her eyes. The decision had been made.

The two of them never discussed it again. He kept his vow not to drink, from that moment until twenty-six years later when he died. She never stopped thinking about those two babies. Every Sunday, she went to church to pray that the mistake had been part of a larger plan. It had saved her husband, of that she was sure. Maybe it required something so awful to do it, but she wanted to believe saving him was in the service of something bigger. He went on to save the lives of so many children over the years. Perhaps that was the reason he was spared from his self-destructive ways.

Even after Paul died, Violet didn't tell a soul what happened in the hospital all those years ago. Now, though, she was dying, and when she died, the truth would go with her. It was time to tell those babies—grown women now—what had happened.

Seated at her husband's desk, squinting in the dim light, she picked up a pen and reached for one of the pieces of stationery. Her fingers were stiff with age, so she wrote slowly.

> *Dear Rachel,*
>
> *You wouldn't recognize my name, but I was a nurse at the hospital where you were born in Lancaster, Pennsylvania . . .*

Chapter 4

Rachel hoisted herself up onto the buggy's front seat and took hold of the reins. Katie jumped in beside her.

They had just dropped off a large container of Leah King's vegetable soup, plus two loaves of bread and enough roasted chicken and potatoes for tonight's supper for the Burkholder family. Sue Burkholder was sick and the family had their farm and eight children to manage, so neighbors were taking turns bringing food and helping with chores.

"That soup has gotten me past many a cold since I was a girl," Rachel said.

"I'm going to ask Grandma to show me how she makes it," Katie resolved. "Or maybe you could?"

"I could, but somehow it won't come out the same way. That's Grandma's special soup, and no one can do it the way she does."

Katie frowned. "I don't think Grandma would like to hear you say that, like she's special or something."

Rachel knew her mother was as keenly sensitive as ever to the dangers of thinking of oneself as special. She glanced over at Katie with a smile. "You're absolutely right. She wouldn't like that. But I think she'd like it if you asked her how to make the soup."

They drove in companionable silence. The morning held the promise of a picture-perfect May day. Wispy clouds crossed the sky as the sun bathed the countryside in bright light. The paved road cut a neat path through the vista of green fields, dotted with houses and farms.

Rachel pulled gently on one of the reins, and Driver turned onto the long dirt road heading toward their barn. She and her daughter disembarked from the carriage and tied the horse to a post. It was Saturday, the day of the week devoted primarily to housecleaning, and Rachel and Katie had taken a short break to deliver the food. Now they would return to scouring the bathrooms and kitchen, and dusting in every room. Then they would help prepare dinner and clean up after the meal before taking on the afternoon's work.

Inside the house, Leah King was wiping down the kitchen cabinets. The kitchen was set within a much larger area that served as dining and family room. Ten chairs ringed a wooden table that could be expanded to seat up to thirty people when necessary. Beyond that, two wooden sofas, multiple armchairs, and a rocking chair gleamed beneath blue cushions. An oak display case contained enough fine china to serve a large crowd. This was the hub of the house where most activities took place, as evidenced by the shelves containing board games and books. A table off to one side held the remnants of a half-finished art project started by Rachel's niece and nephews, the children of Rachel's younger sister, Sarah.

At the moment, those three children were seated at the big table, snacking on home-baked zucchini bread. Sarah was the sibling to whom Rachel felt closest. She loved her youngest sister, Laura, and both her brothers; in fact, she had a special closeness to the baby in the family, Daniel. Rachel and Sarah had been nearly inseparable growing up, and still continued to share everything and confide in each other.

Eleven-year-old Katie, seeing her young cousins, ran over to greet them. The littlest, Christine, was just over a year old, wearing an unadorned powder blue dress, sitting in a high chair and busily making a mess of her snack.

"Funny baby," Katie said, giving the little girl a quick hug. She began to play with her, clapping her hands.

"Katie, you know where the cleaning supplies are," Leah chided.

Nothing more needed to be said. Katie instantly turned and left the room to start work on the upstairs bathroom.

"I'll go with Katie now," Rachel said to her mother.

Leah gave a short nod.

Upstairs in the bathroom, Rachel and Katie resumed their ongoing game, one they had been playing together since they moved into the house after Jacob's death and had wound up sharing this particular Saturday chore. All the hardware in the room, from the faucets to the doorknobs, were characters who maintained a running dialogue, commenting on events that had occurred during the week or whatever else might be on their minds. Katie had designated different voices, typically high for smaller items like the draw pulls, deep for larger ones like the showerhead. Initially, the game had been an outlet for her to express some of her sorrow over the loss of her father, with the running water from the sink and shower representing an outpouring of tears and grief. Over time the game had evolved; sometimes the conversations touched on difficult subjects, sometimes they were simply silly. Katie, Rachel had realized many years before, was a child with many questions, just as Rachel herself had been. These questions weren't necessarily welcomed by her grandparents, so she did her best to handle them herself, out of earshot of those who might fear the girl was probing when she should have been obeying without question. A troublemaker just like her mother, was what Rachel imagined her own mother must think. She chose to look at it as being spirited. In fact, she couldn't help feeling a bit of pride at that, which she knew was terribly wrong. One of her most important jobs as a parent was to teach her child to be obedient. She certainly tried, but she wasn't sure she was succeeding. Katie was always polite and did as she was told, but her questions and some of the discussions they had made Rachel wonder.

Just another way in which I'm unworthy, she thought, her feelings of guilt surging, as always, to do battle with her rebellious impulse.

Katie was almost done with fourth grade. Like the other Amish children in their church district, she attended a one-room schoolhouse that consisted of a single teacher overseeing grades one through eight. School would be over for the year soon; the children finished in May so they could help their parents during the farms' busiest times.

They worked quickly to finish the upstairs bathroom, then headed downstairs to work on the other one. After dinner, when the dishes had been washed and put away, and Rachel had finished mopping the main room's floor, she went to see about dusting in the bedrooms.

At the end of the day Rachel tucked Katie into bed and kissed her good night. Entering her own bedroom, she set down the lantern on a small table next to her narrow bed. She was surprised to see a letter on the bed. She rarely got mail, so, curious, she immediately went over to look at it. The address was faint, as if someone had had a difficult time pressing down with the pen. Strange, she noted; it was addressed to her using her maiden name, Rachel King. Anyone she knew was well aware that her married name was Yoder. Yet she saw from the postmark that it came from Lancaster. Sitting down, she used her thumb to pry open the envelope, then pulled out several pink and white pages, paper-clipped together. She unfolded the pink stationery and smoothed down the pages before starting to read.

Dear Rachel,
  You wouldn't recognize my name, but I was a nurse in the hospital where you were born in Lancaster, Pennsylvania . . .

She read the entire letter, then examined the attachments, a copy of her birth certificate and a birth certificate for a Rachel Lawrence, born two days earlier than she had been.

Rachel took a deep breath, then read the entire letter again. She tried to picture the situation, a nurse covering up for her husband after he had committed an unthinkable act. Rachel felt a pang of sorrow for both of them, having to live with both their mistake and their terrible choice. A choice made out of fear, but one they both knew was wrong, selfish, sinful.

I don't want to know this, she realized. *I don't want this to be happening.*

She tossed the letter down on her bed, then began busying herself with preparations for going to sleep. She kept staring at the pink pages out of the corner of her eye, powerless to stop the flood of questions. Was she really supposed to be this Rachel Lawrence, a girl from New York? She said the name aloud, quietly, tentatively. Was it her real name?

A terrifying thought was forming in her mind. If she was this Rachel Lawrence, born to another family, then her being here was a mistake, and she shouldn't have lived this life. Was she even Amish? Yes, she'd been baptized, but it was all based on a false notion of who she was. Her mother and father, all the Kings, and their enormous extended family weren't her real family. Everything about her life was wrong, not what it was meant to be. Tears stung her eyes.

Maybe none of this was true. Surely it was a mistake. Or a lie.

Yet it occurred to her that, for all the questions it raised, the letter had also answered so many others. *This* was why she was always the child who caused problems, the one who questioned and refused to obey. This explained why she could never over-come her doubts about their faith and way of life. All the trouble and worry she had caused her parents over the years, especially her mother—they hadn't deserved it because she wasn't the one who was supposed to be their child. Of course, she wasn't Amish. She was never meant to be. It was all a cruel mistake. Even Jacob had paid a price; she wasn't truly the girl he thought he had married.

The next thought struck her with the ferocity of a blow. *Katie.* What was her daughter? *Who* was she? This wasn't just about Rachel anymore. If she were revealed to be someone else's daughter, what would that make Katie? Should she be here either? Maybe the two of them would be sent away.

She grabbed the papers from her bed and shoved them back into the envelope. Hurriedly, she went to her dark wooden dresser, and yanked open the bottom drawer, stuffing the envelope beneath the neatly folded pairs of black tights there. No one had to know about this. It could just be as if nothing had happened.

Her heart was pounding. She picked up the lantern and slipped into the hall to look in on Katie. Her daughter was asleep, snoring faintly. Rachel looked lovingly at the peaceful expression on her child's face, the soft, smooth skin and unlined brow. Losing her father had been the worst thing that had happened to Katie. Rachel couldn't imagine what it would do to her child to find out that her mother wasn't who she thought she was. That their entire life was based on a lie—or a mistake. The girl's world would be shattered by such a thing. If her mother's very self was a lie, there would be nothing that could be counted on to be true after that.

Katie must never find out. Far from achieving the goal of

protecting her in life, by telling her daughter about this Rachel would destroy her.

That settled it. Rachel had never read the terrible letter. It had never even come.

Her mouth set, she shut the door and returned to her own room. She was fully aware that she was committing one of the worst sins: lying by keeping silent. Regardless, she was not going to speak of the letter, no matter what, not when it would ruin her child's life. She would simply have to pray harder than she had ever prayed to be forgiven for this sin. After she prayed to be forgiven, she would pray to forget all about this. How fortunate for her that tomorrow was Sunday, and she could be with other members of the community, listening to the hymns and prayers she knew so well, here where she belonged. She changed into her nightgown, desperately trying to empty her mind of everything except what she would do when she awoke in the morning and got ready to begin the day. At last, she turned off the lantern, and slipped under the sheet and light blanket.

She stared up into the pitch-black darkness. A sense of foreboding seemed to seep into her very bones, expanding outward until it filled every corner of the room.

Chapter 5

�֍

The Gate was one of the hottest dramas on Broadway, and the tickets had cost Ellie a small fortune, but she found herself unable to concentrate on the actors onstage. While her mother sat beside her, fully engrossed, Ellie turned over ideas for publicizing a line of organic makeup, manufactured out of Seattle, and recently acquired by one of her larger corporate clients. At intermission, they ran into a woman her mother knew, and, while the two chatted, Ellie excused herself to check her phone for messages and texts. It may have been a Saturday afternoon, but in her business, round-the-clock availability was assumed.

"I really enjoyed that," Nina Lawrence said when the play was over and they emerged onto Forty-seventh Street. "Thank you for taking me, sweetheart."

"It was absolutely my pleasure, Mom. Happy birthday."

"Dad wouldn't have liked it. Definitely not for him. So it was a perfect choice for us."

"Hmm." Ellie felt too guilty to admit she had barely heard a word. She glanced at her watch. "Shall we stroll for a while? We have about an hour until we have to meet everybody."

"Good idea."

The two women headed east. Nina's birthday happened to fall on a Saturday this year, so it hadn't been that difficult to arrange for a family get-together over dinner at her favorite restaurant.

They meandered to Madison Avenue and then strolled uptown, Nina pausing to look in store windows, pointing out things she liked or thought would look good on Ellie.

"Those candlesticks," Nina said, moving closer to a window display and shading her eyes to minimize the glare on the glass. "Perfect for the little table in your entryway."

Ellie laughed. "Mom, do you really see me putting those ornate things on that little table? That's just for my bag and mail. And there's no place in my apartment where they would make sense."

"I admire your ability to keep things pared down," Nina said. "You truly are a minimalist. I'm drowning in all my souvenirs and bric-a-brac. Your apartment is like a breath of fresh air."

Ellie put an arm around her mother. "You're a sentimentalist, that's all." They walked on, Ellie making sure to focus on her mom and not let her mind drift back to work.

"I almost forgot to give you this," Nina said as she pulled her arm out of her bag, a long, white envelope in her hand.

Ellie took it from her mother. "A letter for me? How did you wind up with it?"

Nina shrugged. "It came in the mail yesterday."

Ellie glanced down at the envelope. The writing was thin and wavering, probably that of an elderly person, she thought. No one she knew even remotely would think she still lived at home with her parents. Even odder, it was addressed to Miss Rachel Lawrence, her real name. Outside of her family, few people knew her real name was Rachel, and no one else would use it. There was no return address, and the postmark was faint, the letters broken up. Ellie scrutinized it, finally able to make out the words *Lancaster PA*. That was the town where she had been born, but she definitely didn't know anyone there.

Puzzled, she was about to open it when her mother called her name. Nina had walked a few feet ahead of her. "Coming?"

Ellie dropped the letter into her purse to read later, and the two women continued their stroll uptown. When they reached the restaurant, her father and sister were already there, seated at a large, circular table. A.J. sprang up to hug her mother, whom she hadn't seen in several months. Gil Lawrence, dressed in a navy blazer and gray pants, also got up to kiss his wife, then Ellie.

"Aside from that, Mrs. Lincoln, how was the play?" he asked.

While Nina filled him in, A.J. turned to Ellie, giving her sister a quick hug and a peck on the cheek.

"Hey, Captain of Industry, what's doing?" A.J.'s wide, full mouth opened into a generous grin. She noted her sister's clothes. "Look at how put together you are, and on a Saturday, no less."

Ellie glanced down at her charcoal gray pants and the white

blouse under a lightweight cashmere sweater, her expensive leather bag and shoes, all of it casual enough for a weekend but nice enough to put in an appearance at the office or meet up with a client if necessary. She never knew who she might run into, and long ago she had made it a habit always to look presentable. A.J., in contrast, wore black jeans and a blousy printed top, her dark brown hair hanging loose down her back, large gold hoops in her ears. She was appropriately dressed for this restaurant, but just barely, Ellie decided, immediately rebuking herself for the uncharitable thought.

"I'm glad you got away." The two of them sat down next to each other. "I'm sure you're busy balancing school and your substitute teaching job."

A.J. was getting a master's degree at Brown in urban education policy. "Weekends are precious time for catching up on studying. But it's going well, knock wood." A.J. rapped on the table twice.

"Come on, you don't have to knock anything. You're a model student. And you still love it, right?" A waiter set down a glass of water for her, and Ellie took a sip.

"I absolutely love it. I can't imagine doing anything else with my life."

Ellie wondered if she could say the same about her career. It was succeeding she enjoyed so much, she reflected, not the actual job itself. She knew that her sister would die before signing on for a career to which she wasn't totally committed. Ellie often teased her about wanting to save every child in the world, but she was secretly jealous of A.J.'s unwavering dedication to something bigger than herself. It must be a wonderful feeling to believe you were doing something useful, something so positive.

She changed the subject. "How's Steve?"

"Great. Working on a new commission. Likes the people at the new place. So it's all looking good." A.J.'s husband was an architect. They had met in a coffee shop when A.J. first moved to Providence to begin student teaching in a public school. They had been married for two years, and he had recently been hired by a top architectural firm in the city.

"That's terrific."

"Love that son-in-law of mine," Nina interjected.

"Thanks, Mom. I'm kinda loving him myself," A.J. said. She turned back to Ellie. "What's doing with you? You still seeing that guy?"

"Jason. Yes, we're still together, but it's not really *together*, if you know what I mean."

"Ahh." A.J. nodded. "Well, you basically like to fly solo, right?"

"No, it's not that. It's—" Ellie stopped, unsure what she was trying to say. It was true, she hadn't wanted to get too serious with Jason or anyone else. Still, she couldn't deny feeling a bit surprised, hurt even, by Jason's cheerful willingness to accept her lack of commitment to him after so long. What was worse, even when she was physically with Jason, she was occasionally overtaken by a powerful sense of loneliness.

It had all become very confusing. For the past several years, she was always the one who'd refused to get involved. Now, though, something was changing. Of course, she reflected, it wasn't as if she had always avoided relationships like the plague. She had her first serious boyfriend when she was in college. The years with Mitchell had been easy and happy. Their problems started when he got a small part in one of the school's theatrical productions in the spring of their senior year. He'd enjoyed the whole thing so much, he decided he wanted to become an actor. Surprised as she was, Ellie was happy to support his efforts. After graduation, they both moved into apartments on Manhattan's Lower East Side. He attended acting classes and auditions, while she started working full-time at Swan and Clark. What began to trouble Ellie wasn't that he had performed in just a few unpaid productions, so far off the beaten path that only friends and relatives had attended the shows; the real problem was that she could see he had no talent. She couldn't bring herself to voice this realization to him, refusing to kill his dream. Instead, she'd watched as he waited tables and spent every available moment studying scripts, trying to make connections, and getting nowhere. He was never around to go out with her at night, having taken to drinking in the cheaper bars with other out-of-work actors who, as he explained to her, could relate to what he was going through. Ellie realized she was spending far more of her time with her best friend from college, Bibi, who had also come to New York after their graduation. When Ellie and Mitchell split up two years after graduation, they had drifted so far apart that neither one had any hard feelings. They parted as friends.

Ellie was taken up with her job, socializing with Bibi and the new friends she made in the city, and casually dating. It was then that the company sent her to attend a luncheon for magazine editors so she could make some contacts. She found herself chatting with a tall, suntanned man who turned out to be Claude Hamilton, the editor in chief of a skiing magazine. He wasn't classically attractive, but Ellie found him charming, and was pleased when he asked if he could call her another time. By their third date, Ellie felt she had found the man she could love forever. Claude was kind and attentive. He was knowledgeable about nearly everything, it seemed, and, even better, he made her laugh. Even Bibi, protective of her friend and a harsh reviewer of Ellie's dates, agreed that it seemed she had found "the one."

Which made it that much more of a blow when Claude left her for Bibi. The two moved to California where he had taken a position at another magazine. That was the last Ellie had seen of either one of them.

At the time, Ellie wasn't sure she would ever recover from the double betrayal. Sometimes she wasn't sure which was worse, losing the man she loved or the best friend on whom she had depended. The fact that she had never suspected what was going on left her breathless with humiliation. She barely managed to get into work in the mornings, only wanting the day to end so she could go home and climb back into bed. Friends tried to be encouraging, offering a shoulder to cry on, or a night out for distraction. She refused to talk about what had happened with any of them, and kept saying no to their entreaties and invitations until they gave up asking. Often too depressed to eat, she lost twenty pounds. She simply shut down.

Eventually, she recovered from the hurt, but nonetheless, she never repaired most of her neglected friendships, and the idea of falling in love again flooded her with fear. She never wanted to be in such a vulnerable position again. Until she met Jason, she dated sporadically. He was smart and lively, and they had been going out since the previous summer, but they both knew it was meant to be light and temporary.

Yet, lately, here she was having these hurt feelings about his indifferent behavior. She had become acutely aware that she didn't have anyone to depend upon, anyone who depended upon her. She had recently lost the last, truly close friendship that she had. June Neal had already been working her way up the ladder in fashion magazines when they met several years back after being seated next to each other at a fashion show. The two of them struck up a genuine and deep friendship. Then, last year, June's hard work had been rewarded with a job at *Vogue* in Paris. Emails and texts kept them in touch, but June was now consumed with her job and her upcoming marriage to a man she met over there, and it wasn't the same.

It dawned on Ellie that the solitary nature of her life was wearing upon her. No matter the personal risk, she needed someone in whom she could confide. And it made her sad that no one thought to turn to her when they needed help or support. Maybe it was a good sign, she reflected, a sign that she was ready to put a toe back into the water when it came to forming genuine attachments once more. There was, of course, her actual family, but that was different. She loved them and was grateful for them, but that had nothing to do with what kind of future she might have. Besides, they had their own lives to lead. If her life felt empty, she would have to figure it out for herself.

Well, she thought, she wasn't about to start explaining her confusion to her sister now.

"Don't pay any attention to me," she finally said to A.J. "I'm just being a crab."

The restaurant door opened to reveal her brother's arrival. She observed him as he came toward the table, flashing his lazy grin and waving. He was wearing a powder blue, button-down shirt, half untucked from khaki pants, the sleeves rolled up. She noted the switch from his usual T-shirt and jeans, representing an effort on his part to please their parents. Not that he had to make an effort; in their eyes, he could do no wrong.

Tall and handsome, with a thick thatch of hair in the same dark brown shade as A.J.'s, Nick was whip-smart, and the darling of the household. He was also, in Ellie's view, maddeningly indecisive, always ready to change course at a moment's notice. No matter what it was, Nick made up his mind only at the last second, after agonizing over all the possible choices. Ellie could still recall his high school and college years, when choosing a few electives each semester was an earth-shaking matter. Girlfriends came and went as he tried to decide who he was truly *meant* to be with. Whereas Ellie had followed a straightforward plan of college, then a job, Nick had traveled through Europe and Latin America for a year after high school while deciding if he should even go to college. To his parents' vast relief, he wound up applying to New York University and, though it took him five years, graduated with honors in history.

Ellie couldn't help disapproving of the way her parents encouraged what she saw as simple dithering, paying for his travels, patiently waiting for him to announce his intentions.

In fact, they had also kept silent when A.J. had taken three years off after college to consider her next career move, although her sister had always worked to support herself. Everyone had gotten their act together in the end, but to Ellie it seemed like a pretty self-indulgent road they had taken to get there. Even after college, Nick hesitated to commit himself too fully to anything. He currently had a job writing for a news-related website, but she didn't know if he liked that any more than he'd liked the last job working for a graphic design firm.

Nick greeted his parents, then came around the table.

"Hello, beloved sisters." Nick gave a hurried kiss to A.J. and then Ellie before sitting down next to her.

Nina held up the breadbasket, and looked around to see if anyone wanted any. Gil and Nick each grabbed a piece, but Ellie shook her head no.

"Tell us, are you in charge of everything yet?" A.J. asked her brother.

He laughed. "Absolutely. Actually, I'm getting into a little investigative journalism, which is fantastic."

"That's great," A.J. said. "We could use a crusader in the family."

"You're the crusader," Nick answered. "I'm just talking. You're the one trying to do something."

"The more crusaders, the merrier," Ellie threw in.

"Speaking of merrier," Nick said, "did anybody see that movie *Happier Than Before*?"

A.J. nodded. "I really liked it."

"Wasn't it great?" Nick turned to her.

"I saw it," Ellie offered. "But I can't say I felt the same. I thought it was pretty melodramatic."

"I cried like crazy at the end," Nina said, "but I loved it. And I learned a lot from it."

Ellie had to smile. She virtually never agreed with her family members when it came to movies or books. They had completely different tastes.

The waitress set down champagne flutes at everyone's place.

"I thought we might toast your mother," Gil announced.

"Thank you, darling," Nina said.

The waitress poured champagne all around.

"If I may break with tradition, I'd like to make the toast myself. To all of you," Nina said, picking up her glass and gazing at the bubbling liquid inside it. "This has been a wonderful birthday. My family all together, that's best of all. I mean, what more could anyone ask for? I have all I could want and far more than I need."

"Hear, hear, Mom, nicely said," Nick cheered.

"I love you all so much," she finished. "Thank you. And it's perfect because this will officially be the last birthday I ever have. I've decided to remain the same age from now on."

Gil leaned over to kiss his wife. "I'll love you just as much when you're indistinguishable from a prune."

She slapped him on the arm. "I hate you."

He shook his head. "I don't think you do."

"To Mom!" A.J. held her champagne up high.

They all drank.

It was after eleven that night when Ellie got home to her apartment, a one-bedroom in a building on West Tenth Street.

The apartment was neat, as usual. Ellie couldn't bear being around clutter, or feeling disorganized. She'd always been that way. Having her own place to treat the way she liked never lost its novelty, especially after having to share her childhood bedroom with A.J., an inveterate slob. It drove Ellie crazy to come home from school to her sister's clothes, books—her general junk—all over the floor, on both their desks, burying Ellie's bed. Despite her complaints, there had been no other solution, since her parents had one of the bedrooms, the second was a home office that they shared, and, as the one boy, Nick had the remaining bedroom all to himself. In meaner moments, Ellie had railed at A.J. about being born a girl; if A.J. had been another boy, she would have roomed with Nick, who was also a slob, and the two of them would have been perfectly suited.

She almost laughed, thinking about it. "Control freak extraordinaire," she said aloud.

As she finished washing her face, she remembered the letter her mother had given her that afternoon. She changed into a tank top and cotton sleep shorts, then went to retrieve it from her purse on the hall table. She plucked the envelope out of the bag and took it to her desk in the corner of her bedroom. Grabbing a silver letter opener from the drawer, she sliced it open, then pulled out several sheets of paper. It was a handwritten letter. A rare sight these days, she reflected, as she smoothed down the pages and sat in the desk chair to read it.

> *Dear Rachel,*
> *You wouldn't recognize my name, but I was a nurse in the hospital where you were born . . .*

She read the entire letter through. Paper-clipped to the last pink page, she found two birth certificates, one a copy of her own, and one for an infant girl named Rachel King, parents Leah and Isaac King, with a date of birth two days after Ellie's. The home address was in Lancaster, Pennsylvania, the father's occupation listed as farmer.

Ellie put down the letter. A joke, maybe a prank by a coworker at the office, or a game someone was playing with her. According to the letter, these people, the Kings, weren't just some couple who lived in Pennsylvania; they were Amish. *Amish.* Of all the things a person could come up with, that was definitely way out there. Hilarious. Obviously, it was the Lancaster hospital connection that gave somebody the idea.

She forced herself to put the matter out of her head, getting into bed and drifting to sleep as she considered what she was going to say in an important meeting at the office on Tuesday. Then, at three A.M., she suddenly found herself wideawake.

Being Amish. It was hilarious. Except that it wasn't.

A chill crept up her spine. It was not something she had ever been able to put into words, or even fully admit to herself, but how many times had she felt that, somehow, she didn't quite belong in her family? She was always the one with the different opinion from everyone else's, just like when they were discussing that movie at dinner. And she certainly didn't look like the rest of them. She looked so different from the others that it was assumed she got her looks from a long-gone relative no one could quite remember. A.J. and Nick had that thick, brown hair, while hers was fine, light blond. Their eyes were brown and large, friendly-looking somehow; hers were a cool blue. Her complexion was fairer than theirs. The shape of their mouths, the planes of their faces, their height, their builds—everything about them was similar, clearly derived from one or the other of their parents, and completely unlike her.

She suddenly felt afraid. *Stop it*, she commanded herself. Stop it right now. This was absurd. Completely ridiculous. It was obviously just a joke or some kind of scam.

She decided the fastest way of getting at what was behind this letter was to start with the basic facts. Who would benefit from writing it, and why? She closed her eyes. It was an odd sort of scam, she reflected, with so many intimate details from her past, and that decades-old paperwork.

First thing tomorrow, she would go online to see what facts she could gather about the hospital, that nurse, and her doctor husband. One step at a time. After that, she would decide what to do. Perhaps she would call a lawyer to learn how to make whoever was behind this explain him- or herself, or even better, clear it up and leave her alone.

Ellie lay in the dark for a very long time, trying to figure out what reason someone might have had for making up this strange story—and about her, of all people. She couldn't come up with a single one.

Chapter 6

Rachel was seated at the quilting frame, which was positioned just beyond the kitchen area near a window to maximize the daylight. She typically began her quilting around six or seven, after breakfast was done and she had finished the first cleaning chores of the day. Tending the garden and yard took up much of her time in spring and summer, so she was less productive at the frame in those seasons. During the winter months, she could spend more time on this work, and she particularly enjoyed doing it in the evenings, the family gathered in the room, talking or playing games, her mother making hot chocolate or popcorn. Her favorite evenings were when Katie sat beside her. Rachel taught her about piecing and appliquéing, and they would often sing hymns together while they worked. So far, however, Katie hadn't shown an overwhelming interest in quilting, but Rachel hoped she might develop one later on. Amish mothers usually gave several quilts as wedding gifts to their daughters, and Rachel had already started on the first one for Katie, wanting these to be the most beautiful and complicated ones her talents would allow; she worked on it whenever she could find a free hour or so.

This morning, she was finishing the top of a quilt for a double bed. The pattern, a traditional one known as Log Cabin, featured concentric light and dark diamonds, each composed of many small fabric pieces. Although quilting had always been one way to make use of leftover scraps of fabric from worn-out clothing or sewing projects, like most quilters, Rachel now planned out the colors in advance and purchased fabrics from a store. Her preference was to work on more complex patterns, as she found them more satisfying in the end, but she alternated them with simpler ones such as this so that she could complete several in a shorter period of time. Occasionally, at different points during the process, the other women in the family would help, one of them stenciling, or another one pinning on fabric pieces. They might gather to put the final quilt together, stitching the top to a middle layer of batting and the backing on the bottom, which could be a solid colored cotton or cotton flannel. They would sit around a large frame that kept the quilt stretched taut, each working on a separate section. As they completed their sections, they readjusted the quilt to reveal the next portion by rolling it around wooden poles to which the ends were attached. It generally took a full morning and part of the afternoon to finish a large quilt, and sometimes they were able to help Rachel put together some additional smaller items, like pillows or crib quilts. Spending that time together also gave them a chance to talk about everything from gardening to weddings, while the younger children crawled underfoot or played nearby. Usually, though, Rachel finished the items herself, working on smaller pieces stretched tight on a huge embroidery hoop.

Periodically, Rachel or another family member brought her finished pieces to a quilt shop two miles away to be sold. It was an Amish family-run business operating out of a shed behind the main house. The shop was filled to overflowing with quilts, table runners, and pillows produced by local women. The high quality of the items sold there made Rachel feel honored to have her work among them.

She sat up straighter in her chair and twisted from side to side, stretching her back. A door on one side of the room opened. Hannah King, Rachel's grandmother, entered the kitchen. She was coming from her house, which was a second attachment built onto the main house where she lived with her husband, Amos. A corn-picker accident ten years before had cost Amos two fingers on his right hand and he was losing his hearing, but he still helped around the farm as much as he was physically able. Along with Hannah, he devoted a lot of his time to keeping the farm's financial records, and searching out the best opportunities for well-priced equipment or whatever large purchases might be necessary for the household.

Hannah suffered from arthritis, and moved slowly across the room with the help of a cane, smiling at her granddaughter despite the evident pain in her back.

Rachel stuck her needle into the quilt and hastened over in case Hannah needed help. "Can I get you something?"

"I'm just here for my vinegar and honey," Hannah replied in

a pleasant tone. "I don't know how I could have run out of honey, but I need to use yours today."

Over the years, their grandmother had tried countless remedies to ease her arthritis. For the past few months, Hannah had subscribed to a remedy she repeated periodically, drinking a mixture of vinegar and honey with water several times a day. Rachel knew better than to ask her if it was working. She would, as usual, act as if her condition was a minor annoyance, and the drink just something to quench her thirst.

Rachel helped her grandmother to a chair, then measured out the mixture according to Hannah's instructions. The older woman gripped the glass with her swollen hands and drank, the expression of distaste on her face making her granddaughter laugh.

Even Hannah realized she wasn't fooling anyone into thinking she chose the drink for its flavor. She smiled as she set the empty glass down. "Delicious. I highly recommend it."

"I could tell how much you liked it." Rachel took her seat once more and turned her attention back to her sewing.

The front door opened. Katie came in holding hands with Sarah's two younger children, Nicholas and Christine. When the little ones saw their great-grandmother sitting at the kitchen table, they ran over to her, squealing, both trying to clamber up onto her lap.

"Now, now," Hannah said to them, rising, "we can't all fit there. Let's move to the sofa. I'll read you a book. Katie?"

"I'll get one." She went over to a bookshelf and scanned the titles of children's books there before selecting a short book featuring a picture of a horse on the cover. She brought it to Hannah, who was helping the children get settled next to her, one on either side.

Rachel stuck the needle into her quilt one last time, then got up and went to the kitchen area. It was time to start setting out the midday meal, which was why Katie had come in.

"How are you?" Rachel asked her daughter.

Katie began removing plates from the kitchen cabinets to set the table. She leaned in close to her mother and dropped her voice. "Last night . . . My bed. You know . . ." Her voice trailed off.

Rachel nodded. Katie had wet her bed frequently as a little girl. No one made a fuss over it, and she seemed to have outgrown it, although occasionally she still had an accident. On those occasions, the eleven-year-old was mortified, even though neither Rachel nor anyone else had treated it as anything but normal and unimportant. The two of them had worked out a system that satisfied Katie: She would tell her mother the next day, so Rachel could collect the wet sheets from their spot of concealment behind the door of Katie's room.

Any further discussion was halted by the arrival of Leah King, carrying a basket of newly gathered radishes and lettuce. She greeted everyone pleasantly before setting down the basket and heading for the propane gas–run refrigerator. She, Katie, and Rachel removed food they had prepared earlier that morning, and assembled whatever needed reheating. Without words, they warmed and set out the meal: bowls of chicken soup, three-bean salad, and corn bread.

Katie went out to the barn to call the men in for dinner.

Isaac, his eldest son, Judah, and Sarah's husband Moses were the first to arrive in the kitchen. Within minutes, Judah's wife Annie appeared with Sarah, both women carrying babies, older children trailing behind them. Rachel's younger brother, Daniel, worked for a construction company, and ate his dinner at work; he would, however, be home for supper that night.

The family settled in around the table. After a silent prayer, everyone helped themselves to the steaming food. The conversation primarily revolved around milk production and those cows about to calve, who were now kept mostly outside.

As soon as the midday meal was over, the men went back to the fields while the women cleaned up and dispersed to resume their other chores.

Rachel was the only one left in the kitchen when she picked up the black straw broom to give the front steps a sweeping before going back to her loom. She opened the door to the porch and stepped outside into the bright afternoon. It was a breezy, welcoming day, and, closing her eyes, she lifted her face to the sun's warmth before getting to the task at hand.

She was nearly done when she happened to glance up and notice a car idling at the end of the long walkway in front of the house. Sunshine glinted off its bright red surface, and it was impossible to see who was inside. Tourists, no doubt, Rachel thought, looking back down at her task. They were constantly pulling over in front of the house, obviously delighted when one of the family members appeared, as if they were sighting a rare animal in its natural habitat.

Rachel continued sweeping, but something was bothering her, a feeling of distress. She raised her head. The car hadn't moved. Without knowing why, she moved to lean the broom against the side of the house, her eyes still on the car. She stepped off the porch and took several steps down the path toward the main road. As she walked, she shielded her eyes from the sun, but still couldn't make out who the driver might be.

The car door on the driver's side opened. A woman got out, shut the door and moved to stand by the front of the car, facing Rachel, but made no gesture and said nothing. Continuing down the path, Rachel saw that the woman had shoulder-length blond hair, with sunglasses pushed up on top of her head. She wore a light-colored blouse and dark pants, a gold belt buckle gleaming in the sun. She wasn't old, but she was clearly an adult. She, too, raised a hand to shield her eyes, as she focused her gaze on Rachel.

At that instant, a cloud passed in front of the sun, and the glare disappeared. Both women let their hands drop down to their sides.

Rachel got her first clear look at the woman's features. Stunned, she caught her breath with a gasp. The clothes, the haircut—none of that could hide the fact that the woman looked eerily like Rachel's siblings. Nothing on earth could have been clearer to Rachel than that this woman standing be-fore her was their sister, and a member of the King family.

The missing member that only Rachel knew existed.

She saw the woman stiffen, as if seeing something in Rachel that shocked her as well. They both stood, immobilized, for what seemed like a very long time. Then, the woman made an abrupt move back to the car door, yanked it open and got in-side, slamming it. Rachel watched as the red car sped down the paved road, then made a right turn at the first opportunity, passing out of sight.

As if expecting the car to return, Rachel continued to stand there, staring out at the empty road.

The woman in the car was, without a doubt, Rachel King. The real Rachel King. She had come to reclaim her life.

Chapter 7

Ellie's hands were shaking so badly, she pulled into a gas station and drove around to the side where no one would notice her. Turning off the engine, she gripped the steering wheel, trying to calm herself.

She had never believed she would really go this far, renting a car and driving to Lancaster to find an address she had scribbled on a scrap of paper. In the end, though, she had to see the spot for herself, had to make the facts indisputably real. Just finding the house, with the children playing on swings, and a cat sleeping in the rocking chair on the front porch—that would have been more than enough to contend with. But Ellie barely had time to consider the sight when that woman came out. She was exactly what Ellie pictured when she imagined the Amish, with the white head covering and its thin strings hanging down untied, the simple dark green dress and apron.

Ellie had stared, transfixed, not wanting to acknowledge what she suspected was right in front of her.

She put her head down on the steering wheel. The woman in front of that house was the real Rachel Lawrence of New York. Was *supposed* to be her. Who grew up on Manhattan's Upper West Side, went to college, supported herself in a high-powered job. That was to have been *her* life.

The story, the whole crazy thing, was true. Researching it online had been easy. Within a day, Ellie learned how plausible the situation was. The people mentioned in the letter had all existed, and were at the hospital exactly as described. Every piece of the story fit together, but in the end, the research didn't even matter. One look at that woman coming down the path, even with her brown hair mostly covered, was all it took to confirm the truth. The large, dark eyes, the shape of her mouth and cheekbones—she was the third Lawrence sibling.

She, thought Ellie. Not me. *She* was the eldest Lawrence daughter, her parents' child. Nick and A.J.'s real sister. Even Gramp and Gram—they were *her* grandparents. Every relative up to and including rotten Aunt Lillian belongs to her, not to me, Ellie thought.

She felt a deep sorrow for her parents. They had gone along all these years, loving her, raising her as their own, when, in fact, she was unrelated and irrelevant to their lives. It wasn't even as if they adopted her. They never chose her. They had their own daughter, and it was this woman, living in another state. More like in another world, Ellie corrected herself, thinking of the woman's clothes, her bare feet, the covered hair.

Yet, strangest of all was that something so unimaginable explained so much. All those things she had always sensed, but never allowed to surface in her consciousness. Things that forced her to face how different she was—and felt—from the rest of the Lawrences.

It was, she thought, like those old test questions in school: Which one of these things is not like the others?

That would be me.

Ellie hadn't had a good night's sleep in the week since her mother first handed her the envelope from that nurse. Her distress had only grown as she had been forced to concede that the claims were true. By this point, she was barely eating, distracted at work, practically in hiding from the rest of her family. She didn't know what to say to them, how, or even whether to tell them. This morning, she had gotten up unusually early, knowing without admitting to herself that she was about to rent a car and drive to Pennsylvania. Finding the address of these people had been easy given that the family had lived in the same house for decades. She called the office and told them she had wall-to-wall outside meetings, so they were not to expect her that day. All she had to do was punch in the address on the rental car's navigation system, and she had wound up here.

Now what?

Ellie felt a desperate need to leave this place and get back home to New York. She turned on the ignition, jerked the wheel to pull the car around, and sped out of the gas station. Turning on the radio, she raised the volume so the blaring music would drive all thought from her mind.

By the time she dropped off the car and got back to her apartment, it was nearly six o'clock. She kicked off her shoes and poured herself a glass of red wine, taking it over to the sofa. She sat down and gazed out the window at the view, the familiar skyline she loved so much. The sight of those buildings was alternately soothing, glamorous, mysterious, dangerous, hopeful. New York was her city, her home.

But it's not mine, she thought. None of it is mine. I should be living on a farm. She glanced down at her outfit. None of this stuff, she reflected, that's for sure. No expensive clothes or makeup. No cars. No computers or cell phones, maybe no telephones at all. Certainly no public relations job—she didn't know much about the Amish, but she could guess that wouldn't be a profession they would particularly admire.

She took a large drink of her wine. Finding out she came from another family would have been terrible enough. But this—an Amish family. It was so far beyond her comprehension. She had no reference points, no way to understand what it meant.

Still, she knew better than to tell herself the visit today had been the end of it. Whoever else was in that pristine white house, behind those green shades, were her real family. Her biological parents. She grimaced at the notion that she would suddenly need to use such a phrase. The children playing outside today—were they related to her? Nieces and nephews?

Maybe some of them were the other Rachel's children.

Ellie set down her wine on a side table with such force, the burgundy liquid splashed over the top of the glass. She didn't move to clean it up. The idea that this woman might have children hadn't crossed Ellie's mind until now. But it would hardly be surprising, given that she was thirty years old, the same age as Ellie, of course, almost to the day. It dawned on her that the children would be nieces or nephews to Nick and A.J. And they would be her parents' grandchildren.

Gil and Nina had encouraged their children to make their own decisions about most things in life, but they were shameless in demanding a grandchild from all of them. Ellie could hear her mother's voice, cajoling, teasing. "We've waited forever. The heck with school and your jobs. We need a baby in this family. Immediately!" They didn't truly expect any of the three to produce an offspring any time soon, but everyone knew that they were dying to see one of them take that next step. Behind the humor, they were expressing a serious wish. They wanted to fuss over an infant, to love it with the joy of never having to discipline it. As they said, a grandchild was the only thing in the entire world they lacked. "If you really loved us, you'd give us that grandkid!" their father often joked.

That grandkid was probably here, Ellie thought, maybe still an infant, maybe an older child, but likely to have been in that house. She tried to picture what her parents' reaction would be to the fulfillment of their wish by a daughter they had never known. She couldn't do it.

One thing she could do, though, was put an end to the secrecy. The rest of her family had to be told the truth. Even if she wanted to, Ellie couldn't sweep it under the rug any longer. No matter what happened, she had to follow this wherever it might lead. Somehow, she had to find out who she really was, or was meant to be.

She got up and went to the phone.

"Hello?"

"Hi, Mom." It occurred to Ellie that it wasn't even correct for her to call this woman Mom, but she pushed the thought aside. If I go down that road, she realized, I'll lose my mind completely.

"I need to see you and Dad. It's important. Are you two home tonight?"

Ellie was at her parents' apartment, ringing the doorbell at eight-thirty, wondering how she was going to explain the situation to them.

She heard her father approaching the door.

"Who could that be?" Smiling, she murmured her father's trademark phrase to herself from her side of the door at the same moment he called it out.

Once inside, she gave him a long hug, wondering if and how things between them would change after tonight. She wasn't sure she would be able to stand it.

"What's the mystery, sweetheart?" Nina emerged from her bedroom to give her daughter a kiss. "It's not like you to call a summit meeting." Her tone was light but Ellie heard the concern beneath the words.

"Let's sit." Ellie led them into the dining room.

"In here? This really is a summit meeting," her father said as he sat down beside his wife. "Is everything all right?"

Ellie tried to collect herself. "I have something to tell you, so please let me get it all out." She reached into her purse for the envelope, extracting the letter and documents within and spreading them out on the table. "I received this earlier in the week. You remember, Mom, the letter that came here—you gave it to me when we were out shopping. On your birthday."

"Yes, I remember." Nina nodded. "It came here by mistake or something."

"No, not by mistake. This was the only address for me the person had. It . . ."

Ellie trailed off. She didn't know how to get through this story. She couldn't. She pushed the letter across the table to her parents. "Read this, please."

Both of them reached into pockets to pull out reading glasses, and Gil moved his chair closer to his wife's so they could read together. They each held one side of the page. Ellie watched their expressions go from mildly expectant to serious. Then, her father turned pale. Her mother clasped a hand over her mouth, and her eyes grew large. She finished first, and let go of the page, putting both hands flat on the table and staring at them. Gil put the letter down, and picked up the birth certificates Ellie had slid over, sharing them with his wife. Ellie waited while they took in the information, the tension unbearable. Finally, they lay everything back down and turned to each other. Ellie saw a rush of emotions pass between them. She couldn't decipher the unspoken communication between a couple of more than thirty years, but she easily recognized their anguish and shock.

Her father spoke first, his voice husky. "Is this true?"

Ellie nodded. "It all checks out, yes."

"But how could it have happened? These things just don't . . ." Nina looked off to the side, clearly trying to remember the events of those long-ago days. "Yes, there were some problems, but I would know my own baby."

She looked over at her husband. "Gil? Is this possible?"

"Well, technically it's possible, yes. There are errors made in hospitals like anyplace else. But I don't see—the baby was ours. I mean, you, Ellie, you were our baby."

Ellie resisted giving in to the tears welling up in her eyes. "No, Dad," she got out. "I wasn't."

Nina's voice rose with indignation. "Of course, you're our baby. Our child, I mean. This is ridiculous! I raised you. I should know."

Ellie could only shake her head.

Anger replaced Nina's indignation. "Who wrote this? What kind of person sends such a thing and just signs their name, no address, no nothing? Someone who's not telling the truth, that's who!"

"Nina," Gil said, putting a calming hand on her arm. He gazed over at Ellie. "Sweetheart," he said, his tone gentle, "how can you be sure about this?"

She raised her eyes to his. "Because I saw her."

"Who? You saw who?" Fury and fear were evident in Nina's voice. "This nurse? Where? I want—"

"Rachel." Ellie looked from one to the other. "I saw Rachel. Your real daughter."

There was silence at the table.

"I drove to Lancaster today." Rachel spoke slowly, as if she were painting a picture for her parents. "I saw where these people, the Kings, live. And Rachel came outside to sweep the steps. That's all. I didn't speak to her."

Gil sat back in his chair, as if to distance himself from the entire situation.

"How do you know it was her? She could have been anyone."

Ellie rubbed a hand across her eyes, suddenly exhausted. "I saw her face, Mom. It was like looking at A.J. and Nick. And you."

Nina stared at her.

"Maybe that's just what you expected to see. Are you certain, Ellie?" Gil asked.

"Beyond the shadow of a doubt, Dad." Ellie said. "Listen, put aside the fact that the whole story checked out, every bit of it. I researched it myself, and I assure you, I did it thoroughly. But, Mom, this woman was you. I don't mean she looked a little like you. I mean, *she was you.* Both of you, really. Like A.J. and Nick, the way they look just like you. Your DNA, your genes, whatever you want to call it. She's your child. She's Rachel Lawrence."

Ellie stopped, feeling almost physically ill. It wasn't her fault this had happened, but she felt as if she was torturing her parents by bringing them this news.

"And you?" her mother got out. "What about you?"

Ellie looked down. "Like it said, I'm—or I was supposed to be—Rachel King. A member of an Amish farming family."

"Dear God." Gil ran one hand through his graying hair. "It can't be."

"Ellie, honey . . . what are you saying?" Nina asked.

"Mom!" Ellie understood that her mother didn't want to hear the words, but she was powerless to stop her own growing agitation. "You read the letter. It was an *Amish* family that de-livered the other baby. The Kings are Amish! They're my real parents!"

"No!" Her mother drew herself up and smacked the table with the palm of her hand. "Don't you ever say that again! We're your parents, no matter what! You were raised here, in *this* family. We're your real parents, always. Nothing can change that, not ever!"

Gil reached over to take Ellie's hand. "Mom's right, of course. You're our daughter, the same way you were yesterday, and the day before that, and every day for thirty years before that. This doesn't change anything at all."

Ellie sighed. "I hope that's true."

"How could you say that?" There was pain in Nina's voice. "You can't possibly think this makes any difference to us."

"You didn't see her, Mom. Her face . . ."

"Ellie, are you suggesting we're going to feel differently about you because this other person is in the world?" Gil was clearly hurt by his daughter's words. "It has nothing to do with loving you."

Ellie attempted to smile. "I know, I know. I'm sorry. It's just overwhelming. I don't know what to think about anything anymore."

"What do you want to do about this? What happens now?" Gil looked at his wife. "What do we *all* want to do about this?"

"Don't know, Dad." Ellie shrugged. "We're going to have to do something, though. I have to see these people, I realize that. Meet them. Amish or whatever, if they're related to me, I have to."

Nina spoke quietly. "Do we know if this girl wants to meet us?"

Ellie shook her head. "We don't know one single thing about her. You read in that letter that we were each getting a copy, so she knows the whole story. I have no clue what her feeling is about all this."

Gil seemed to be thinking aloud. "If she got the letter the way you did, just addressed to her, she may not have told anyone else about it. So we can't really go barging in there." His face was regretful. "Ellie, it seems this nurse made it be about the two of you. She left it to you two to decide if you wanted to tell people."

Ellie considered this. "I guess I need to tell her I want to meet her parents. My parents."

Nina winced but said nothing.

Ellie sighed. "Of course, they don't have a phone, just to complicate things."

"Write her a letter," Gil suggested.

"Another letter," Ellie echoed. "It's almost comical, having to resort to that. Who the heck writes letters anymore?" She stood. "I'm sorry, but I can't think straight anymore. This has been the strangest day of my life."

Her parents jumped up and came around to her, Nina wrapping her in a fierce hug. Gil gently rubbed her back.

"Sweetheart," Nina murmured into Ellie's hair. "This isn't anything bad. Life will go on, nothing will change. Maybe it will be like having another sister. Something wonderful."

"Thanks, Mom. I love you," Ellie said. "Here you are trying to make me feel better when I just dropped a bomb on you."

"That's true." Nina pulled back to look into Ellie's eyes. "You've brought us quite a piece of news, sweetie. I haven't had a chance to take it in."

Ellie's heart broke for her mother, whose crooked smile made it clear she was struggling to put on a brave face. She wondered what her parents would do once she left the apartment.

"So you'll write to this girl?" Gil asked.

Ellie nodded. She leaned over to kiss him on the cheek, inhaling the familiar scent of his aftershave. "I'll keep you posted," she said in as light a tone as she could manage.

"Okay, Champ," he said, using one of his old nicknames for her. "And don't you worry. Everything will be fine."

Famous last words, Ellie thought.

Chapter 8

�֍

Rachel stabbed at the dirt with her spade, paying little attention to the gardening. It had been nearly two weeks, but every day she was haunted by the memory of the woman in the red car. When Rachel got dressed in the morning, she imagined that woman putting on her clothes, closing the snaps designed to look like buttons, slipping on the apron. When she worked on her quilts, she envisioned her making the same detailed movements with a needle. In Rachel's mind, the other woman always did a better job at being Rachel King. *That* Rachel was satisfied with her life, and didn't cause trouble. In every way, she was more competent and she radiated contentedness. She *belonged*.

Then Rachel would think of Katie. No matter what, the other woman wouldn't have had her. Nor would she have married Jacob Yoder. Those parts of Rachel's life were hers and hers alone. Katie was the miracle for which Rachel never stopped feeling grateful. Those thoughts comforted her. Until the next time she found herself wondering what if . . . it should have been. . . .

"Rachel, please get the mail—I'm expecting something," her father said, as he passed her on his way back to the fields. Shaken out of her reverie, Rachel hastened down the path to the mailbox and retrieved the small pile of letters and notices inside. She saw a letter with her father's name on it and turned in the direction he had gone to bring it right to him.

What surprised her was a letter just underneath it addressed to her, although, again, the name was Rachel King, her maiden name. This time, though, there was a return address. Rachel stopped walking. Ellie Lawrence, New York, NY.

Lawrence. The other Rachel.

Rachel changed course and walked off toward the far side of the house where she could be alone and unseen. Sitting on the grass, her heart beating rapidly, she opened the envelope.

It was a friendly letter, but the intent of the writer was clear. She started out by apologizing for driving off so quickly the day they had first encountered each other outside the King home. Then she laid out a few details about her life, how she had grown up in New York City where she lived and worked now, some information on her immediate family members, how she got the nickname Ellie. Now that she knew about them, she wanted to meet her biological parents and the other members of her family. She asked Rachel to contact her, providing a list of addresses and phone numbers. The letter finished with her speculations about Rachel's reactions to the nurse's letter they had both received, and how it was understandable if Rachel were reticent about sharing the news with her family. This might not be the case at all, but, either way, Ellie felt she had to see and talk to the parents she had never known; she only hoped Rachel would work with her to make this happen. Of course, it was up to Rachel whether she wanted to meet her own biological parents in New York, but they now knew the story and would welcome her with open arms.

Rachel reread the last sentence. It had never occurred to her to go to New York and meet the Lawrences. She wondered why. It wasn't only this Ellie who had another set of parents to meet; she did as well. And a new sister and brother. Who were also a new aunt and uncle for Katie. Rachel's head drooped as she envisioned having to explain the story to her child.

Well, she said to herself, it didn't matter what she wished or feared. It was obvious that this Ellie Lawrence was coming to see the Kings, all of them, whether Rachel wanted her to or not. That meant she had to tell her parents.

Surprisingly, the idea of sharing it made her feel lighter; she hadn't realized the almost physical weight of carrying such a burden. *This is exactly why we don't tell lies*, she thought. Despite her dread of revealing who she was—and was not—Rachel saw that telling the truth was the only way. Come what may, she was going to do what was right.

It wasn't until later that night, afer Katie and the other children had gone to bed, that Rachel had a chance to tell her parents she needed to talk to them. Leah King was already seated at the kitchen table, in the middle of mending a tear in a bedsheet, a basket of other sewing still to be done beside her.

"I may fall asleep while we're here," Isaac said, "but you have my full attention until then." He sat next to his wife, regarding Rachel with a sleepy expression. Leah continued to sew.

Just then, Sarah came into the kitchen. "I left my favorite tea here," she said by way of explanation.

"Would you sit with us?" Rachel realized having her sister there would be good for moral support. Besides, Sarah was the other person with whom she was most anxious to discuss this. "I want to tell everybody something."

Sarah nodded, filling the kettle with water and turning on the stove's propane gas–powered burner. She stood there, waiting for the water to heat up as Rachel began to speak.

She tried to lay out the whole series of events without leaving anything out. When she got to the part about the doctor's error back at the hospital, Leah King put her sewing down on the kitchen table and folded her hands in her lap. She sat, listening, her face expressionless. Isaac King tilted his head, as if trying to take in every word, but avoided looking at his daughter. Sarah said nothing, but made her cup of tea and brought it to the table, where she sat sipping the hot liquid, her eyes locked on her sister. At the mention of Ellie having been right outside the house, Sarah started. Isaac King put his elbows on the table and rested his head in his hands. Rachel described how much she resembled the other King siblings. Leah rose and went over to the sink, pretending to be washing something that was already clean, apparently needing an excuse to turn her back to them. Rachel saw all this, but forced herself to go on. When she finally explained that Ellie wanted to come to the farm to meet all of them, Leah whirled around to face them again, unable to hide her shock. No one spoke.

Sarah broke the silence first. "Is this person really part of our family?"

Rachel bit her lip. "She's your sister. I'm the one who's not really related, not by blood."

Isaac shook his head. "No, Rachel," he said fiercely. "You are ours. You are Amish. You've been baptized. This is your life and we are your people, forever."

Rachel looked at her mother, standing by the sink. She hadn't spoken or moved. "Are you all right?"

Leah seemed confused. "This girl, this woman . . . You are saying she's our child. But she's English, not Amish. She lives in New York City. No husband, no children. She works at a job to take care of herself and lives alone." She frowned. "How can we hope to know this person as our child?"

"If this is true," Isaac said, "she is also our child whether we know her that way or not."

Anger flashed in Leah's eyes. "I knew it was a mistake to go to the hospital." She glared at Rachel. "You were the only one not born at home. Look what they did!"

Rachel recoiled at the outburst. Her mother quickly collected herself.

"I didn't mean that. I shouldn't say such a terrible thing." She put her hands over her face, distraught.

Isaac went over to stand next to his wife, as if to transfer strength to her, but he addressed his words to Rachel. "You are our daughter." There was pain in his eyes.

Sarah reached across the table to take her sister's hand. "We are all united in one family. We live our lives by our faith and in the best way we know how. Nothing can change that."

Rachel was filled with gratitude. "Thank you," she whispered.

She glanced over at her mother and was stunned to see tears rolling down her cheeks. Rachel couldn't remember ever seeing her mother cry. She was afraid to ask if she was upset because she had been given the wrong child instead of the one who was truly hers, the one who might have brought her far more happiness over the years. Leah, seemingly unable to bear any more, left the room. Her husband went after her.

Rachel turned to her sister. "Did you see that?"

"She was crying! I can't believe it."

"What will happen now?"

Sarah opened her mouth to speak but seemed to be at a loss for words. "Oh, Rachel," she said at last, "I don't know. I guess this woman from New York will come here."

"What about Katie? What do I tell her? She's not actually related to anyone else here."

Sarah's eyes widened at the reminder of her niece. "No! It's not possible!"

"Think about it. If I'm really this Rachel Lawrence, then Katie is related to them, too. Not to this family at all."

Sarah shook her head. "This is too much to understand right now." She stood up. "We should go to sleep now and talk it over in the morning."

"No," Rachel burst out, "we're not going to understand it any better in the morning. I've been trying to understand it for weeks, and I still don't." Stunned by her own vehemence, Rachel took a deep breath.

Sarah, anguish on her face, put her arm around Rachel's shoulders. "It will all work out. Things always do, right?"

"Yes, of course," Rachel murmured. She did her best to smile as Sarah headed for the doorway leading back to her house.

The next morning, Rachel went with Katie to help her in the chicken pen, collecting eggs and feeding the chickens. The sense of dread she had felt upon first learning the name Rachel Lawrence had returned in full force. The familiarity of the noisy pen, chickens clucking and running around their legs, was soothing. She wanted to treasure each moment of her life before it was permanently altered by the arrival of this woman, Ellie.

Katie clucked back in amusement at the chickens as she tossed out the feed. While she checked the birds' water supply, Rachel watched Katie, the side sections of her blond hair tightly twisted in the traditional Amish style and all of it neatly hidden beneath her white *kapp*. Her hazel eyes were bright. The little girl caught her mother's gaze and smiled. It had been such a long road back from Jacob's death, Rachel thought. She could only pray this new situation wouldn't be too much for Katie to bear.

Impulsively Rachel put her arm around Katie. "There's nothing like family. You love them, and they love you, always."

Katie looked at her questioningly. "Well, of course. How could they not love you?"

"They do, yes, absolutely. Always."

Katie made a face to express how odd she found her mother's remarks. But Rachel wasn't looking at her. She was just hoping that what she said would turn out to be true.

Chapter 9

�֎

Ellie was so nervous, she felt like she was about to jump out of her skin. In the brief note she had received the week before, the Kings had invited her to come at noon. The note was handwritten by the mother—*her* mother, she corrected herself—on a piece of plain white stationery, suggesting she join them for dinner this Saturday at twelve o'clock. It was signed "Sincerely, Leah King." Ellie wasn't sure what to make of the formality, or the fact that the woman made no reference to the circumstances of such a meeting. But she would be there, and at noon on the dot.

She thought carefully about what to wear and decided that overdressing would be weird and underdressing would be insulting. She settled on navy pants and flats, and a pale pink blouse.

At last it was time to leave. For this trip, she chose a black rental car, more sedate than the previous red one. She recalled driving these roads the last time, almost in a daze, not knowing what she would find or if she was sure she even wanted to find anything, but compelled to continue. Today, she felt only panic, plus her usual stomachache in one of its stronger phases. Even though she was the one who had pressed for this meeting, she wondered if she would live to regret it. She might hate this family, or—and this could well be much worse—love them so much she would be embittered by what she had missed. Her mind raced, considering the various reactions she could have to them, or they might have to her. Each scenario was grimmer than the last.

At eleven-forty, she pulled off the road in front of the Kings' farm. She glanced in the rearview mirror to be sure she was presentable. Her palms were damp, her mouth dry. She took a quick swig of water from the bottle she had stashed in her bag. As she capped and set it in the cup holder, she looked up to see Rachel King come out of the house. She must have been watching from behind one of the green window shades. Perhaps she was nervous as well. That possibility had never occurred to Ellie.

She turned the car onto the driveway, which led to an open space toward the right of the house. Her fearful anticipation grew almost unbearable as she got closer. She could see behind the house to make out what was probably a stable, plus an enormous barn and large fields of crops in the distance. Rachel King stood on the porch, dressed just as Ellie had seen her that first time, in a simple, midcalf-length dark dress and an apron, with her hair beneath a white head covering with untied strings hanging down. She had no expression on her face. Ellie forced herself to smile as she reached for the door handle.

Deep breath, she told herself, as she stepped outside.

"The other Rachel," Ellie said, coming toward the porch steps. She smiled again.

"You are Ellie. We're expecting you." She stuck out her hand.

Ellie heard the faintest lilt of a slight accent, but nothing in her words or expression could be interpreted as welcoming.

Sticking out her hand in return, she received a quick, firm handshake. "Thank you for having me. I know this is an odd situation." She gave an awkward laugh. "That doesn't begin to describe it, really."

Rachel's small smile was forced. "This is what you wanted."

Ellie tried to hide her surprise at how sharply she spoke the words.

"Please come in." Rachel held open the screen door. "Our parents are waiting."

Our parents. Apparently, she had come to her own terms with this mess, and chosen the approach she would take. It was a good one, Ellie realized, reasonable and workable. She hadn't ever considered it that way.

She followed Rachel into a large room, painted pale blue and lit by the sunshine of the June day. There they were. Her real parents. A man seated at a large table set up for lunch, a woman stirring one of several pots sending up steam on the stove. He got to his feet as soon as Ellie entered the room, and she could see he wore black pants with suspenders and a dark green shirt. The woman, wearing glasses, her face scrubbed clean and devoid of makeup, was dressed in an outfit nearly identical to Rachel's, a full black apron over a long, plain, burgundy-colored dress, her light brown hair hidden under a white cap. She stared at Ellie. Then, she murmured something in another language, and put down the spoon she was using, coming toward her. She took both of Ellie's hands in her strong ones and stared into her eyes as if drinking in the sight, saying nothing.

Ellie felt herself getting lost in that stare. She *recognized* this woman. Not as someone she had seen before, but as someone deeply connected to her. Was it possible to recognize your mother if you had never met? She didn't believe that. Maybe it was the familiarity of seeing her own skin coloring and eye shade, *her* nose and *her* lips on someone else. It was as if she were looking at a picture of herself that had been aged by computer.

The woman's face broke into an enormous smile. "You are Ellie."

The same words Rachel had used outside, but a different world of meaning in them this time. Wonder and warmth.

She turned to her husband. "Isaac, it is our Rachel."

He joined them, his smile genuine if not quite as wide. It dawned on her that these people might have their own mixed feelings about opening up this Pandora's box.

She took in his beard, the lack of mustache, and the bangs across his forehead. This odd-looking man is my father, she thought in amazement.

"Welcome, child," Isaac said. "Come and sit down."

She followed him and Rachel to two large chairs near a sofa, where they sat as Leah King hurried to the stove to turn off burners and give a final stir to her food before joining them. No one said anything, and Ellie was unsure if she should speak first. The huge room, she saw, was simple, only a calendar and a clock on the wall, as well as a framed document of some sort, done in calligraphy. The windows let in daylight, but it was still too dim for Ellie's taste. Shelves in one corner revealed neatly arranged books and games. Several hooks by the front door held straw hats with black bands, plus a black bonnet, and over the doorway, she saw a painting of a farm that appeared to be done on the extra-long blade of a saw. A wall extended partway into the room to divide the kitchen from the living room area where they sat. Everything was spotless. She took it all in, from the unsophisticated furniture to the bucolic scene of the saw painting. It didn't seem possible for her to feel any more out of place than she did at that moment. She noted with some apprehension that the kitchen table was set for a huge group.

She actually felt a childlike urge to squirm with discomfort as she felt all eyes upon her. "I'm sorry I'm a little early," she began.

Leah sat down beside her and waved her hand dismissively. "We are glad you are here. It was a long drive?"

"Less than four hours."

"And you make that trip whenever you want." Rachel's tone was cold.

Ellie looked at her in annoyance. "The road travels in both directions. You could make it whenever you want, too."

Another silence.

"So," Leah said, "this is a big shock for everyone, no? The hospital and that doctor did the biggest mistake they could do. And here we are."

Ellie noted that Rachel looked at her mother in surprise, as if she hadn't expected her to get right down to it. For her part, Ellie was grateful to Leah for breaking the ice. She turned to her.

"I didn't know what to do when I found out. But once I was sure the story was true, I had to find you. Thank you for agreeing to see me."

"Of course we would agree," Isaac said. "We—"

He was interrupted by the arrival of a young girl, around ten or eleven, Ellie guessed. She recognized her at once as the girl who had been pushing the younger children on the swings outside the day she had first driven here.

The girl stopped short when she saw they were seated with a guest, and waited, as if for instructions.

"Katie," Rachel said, her tone softer than Ellie had yet heard it. "Come here." She waited until Katie had approached. "This is our guest, Ellie Lawrence. She is a friend of Grandma and Grandpa's. Ellie, this is my daughter, Katie Yoder."

Her daughter. Ellie struggled not to stare. "It's very nice to meet you, Katie," she managed to get out. From Rachel's description of Ellie as a family friend, it was obvious the girl hadn't been told anything.

"Nice to meet you, too." She looked directly into Ellie's eyes, her gaze expectant and open. Ellie was struck by what seemed like a sense of innocence combined with maturity.

The little girl turned to her grandmother. "Should I put out the food yet?"

Leah stood. "Yes, it is time for dinner. The others will be here soon." As she moved toward the stove once more, she turned to Ellie. "Rachel's sisters and brothers will be here, too."

Ellie surmised that Katie might not have been told the truth, but the other family adults had been, and they would all be there to look her over. That's not fair, she reprimanded herself; maybe they were coming to welcome her. She wished she didn't feel so uncomfortable. This visit wasn't going at all the way she hoped. It was like swimming through molasses, trying to guess everybody's feelings and intentions.

Suddenly, it seemed, the room was full of people, men and women approaching to be introduced. It was difficult to keep them all straight. Rachel had two younger sisters, and Ellie got those two names down first, Sarah and Laura. There was a brother, Judah, a tall, broad-shouldered man with a beard but, like Isaac, no mustache. He had glasses and an open smile, and looked to be between thirty and thirty-five. There was another brother who seemed much younger than Rachel, but whose name she forgot, along with those of the various spouses. Lastly, Rachel's grandparents came in. They moved slowly, and looked as if they had led lives of hard work, but not unhappy ones. Ellie wondered where Rachel's husband was; she expected to see him among the family members. Perhaps he was away, or they were divorced. No one mentioned him, and she decided it was probably wiser to follow their lead.

Everyone offered words of welcome that were polite, but

their faces remained impossible to read. The group assembled around the table, men on one side, women on the other. Ellie was vastly relieved that she noticed the arrangement before plopping herself down on the wrong side. She caught sight of Rachel's youngest brother looking at her from across the table with outright curiosity, but a broad smile. Grateful, she smiled back at him. Daniel, she remembered, this one was Daniel. That should be easy to remember. He was the only man without a beard, and without a wife. And, she thought, startled by the idea, he looks a lot like me.

There was a silent prayer before the meal started. Ellie sat, motionless, confused about what was expected of her, and hoping she wouldn't commit some horrible faux pas. All the women plus Katie started bringing what seemed like countless platters and bowls of food to the table. Ellie was afraid to offend her hosts by refusing what was offered to her, so she filled her plate with a little bit of everything: pot roast, macaroni and cheese, beets, potato salad, and asparagus. For dessert, she accepted chocolate pudding, ginger cookies, pineapple upside-down cake, and apple fritters, which she recognized as such only when someone offered them by name. She took the smallest bites she felt she could politely get away with, thinking that she normally didn't eat this much food in a week, much less one meal. Not to mention, she said to herself, that this meal was a cholesterol festival. The others had no trouble finishing whatever they took, most of the men having additional portions.

The conversation was limited. Only Leah King seemed animated, her eyes sparkling, as she chatted about the farm, and the milk and food crops they sold. It was apparent to Ellie that she was trying to relay information without alerting little Katie to the fact that something odd was going on. Ellie wished she could stare at each person at the table in turn, maybe learn something about them. Of course, that was impossible. Besides, she knew she was the one under their scrutiny that day.

When Isaac King asked about Ellie's family in New York, there was total quiet in the room as she explained that her father was a surgeon, and her mother did a lot of charity work. She described Nick and A.J. as well. She could see them all running this information through their minds, assessing it and then probably attempting to connect their Rachel to these people. Ellie added that her parents were extremely anxious to meet Rachel, and hoped she would come to New York as soon as she felt ready. No one commented. Ellie wanted to kick herself for adding that; this wasn't the time to bring it up, nor should she have mentioned it in front of the whole family. She quickly changed the topic by describing the neighborhood where she lived, which led to a brief explanation of her public relations job.

When the women cleared the dishes after dessert, she tried to join them but was quickly waved back to her seat. One of them, the older brother's wife, glanced at all the leftover food on Ellie's plate as she picked it up. Her name suddenly came back to Ellie: Annie King.

Annie smiled. "You don't eat. That's why you are too thin. I hope you are healthy."

Ellie gave her a slight smile in return, not appreciating the insult behind the seemingly well-intentioned remark. Good Lord, she thought with a start, did every family have an Aunt

Lillian, even Amish families? For the first time that day, she wanted to laugh.

Rachel and her daughter, Katie, had spent the meal at the far end of the table, and were now cleaning up in the kitchen area. As everyone finally left the table, Ellie worked her way over to them. Rachel was wrapping up the little leftover dessert there was and scraping table scraps into a dog's food bowl. Ellie put a hand on her arm.

"This is so hard," she said, speaking quietly so that no one else could hear over the multiple conversations going on in the room. "I'm sorry for any trouble it's brought to you."

Rachel continued with what she was doing without looking up. "Fine."

"I hope we can be—" Ellie was about to say friends, but that seemed ridiculous. "I hope we can have some kind of relationship."

"Perhaps." Rachel set the plate in her hands down on the counter. "Did you get what you came for today?"

Ellie was taken aback, unsure whether it was a sincere question or Rachel's way of asking if she would please go now and not come back. It was also a good question, Ellie realized, but one to which she didn't know the answer.

"Excuse me, but I have to go to help my Uncle Judah." Katie appeared beside Ellie and was addressing her. "It was very nice to meet you."

"Oh, I so enjoyed meeting you, too, Katie. Thank you." She knew her parents would give anything for a photograph of their grandchild, but she had vaguely recalled once hearing that the

Amish didn't pose for pictures, so she hadn't bothered to bring a camera. Ellie tried to commit the details of her appearance to memory so she could describe her later.

She ignored the protests of Rachel's sisters, and helped them finish clearing up. The elder Kings, Isaac's parents, came over to say good-bye, explaining that they had promised to visit Amos's brother that evening and needed to be on their way.

"Buggy's not quite as fast as your car," Amos said with a grin, "but I'll bet you knew that."

"I guess I did." She smiled back at him.

"Next time you come, you will take a ride with us," his wife, Hannah, added.

"That would be wonderful." Ellie decided she liked these people. They had a welcoming manner. They must be nice grandparents. And they would have been mine, she couldn't help thinking. Heck, they *are* mine. With a start, she pictured her grandparents back in New York. If she had been living here, she never would have known them. A terrible thought.

The rest of the men began drifting over to say their good-byes to her. They all had work to do, chores to which they had to get back. Saturday was not a day off around here. The women were washing and drying dishes, talking quietly among themselves but repeatedly glancing in her direction.

She had planned to stay longer. Now, she couldn't wait to leave. She went over to Leah.

"I realize you have a lot to do, and I should drive home before it gets dark." Ellie hoped no one would call her on the fact that, considering this was June, it would be many hours before it got dark. "Thank you." That seemed hopelessly inadequate, but she couldn't decide what words would be appropriate for this occasion.

Leah gave her a hug, then quickly stepped back, seeming startled by her own impulsivity. "To learn this, to see you . . ." She trailed off.

The other women offered their good-byes. Rachel said she was on her way to finish some work upstairs and disappeared from the room without any further discussion. Isaac came over to walk Ellie out, grabbing one of the straw hats from a hook near the door. She took a closer look at his haircut, his beard, his clothes. So strange. She couldn't recognize this man as her father, not in a million years.

He might have been having the same thought. Taking her hand again as they paused by her car, he gave her a searching look. "So. You are my daughter."

She nodded. "Can you think of me that way?"

He considered her question. "I am trying."

"I appreciate your honesty."

"Rachel is also our daughter. She has been a good daughter."

"Of course! Please don't think I would ever dream of trying to replace her."

"No, I do not think that. But this is not easy for her. Her Jacob died only three years ago. She has Katie to think of."

Ellie was stunned. Why hadn't it occurred to her that Rachel might be a widow? She had assumed the husband was away or they were divorced. Idiot, she said to herself, the Amish probably don't even have divorces.

"I didn't know . . ."

He smiled. "We must give this time. We need to know each other. To understand each other." He reached over to open the car door for her.

She squeezed his hand. "Thank you." Isaac? Father? She didn't know what to call him, so she stopped there. She got into the car.

"We will talk again?"

She nodded. He raised his hand in farewell, then turned and went back toward the house. Ellie buckled her seat belt, then looked once more at the pristine house, the bucolic setting. In under four hours, she would be back home in her apartment. Would this day even seem real to her?

Chapter 10

�֍

Rachel sat in her chair, struggling to concentrate on the quilt piece she was working on. Ever since the night before, she had been unable to think about anything other than Ellie Lawrence's visit.

She had done absolutely nothing to make Ellie feel comfortable or even wanted there. On the contrary, she had said little, sat with Katie at the far end of the table to avoid conversing with their guest—or answering what must have been dozens of questions the woman would doubtless have liked to ask—and made it plain that she had no interest in pursuing this further. She had acted like a child, she thought. No—far worse. The children would never have behaved as badly as she had.

No doubt it had been difficult for Ellie. A roomful of strangers, an impossible situation with which they were all trying to contend. But Rachel hadn't been able to make herself care. All she could think about was seeing her mother's face transform with joy over the sight of her newly discovered child. Even worse was standing by while Leah gazed at Ellie, and hearing her mother utter those words of love and recognition: "Isaac, it is our Rachel."

Our Rachel.

Her mother had been practically giddy over dinner, talking more quickly and animatedly than Rachel could ever recall her doing. It was as if she was trying to impress Ellie, going on about the farm and everything they produced on it. Certainly, Rachel had never seen her mother try to impress anyone. That went against everything she believed, everything the Amish believed. The whole thing had been so out of character for Leah King, Rachel wouldn't have believed it if she hadn't seen it.

Her father had been more circumspect, but she had seen the wonder on his face as well, and the way he took those special moments alone with Ellie to say good-bye. She wished she knew what he said.

She resumed working. She realized she was succumbing to jealousy again, that and about a dozen other ugly, unacceptable emotions. Her shame returned in full force. Ellie hadn't done anything to Rachel, or done anything wrong at all. She was in the same position Rachel was, a person who had lived her life and suddenly been informed it wasn't actually meant to be hers. It wasn't as if they were being asked to take over the other person's life and give up their own, she reflected. Still, it felt as if everything she took for granted was no longer true. Even though she knew it didn't make sense, her life didn't seem quite . . . legitimate anymore.

Unhappily, she focused on her stitching. She looked up when her sister Sarah came into the kitchen. Rachel smoothed the front of her dress, as if her distraught feelings were somehow reflected in her appearance.

Sarah was carrying a basket of potatoes, and set them down on the counter to retrieve a knife from one of the kitchen drawers. She picked up a potato, then glanced over at Rachel as she prepared to start peeling.

"I'll put these up for mashing later," she said.

There was a brief silence, and Rachel found herself raising the one subject she thought she wanted to avoid.

"What did you think of Ellie Lawrence?"

Caught off guard, Sarah paused in what she was doing, then went back to peeling as if nothing had been said.

"Sarah?"

Her sister sighed, putting down the knife. "I don't know what to think. We didn't get to know her at all. It was like she didn't want to say too much. Maybe she was afraid for some reason. Or she isn't so friendly? Maybe there were too many of us all at once and she was nervous." She grinned. "Guess we scared her off."

Rachel's sense of relief that Sarah didn't proclaim undying love for Ellie was immediately replaced by disgust with herself for having had such a reaction.

Sarah went on. "She is an unmarried woman from New York City. She seems to have a great deal of money—you saw the clothes and jewelry she wore, the car she had. I guess her job pays well. That's what I know, but it's all on the surface and doesn't tell me anything important about her. I can't say what kind of person she is."

"Did she seem like she could be your sister?"

Sarah picked up the knife again. "You are my sister. What may happen in the future with this other woman—" She shrugged.

Rachel nodded, looking down at her design of interlocking circles that would eventually be part of a queen-sized quilt in the Double Wedding Ring pattern. She was unprepared for Sarah's next question.

"Will you be going to meet your own new parents in New York?"

Rachel's head came up sharply. "I . . . I don't know. Why? Do you think I should?"

"I truly don't know what you should do. I suppose I'm asking if you want to meet them."

"I don't see what good it would do."

Sarah considered her words. "It won't do any good. Or maybe it will. But there they are, out there. You don't wonder about them, not even a little?"

Rachel didn't reply. Then, she stood. "Excuse me, Sarah. I have to leave."

She let the screen door slam behind her. This was the question she had been dreading. She knew that she was going to have to face the decision sooner or later, but she was afraid such a meeting posed dangers of which she couldn't even guess. The stability she had struggled to achieve for herself and Katie after losing Jacob could be jeopardized. Her life was inextrica-bly bound up in the close bonds of her family and the commu-nity; to have those bonds broken, or even loosened, would leave her lost and adrift. She felt the only safety lay in staying where she was, close to home and everything she knew and loved.

She walked over to sit on one of the children's swings, idly sweeping her bare toes back and forth in the dirt. No one was around at the moment, everyone occupied with their work. As she should be.

Nina and Gilbert Lawrence. They were indeed, as Sarah had put it, out there, living in New York City. What on earth would it be like to grow up in a big city? She hadn't minded city life when she was a teenager; it had seemed exciting. Now, though, she wanted no part of the noise, the hurry, and the dirt. But to be a young child actually living in a city day in and day out— she had never considered that. Maybe city life didn't bother you if you didn't know anything else.

Still, she reminded herself, whatever she had and hadn't ex-perienced while growing up didn't matter anymore. The ques-tion was what she was going to do now. If she was going to be truthful, she had to admit that, on some level, she had believed Ellie might not cause as much of a disturbance in their lives if she was allowed that one visit and then, hopefully, went away. It was obvious now that this was wishful thinking. Ellie had set something in motion, and Rachel was powerless to stop it.

Rachel realized she wanted to meet the Lawrence family. Her parents here belonged to Ellie as much as to her, but it worked both ways. She needed to see who her real mother and father were. Acting as if she never thought about going to New York was just posturing on her part, trying to minimize Ellie's connection to the Kings. It was time for Rachel to stop pouting and pretending that she didn't care about any of this. She cared deeply.

She went back to the house. She would contact Nina and Gil Lawrence and ask if she could visit. Someone would take her to the bus station early in the morning, and she would come home that same day. She wouldn't bring Katie, though, that was definite. For now, she needed to do this alone.

While still apprehensive, Rachel was greatly relieved she had decided what her next step would be. She entered the kitchen to find her mother setting the peeled potatoes into a huge pot of water. Next to her were a large pile of string beans and the ingredients to prepare fried chicken.

"May I speak to you about something important?" Rachel asked.

Leah glanced up. "Will it take very long?"

"No, I guess not." Rachel hesitated, then blurted it out. "I think I'll go to New York to visit the Lawrence family."

"Fine."

"So that's all right with you?" Rachel asked. She was suddenly anxious about what effect this might have on her mother.

She looked up in surprise. "Of course. I expected it. You have to go. I understand that."

Rachel waited. Leah had transferred her attention to the string beans. As usual, Rachel thought, her mother was unflappable. Rachel wasn't sure if she was grateful to her for being so understanding or shocked that she showed so little interest in the subject.

"But remember, Rachel, you are Amish. Do not forget this for even one minute."

She turned back to see her mother gazing at her. She wondered if her mother was warning her to behave properly on her visit, or offering some support, reminding her that she was a member of this family for good. But her mother looked away, and neither of them said anything else.

Chapter 11

Jason Phillips and Ellie settled into their seats at the Japanese restaurant. It was noisy in the small room, a recently opened hot spot they both wanted to try. Despite the late hour on a weeknight, the restaurant was still crowded, but, fortunately, a table opened up almost immediately.

"Should we get some sake?" Jason picked up a menu.

"Sounds good." A little something to fortify her, she thought. She had promised herself that this was the night she would tell Jason the truth about her background. Soon she would lay it all out for him. She was both afraid and eager to hear his reaction.

Once they ordered their dinner, she had run out of excuses to put things off. She absentmindedly played with the gleaming black and gold chopsticks, wishing her stomach would stop hurting.

"There's something I found out about myself that I have to tell you," she said. "It's so crazy, you may not believe me."

"Really?" His eyebrows shot up. "Something crazy about you? I would hardly have expected that. You're the furthest thing from crazy."

"Well, not anymore."

The waitress set down two seaweed salads, giving Ellie a chance to collect her thoughts.

"Okay, here goes. A little while back I got this letter . . ."

She went through the story again. Jason's handsome face wore its usual expression of bemusement until she got to the details of the switching of babies. At that point, his expression turned to incredulity. When she revealed that her biological family was Amish, he burst out laughing.

"You're making this up!" He leaned back in his chair, his laughter growing louder.

She watched him, her heart sinking. This was the reaction she had dreaded. Disbelief, concern, confusion—anything along those lines would have made sense. From there they could have gone on to discuss the situation in more depth, and she might have gained some insight or felt some kind of support from him. She didn't want to burden her parents with her difficulties when they had their own emotions to deal with in this whole mess, and, so far, they had agreed to put off telling A.J. and Nick until they could do it in person, all of them together. It had occurred to her that talking to an outside person might help.

After the discouraging day she had spent at the Kings', she desperately wanted to forget the whole thing. There was no way she was going to become a beloved member of that family, or even be able to connect with them. The gaps between them were too wide. Instead of forgetting the Kings, however, she found she could think of little else. At work on Monday, she sat at her desk in a daze, recalling the way Leah King had looked into her eyes. On the subway ride home, her mind roamed over vividly green grounds surrounding the house. In bed last night, unable to sleep, she saw a parade of images: the food spread out on that long table; Daniel King smiling his friendly smile at her; the smooth, efficient way the sisters served that enormous meal to so many people. Again and again, she replayed the instant she had seen Rachel that first time, stopping to feel the warm sun on her face before sweeping the front steps.

On the phone with her parents right after her visit to the Kings, she presented a highly edited, bland version of the day, feeling bad that she was denying them the details they clearly craved. This was something she needed to mull over for a while, without allowing their feelings to muddy the waters. Before they could probe more closely about Ellie's reactions, she told them that Rachel had a child, their granddaughter. Shock immediately turned into a thrilled fascination, and for the rest of the conversation they kept Ellie busy recalling every detail she could about little Katie.

When Jason called this morning to suggest dinner with him tonight, it occurred to her that he might be the one to lend a sympathetic ear. Big mistake, she thought now, noting the mirth in his eyes, even as his laughter died down. The waitress looked at him curiously as she set two plates of sushi in front of them.

"Oh, honey," he said, smiling, "you can't be Amish. Tough New York career girl wielding a pitchfork. Not you, Ellie, that's not you."

She looked at him without amusement. "That's not the point."

"Oh?" He picked up a piece of a complicated-looking sushi roll with his chopsticks. "What is the point?"

"Jason, come on," she said in exasperation. "I have a different identity than the one I grew up with. Don't you think that might mess up your mind a little bit?"

"I think the point is that you're thirty years old, and it's a little late for this. It might be good to know your background, for medical records and stuff. But it's like finding out you were adopted. You don't have to make it into a huge deal. You can just know it."

"Is that how you would handle it?" Such a simple approach. Could anyone actually do that, she wondered.

He poured soy sauce into a small side dish while he considered her question. "Yes, definitely. I'd go take a look at them, like you did. If they weren't people I could get along with, or if they were part of some weird group like this, then I'd take it in stride and move on."

" 'Move on.' Just like that." Ellie realized that moving on was what Jason did in every situation he had ever told her about, from his jobs to his friends, so why wouldn't he do the same in this one? That's who he was and what he did. She could never be as detached from people as he was, or from life generally.

She pressed on, not sure why she was bothering to continue the conversation. "Remember there's the other baby from that hospital, who's also now a thirty-year-old woman. She's the real child of my parents. What about her?"

"Do you know for a fact she wants to get involved with your family?"

Ellie shook her head. "Not at all. I haven't heard from her since I went there. Although that was only two days ago."

He gestured with his chopsticks. "Well, then. She may have washed her hands of the whole thing." He grinned. "Using cold water, of course. You know—the no-electricity thing."

He chuckled at his joke. Ellie regarded him in silence as it suddenly dawned on her that she simply didn't like him very much.

"Okay, okay, I shouldn't have said that," he conceded, reading her expression. "It's just—what are you going to do? Convert? Why would anybody want to go back to living like some peasant in the Middle Ages? Can you even do that, convert to Amish, or however you'd say it?"

"I don't know." Ellie pushed her mostly untouched plate away from her. She had lost interest in pursuing this with him any further. "I've got an early morning. We should get going."

He looked startled. "Hey, come on. You've got to give me some time to get adjusted to the idea. Let me sleep on it and we can talk about it again tomorrow."

Too little, too late, Ellie thought. Jason had shown his true colors before he had thought to hide them. She might not be in a serious relationship with this man, but whatever their relationship was, if she was going to be with him, he at least had to be a decent human being. She'd been trying to make Jason appear to be one, when he wasn't. Simple, really. Pushing back her chair, she started toward the door.

He put down some bills on the table and followed her. Outside on the street, he took her arm. "Ellie, don't be angry. This is a lot to ask someone to take in. I promise to give it the gravitas it deserves. But don't lose your sense of humor, okay?"

"Sure, Jason, whatever you say." She just wanted this evening to be over.

"Come on," he said with a smile, "I'll hail you a buggy."

She stared at him. Then, without another word, she turned and strode in the direction of the subway station. Interesting, she thought, that without even trying, her Amish family had helped her face the truth about a relationship that had gone on in her life far too long.

Chapter 12

�֍

Rachel tried to ignore the stares from other passengers as she searched for an exit. She was used to being stared at by tourists back home, but here in New York, she seemed to stick out even more. Maybe, she thought, she was overly sensitive because this entire day was so unbearably nerve-wracking.

The street outside was crowded. She saw a line of taxis by the curb and went to the first one. Settling inside, she ignored the curious stare of the driver in his rearview mirror and told him the address she now knew by heart. At times, the car crawled along in traffic, and she felt she was being enveloped by the humid air and car exhaust coming in through the open window. Then the taxi would pick up speed, and the streets went by at what seemed like breakneck speed, too fast for her to take in everything—or hardly anything.

By the time they got to their destination, she had a headache. When she got out at the curb, she paused to stare at the enormous gray building before her. It took up much of the block and rose majestically, with columns beneath intricate carvings of faces and cherubs lining the façade. She found it strangely beautiful and a bit scary at the same time.

"Miss?" The doorman was holding open the door for her.

"Good morning." She entered the dark, air-conditioned lobby, disconcerted by how cold it was after the July heat outside. "Thank you."

He was an older man in a gray uniform and hat. His eyes were kind. "How may I help you?"

"I'm here to see Gilbert and Nina Lawrence, please."

He went behind a small desk. "Who may I say is calling?"

"Please say it's Rachel Yoder."

The doorman finished talking on a telephone and gestured toward the elevator. "Apt 11C. When you get out, make a right."

She thanked him and went toward the elevator. She had ridden in an elevator before, but not one as luxuriously appointed as this one, nor as fast. Her stomach seemed to flip over repeatedly as it ascended.

Ringing the apartment's doorbell, she thought she might actually be paralyzed with fright.

The door started to swing wide, a woman's voice speaking brightly before it was fully opened. "Welcome, Rach—" The name died in her throat as she took in the visitor before her.

"Oh, my God," she whispered.

Rachel was confronted by a woman with short black and gray hair, wearing black cotton pants and a white tunic. Her mother. Rachel felt as if her heart had leaped out of her chest.

This woman had the same dark eyes as Rachel's, the same shaped face. A flash of recognition passed between them. This woman was a total stranger, but totally familiar to her. Suddenly, she understood why Ellie and Leah King had been frozen to their spots when they first met.

"Nina, did you get the door?"

A man's voice filtered down the hallway, and Rachel heard his footsteps approach. He came up to stand behind his wife. Rachel saw he was a nice-looking man with thinning gray hair, dressed in khaki pants and a white shirt. When he reached the doorway, he stopped short and stared.

"Oh, my," he murmured. "I can't believe it."

"Gil?" Nina Lawrence's voice was unsteady. Suddenly recovering, she stretched out an arm to Rachel. "Please, forgive us. Come in. It's just that you look . . . Well, I guess you know."

She put her hand on Rachel's arm and Rachel saw that even their skin coloration was identical, not as fair as the rest of her family's back in Lancaster. She allowed herself to be brought inside, trying to find words.

"I'm glad to meet you," she got out.

"This is incredible," Gil said. "I never dreamed . . ."

"Come in, please," Nina said. Words started tumbling out of her. "Ellie isn't here today. She thought you might want to meet us without having her around. That it would be easier for you. Our other children are here to meet you. My daughter, A.J., brought her husband Steve, as well."

Rachel remembered the shopping bag she had brought and extended it to them. "This is for you. I made it." She wished she didn't feel so awkward.

The woman's face lit up. "Did you really? That was so nice of you."

They reached the end of the hall where Rachel saw a young woman and two tall men standing up in the living room. It was easy for Rachel to pick out which were the brother and sister. They looked exactly like her. And they regarded her with the same shocked fascination that she imagined was on her own face.

Nick stepped forward and they shook hands. "Welcome. It's quite a surprise and pleasure to meet you."

"I don't know what to say." A.J. shook her hand as well. She gestured toward the other man in the room without taking her eyes from Rachel's face. "This is my husband, Steve."

He extended his hand. "I'm very glad to see you, Rachel."

Gil Lawrence joined them. "Why don't we all sit down and get acquainted?"

"Let me get something to drink for everybody," Nina said. "I'll be right back."

Rachel looked around the room, noting its rich-looking sofa and chairs, intricately worked lamps beneath large pleated shades, the enormous Oriental rug. She saw numerous paintings in groupings on the walls, and objects interspersed with books lining the bookshelves. So many things. Too many to look at.

"Please make yourself comfortable." Gil Lawrence led her to a club chair upholstered in a dark green silk, and gestured for her to sit down as the others settled in on the sofa. "We're all somewhat tongue-tied, I think, but I'm sure we'll get over it."

Rachel sat a bit stiffly on the edge of the chair's thick cushion.

"We're also afraid of making idiots of ourselves," Nick added, with a smile. "We wouldn't want you to start out hating us."

"Or worse," A.J. picked up his thread, "we don't want to do anything that would offend you in some way. We aren't exactly well-versed in Amish ways."

"You're not going to offend me," Rachel said. "Please don't worry about such things."

Nina entered the room carrying a large silver tray laden with ice-filled glasses and a pitcher. As she set it down, she shook her head. "Rachel, it's so strange. Coming in from the kitchen, I could have sworn that was A.J.'s voice. You even sound like her." She looked from one girl to the other. "Like your sister."

Rachel shifted uncomfortably.

"Okay, Mom, let's not scare her too much." A.J. picked up the pitcher and starting filling glasses.

Nina set one of them down on a table beside Rachel. "I hope you drink iced tea . . . Is that okay?"

"Thank you."

Nina retrieved the shopping bag Rachel had given her.

"Our guest was kind enough to bring us a gift." She smiled at Rachel as she extracted the bag's contents. It was a small quilted pillow, white stitching in an intricate design over bright pieces of fabric. Rachel hadn't had enough time to prepare anything bigger, but she was proud of the fine stitches and detailed work.

"We do a great deal of quilting," Rachel explained, "and I make quilts, bags, things like this. We sell them at a shop. It's all mostly handmade."

"You made that by hand?" A.J. asked in disbelief.

"It's absolutely lovely." Nina ran her fingers over the stitching. "Look at this. What beautiful work." She passed it over to her husband for his inspection.

Rachel saw they both looked genuinely impressed, but all she could think was that the pillow could not have been more out of place in this apartment. There was absolutely no spot, at least in this room, where it would look as if it belonged. Like her, she couldn't help adding.

"Why don't we start at the beginning?" Gil said, setting the pillow down. "Rachel, would you like to tell us about your family in Pennsylvania, and we'll tell you all about us?"

Rachel took a deep breath, then began. "Well, my family has a dairy farm. After my husband died three years ago, my daughter and I went back to live there."

"Ellie told us about your husband. We're very sorry," Nick said.

"She also mentioned that you have a daughter. Eleven years old, right?" A.J. asked.

"You know what, everybody?" Nina interjected. "We're throwing a lot at Rachel all at once. Let's go into the dining room to have lunch and we can take this a little more slowly."

They got up and filed into the other room, Gil walking at Rachel's side. "We have a great deal to talk about, don't we?" he asked her. "So much for us to learn."

Rachel went through a set of French doors into the dining

room, where she saw a long table set with gleaming dishes and vases of pink peonies, platters of food already set out along a buffet table against the far wall. She took in the heavy chandelier and drapes at the window, pulled open to let in the daylight.

"Please sit here next to me," Nina said, pulling out a chair for her. "If you need anything, just say the word and I'll get it."

Rachel appreciated the kindness in her voice. These people, though—it was as if she knew them, but at the same time they were complete strangers, and she didn't understand or like the feeling. They weren't Amish, and knew nothing about her or her world. They might be her relatives but she had nothing in common with them.

Gil had said they had a great deal to talk about. Rachel wasn't actually so sure.

Chapter 13

Rachel and Sarah settled down into two chairs in Laura's backyard, waiting for her to join them. The three sisters and their families had just finished having supper. Moses and Laura's husband, Lonnie, were off talking together, the children scattered about, with those old enough to be on their own having gone off, out of sight, and the littlest ones playing several feet away. The early stages of sunset were painting the clouds pink. Without speaking, the women watched the sky, as darkness began to assert itself to end the August day.

Laura came out of her house and made her way to them. She pulled a chair closer and sat down. They continued to watch the clouds, not speaking.

Sarah broke the silence. "Your cherry pie is my favorite."

Rachel nodded, her eyes still on the sunset. "Not too sweet, but exactly sweet enough."

Laura accepted the compliment with a simple "Good."

"It's almost time to go," Sarah noted.

"Hmmm," said Rachel, relishing the last few minutes of this warm night and the treat of sitting quietly with her sisters in the fragrant night air.

"Rachel," Sarah went on, "that means it's time to talk." She gave her a meaningful look. "We heard the official story of your visit to New York. Now tell us the rest."

"Sarah, don't make her go over it anymore if she doesn't want to," Laura interjected. "She's already answered so many questions."

"Oh." Sarah gave a dismissive wave. "Their names, and a little information about lunch. This is meeting her real parents! I want to know more."

Rachel sighed and answered in a whisper just loud enough for the women to hear. "As I said at supper, they were very nice. They did their best to make me feel at home. But I definitely didn't. It would be impossible."

Sarah looked thoughtful. "Whether you like it or not, you still have a connection with these people. How do you see yourself fitting in with them?"

Rachel paused. "I'm not sure how I could. Fitting in—I don't know what that means."

"It's not as if she's going to become one of them," Laura remarked.

"Of course not," Rachel replied. "But I don't know what the right thing is here. Those people are my family, too. Should I ignore them? Say, 'okay, we met, and that's all, thank you'? Maybe that's what they're going to say to me. They don't have any idea what it means to be Amish."

"What about what Ellie wants?" Sarah asked.

"I don't know that, either. She really surprised me, not being at lunch yesterday. They said she was trying to make it easy for me, but I thought she would come to introduce me, maybe tell me more about the family." She was silent for a moment. "Of course, I didn't help her out when she came here. Maybe she was paying me back."

"You really don't know what to think about her—or any of them, do you?" Sarah asked.

Rachel shifted uncomfortably in her seat.

"It will be fine, you'll see," Laura said.

Rachel smiled at her youngest sister. "You always have the right attitude about things."

"I have faith."

They turned at the sound of more children approaching. Laura's two daughters were talking and giggling with Katie as they came into view.

"Time to get home. Katie," Rachel called out to her daughter, "say good-bye to your cousins. It's late."

The three women rounded up the children and walked toward the two buggies that would take the guests back to the King farm. Sarah's and Laura's husbands were visible through an open window, their heads bent close together over something in *The Budget*, the newspaper read by so many Amish families.

"Moses," Sarah called as they passed the window, "we're ready to go when you are."

He glanced up and nodded at her, then resumed conferring with Lonnie.

Sarah hoisted baby Christine on one hip. "Rachel, we haven't helped you."

Rachel smiled. "You are helpful, always. Having you two as sisters is a gift."

"All family is a gift," Laura said. "Sisters, brothers, children . . ." Smiling, Rachel gestured to Katie to get in their buggy. Sarah and Moses would be taking their children in their own. Laura said good night and went back to the house. As Rachel untied Driver from the post, she stroked the horse's neck while continuing to gaze at the sky, now a blazing crimson and orange. There was nothing more beautiful than a summer evening at home, she thought. Here, in her real home.

"I'm sleepy." Katie came up to her and rested her head against Rachel.

Rachel moved to put her arm around her child, overcome by a wave of love for her. This was their life. It was, and always would be.

As soon as they returned to the farm, Katie got ready for bed and was asleep almost the instant her head hit the pillow. It was then, when Rachel went to her own room and sat down tiredly on the bed, that her doubts arose again.

She had tried to keep things simple when she described her visit to New York to her family. Now, alone in her moonlit room, she could try once more to untangle the knot of emotions that formed in her stomach yesterday as soon as she had gotten on the bus back to Pennsylvania, and refused to leave her.

The truth, she thought—or was it the *problem?*—was that she had genuinely come to like the Lawrences by the end of their afternoon together. They were direct, which her family here was as well, but they said more, spoke more about their feelings, opened up in ways that Rachel wasn't used to. She felt a connection with A.J. and Nick that amazed her, as she quickly grew comfortable talking to them, something that was completely uncharacteristic for her when she encountered people she didn't know. At one point, the conversation had turned to some of the places Gil and Nina had traveled to, and Rachel found herself rapt as they described different countries and some of the places they had seen. Being with the Lawrences, listening to them, stirred up a curiosity in Rachel that she hadn't felt in years.

That was what troubled her now. Her life wasn't about traveling and asking questions, or eating fancy food in fancy dining rooms. It was about service and family and community. She feared she had allowed herself to be drawn in by what were, in fact, strangers in the course of only one day. She felt disobedient and disloyal to her parents.

She leaned forward and buried her face in her hands. There was no way to straddle these two worlds. It was impossible. She couldn't be Amish and English. She had to choose.

The list of sins Rachel knew she was committing continued to grow. She hadn't drawn a true picture for her family here of her visit to New York; she hadn't confessed to her inappropriate questions and interest in the worldly pursuits of the Lawrences; worst of all, she was hiding the most important fact.

She wanted to go back to see them again.

Chapter 14

�֎

Ellie slung the gym bag containing her tennis gear and racket over her shoulder and started walking downtown in the direction of her apartment. She wanted to enjoy the summer evening for a while instead of getting right into a cab or the subway. Tonight, there had been a few moments when she thought she might confide her situation to Samantha, whom she had known for over two years. In the end, she couldn't bring herself to do it. Samantha was an acquaintance through work, a publicist for a movie distributor, and their relationship hadn't ever progressed much beyond the tennis and an occasional quick bite of dinner afterward. Which left Ellie still frustrated by her inability to get an outsider's view on her peculiar situation.

She fished her cell phone out of her purse and tapped on the screen a few times. Still walking, she listened to the ringing on the other end. She was relieved when her brother picked up.

"You're there," she said.

"I am indeed. What's up?"

"What? What on earth do you think is up? You never called me after your big lunch with Rachel King. Or Rachel Yoder, I guess it is."

"I didn't know you were waiting for a call from me."

"Nick," she said in exasperation, "you didn't think I wanted to hear from you? Like it's an everyday occurrence, meeting your new sister."

"Didn't you talk to Mom and Dad?"

"I avoided their calls today. I know, I know. But I wanted to hear from you and A.J. first. And she's not answering her phone."

There was no answer.

"Nick?"

"I'm here. I guess I feel kind of weird, being the one to explain such a big deal."

"I won't hold anything against you. Tell me how it went."

"Ellie, don't make me do this. You could have seen it all for yourself if you'd shown up. Why didn't you?"

She ignored the question. "Come on. It's not such a big deal for you to tell me."

He gave up. "Oh, all right." He paused, thinking. "At first, it was strange and awkward. Then, somehow, everybody seemed to relax. We talked a lot. Everyone liked everyone else quite a bit."

Ellie wasn't prepared for such an upbeat report, and she wasn't sure how she felt about it. "What did she act like?"

"You've met her. She was nice."

Ellie didn't voice the thought that Rachel hadn't actually been all that nice during Ellie's visit.

"We must have freaked her out when she was introduced. I could see how uptight she was, sitting in the living room. But, I have to give her credit, she got over it. She was genuinely interested in Mom and Dad's traveling, and they, of course, ate that up. They were able to trot out all those old stories we've heard a million times."

"She was interested in their vacation stories?"

"Well, that was just one thing. She wanted to hear about what A.J. and I did for a living. Our jobs seemed to fascinate her. Obviously, they don't do anything like what we do." He laughed. "They actually produce things, instead of just talking about them."

"Did anybody comment on how much she looked like you guys?"

"Oh, wow, how freaky was that? After she left, we all talked about it. Mom was especially thrown by it."

"Like the one that got away, this daughter." She wished she could take back the words as soon as she said them. She didn't want to sound petulant, or as if she was jealous.

Her brother immediately sounded contrite. "I didn't mean it like that. I'm sorry. And, hey, it had nothing to do with you. It was a big shock. She said you looked exactly like her family in Pennsylvania. Is that true?"

She stopped at a curb to wait for a red light to change. "Yes, it is. The sisters, and especially the youngest brother. The mother is me, but older."

"Incredible."

Ellie crossed the street, barely avoiding banging into a man who was walking with his head down. "You have no idea."

"So, what else? Oh, she brought Mom a pillow that she made. I think she likes to laugh. She wasn't exactly cracking jokes, but after she relaxed, you could kind of tell she enjoyed the kidding and stuff around the table. Not that we were kidding her. Each other, I mean."

Ellie thought back to the grim feelings she had had during her lunch at the King farm. Not much laughing going on there.

"How did A.J. take to her?"

"She liked her, definitely."

"And Mom and Dad?"

He hesitated. "Sure, they liked her fine."

"Nick? Come on."

"Look, they just discovered they had another child. They were pretty excited. And she has a daughter, too. The much-longed-for grandchild! It was huge for them."

"Oh."

"Ellie, are you upset?"

Her voice was quiet. "No."

"You are! I *knew* I shouldn't have had this conversation with you."

"No, no, I appreciate it. I'm fine, really. It's a lot to deal with, that's all."

"Of course it is! For everybody. I mean, you most of all, obviously. But none of us knows how to handle this. We don't know how to be, what to expect. Are we going to see this new family member all the time, or just exchange Christmas cards, or what? What are *you* going to do?"

"I wish I knew."

"How did you feel about your other family? I never heard anything other than that you met a bunch of people."

Ellie stiffened. "Sorry, I'm getting another call and I have to take this. Talk to you later."

"But—"

"It's work. Gotta go. Bye!"

She tapped the phone's screen to end the call, and put it back into her purse. She felt bad about hanging up on her brother, but she wasn't prepared to discuss the Kings with him. The disappointment she felt over her lack of rapport with them was growing stronger each day. She didn't know if she was disappointed with them or herself for being unable to see past the surface differences. Not that those differences were so minor, she said to herself; they couldn't be much greater. Still, the letdown of that meeting had left her unhappy and out of sorts. She was embarrassed to admit it, but she couldn't bear to see Rachel make a success of her equivalent moment.

She shifted the heavy gym bag to her other shoulder. That bit of jealousy, she thought, was only one on a list of horrible feelings she had to admit to. Let's really lay it all out, she told herself. For starters, she didn't want her parents to decide they loved this new daughter more than they loved her. Nor did she want her siblings to transfer their loyalty to their real sister. Nor did she want everybody thinking she was an unimportant interloper about whom they could now happily forget. Ellie had a powerful urge to get down on her hands and knees and pound her fists on the sidewalk, shouting, "Get away from my family! They're mine, not yours!"

Her cell phone played the first notes of "Bad to the Bone." Jason. She ignored it. He had called several times since the dinner when she left him on the sidewalk outside the Japanese restaurant. The first few times she claimed to be busy when he asked to see her, but he refused to be deterred. She found it doubly annoying that he had been indifferent to her for so long, but was suddenly longing to be with her as soon as the situation was reversed. She was glad to be rid of him.

Which left her where? she wondered. Did she have any attachments that were much deeper than Jason's? Keeping so busy with her job had allowed her to ignore the truth about how few people she was close to. Now this other woman was descending upon her family from out of the blue, displacing Ellie from her position as eldest daughter and sibling.

Feeling increasingly sorry for herself, Ellie lost interest in what had started out as an enjoyable walk, and ducked into the nearest downtown subway. Back in her apartment, she took a shower, threw on a robe, and sat down to comb out her wet hair.

This is ridiculous, she told herself. She was wallowing in self-pity and paranoia. There was no reason to think anybody was trying to replace her, or that her family would forget she was alive at the first opportunity. If this other Rachel was going to find a way to connect with her biological family, then Ellie needed to take a lesson from her. Maybe they hadn't made a connection during that first visit, but that didn't mean she should give up.

Ellie put down the comb. She knew what she had to do. It was the only way she would ever find out who she really was.

Chapter 15

�֎

Ellie could feel her heart beating faster as she ripped open the envelope from Leah King, wondering what she would find written inside. She had mailed a letter to Leah, asking if she could stay with the family for a week. In it, she explained that she didn't want them to treat her as a guest, but instead to let her be a useful part of the household. Here she was, holding the answer in her hand, yet she wasn't sure if she was hoping for a yes or no.

Leah had used the same plain white paper she'd written on the first time. Now, though, the tone was friendly, if still proper. Ellie was welcome to come; they had been looking forward to another visit, and this would be a chance to get to know each other better. It was signed "Best Regards."

She couldn't help wondering if anyone other than Leah was truly looking forward to another visit. Every time Ellie thought about how she'd acted the first time she'd been there, she felt even more uncomfortable about her behavior and the reactions she had received from the King relatives. She was pretty sure the others hadn't much liked her. And they had good reason to feel that way. Looking back, she could see how guarded she had been. Even worse, she had shown actual disdain toward their house, their food—toward them, in fact. Which was because she had *felt* actual disdain.

The question, she asked herself, was why? It wasn't like her to look down on things or people she didn't understand. Apparently, she hadn't been able to face how scary it was to meet the strangers who were really her family. She had retreated behind snobbery to protect herself. The realization was mortifying.

The next morning, she headed straight to her boss's office to tell him she would be taking vacation the first week of August. The timing couldn't have been better. No explanation was necessary in midsummer. She had completed whatever advance work had to be done for events in the fall, and August was a dead month at the office. Everyone in the business was on vacation as well.

Robert Clark had a large office, decorated with plush leather chairs, a conference table, and a gleaming black desk with a silver computer screen and little else except a tall vase containing a single, exotic flower in it, always white, a different one each week. Ellie stuck her head inside his office door. As usual, he was wearing a perfectly fitted dark suit, looking polished and impeccably dressed. Robert was well liked in their business, driven, but professional and good-humored.

He was standing behind his desk, looking through a sheaf of

papers. Ellie said a quick good morning, and informed him of her plan.

"Okay, as long as everything is nailed down here while you're gone," he said without looking up. "Could you tell Barry to come in here?"

She ducked back out into the hall. Now she was truly committed. One way or another, she would be getting to know the Kings and the world they inhabited.

Over the next few weeks, she grew increasingly nervous about the trip, fearing she was making a mistake, that she would feel trapped if she wanted to leave. She didn't know what accommodations she would have to make to live as they did, and hoped she could handle it.

Several days before she was due to leave, she called her mother, and shared her fears. Nina reassured her.

"We're all stunned by this, sweetheart. And confused. This sort of situation would be impossible for anyone to deal with. That they're so different from us, from anything we know, means we have to figure things out as we go along."

"I don't know, Mom. Rachel at least knows how to deal with people who aren't Amish. I'm at sea here," she said. "I feel like a fool, not knowing what to say or how to act."

"It's not easy. But since when did I teach my children to shy away from difficult things? More to the point," she added, "it might well turn out to be wonderful. These people have been nothing but nice to you. You're more likely to be gaining a second, fascinating family."

"Right," Ellie said, far from convinced.

At last, the Monday she was scheduled to begin her visit arrived. She realized her toned-down but expensive outfit last time had been a mistake, so she put on jeans and sneakers. She packed a few pairs of pants, and several longer skirts and dresses that she bought specifically for this visit; summer heat or not, she assumed no one there would appreciate her shorter hems. She rejected tank tops and sleeveless shirts, opting for items with a more modest cut that covered her shoulders. Beyond that, she wasn't sure what else to bring, so she tossed the suitcase into the trunk of yet another rented car and crossed her fingers.

When she pulled up to the house in the midafternoon, she saw three women off to one side of the backyard, hanging laundry on a long line. They turned at the sound of her car coming up the driveway. Ellie could make out Rachel and her mother, Leah, as they put down the garments in their hands to come greet her. A small black dog appeared from far away, barking excitedly as it raced toward her.

Rachel got there just ahead of her mother. "Welcome."

Ellie, getting out of the car, was surprised at the friendliness in Rachel's voice. "Thank you. It's nice to see you again."

The dog proceeded to jump up and down, vying for Ellie's attention.

"Noodle, down!" Leah was shaking her head. "He's always like this with new people."

Ellie bent over to pet the dog, who stopped jumping to get scratched behind the ears. "Hey, Noodle. Hey, boy." She straightened up. "What a sweet face he has."

"And he knows it," Rachel said. "He's full of mischief, but gives you the big eyes, trying to get out of it."

Leah took one of Ellie's hands in hers, giving her a broad smile. "It's good that you have come."

By now, the other woman by the laundry line was approaching. Ellie recognized her as Rachel's sister, Sarah.

"Have you come to help with the laundry?" she asked, smiling.

"Well, why not? Just show me what I have to do. As I said in my letter, I want to do whatever everybody else does."

A smiling Leah hooked one arm through Ellie's, and led her back in the direction of the wet laundry. "Good. We will work and talk. That's always best."

Ellie saw that every item had been neatly attached to the line with wooden clothespins, the men's pants together, then the boys', women's dresses next to girls' dresses and so on. She admired the picturesque effect, like a family standing in a row. Leah handed her several clothespins and two ends of a wet sheet. She held the other two, and they stretched it taut before attaching it to the line.

They passed the rest of the time exchanging small talk, but Ellie was far more comfortable hanging out wet pillowcases than she had been sitting in their living room. She found she was better able to pay attention to what they were saying, less consumed by her own distracting thoughts. She got the sense that, even though they all didn't share one house, the siblings spent a great deal of their time together.

As they were about to go inside, Isaac King emerged from the dairy barn. He came over to the women, and gave Ellie a smile, his eyes twinkling.

"You have come back. Maybe this week will give us time to know each other better."

"I hope so." She smiled back. "That's why I'm here."

He nodded. "Good."

"I wonder if you might teach me something about the animals, when you have a chance."

"Even better. Tomorrow morning, you'll help me milk the cows."

"Oh." Ellie tried to hide her surprise. "Okay. Great."

Isaac gave a quick wave, and turned to go back to his work.

Rachel picked up the empty laundry basket and accompanied Ellie to her car to get her suitcase. "There's a bedroom upstairs for you, near mine."

They made their way to the small room, which had two single beds made up with colorful quilts, a nightstand in between, and a low double dresser. Short, pale blue curtains framed the windows.

"This used to be my sister Sarah's room, but now it's for guests," Rachel explained. "My daughter's bedroom used to be for my other sister, Laura. Years ago, we three sisters were together up here at this end of the house."

"Sounds like you must have had fun, sisters together like that."

"We did, yes. A lot of laughing and teasing."

Both women were silent, each one struck by the significance of Rachel having memories that, under different circumstances, would have been Ellie's.

"I'll leave you to get settled in."

"What will you do now?" Ellie asked.

"Start cooking supper."

"If I finish up here quickly, may I help?"

Rachel nodded as she left the room. Ellie unpacked, her nervousness returning, then went downstairs to offer her assistance in the kitchen. Leah stood over a large pot of chicken in gravy, while Sarah assembled a salad and Rachel cut up potatoes. Katie, carrying silverware toward the table, stopped when she saw Ellie.

"Hello, again," she said with a bright smile. "You're going to stay with us this week."

Ellie smiled back. "That's right. I hope I can spend some time with you."

"That will be nice."

Katie set down the knives and forks on the table, and Ellie helped her lay out the place settings.

"Come over here by me," Leah called to Ellie. "You can cut these onions. Wash your hands first."

Leah talked to her as she cooked, going over what she was serving that evening and which of the ingredients they had grown on the farm. Later, she said, after they ate and the animals were attended to, most of the family would sit together outside to enjoy the summer night.

"Then you will find out all about us," Leah said. "Not just the little things, like before."

She and Ellie exchanged a smile. So, Ellie thought, she also feels like we didn't accomplish anything the first time. They both wanted to get past that initial awkwardness and start again. It made her feel a lot better.

At six o'clock, the family gathered for supper. Ellie exchanged greetings with Moses, Sarah's husband, and was introduced to their three small children. Isaac came in with Rachel's younger brother, Daniel.

"You couldn't stay away, could you?" Daniel asked with a grin as he hung his straw hat on one of the hooks beside the door. "We are irresistible."

"Daniel!" Leah King reprimanded her son, but she couldn't suppress a smile.

It wasn't clear to Ellie why Daniel deserved the reprimand, so she kept her answer neutral, "I'm happy to be here."

"We are happy to have you here," Leah put in.

Ellie noticed that Rachel was watching her mother with obvious surprise, and what seemed like displeasure. The situation with Rachel was fraught with emotional peril, as Ellie knew all too well. It wasn't going to be easy for either one of them.

"Are Amos and Hannah here?" Ellie asked.

"They are visiting Amos's brother tonight," Isaac said. "But you will see them tomorrow morning."

Ellie was able to relax a bit during supper. Perhaps it was because there was a smaller group at the table than the first time, she thought, although eleven people hardly qualified as a small group. Or maybe it was just because she was exhausted by that point. She was a long way from comfortable, but it was a start. As opposed to her previous visit, this time she bowed her head during silent prayers before the meal, then listened to the conversation, which was minimal, while the family ate their meal. She didn't try to fill the quiet with words, or ask questions about things she didn't understand. Instead, she concentrated on taking in what was going on around her without making assessments or judgments. She took some of the food offered to her, but not everything. No one seemed to notice.

After supper, she helped with the cleanup, and then followed the women and Katie outside to make sure everything was neat and in its proper place. At last, they sat down on the side porch to enjoy the summer evening. Isaac emerged from the house, reaching into his pocket to produce a small mouth organ. He started to play, the notes ringing pure and clear in the night air. The children gathered on the ground in a circle around him. Everyone stopped what they were doing to listen.

Ellie observed it all in fascination. These people had been working hard for hours without rest—her own fatigue could vouch for that—and now they were taking the time to appreciate the idyllic summer evening. No computers or phones with which to contend, or on which to waste time. Nor, for that matter, any meetings to plan, or clothes to lay out for presentations to be made in the morning. No rushing around. Just being there, together, smelling the perfume of the summer flowers, speaking softly below the darkening sky. She was still a stranger, but she could see how appealing this could be. And it couldn't be any more different from her own life. Of course, maybe a week of this would drive her crazy. In fact, she wasn't sure how she would feel after just a few days of playing at being an Amish farm woman.

When Isaac finished, his wife began to sing a slow hymn. Leah's voice was only average, but the words were heartfelt.

Beautiful, Ellie thought, genuinely moved. She looked up at the vast night sky, visible everywhere she turned, nothing to obstruct the view. Whatever might happen, at this moment she was glad and grateful that she had come to this place, and to these people.

Chapter 16

Ellie was awakened by a series of loud knocks at her bedroom door.

Disoriented, she managed to get out a weak, "Yes?"

"Time for the milking." It was Isaac's voice.

"Oh . . . of course." It was dark in the room. "I'm up." She reached out to the night table and felt around for the travel clock she had put there the day before, struggling to focus on the numbers. Four-thirty. "I'll be right there."

"Come to the barn."

His footsteps faded away as he went downstairs. Ellie threw back the covers, groggy and panicked at the same time. She recalled their conversation about her joining him to milk the cows today, but she had not been sure he was serious. He certainly hadn't warned her they would be doing it in the middle of the night. Apparently, this was when the day began here. Not so surprising, she thought, considering that everyone had gone off to sleep last night by nine-thirty. She had followed their lead, but lay in bed, wide awake, her mind darting everywhere, from the events of the day to the office to what she had left undone in her apartment. The last time she had looked at the clock, it was past midnight.

She fumbled to find her jeans and a T-shirt in the darkness, trying not to cry out when she banged her knee against the bed's wooden footboard. After hastily jamming her feet into sneakers and a quick stop to brush her teeth and throw water on her face, she hurried outside, still hopping on one and then the other foot as she struggled to tie her sneaker laces, embarrassed to see that it was already ten minutes to five. And that's without stopping for even a sip of coffee, she noted, which she would have dearly loved. She made her way in the dark toward the enormous white barn. At least it was warm outside. She shuddered to think what it must be like to do this in the winter months.

Entering the barn, she tried not to show any reaction to the strong smell. She saw two long rows of black and white cows, all facing away from the center aisle that ran the length of the building. They were huge animals, she realized, larger than she had expected, some swishing their tails, a few letting out gentle mooing now and then. Some rested on the ground, but most were standing. The floor had been swept completely clean. The smell, she realized, was the unfamiliarity of animals and the manure they produced, passing through grating on the floor beneath their hindquarters.

She spotted Judah, Moses, and Daniel at the far end of the barn.

"Good morning," she called out. Her voice seemed to boom through the building, making her cringe. The three men looked up and each gave her a quick wave.

"Morning to you," Judah replied, his words softer, but loud enough to carry.

She noticed they were all wearing tall rubber boots, and made a mental note to buy a pair when she had a chance. Taking a few steps down the row, she located Isaac, seated on a low stool between two cows. He held up a collection of tubes and metal, immediately launching into an explanation of what he was doing.

"This is a milker. I attach a tube to each of the cow's teats, and it milks the cow, easy, like a person." He pointed as he spoke. "The milk goes through this hose from the barn to the cooling tank in the milk house, which is a separate building outside."

Ellie tentatively reached out to pat the cow on the back.

"We also put disinfectant on the teats after milking to stop them from getting any infections or cracking and such." Isaac smiled. "You have milked a cow before?"

"You can tell I haven't, I'm sure."

"That's all right. Try it."

He turned to the cow on his other side and moved the stool closer as he put a bucket beneath the cow.

"This is the udder. These are the teats. Put your hand around one, like this." He demonstrated. "Then squeeze. That's all there is to it."

She sat down and reached to take the cow's teat in one hand, giving it a squeeze. Nothing happened. She tried several more times, still with no results.

"Don't be afraid. You're not hurting her."

"I can definitely do this," she said with exaggerated determination.

Suddenly, milk squirted out into the bucket.

"There you are," Isaac said.

Grinning, Ellie kept at it, amazed, not only that she was actually milking a cow, but at how thrilled she was to be doing it. She felt somewhat ridiculous; here she was finding something people had been doing for centuries such a big deal. For all her talk about organic this and green that, she knew next to nothing about animals or growing anything at all.

Before she knew it, they were leaving the barn, and her watch read six-fifteen.

"You do this twice a day, every day, right?" she asked.

"Three hundred and sixty-five days," Moses answered. "Cows don't take holidays or vacations."

"It went quickly today," added Judah, "because we were all there. Doesn't always work out that way." He smiled. "And today, you were also there. Our special assistant."

"Ready for some breakfast?" Isaac asked her as they got close to the house.

"I am, but it's not like I did anything to work up an appetite." She smiled. "Mostly hungry from asking questions."

"Test on everything tomorrow." Daniel grinned.

She entered the kitchen with them to a table already set up for breakfast. Leah, Sarah, Rachel, and Katie busily set out platters and bowls of food, Sarah's children darting among them. Everyone took their seats.

Leah put a glass pitcher of orange juice on the table. "As

soon as Amos gets here, we'll eat," she explained. "He's fin-ishing up with the horses. His wife, Hannah, went to bring some of her special medicine to a friend a few miles from here."

As she spoke, Isaac's father, Amos, appeared in the doorway and said a general good morning. Ellie hadn't seen him since her last visit, so she went up to the older man to greet him.

The corners of his blue eyes crinkled as he smiled. "I heard you were back. You are learning how to be Amish, yes?"

"I think that could take me a long time to learn."

"Maybe not. Maybe it is in your blood."

Ellie wanted to tell him how much she wished to know if such a thing might be true, but she wasn't sure if he was joking or not.

"We will do our best to teach you," Amos added.

Ellie felt a rush of warmth toward him. He seemed truly kind. As did everyone here, she realized.

After the silent prayer, they helped themselves to pancakes, sausages, oatmeal, fruit, doughnuts, and bread with butter and strawberry preserves. Ellie usually had only coffee in the morn-ing, but today she was glad to accept the offer of a bowl of oat-meal with fresh blueberries. It was beginning to dawn on her that there was a reason these people ate so much at meals; if they always worked as hard as she had seen them working since she'd arrived, they needed those calories to get through the day.

"Ellie," Leah said, as she refilled coffee cups for the adults, "maybe you will spend today with me. I am ironing in the morning, and later, we can work in the garden."

"That would be lovely. Thank you." Ellie took another sip of the steaming hot coffee.

"If Ellie is with you," Rachel said to her mother, "then I can finish a quilt instead of working in the garden. Is that all right?"

Leah nodded, then turned toward her granddaughter. "Katie, you come with us as well."

Ellie saw Rachel give her mother a sharp look and open her mouth as if to speak, then apparently think better of it. Katie only smiled in agreement as she smeared strawberry preserves on a slice of bread and bit into it with obvious satisfaction.

It was a morning of constant activity, as Ellie helped clean up after breakfast, then straightened her bedroom and the nearby bathroom before assisting Leah in bringing clothes in from the line.

Leah ironed while Ellie folded the pressed clothes or put them on hangers. They had said little while collecting the laundry outside, but Leah began to talk as she moved the iron back and forth across the brightly colored dresses and shirts.

"My husband's grandparents—Amos's parents—built this house, the original part. When they were older and Amos took over the farm, he built that attached part for them to live in. They died, and after Isaac and I got married, we got the farm, and Amos and Hannah moved into that part. Many Amish families do this, you know."

Ellie nodded, although she hadn't known.

"When our daughter, Sarah, married Moses, we built their part of the house. But each is separate, with its own kitchens and all. Judah is across the street with Annie. We are together. It's good. Many hands to help, and we are never lonely."

She looked over at Ellie. "Do you get lonely? You live by yourself, and your people are not near you. You go to an office every day. What is your life like?"

Ellie positioned a man's royal blue shirt on a hanger and smoothed the front. "I guess I was brought up believing I might get married or I might not, depending on what I chose to do. And that I should be able to support myself, so I would be free to choose. But my parents are nearby, and I see my brother and sister. Not like you do here, of course . . ."

Leah frowned. "I cannot understand this kind of living. You are happy this way?"

"Yes, I suppose. I like my job, and I meet a lot of people." She paused, wondering why she was having trouble displaying a lot of enthusiasm for her life. "My work is interesting, I get paid a good salary, I have a nice apartment."

Leah set down the iron as she thought about Ellie's words. "But the people around you? You are part of a community?"

"When you work as much as I do, the people in the company become like a community, because you spend so much time with them. I have some friends. I date."

Uncomfortable, Ellie turned away. For some reason, she felt obliged to defend her life, but she wasn't being truthful. The people in her office weren't a community by any stretch of the imagination; they were competitors who occupied a spot on the corporate ladder either above or below her, and not much more. She had few friends, since she allowed her job to consume most of her life, maybe, she understood, as an excuse not to face her distrust of people. To say she dated was also a stretch, as spending time with Jason hardly qualified as such, and even that was over. She certainly hadn't mentioned the number of times she had recently been struck by unsettling feelings of deep loneliness.

Leah was quiet for a while, sliding the iron back and forth over a pair of black men's pants.

"I'm sure your life is very nice," she said.

Ellie doubted the other woman thought anything of the sort.

"I hope," Leah continued, "you'll think our life is very nice, too. To have another daughter is such a gift. It is hard to understand what happened, but I have faith that it was supposed to be this way and I am happy you are here. I do not expect you to become Amish; that would be very difficult to do. But I want you to understand who we are. And that we are your family."

"Thank you for saying that. This has been hard."

"Hard for Rachel as well. You can see that we have not said anything to her daughter Katie about this, but while you are here, you two should get to know each other. At some time, Rachel will have to tell her the story. It would be good if the child has some knowledge of you, more than just a guest in the house."

That explained Leah telling her grandchild to work in the garden with them, Ellie thought. It was to start preparing her for hearing the truth. Very smart.

"Finished," Leah announced, handing Ellie the last dress, still warm from the iron. "Now it is time to get dinner ready. Stew and noodles."

She smiled, and Ellie saw the genuine warmth in her eyes. She was filled with admiration for this woman who ran such a tight ship and seemed to know how to do everything and, equally important, how to handle everyone. An image of Nina Lawrence flashed in her mind's eye, smiling with pleasure at the sight of her daughter, the way she did every time she greeted Ellie. Their lives were as different as any two lives could be, yet both were so loving.

"Come quickly, now," Leah said, interrupting her reverie. "We still have to gather a few herbs for the pot."

Ellie felt as if the women in this house spent practically as much time preparing food as they would if they were running a restaurant. By the time she was done here, if she paid attention, she could be an expert Amish cook. Which would serve no purpose whatsoever in her life.

The sun was high in the sky when Ellie, Leah, and Katie went to work in the garden after the midday meal, each carrying several empty bushel baskets. They left Rachel inside, sitting by the window, her head bowed over a large, rectangular quilt. It was, she explained to an admiring Ellie, a pattern known as Sunshine and Shadow, with a wide border surrounding small bright squares stitched together to form a series of concentric diamonds.

Outside, it was probably close to ninety degrees. Ellie had on a baseball cap and sunglasses, and forced herself to leave them on even though she felt silly next to the other two, who had only their thin white *kapp*s as protection against the sun. Leah directed Ellie and Katie to pick tomatoes and zucchini, which were planted next to each other, while she gathered lettuce in another section of the garden.

Ellie stopped to inspect the first tomato plant she came to, and tentatively grasped a large, deep red tomato. She gave it a yank, but the plant refused to cooperate.

"It's embarrassing," she confided to Katie, who stood nearby, "but I've never done this before."

"It works better if you twist it a bit," the girl offered.

Ellie followed her instruction, pleased to see the tomato come right off the stalk into her hand. "So heavy," she said, moving her hand up and down slightly to illustrate its heft.

"Do you want to eat that one? I always like to eat the first one I pick at the start of the season. And this is your very first one you picked, ever."

"It's okay?"

"Oh, yes. We have lots of them."

Ellie rubbed it against her shirt a few times, then took a bite. It was warm, fragrant, and delicious.

"Wow, that's incredible. This must be what they mean when they say a tomato is meaty. I never quite understood that before. This has to be the best tomato I've ever had."

Katie looked curious. "Don't your tomatoes taste like that? It's just a regular one."

"No, they don't. I guess what I usually buy in the store is from some other country or someplace far away. It's probably been shipped for days. I mean, I've had really good ones like this, but those are the exception, not the rule. It's fantastic."

"I'm glad." She moved away several feet to attend to the zucchinis, growing close to the ground, hidden beneath huge leaves.

Ellie wondered what to talk about with Katie.

"Your mother makes beautiful quilts," she ventured.

"Thank you. She is trying to teach me how, but I don't know if I'll ever do it like she does."

"Do you want to?"

"It's useful to be able to do them well. All skills like that are useful. My mother sells them, but we make them for each other, too. When a girl gets married, she gets them to start her new home." She lowered her voice conspiratorially. "I know my mother is working on some for me to have when I marry, even though she is trying to keep them a secret. She's so good at it, they'll be very beautiful."

"That will be a wonderful thing for you to have."

"Do you get something like that when you marry? English families, I mean?"

Ellie added another tomato to the growing pile in her basket. "I guess there are traditions like that. Dishes or something. At this point, people can ask for or get all different things. Not like the quilt tradition, which sounds really nice."

Katie brightened. "We also get dishes."

Ellie tried not to smile. "You're thinking about getting married?"

"Not really. But it isn't really too many years away, if I find someone I want to marry. First, I have to get baptized, of course."

"You have to be baptized before you get married?"

Katie paused in her task, trying to figure out how to explain. "You have to be baptized to be Amish, and then you could marry to start an Amish family. That's how it goes, in that order."

"Ahhh, I see."

"My parents were baptized, and then got married right after that."

Ellie knew nothing of Rachel's husband, but she hesitated to ask anything about him. She didn't want to pry.

"My father was Jacob Yoder. He died of cancer." Katie spoke matter-of-factly, as if reciting a list. "He and my mother had a farm, but after he died, we came back here to live with my grandparents and great-grandparents."

This was what Ellie had been told by her parents in New York, after Rachel had visited them. The information had been merely factual then, but today it seemed personal, and she felt a surge of sorrow for this child beside her. One day, she was living on a farm with her young parents, and, the next day, everything changed.

"I'm so sorry about that. Your father, I mean."

Katie kept her eyes down. They continued working in silence. Ellie was intrigued by the maturity of this child. She was so open and direct with adults, but there was nothing rude about it. In fact, it was disarming. She also did what she was told without question or protest. Rachel's sister Sarah had much younger children, but they were also remarkably well behaved.

Ellie added the last tomato she could fit into her basket without toppling the lot of them. "I think I'm about done here."

Katie looked up and nodded. "I've got some more to get."

"What will your grandmother do with all these tomatoes?"

A shrug. "Lots of things. She likes to make big slices, just to eat by themselves. Those are good with everything. And she puts them in tomato sauce, and soup. Oh, and salad."

"You could make a hundred things, I guess. They're so good."

"You should eat with us more if you like our food. I'm sure that would be okay with everyone." She smiled in encouragement.

Ellie had to resist the urge to give the little girl a hug. She was, after all, still something of a stranger, and it might not be all right for her to be demonstrative. Given the complexities of the situation, it might never be all right, especially in Rachel's view. But her heart melted at the generosity of Katie's spirit and her sweet nature. Were all Amish children so loving? Had Rachel been like this as a child? Before she could stop herself, the question popped into her head: Am I looking at an alternate version of myself, if I had been raised here as I was supposed to be?

Later that afternoon, Ellie was in the kitchen chopping up vegetables for the evening meal's salad when the door opened and Judah stuck his head in. Leah, preparing to make macaroni and cheese, turned to her eldest son.

"Yes?"

"Dad and I must go talk to Lonnie. Grandma is also going so she can see Laura. Ellie, do you want to come, too?"

Ellie turned to Leah. "That would be great. Is it okay if I leave you with this work, though?"

She nodded. "Go. You need to spend some time with your sister Laura."

"We're ready to leave. We will wait for you outside." He was gone.

"Thank you." Ellie began to clean up.

"Stop. I can do that. Don't make them wait." Leah made a shooing motion.

Ellie hurried outside to see Judah helping his grandmother into the buggy, a sleek, dark brown horse harnessed to it. The front seat folded down so passengers could get into the back. Judah gestured for Ellie to get in next to Hannah. When the women were inside, he flipped up the seat, and he and his father got into the front. Isaac took the reins and gave a quick click of his tongue, which signaled the horse to take off at a gentle trot.

Ellie smiled at Hannah before taking a look around. The buggy, black with a gray covering, had just a few knobs and levers in the front, the simplest of dashboards. Its seats were covered in what looked like a sturdy cotton velvet. It was a surprisingly comfortable ride, a gentle jogging up and down, although she supposed it could be pretty jarring on bumpy roads or in bad weather. Today, though, she found it delightful to look out onto the grazing cows and horses, the endless rows of corn, the low farmhouses and their silos.

"What do you think of our farm after living in New York City?" Hannah asked, interrupting her thoughts.

Ellie was embarrassed to realize that she had been rudely ignoring her—my very own *grandmother*, she reminded herself. "Your farm is a wonderful place. To be honest, I had no idea how little I knew about farming. Actually, not that I knew so little—I knew absolutely nothing. But everyone is being very kind, trying to teach me."

"And what about everything else?" She gestured to her clothing and the buggy. "Can you imagine this as the place where you grew up?"

Ellie smiled, appreciating Hannah's directness. It reminded her of the people she worked with. Although, she reflected with a frown, their directness was often unkind, in the service of some other, hidden agenda. Here, it seemed, what you saw was what you got.

"If I'd grown up here, I would call you Grandma," Ellie said. "I think I would like that."

Hannah laughed. "A good answer. But, surely, you have more to say than that."

Ellie sighed. "It's pretty hard to imagine me growing up here. But should I even try to imagine it? At best, it may be pointless. At worst, it might lead to a lot of unhappiness."

Hannah put a hand over Ellie's and gave it a gentle squeeze. "I should not have asked that. I don't want to make you sad. We have each day that we are given, and we must live it as best we can."

Ellie had never lived a single day, perhaps not a single moment, she realized, thinking about the day she had been given. She was too busy thinking about the day to come. The challenge to come, the client to come. The failure to come.

"Here we are," Judah said, as his father turned the buggy onto a paved driveway, leading to a white house with green shutters, so similar to the other Amish homes she had seen.

"This is where Laura and Lonnie live." He pointed to a much smaller white building over to the left. "And that's his shop, where he builds the furniture he sells."

As the buggy pulled up to the front of the house, Laura came outside, barefoot, in a green dress beneath her black apron. The men jumped down before helping Hannah and Ellie out. There were greetings all around.

"Lonnie out there?" Isaac jerked a thumb in the direction of his shop.

Laura nodded, and the two men walked off in that direction.

"Come in. I have cookies that are just out of the oven."

Ellie was interested to see that Laura's house was remarkably similar to the Kings', though much smaller. The same type of furniture. A large wooden cabinet displaying china bowls and platters. A calendar and little else in the way of decoration. Steam rose from a large pot cooking on the stove, the fragrance of a meat stew filling the air. Everything appeared spotless.

Laura took some chocolate chip cookies and set them on a plate. "Root beer?"

The three women took everything out a side door, where they settled onto wicker chairs on a screened-in porch. A brown and white cat sauntered over to sit at Laura's feet.

"Where are the children?" Hannah asked.

"The boys are bird-watching with some of the Smucker children." Laura said, picking up the plate of cookies and extending them to her guests. "My two eldest. They're eight and nine. They love bird-watching. My little one is Susie, who's five. She's with Lonnie's sister today."

Ellie marveled to herself at the way these people took care of

each other, as if the entire community was one big neighborhood street, where kids could run in and out of houses, and
everyone seemed to look after everyone else's kids.

"Laura makes candy here on many days to sell at the family's
roadside vegetable stand and other tourist markets," Hannah
said to Ellie. "We should arrange for you to come over when
she's doing that."

"Oh, yes," Laura agreed. "Not tomorrow, but the next day
I'll be making it. Would you like to come see? Tomorrow I
make noodles. Maybe that would be more interesting to you."

These women were unreal, Ellie thought, taking a bite of
the warm cookie. As if they didn't have enough work running
these busy farms and families, they did all these other things on
the side, as if it were nothing. And it was pretty clear they
didn't take classes to learn them—these were skills obviously
passed down from one generation to another. Ellie couldn't
think of a single skill her parents had passed down to her. Not
that it was their fault, she reflected. That just wasn't the way
their world worked. She learned her skills in school, and it was
quite a different set.

"So, Ellie, do you have any questions you want to ask? You're
trying to find out all about us, but there's a lot to learn." Laura
smiled. "I want to help if I can."

Ellie laughed. "Only about a million questions."

"Give me a try. If I can answer them, I will. Anything. Don't
be shy."

Ellie sipped at her root beer. "Okay, here's a silly one. How
do you get your hair like that?"

It was Laura's turn to laugh. "That's easy. We twist the pieces in front tightly. We keep our hair long, but our hairpins are a bit sturdier than yours."

"Here come Isaac and Judah." Hannah nodded in the direction of the approaching men.

"Ready?" Judah called out as they got closer.

Laura gestured for them to come closer. "I'm answering questions for Ellie."

"Do you have any we can answer?" Isaac asked her.

"Here's one for anybody who wants to take it. How are you able to power so many things without electricity? I'm a little confused."

"There are several answers to that," Isaac said. "Some things we can convert from electric to gas power. We also use diesel power."

"Plus hydraulic or compressed air systems," Judah put in.

Ellie hadn't realized there were such sophisticated systems in place. Another example of me patronizing these people, she thought, ashamed. They might choose not to use electricity, but that didn't mean they couldn't use their own resourcefulness to get things done. It was more as if they didn't want to be connected with the outside world, or dependent on it, not that they wanted to live in another century, as they were often depicted.

Ellie got up and, without thinking, extended a hand to Hannah and leaned forward slightly to help her get out of her chair. Surprise flickered across the older woman's face as she took Ellie's hand.

Was she being too aggressive for an outsider, Ellie wondered. She hadn't meant to be presumptuous. It was more that she felt affection for Hannah, the same kind of protective affection she felt for her grandparents in New York.

"What would you like to see, noodles or candy?" Laura asked.

"Both sound good. Whatever day would be easier for you."

"Fine. We will arrange it." She smiled broadly. "It will be fun working on it together, and it will go very quickly with two of us."

Ever practical, these people, Ellie thought. She loved the way they got right to it: Get things done, have a good time but don't waste effort.

Chapter 17

✖

"Will you tell me now? Please, please, *please?*" Katie could barely sit still in her seat.

Rachel held up a finger. "One second, let me just get this bag settled."

She hoisted their suitcase onto the overhead metal rack and sat down next to her daughter. They soon felt the motion of the bus starting to pull out of the station.

"We're moving! Where are we going?" Katie held on to her mother's arm as if to prevent her escape until she answered.

Rachel had been contemplating how to handle this moment since she made the decision to bring Katie to New York. She wasn't proud of the way she had done this, her motive based mostly on a desire to get away from the farm while Ellie was there. In just the three days since she had arrived, everyone, it seemed, had fallen in love with Ellie. Worst of all was having to watch her mother dote on her. It was as if Rachel came upon the two of them every place she turned, working at something or other, their heads close together, talking, occasionally laughing, engaged with one another to the exclusion of everyone else. Her mother might as well have been a stranger, the way she was behaving. Then there was the way Ellie caught on so fast to everything they taught her. Although no one expected her to, she was up to milk the cows in the morning, and back for the evening milking later on. Leah and she cooked together at every meal. Ellie was everywhere, in the hen house with Katie, feeding the calves, sweeping the house, going to town for supplies with Isaac or Judah. She never appeared tired, and happily dove into each new task, the hesitation of the first day apparently gone for good. Leah never had any criticisms of the way she did a job, either; apparently, Ellie more than met her harsh standards for cleanliness and efficiency. The spillover effect meant that Leah criticized everyone less as well, or perhaps she was too distracted to pay attention to anyone else's shortcomings.

Rachel berated herself, praying that she would stop harboring such petty, mean-spirited thoughts. Yet she still felt a pang when she saw Daniel teaching Ellie how to play Rook, the card game her family played together on so many nights over the years. Rachel started to wonder if her fears that Ellie would prove to be the perfect Amish woman were coming true. But it was when Katie started talking about how nice their guest was, and how she hoped she would stay on with them after the week was over, that Rachel decided she couldn't take any more.

Their neighbors had a telephone in a small shack behind their farm, and Rachel used it to call the Lawrences. After assuring them that Ellie was having a good visit and everyone was doing well, she proposed that she take this time to introduce her daughter to them. They were thrilled, and insisted on picking them up at the bus station.

The next morning, while Katie and Ellie were still out gathering eggs, Rachel informed her parents that she and her child would be going to the Lawrences' for the next few days. It was to be a surprise for Katie, and she asked them not to say anything about the destination. Her father looked somewhat taken aback, but Leah gave a quick nod of agreement. Rachel packed one suitcase for the two of them, then informed Katie they were taking a bus ride to a mystery destination. Her daughter was beside herself with anticipation. After breakfast, Isaac took them to the bus station.

"You said good-bye to Ellie?" he asked as Rachel stepped down from the buggy.

"I didn't have the chance," she said, knowing she had made no effort to find such a chance.

Isaac shook his head. "Something is not good here. Please be careful. We can make this a happy event, or we can make it trouble."

Of course, Rachel thought, *he knows exactly what I'm feeling.* She avoided his gaze by turning to take Katie's hand. "We'll see you soon."

"I will tell everyone you have gone on this trip."

"Okay, thank you." She turned away.

"Good-bye," Katie called out to him, waving.

He waved back and clicked his tongue twice, signaling the horse. Driver took off at a brisk trot.

Now that Katie and she were on their way, it was time to tell her daughter where they were going and why.

"I have a big, big surprise for you," Rachel began. "We're going to New York City for a few days."

Katie's eyes opened wide. "*What?* Why?"

"We'll be visiting some nice people who live there. They're actually the parents of Ellie."

"Ellie?" Katie happily echoed. "Is she going to be there, too?"

"No, she's staying at the farm. We're kind of trading. She'll be with our family, and we'll be with her family."

Puzzlement was evident on the little girl's face.

"You see," Rachel said, choosing her words with care, "we have a very unusual situation here. The most giant surprise you ever heard. Ellie's family is yours and mine, too."

Katie tilted her head in bewilderment. Then she laughed. "That's so silly. We have our family. We can't have two."

Suddenly, Rachel wished with all her heart that Jacob was alive to help her make sense of things. He would know how to deal with this.

"I'm going to tell you a strange, funny, weird story," she said, leaning in as if she were going to share a great treasure with Katie. "But, mind you, this is a true story, it actually happened."

Slowly, Rachel relayed the necessary facts. She omitted everything about the cause of the doctor's error, and the nurse's horror at discovering the mistake. She also skipped over the implications of going home with the wrong family, trying to depict it as a tale in which everyone was living the life they were supposed to live and they were all reunited as part of a happy ending.

Katie listened without interrupting until her mother was done, then sat very still without saying a word. At last, she turned her face up to Rachel's and asked, "Who am I, then? Am I Katie Yoder or Katie Lawrence? Who is my family? Who are *we*?"

Rachel froze. It hadn't taken her daughter more than a minute to unearth the essence of confused identities. To discover that the sense of belonging they had always known, as sturdy as a rock, was perhaps not so sturdy after all.

"I like to think we're part of both families," she said. "As if we're so lucky, that we can have two. You and I are Amish. That's who we are. But we can also know this other family and be part of their lives."

"What about Papa's family? Are we still related to them?" Katie's voice was anxious.

"Oh, yes, of course. Nothing has changed. They're still your aunts and uncles and cousins. Papa's parents are your grandparents, just like Grandma and Grandpa are."

Katie took this in, then sat up straighter as something dawned on her. "Wait," she said, "what about Ellie? Is she Amish, too?"

This was harder for Rachel to answer. "She hasn't been baptized, so that's one thing. Right now, no, she's not Amish. I don't know what the future holds. She is spending time with us, learning about us and our ways."

"I like Ellie."

"I know you do. She's very nice." She was, in fact, very nice, Rachel thought. It wasn't Ellie's fault that she was so jealous of her. That was Rachel's own failing.

"What do you think these people in New York will be like?"

"I've met them once before."

"What?" Katie was stunned.

"I was at their apartment in New York City last month. For a couple of hours. They were very kind. And they are very excited about meeting you."

"They know about me?"

"Oh, yes! They can't wait to see you."

Katie face showed traces of both excitement and anxiety. Then, suddenly, she burrowed into her mother's side and said nothing else. Rachel put an arm around her, guessing that her child had absorbed all she could bear to at the moment about such an overwhelming situation. They rode that way in silence until Katie's regular breathing told Rachel that her daughter had fallen asleep.

By the time the bus pulled into Manhattan, Katie was wide awake once more, ready to begin their adventure. Rachel had to admire her child's resilience; she wasn't going to ask any more questions, but would be enthusiastic about greeting whatever might come next. It was clear to Rachel that meeting Nina and Gil Lawrence in the station was, for now, less significant to Katie than seeing the throngs of people. She greeted her new grandparents politely as they exclaimed over her, but her eyes were drawn to the crowds around them. When they got outside, it was as if Katie didn't know where to look, at the faces or the tall buildings or the endless stream of traffic. The

Lawrences ushered them into a taxi, where Katie sat, one hand tightly gripping her mother's, with her face glued to the window while the adults talked.

Riding in an elevator was another new thrill for Katie. Once they got into the apartment, Nina took the two of them on a brief tour to explain where to find whatever they might need.

"You have your choice of bedrooms," she said to Katie. "If you want, you can stay with your mother in here." She opened the door to a room with twin beds. "Or, you can have your own room." She moved down the hallway to another bedroom, this one with a double bed.

"Thank you."

Katie was taking in the expensively furnished surroundings. Rachel watched, forcing herself to stay quiet. She had been overwhelmed when she first visited; she could only imagine what Katie was thinking. Neither of them had ever been in a home like this one.

"These were my children's bedrooms while they were growing up," Nina explained.

"They don't look like children's rooms." Katie touched the duvet cover on Nick's former bed, stark white linen with a thin navy blue rectangle outlined within its borders.

Nina smiled. "It's been a long time since a child lived here. They all live in different places now, so we've made the rooms more like guest rooms. Anybody can stay here." She rested a hand on Katie's shoulder. "It's a big treat to have a child here again. If there's anything you can think of that would make you feel more like you're in your own room, please tell me."

Katie looked at her in surprise. Rachel knew she was thinking that the only way this would feel like her own room would be if they moved nearly everything out.

"Help yourself to towels, extra pillows, whatever you like." Nina took them back into the hall and opened a closet door to reveal shelves of neatly stacked linens. "Of course, any time you're hungry, you should go into the kitchen and take whatever you want. We stocked up on things we hope you'll like, but you have to tell me what I missed."

Katie gave her a reassuring smile. "Oh, no, we won't need anything else. I'm sure it will be just right."

Rachel nodded, pleased by her daughter's appropriate manners. "You have been too kind to us already."

Gil, coming to join them, interjected. "Come now, we haven't been kind at all. We have yet to do a thing for you. But we hope to."

"I thought you might like some time to unpack and relax, maybe lie down. If it's all right with you, we arranged to go out to dinner with my son, Nick. That won't be until seven." Nina looked at Rachel. "Will that be okay?"

Rachel smiled. "I look forward to seeing Nick again and introducing him to Katie. But we don't need to lie down. We have done nothing at all today except sit on a bus. So I'll unpack, and then we'll be ready to do whatever you like."

"But why do you have dinner at seven?" Katie asked in confusion. "Don't you get hungry if you don't eat all day? What time do you have supper?"

Gil was the first to understand. "We call them different

names, that's all. We call our midday meal lunch, and our evening meal dinner. But we can do it the way you're used to. Breakfast, dinner, supper. Easy."

"No, no, please don't change anything. I see now." As she spoke, Katie went over to the window in Nick's room to look at the view below. She gasped. "It's like we're in the clouds. The people are so small! The cars!"

"At home, we have no reason to be so high up," Rachel said.

"Oh, Katie," Nina said, going to stand beside her, "we have so many things to show you. We want you to have a wonderful time, and New York is a wonderful place."

"We hope you'll come to love it as we do," Gil added.

Rachel felt a twinge of nervousness at the words. "Why don't Katie and I put our things away now?"

"Whenever you're ready, we'll be in the living room." Nina went over to her husband and hustled him away.

Katie sat down on the bed and bounced up and down, gingerly at first, then with more energy. "So thick and soft," she marveled. "I want to sleep here if it's okay." Her eyes darkened. "Did you bring the rubber sheet?" she whispered.

Rachel nodded. "Of course. Don't worry."

Katie stood up and moved around the room. "This is how the people in New York live, in places like this?" she asked in amazement.

"No, no, not all in places like this," Rachel hastened to correct her. "From what I know, most people live in smaller places, and they don't have so many things."

"Do they want so many things?"

"I guess some do and some don't."

"I wouldn't know what to do with so much. It's a lot to dust."

Rachel smiled. "I like our house, don't you? Simple, clean. It leaves us free to spend time on what's important."

Katie came over and reached up to hug her mother. "I like our life. This is so strange."

Rachel stroked her hair, relieved. She hadn't realized until now how worried she was about Katie's reaction to the opulence of the Lawrences' world. Instilling the seeds of acquisitiveness in her child would have been unforgivable. "I like our life, too."

Still, she thought, they had only been there an hour or so. They would have to see what happened by the end of the trip.

By late afternoon, Katie had regaled her new grandparents with tales of the farm, her favorite calves, their cat and two dogs, and what they grew in the garden. She told them that her grandmother at home could do everything, and how they preserved fruits together. After the Lawrences showed Katie the pillow Rachel brought them on her last visit, they heard more about her quilting skills—until Rachel stopped her daughter, reminding her that boasting, even on someone else's behalf, was not to be done. Nina served lunch, an assortment of breads, meats, and salads. Katie happily munched on a tuna fish sandwich with carrots and strawberries on the side, while talking about how much she liked Ellie.

Afterward, they all went out for a walk to get ice cream. If Katie noticed the stares from people on the street, she didn't comment; having tourists in Lancaster County whisper and point at her family's clothes had prepared her. In fact, it was Katie who was busily whispering about people they passed. She was intrigued by the women in business suits with briefcases, and the teenagers in leather jackets and miniskirts. Rachel was amused to see that, by the time they strolled back toward the apartment, everyone trying to enjoy their cones before the August sun melted them, Katie looked as at home on the New York streets as a little girl in a white *kapp* and long gray dress could look. Obviously, she liked the Lawrences and was happy to learn about this city, as foreign to her as another world would have been. When Katie missed her step coming off a curb and nearly fell, she grabbed Nina's hand to steady herself. Rachel saw the look of joy that crossed the older woman's face when the girl continued to hold her hand as they resumed their walk.

This was either a wonderful, miraculous reunion or the worst idea she'd ever had.

That evening, before they left to meet Nick, Rachel went to check on Katie. Her daughter had settled into Nick's old room, putting away her clothes in his closet, remaking the bed to put her rubber sheet on it. Rachel opened the door to find her in front of a television set on a stand in the corner, mesmerized by a cartoon. Rachel hadn't noticed the television was there earlier.

"Katie!" She couldn't keep the shock out of her voice.

The little girl whirled around. She quickly pressed the power button and the screen went dark.

Rachel went over to her, and put a firm hand on her arm. "We don't do this. We are visitors, and, yes, they have offered us to help ourselves to everything here. But we are Amish, and you know this is not for us."

"I'm, I'm sorry. It was just, it . . ." Katie was stammering in guilt and fear.

Rachel stopped herself, taking a deep breath. She had put her child in this situation, and then expected her to know what was allowed and what wasn't. It wasn't fair. She brought Katie over to the bed, and they sat down on it, facing each other.

"I shouldn't have yelled at you like that. This is confusing for you, I know. It was just a bad surprise when I saw you like that. We will have to figure out how to do these things we don't usually do, and when we have to say no. So . . . how about we agree that we stay away from television, computers, and telephones unless we have no choice. Okay?"

Katie, her head down, nodded.

"If I think of other things I'll tell you, but I promise not to yell at you if you accidentally do something you're not supposed to. Okay? And will you promise not to yell at me if I do?"

Katie looked up, a small smile on her lips at the notion that she would yell at her mother. Rachel gave her a long hug.

"You are doing very well here."

Katie hugged back even more tightly.

"Now let's go out to, as they say, dinner. Or will they be calling it supper from now on? Maybe we'll start calling it dinner and they'll call it supper."

"That would be funny." Katie laughed.

"Either way, wash your face and hands."

The four of them walked to the restaurant, which was only a few blocks from the apartment. They arrived before Nick, and sat down at a round table. Katie was quiet once more, taking in the well-dressed patrons and waiters dressed in black. Her mouth opened slightly in astonishment when she saw the menu's prices.

Gil must have noticed and understood her concern, because he spoke at that very moment. "I hope you know, Katie, that you and your mother are our guests for this entire visit. That means we take you and pay for it and celebrate this very special occasion of having you here. It's the way we can show you all the special places we like."

Nina caught on at once. "You order whatever sounds tasty to you, Katie. The food is good here, but you'll have to tell us if it's really as good as what you grow and eat at home. Fresh food is the best."

"Hello, again."

All eyes turned at the words to see Nick approaching Rachel, a broad smile on his face. He put out his hand to shake hers. "This is a great surprise, getting together again—but now I get to meet your daughter." He moved to stand next to her. "Hello. You must be the Katie about whom I've heard such wonderful things."

Suddenly shy, she nodded.

"This is our son, Nick." Nina jumped in to spare Katie from having to say anything.

He knelt down so he was no longer towering above her. "I'm very glad to meet you."

Katie considered him. "You're Ellie's brother, right?"

He nodded.

"Which means you're my mother's brother, too. So you would be my Uncle Nick, wouldn't you?"

The adults were caught off guard by her comment. Startled,

Nick thought about what she had said. "Well, yes, of course, you're absolutely right. I'm your Uncle Nick. And you're my niece." He grinned. "Wow. I have a niece!"

"Okay." Satisfied, Katie smoothed her napkin in her lap and reached for her glass of water. The adults exchanged looks with one another, not sure what to make of how quickly and calmly she had assessed the part she played in this puzzle.

Nick took the empty seat between his mother and Katie. "What do you think of New York City so far?" he asked her.

Her face lit up. "I love it!"

Again, Rachel felt uneasy, wondering what she had opened up by bringing her child here. The Lawrences, however, grinned with pleasure.

"And we haven't even gotten started," Gil said to Katie. "Tomorrow, The Metropolitan Museum of Art, the Empire State Building, and a ride on the Staten Island ferry to see the Statue of Liberty."

"You can't come to New York without seeing the things it's famous for," Nina added. "We'll start with the big ones and work our way down the list."

"Um, maybe that's a little bit much in one day, guys?" Nick said to his parents.

They looked at one another. "You're probably right," Gil said to his son. "We're going overboard, huh?"

Nina looked at Rachel. "It's just that we're so excited to be able to show you around."

"Whatever you want to do will be perfect," she reassured them.

"Hey, it's summer," Nick said. "How about listening to a

steel drum band in Central Park? Rent a rowboat there and bring a picnic. You can people-watch and still see the skyline all around."

Katie brightened at his words. "That sounds like fun."

Nina nodded. "Central Park it is. That will be our day, and then, the next night, we're having some of our relatives over to meet you in the evening. You can understand, I'm sure, that they're dying to see you both."

Rachel wasn't sure if she was ready for all that, but she recalled that Ellie had been faced with a group of King relatives on her very first visit to the farm. It was only fair, she supposed. "That will be very nice."

Nick smiled. "Oh, you think so, do you? You haven't met them yet."

"Nick!" Nina took an ineffectual swipe at him with her napkin. "They don't know you're just teasing."

"What makes you think I'm just teasing?"

Nina turned to Katie and rolled her eyes. "Ignore him, sweetheart. He's joking. They're lovely people."

The waiter came over to ask if they were ready to order.

"Katie," Gil said, "do you know what you'd like?"

Rachel bit her lip. It was also not right for an eleven-year-old to be the center of attention this way, all the grown-ups fussing over her and allowing her to order her food first. This was not their way. She could imagine how upset her mother would be if she knew.

"Why don't you go first?" she said. "Katie and I need a few more minutes to look."

The others listened while the waiter recited the specials.

Rachel leaned over to her daughter, whispering in her ear to remember her manners, no matter how nice and casual everyone was to her. Katie nodded, slipping her hand into her mother's. Rachel gave her an encouraging smile. She felt a stab of guilt. Monitoring Katie's behavior so closely gave her an excuse not to face her own apprehensions about the situation. These people were family, but they felt nothing like it.

Chapter 18

Rachel poured herself a glass of milk and took it to the dining room. She sat down at the table and gazed out the window, marveling at how bright the streets were at three A.M. Even at this hour there were lights everywhere, on the streets, in signs, some still blazing in apartments. The outside glow made the kitchen more than bright enough, with light glinting off the stainless steel of the appliances. Between the lights and the noise outside, she wondered how people got a night's sleep. It was hard to believe that she could hear the cars below all the way up here on the eleventh floor. She took a sip of milk. It was cold, but certainly not as good as the fresh milk at home. *Every single thing here is different*, she thought.

"I thought I heard someone," Nina said, tying the sash on her robe as she came in to sit down. "May I join you?"

She smiled. "Forgive me if I'm staring. Obviously, this is the first time I've seen you with your hair down. It's the strangest thing, how you look so much like A.J. and Nick. I think, she's not even related—but then I remember that you are related, as closely as any family members can be. It's just an indescribable sensation. The confusion of it all, emotionally."

Rachel sipped at her milk. "I understand."

Nina sighed. "I'm not sure I could ever understand what this is like for you two girls. I mean, I'm so furious at that doctor and nurse for allowing this to happen, and then keeping it a secret. It was an unforgivable crime, and I can't even confront them. Yet, I can't picture life without Ellie."

"Exactly. I can't picture my life being any other way."

Nina nodded. They sat in silence for a bit.

"Tell me." Nina put a hand on Rachel's arm. "Are you close with your family? Have you had a happy life so far? Maybe I'm overstepping. But can you imagine how much I want to know if my child has led a good life, the one we would have hoped for? If there are people who love her, and are kind to her."

"Oh, yes," Rachel replied. "You don't have to wonder about that for a minute. My family is very close. I'm surrounded by people who care for me, and for Katie. We work hard, and we try to live the best lives we can. In that, we find our happiness."

"Was your husband a kind man?"

Rachel smiled. "The kindest man you could ever hope to meet. We had a very good marriage for nine years. Happy, as you say. And he left behind our Katie, my most precious gift in the world."

"I'm so sorry you lost him."

"Thank you." Rachel didn't wish to elaborate on her feelings for Jacob or how his death still hurt.

Nina got up. "I'll leave you to your milk and your thoughts. But I hope you see that my husband and I desperately want to know the two of you. We want you to be part of our lives. The one thing we don't want is to make your life difficult. We'll have to follow your lead on this."

"Thank you. I already know that you two are very kind as well." Rachel smiled. "I can tell I would have had a good life here, too."

Nina smiled, but there was pain in her eyes as she left.

Rachel had no right to expect these people to care for her, regardless of their biological connection. Yet they did. She took a last sip from her glass and went to wash it and replace it in the cabinet. She felt sure she would sleep now.

The next day, she and Katie were up by six, dressed by six-thirty. Rachel couldn't recall the last time she had slept so late. When Nina and Gil emerged from their bedroom at seven-thirty, still in their robes, they took a look at their two fully dressed guests and immediately retreated back into their room, emerging in their clothes twenty minutes later. After a breakfast of eggs and toast, the four of them ventured into the bright, hot day, Gil carrying a fully packed picnic basket. They went to the zoo in the morning, an excited Katie running from one animal to the next.

Next, they followed Nick's advice, renting a rowboat for a ride on the park's lake. Katie and Gil shared the rowing duties, sitting side by side on the narrow bench, each holding an oar. They spent much of the time taking the boat in a circle, as his stroke was stronger than hers, and he was enjoying Katie's laughter at their inability to get anywhere. His clownish bewilderment at her instructions to row less forcefully made her laugh harder. Late in the afternoon, they settled down on a shaded patch of grass to enjoy their picnic of peanut butter and jelly sandwiches, broiled chicken, cherries, and potato chips. Rachel was growing weary of having passersby point at her and her daughter, but Katie was oblivious, happily chatting with the Lawrences about the animals at home, how much she liked rowboats, and what it was like when they were in the countryside back in Pennsylvania.

Later, at her request, there were more ice-cream cones, followed by a happy, tired walk back to the apartment. Nina cooked dinner that night for them, spaghetti with turkey meatballs, sautéed spinach, and a salad, refusing all of Rachel's efforts to help. Rachel was proud of Katie for praising the meal, even though she could see her daughter didn't enjoy the unfamiliar recipes. This time, the two of them ignored Nina's protests, and insisted on cleaning up the kitchen by themselves. Rachel felt much better, having something useful to do. Two days without a schedule of any kind, and no responsibilities to which she had to attend, had left her restless and a bit anxious. She didn't enjoy the sensation of floating along with no purpose, letting others take care of her.

The next morning, they took a ferry ride to see the Statue of Liberty. Both Rachel and Katie were stunned by the vision of the majestic green woman, and couldn't stop marveling at it throughout lunch and all the way back uptown. Later, Nina took Katie out for a stroll around the neighborhood.

Still feeling unsettled, Rachel was glad when Katie and Nina returned from their walk, Nina informing them that she was taking them out for tea with Gil's sister, Lillian. When they were in the bedroom getting ready to go, Katie asked her mother why they couldn't make tea right there, and Rachel could only shrug.

Rachel's voice was quiet. "There is a lot here we don't understand."

Rachel wrapped her daughter in a hug.

"Everybody ready?" Nina's voice rang out from her bedroom.

"Coming!" Katie raced from the bedroom. Through the doorway, Rachel could see her giving her new grandfather a good-bye hug.

A taxi took them to the Plaza Hotel. Rachel and Katie had to pause outside to take in the sight.

"Beautiful!" breathed Katie. "Look, carpet outside, on the steps!"

"It's a very, very old building," Nina informed her. "It was one of the grandest hotels anywhere. Gil and I stayed here on our wedding night."

"You had no place to go?" Katie asked in concern.

Nina smiled. "We did, but this was a special treat. Then we left the next morning for our honeymoon in France."

Katie looked confused. "When people back home get married, later they visit the people who traveled to their wedding.

But the two of them don't go anywhere alone to another country. Why would they?"

"More traditions." Nina took Katie's hand. "Come, let's go meet Aunt Lillian."

Katie discovered the fun of going around and around in the revolving door. At first, they could see she was afraid she wouldn't get out in time, but then she started to enjoy the ride. They waited patiently until she took one last turn and practically leaped out into the lobby.

"Ohhhh . . ." Her eyes traveled everywhere at the sight of such luxury.

Nina led them toward the Palm Court, the three of them ignoring the stares of the people walking past. Both Rachel and Katie were spellbound by the enormous space of glass and mirrors, the lavish table settings, the palms in pots strategically stationed around the room.

"There she is." Nina waved at a woman seated at a table for four, who immediately rose and waved back. Rachel saw a tall, very thin woman in a short, tight, white dress with huge flowers printed on it.

"Hello, Lillian." Nina approached in front of the other two, leaning in for a kiss on the cheek. "I'm pleased to introduce you to my daughter and granddaughter."

At the sight of Rachel, Lillian put a hand to her heart, the motion making her numerous gold bracelets jangle. "Oh, Nina, would you look at that?" she said, as if her sister-in-law was the only one who could hear her. "The resemblance . . . I'll be da—"

"And this," Nina cut in, "is Rachel's daughter, Katie. My granddaughter."

Lillian forced herself to turn her gaze to the little girl. She gave her a big smile. "Well, aren't you as cute as a button?"

"Thank you," Katie replied. "But we don't use buttons. Do people here think they're cute? I didn't know that."

Lillian let out a raucous laugh. "Precious!" She sat down again and the others settled into chairs as well. "I've taken the liberty of ordering. There's a special tea for children," she turned to Katie, "so I told them to bring that for you."

"Thank you." The girl clearly didn't understand what could be special about a cup of tea for a child, but she knew better than to ask.

It became evident when the food started to arrive, trays of tea sandwiches, pastries, and scones. The waiter brought a different selection of items for Katie, including peanut butter and jelly sandwiches, chocolate cupcakes, and peppermint iced tea. While Lillian threw questions about their lives at them, Rachel and Katie tried the delicacies set before them. They were loath to leave food after being taken for such a fancy treat, but neither one could finish. Rachel reflected that they had done no physical work since they had come to New York, so it wasn't surprising all the food they were eating had left them stuffed to the point of discomfort.

After tea, they decided to go for a stroll around the lobby.

Lillian turned to her sister-in-law, lowering her voice only slightly. "I hadn't realized how complicated the Amish thing would make this. Must be keeping you and Gil on your toes. How are you managing?"

Nina put an arm around Katie. "It's as easy as could be." She looked at the little girl and gave her an affectionate squeeze. "Right, kitty-cat?"

Katie smiled up at her. "Right."

Rachel had been watching, holding her breath. Finally, she could exhale. Whatever else might happen, Katie seemed okay. She might even benefit from this unnerving acquisition of a new family. They could go home and tuck away the memory of this trip as a happy adventure they would always remember.

Chapter 19

�֎

Ellie stared at her cell phone. This was the first time she could remember ever letting the power drain completely. It wasn't that she couldn't charge it at the Kings'; she could plug it into her car lighter with a special adapter, as she had the first few days she was here. The point was that she had forgotten to charge it. She'd forgotten even to look at it. She thought back. It must have been three days since she last checked for messages. She had sent a few work-related emails and texts, and then put the phone in a dresser drawer, beneath her makeup case. It was only because she was packing to leave that she had come upon it now.

The strangest part of it, she realized, was that she had no interest in charging the phone and finding out what she was missing. Normally, her instinct would be to run and to find a power source so she could start frantically replying to what had to be a massive pileup of messages. Yet she felt no urge to do so. She had told everyone at the office to refrain from getting in touch with her this week unless there was an emergency. They ignored her instruction as she knew they would, and sent a barrage of information and questions, some of which were important, most of which could wait. Why, she thought, couldn't she take a few days off without constant interference about every stupid thing that went on at Swan and Clark? The world wouldn't come to an end if she didn't know the exact second an actor client walked off a picture in a huff, or a corporate merger important to one of their clients had fallen through. She wasn't there, she wasn't going to do anything about it now, and she didn't care.

Ellie sank down on the bed. There it was. She didn't care. Never, never, never would she have imagined those words could come out of her. What had happened to her in the course of less than a week? She had taken plenty of vacations over the years, but she had always stayed on top of what was happening back at work, and felt recharged when the week was over, eager to get back to her desk. This time was different. She didn't want to go back to New York and her apartment. And she definitely didn't want to go back to Swan and Clark.

She liked it here. She liked the people, the farming, the animals. At home, when she worked hard, she was rewarded by some celebrity's indifference at having been spared a public humiliation he deserved, or by a corporate spokesperson who only wanted to know why Ellie hadn't put out some proverbial fire even faster. Here, she was rewarded by plants that would grow, cows producing milk that supported the family, a smoothly running farm where everyone pitched in. No one was praised, but all were appreciated. When she worked hard here, she felt as though she was actually producing something tangible. No office politics, no gossip, no making nice to people she couldn't stand. She and Leah could work side by side, either talking or in comfortable silence, cooking, weeding, washing. There was less physical demonstration of affection among the family members—that was something Ellie saw right away, a notable contrast from her parents, who were big on hugs and kisses. It didn't bother her, though. She could tell Leah felt genuine affection toward her, and she hoped Leah knew it was returned. Rachel's siblings were more guarded toward her, with the exception of Daniel, who was clearly the most easygoing, but Ellie could understand their hesitation. Their allegiance was to Rachel rather than to some interloper who appeared out of the blue. Still, they were invariably kind, and always helpful to her. Isaac seemed to be trying his best to welcome her, although she could see it was a battle for him, as if he didn't want to betray his loyalty to his other daughter. Still, it made no sense to expect everyone to open their arms to her in under a week. Whatever emotional terms they all came to would take a long time. In the meantime, they made her feel as if she were a valued member of the group, her contributions important.

She was struck by another realization. Her stomach no longer hurt. The stomachache that had been her constant companion for years was gone.

"It can't be . . ." she whispered.

Nonetheless, it was time to go. She wanted to stay another week, but she felt the obligation of her job. It would be unfair to impose any further on the Kings. She—and they—had to think about all that had transpired that week. Ellie wasn't sure what would happen next. She knew the Kings weren't coming to visit her in New York. If they were to see each other, it would be because she came back here. Yet she wasn't sure if she could keep coming back as a guest, especially with Rachel here again. In fact, Rachel and her daughter were returning that night from their few days in New York, and Ellie was relieved she would be gone before evening so they wouldn't have to cross paths. She had been unpleasantly surprised when she learned that Rachel and her daughter had taken off for New York. It was almost furtive, leaving without so much as a good-bye. As if Rachel wanted to sneak off to see the Lawrences specifically because Ellie wouldn't be there.

Ellie pulled her suitcase out of the closet and set it on the bed. It was odd that after nearly a week, she understood no more about what it meant to be part of another family than she had before. She assumed she would get some clarity about it, but the reverse was true. She had developed a deep admiration for these people, particularly Leah, but she felt fiercely devoted to her parents at home. She also wasn't sure how to address the fact that they were Amish. If her biological family had been, say, another family in New York, what would that have meant? Maybe she would have liked them, everyone would have gone out to dinner together, and the two families would get along swimmingly. It was impossible for her to judge what part their being Amish played in her feelings. At first, it made her want to retreat from them. Now, it was just the reverse.

The next morning began as usual, Ellie helping with the milking before breakfast. She was sad to be leaving, but everyone else was caught up with their usual duties, and made no reference to her departure. She understood that; they attended to their priorities as a matter of necessity in their way of life.

After breakfast, the family members made it a point to say good-bye to her before their daily chores took them away for the day. Laura and Lonnie even drove over in their buggy just to wish her well. Ellie could see that Isaac was warming up but was still a bit hesitant about how to treat her. He gave her a handshake and a kind smile, telling her to be careful driving and come back to see them very soon. Leah was clearly sorry to see her go. She gave Ellie a hug, telling her that she would always be grateful for this gift.

"I will wait to see you again," she said. "You must come back. You must. Yes?" She searched Ellie's eyes for a reply.

She nodded. The connection between the two of them was unspoken but powerful. "As soon as I can."

Leah walked her out to the car and waved as Ellie went down the driveway. In the rearview mirror, Ellie saw her fold her arms and go back inside, no doubt to start preparations for the midday meal. Schedules, the day proceeding like clockwork, Ellie thought. That notion somehow seemed right to her. Being pulled in a million directions at work sometimes left her feeling suffocated, unable to think. She was always having to choose what to deal with first, running from problem to problem. Here on the farm, with more restraint, oddly, came more of a sense of freedom. Everything had its time and place, within the cycle of the day, the week, the season.

Hours later, when she saw the New York City skyline ahead, she felt disoriented, as if she were traveling between two worlds. Disappointment flooded her when she unlocked the door to her apartment. It was so small and quiet. Just a place to sleep, without any joy to it. She wondered what the Kings were doing now.

The light on her message machine blinked on and off. Her parents, Nick, and A.J. had all checked in, wanting to hear about her trip. Before she got into it with her parents, she decided to talk to her sister to find out what had transpired in her absence.

A.J. answered her phone right away, obviously having checked her caller ID. "Hey! How was it?"

Ellie smiled, happy to have an excuse to talk about the Kings. "Amazing. The way they lived, A.J.—in a different era, with completely different ways of looking at the world. It was hard work, but so peaceful."

"How'd you get along with them?"

"Leah, my mother, was incredible. She—"

"Your mother?" A.J. interrupted. "You planning to call her that when you see Mom?"

Ellie stopped. "Um . . . no, I guess not, huh?"

A.J. sighed. "Oh, what do I know? It kind of caught me off guard. But she *is* your mother."

"Well, what about Rachel? Did Mom describe her as her daughter?"

"Oh, that was nothing compared to being able to introduce their *granddaughter*."

"Katie. Of course. That must have been huge for them."

"They had a family dinner, but we couldn't go down for it. Nick said Katie was the hit of the evening. Apparently, she's a very polite and self-possessed child. Not your basic obnoxious preteen at all. Everybody loved her."

"How did Rachel do?"

"From what Nick told me, she was great. Mom and Dad pulled out the stops to show them the city, ran them all around. The four of them got along like a house afire."

"Really?" Ellie tried to sound enthusiastic, feeling left out and knowing she was being ridiculous.

"They adored Rachel. You know, another daughter, as far as they're concerned. Mom couldn't stop raving about her to me on the phone. Even Dad told me what a fine individual she was, or some Dad-like phrase. Nick liked them both a lot, too. He said the little girl was really smart."

"Oh." Ellie wondered if any of the Kings would rave about her. Then it occurred to her that raving about anybody was not something she could imagine them doing. It wasn't their way. They didn't boast and they didn't rave. She felt her shoulders relax.

"I better check in with Mom now."

"Definitely," A.J. agreed. "She'll be dying to hear the details. So you're okay?"

"I am. It was like nothing I've ever experienced on pretty much every level."

"I'll bet."

"Let's talk later."

" 'Kay. Bye."

After she hung up, Ellie went into her kitchen and poured herself a glass of red wine. She took a sip only to find she had no interest in drinking it. As she poured it down the sink, she thought about work on Monday. She could only assume that what she was feeling now—dread at facing her own life, longing for what she had just left behind—would fade, the way a suntan and the sense of relaxation that followed a vacation inevitably did. She needed to get back to reality, and the sooner the better.

The next day, she took care of a few errands and talked to her parents, but she spent most of it in her apartment, thinking about the Kings.

It wasn't until the evening that she checked her texts and emails. She noted how many of the so-called emergencies had sorted themselves out without anyone's help. People changed their minds, issues faded in importance and were replaced by new concerns. There's a lesson, she thought; half the time I'm running around frantically to fix something that would fix itself. The terror that she would fail or overlook some critical point was, in fact, a waste of time. Apparently, much of what terrified her vaporized on its own if she just let it be. The idea depressed her even more.

On Monday morning, she was at her desk by seven-thirty, determined to shake off her dark mood. Coffee in hand, she got right down to reading the online releases and new emails about what she had missed and what was coming up.

"Hey, good to have you back." Chris, one of the account executives, stuck his head into her office. "How was the vacation?"

She looked up from her computer. Chris and she had little interaction at work, and she knew his inquiry was just a formality. "Great, thanks."

"Look at you, all natural and stuff. I like it!" He grinned and walked on.

What did he mean? She got up and went to the mirror on the wall near her office door, part of an arrangement of photos and paintings. Having it there gave her a chance to check her hair and makeup as she was walking out the door without stopping anywhere or even appearing to be doing so. Her reflection surprised her. Usually, she wore a bright lipstick and lip gloss; today she had put on only the gloss. Her eye makeup always consisted of three carefully blended eye shadows, liner, and lots of mascara; this morning, she had brushed on two shadows and a touch of mascara. Without being conscious of it, she realized, she had gotten used to going without makeup, so this amount had seemed like a lot. She noticed that she had even forgotten to put on earrings. She did, in fact, look very different.

It was a busy day, everyone wanting her attention so they could complain to her about some situation or other. Her attention drifted. Nothing seemed particularly compelling. She snapped back to attention when she was called into Robert Clark's office for an emergency meeting late in the afternoon, along with Iris Herbert, a senior person with whom she typically shared projects. They hurried in to find Robert seated at his desk looking displeased.

He greeted them with a terse "Sit down," then waited while they quickly found chairs. "Just got off the phone with Jeffrey Kirk. Kip Dawn was arrested walking out of a jewelry store on

Madison with a three-thousand-dollar watch in his pocket. He claims he indicated to his assistant that she should pay for it. They have video cameras, though, and they say there's no sign of that, nor did anybody in the store see anything that could be construed as even a signal. The assistant says she didn't know she was supposed to pay, and didn't see any signal. She's not going to take the hit for him. P.S., the cops didn't like his behavior, so they tested him, and he was legally drunk. P.S. again," here he looked directly at Ellie, "remember he had that DUI a little while back."

"Seems our boy has a couple of, shall we say, issues," remarked Iris. "Does he have any prior problems with shoplifting?"

"Find that out, Iris, and see what this qualifies as—it's got to be a felony or maybe worse, whatever that is, but get the details and what he might be facing in court. Jeffrey can give you the numbers for Kip's lawyers. We have to know what we're dealing with, first of all."

Hands in his pockets, he came around to stand in front of his desk. "Okay, now what are we going to do? We need to get out a statement pronto. Nobody knows yet, but that's probably going to last for another five seconds."

As she always did in a client crisis, Ellie immediately started sorting out pros and cons, mentally flipping through what she knew and how that might work in the client's favor. She recalled the days she spent about two years ago cleaning up the hot young actor's DUI mess, when he was arrested driving home drunk from Vermont. That had blown over quickly. He had gotten a lot of good press since then, partially because he was so good-looking and considered talented, and partially because he had started dating an older, very successful actress. The public liked him for all that, which translated into points on his side. But a drunken thief—nothing likeable there. His last film had come out nearly a year before and was a romantic comedy. No help from that corner. He hadn't enjoyed comedy, and his next one was going to be completely different. She searched her memory trying to recall the subject.

"Wait." She sat up straighter. "He's scheduled to start shooting *Just One More* in October. He's playing a cop. Cops arrest bad guys. Couldn't he have been doing research for his role? Wanted to know what it's like to steal something, but still planned to have his assistant pay for it so he could experience walking out the door with it."

Grinning, Robert pointed a finger at her. "And that, ladies and gentlemen, is how it's done. Write it up, Ellie. Be sure to get with his lawyers first so we're all coming from the same place on this. Thanks for your help. You both can go."

The two left his office. Ellie headed directly to the ladies' room, thinking she might be sick. She bent over a sink to splash cold water on her face. She couldn't believe it. Almost without thinking, barely making an effort, she had spun a story to excuse the despicable behavior of a client simply because he *was* a client. He might go to trial, he might even get convicted—although she doubted he would ever serve a day in jail—but she was helping him get away with it, if not in court then with the public. And this was the second time she would be helping him avoid the consequences of his actions.

It wasn't until this instant that she understood. She hated her job.

If she had never found out the truth about her background, she wondered if she would ever have come to this moment. Ashamed, confused, afraid, she covered her face and cried.

Chapter 20

✖

Despite his silence on the subject, Rachel could tell her father was still glad she was back and apparently unchanged by her trip to New York. At supper, she saw him repeatedly raise his eyes to look at her, a new anxiety showing beneath his calm exterior. He was more strict than usual with Katie, correcting her nearly perfect table manners and uncharacteristically criticizing the pace at which she served the food and cleared the plates. It was obvious he was trying, in his way, to counteract any bad outside influences she may have encountered on her trip. Rachel knew it wasn't her place to say anything about it, though. One didn't criticize one's parents or elders.

Leah, on the other hand, seemed neither affected by anything that had transpired nor interested in searching out any possible changes in Rachel or Katie. She was her usual brisk self, busy with canning and preserving the many items from the garden coming in as the month of August wound down. As she was working with Katie by her side doing the canning, she may well have questioned the girl about her trip or discussed Ellie with her, but, if so, Rachel heard nothing about it from her daughter. Rachel wished that she could be more like her mother, steadfast in the face of any change. She also wished she could shout at her, demanding to know how she could go on as if nothing had happened. Although Rachel knew she had always given her mother a more difficult time than the other children had, it wasn't until now that she started wondering if her mother's feelings for her had always been different from her feelings for the others. Was it possible, she wondered, that her mother had felt a little less for her? Did she sense, on some level only a mother could reach, that something was wrong, was not as it should be? It was a chilling idea.

Sitting on the porch that evening as the sun left the sky, Rachel listened to the children singing choruses, letting the pure sounds wash over her. She had gone too far, she told herself. All this thinking about what everything meant, how everyone felt—far from being helpful, it was destructive. This is why they should have stayed at home and not ventured out into the craziness of New York City. A mistake made in a hospital shouldn't be allowed to destroy a lifetime of thirty years and a child whose mind was still impressionable.

No more, she decided. She didn't want to see the uncertainty in her father's face. It made her doubly unhappy, since she was the cause of it. Nor was it fair to put her sisters and brothers through this. She had met her birth parents, and that was enough. It was time to put an end to it.

She tried. Day after day, she awoke determined to do her

chores as well as she knew how, to be a good daughter, and to be a good mother. Her goal was not to speak of what she wanted to accomplish, but to do what needed doing. A life of action, of doing the right thing, was more important than any words. She said little, and she worked hard.

No matter how she tried, though, she couldn't contain the wanderings of her mind. When she glanced at her hands, she recalled the similarity of her skin tone to Nina Lawrence's. When she drank tea, she remembered the delicate cups and dream-like surroundings of her afternoon at the Plaza Hotel. She recalled the gathering of relatives at Gil and Nina's apartment and how welcoming everyone was. Even her quilt stitching reminded her of the pillow she had presented to the Lawrences on her first visit there, which had, in fact, been given a prominent home on one of their living room chairs. Only a few days after returning home, she received a long letter from Nina and Gil, letting her know how much they enjoyed the visit, asking the two of them to come again soon. They spoke of the depth of their affection for her and Katie, and marveled that such a strange situation could produce this miraculous addition to their family. A couple of days after that, Katie received a package from them containing a box of chocolates and a tiny, intricately carved wooden rowboat to remind her of their time in Central Park. Katie, in turn, wrote them a note of thanks in which she expressed her affection, and Rachel added a few lines to send her thanks and good wishes. The Lawrences, it seemed, were never far from their consciousness. Katie repeatedly asked when they might go back, until her mother's silence on the subject told her to drop the question for good.

Two weeks had passed since her visit when she received a letter from Ellie. Taking it to her bedroom so she could be alone, Rachel noticed her fingers trembling as she opened the envelope. It was a short note. Ellie wanted to talk in private, and they could do it anywhere Rachel liked, in Pennsylvania, halfway between them, or anywhere else, as long as it was just the two of them. Rachel sat on her bed, unmoving. She didn't know what the meeting would be about, but she understood that it would be the end of her efforts to put this behind her.

Chapter 21

�֎

The restaurant had posts for Amish buggies and numerous parking spots for cars. Rachel made sure she tied Driver securely before turning toward the entrance. Steeling herself, she walked over to the door, beneath the shade of the awning, past the Waitress Wanted sign, and into the air-conditioning of Carson's. It was a small restaurant, rarely frequented by the Amish, and she hoped it was far enough away from home that she wouldn't see anyone she knew.

She saw Ellie waiting at a table by a curtained window, a glass jar with fresh flowers in front of her. Rachel's immediate thought was that she looked nervous.

Nervous or not, she managed a smile as Rachel approached. "Thank you for coming. It means so much to me."

"I'm not sure why," Rachel said, "but I guess it will become clear soon."

Ellie held out her menu. "Do you want to order something? I'm getting coffee."

The waitress came over to the table, a cheerful girl around twenty or so, with spiky, black hair and bright red lipstick. Rachel asked for iced tea and a corn muffin. Then the two women faced each other again. It seemed to Rachel that Ellie wanted to speak, but something was holding her back.

"How are Nina and Gil? And everyone else?" Rachel inquired.

Ellie looked startled, as if she had forgotten that Rachel knew the members of her family. "Oh, they're fine." She seemed to warm to the subject. "They talk about you and Katie all the time. In fact, they're driving me and themselves crazy wondering when you'll come back."

Rachel picked up her spoon, examining it to avoid the other woman's eyes. "We don't have any such plans right now."

"Right. Let me guess. You're going to get back to your regular life and try to forget all this. Too much confusion, too difficult for everyone. Especially you."

Rachel couldn't hide her surprise. "How did you know?"

"Because that's what I was thinking when I got home from here."

She voiced her question with hesitation. "But you're not thinking that anymore?"

"No."

Interrupted by the reappearance of the waitress, they waited while she put down their drinks and a large corn muffin alongside two bowls containing butter and raspberry preserves. "Anything else I can get you?"

"No, thank you," Rachel said.

In silence, they poured cream and sugar, unwrapped straws, spread butter. Finally, Ellie spoke.

"I thought it would be a big deal to meet my real parents and the rest of my real family. I knew it would be complicated because they were Amish. What I didn't know was that it would show me that I hated my life, the life I've been living until now."

Rachel, in the process of chewing a bite of her muffin, swallowed and put the piece she was holding back down on the plate. She had tried to guess what Ellie might want to say at this meeting, but was unprepared for anything like this.

"I love my family in New York dearly, please don't get me wrong. But I don't love my work and the life I've made for myself. I've just been too caught up in my own ambitions and self-importance to see it. Until now."

Rachel sipped her iced tea.

"I realized this almost as soon as I got home from here a couple of weeks ago," Ellie continued, "but I didn't do anything about it. It was such a frightening idea. Of course, I also figured it might just be the effect of spending time here on the farm. Except the feeling got stronger. I don't know what is right for me, but I see now that what I've built for myself is wrong. And I want to change it before it's too late, while I still have the ability and the courage."

"Do you know what you want to do instead?"

"Not exactly." Ellie picked up her coffee cup. "What I'd like to do for now is come back here, but stay longer, at least several months. Maybe forever, I can't say. Rent a small place near the family. I need a fresh start."

"Oh," was all Rachel could manage.

"I don't mean to sound ridiculous. I'm not trying to renounce everything and pretend to be Amish. But this is an opportunity to learn about another way of life. I really admire you and your family—our family." She gave a slight smile as she set down the coffee cup. "I'll never get that right. Anyway, I want to see what other way there is that I might live, or try to *be,* if that makes sense. And I want to take the time to build real relationships with everyone here, not just come as a guest, then take off again."

"I see. But why did you want to meet me alone to tell me this?"

Ellie ran her fingers through her hair, pushing it back from her face. "Because I have a suggestion for you as well. I'm not for one minute suggesting you hate your life. Please don't think that. But this is an opportunity for you to build something bigger with the family we share in New York. If I come here, I would sublet my apartment in New York. It occurred to me that you and Katie could take it over if you wanted to. You know, spend a few months living in New York."

Rachel didn't bother trying to hide her shock. "Do you know what you're suggesting? Why would I do that?"

"Because the question of who we both are is not resolved. Not to my satisfaction, and I'll bet not to yours, either. A few days together, some hugs, warm feelings—that doesn't do it. I don't know who I am or who I was supposed to be. Do you?"

Rachel looked out the window, unwilling to reply.

"Truthfully," Ellie went on, "I don't think I ever knew who I was, and maybe that's because I'm not living my life, the life I was intended to have."

"Do you really think that?" Rachel turned back to her.

"I wish I had the answer." Frustration was written on Ellie's face. "I'm not sure I ever will."

"I do know what you mean." Rachel's voice was barely above a whisper. "I'm not unhappy with my life, not at all, but I always felt there was something . . ."

Ellie nodded.

"But you're talking about me leaving the farm, and all the work there. I couldn't do that to my family."

"I'll do your share of the work. Except for the quilts, obviously. Hopefully, they can teach me to bake a reasonably acceptable pie."

"And Katie. What about school?"

"There are tons of schools in New York. My parents could arrange for her to go to a good one for however long you want."

"An English school?" Rachel shook her head.

"I suppose. But I don't see that a few months would be so terrible."

There was a long pause while Rachel considered the situation. "Let me ask you something. Why do you care if I go to New York? Why do you want me to leave?"

Ellie sighed. "You may not believe this, but I don't have any ulterior motive. My parents desperately want to get to know you and Katie better. You barely know Nick, and you met A.J. once."

Rachel must have looked skeptical, because Ellie hurried on.

"Okay, I don't deny that it would probably be easier for me if you weren't there. It's downright weird being in the same room with your family when you're there. That means it has to be easier for you if I'm not around, breathing down your neck. Do you think you'd enjoy being with my relatives if I were there at every turn?"

"No, I guess not."

"I would have liked for us to be friends." Ellie's tone was wistful. "It doesn't seem to be working out that way, though. Why pretend?"

Rachel wasn't used to such a frank dissection of emotions. Her family wasn't prone to laying out their feelings to be analyzed this way. Nothing on earth could have induced her to say such a thing to another person. Even though the words were true. She didn't answer.

"Still, I think this is a good solution," Ellie went on. "Instead of just leaving everything half finished, let's get to the bottom of what this means. Was the switch a mistake that thwarted our destinies? Or was the switch *meant* to be our destinies?"

Rachel didn't want to admit to Ellie that these were the same questions that had been tormenting her. "I don't know," Rachel murmured. "I just don't . . ."

"Please, I don't want to browbeat you about this. I'm offering you a place to stay with your daughter if you want it. Whether you do or you don't, I'd like to go ahead with my plan." She put a ten-dollar bill on the table and got up. "I've already written a letter to tell Leah and Isaac my idea. That seemed the best way to approach this—give them time to discuss it. I'll drop it in the mailbox right outside and they should get it tomorrow. I'd like to think they'll feel good about it. So you let me know what you want to do. Okay?"

Things were moving too fast for Rachel to take in. "Wait— when would this happen?"

"As soon as possible." Ellie slung her purse over her shoulder. She regarded Rachel, continuing in a softer tone. "Will you be okay if I go? You look shell-shocked."

Rachel didn't know what the term meant, but she could figure out the general drift. "No, it's fine. You . . . you don't waste any time, do you?"

She was surprised when Ellie came closer and put a hand over hers. "I'm sorry if I blindsided you. I can be a little blunt. Please understand that I don't want to do anything to hurt you or anyone else in the family. Either family."

Rachel looked up to see concern in Ellie's eyes. "Thank you for saying that."

Ellie gave her hand a squeeze and left.

She shifted back around in her seat, gazing at her half-eaten food. She had a huge decision to make, and no one else in the world could help her make it. If only Ellie could have left things alone, instead of coming up with this plan. From the first, she had instigated everything, throwing Rachel's—and, apparently, her own—life into turmoil. It would have been much better if she had reacted to the initial letter from that nurse the way Rachel did, burying it and pretending it had never arrived.

Yet, everything they talked about had been true. Rachel was unsettled since coming home from her trip. Too much had been left unresolved. She had redoubled her efforts to do her best at everything, but it felt almost mechanical, as if she didn't know whether she was even supposed to be doing any of it. It was, she realized, as if she were waiting for something, although she had no idea what.

Chapter 22

�֎

"You're *what?*"

Alarmed, Robert Clark leaned forward in his chair. The two were seated close to each other at the conference table in his office. When she arrived for the private appointment she had requested, he led her to sit down with him, understanding that their meeting was going to be about a personal matter.

"That's right. I'm resigning. Leaving." Ellie hoped her voice didn't betray her perspiring palms and the way her heart was pounding in her chest. "I need to stop working for a while."

He sat back, regarding her. "Okay, Ellie, what's this about? I know you. You're happy here, you do a great job. You're not a person who just up and quits. You've been with us for, what, ten years? What could possibly induce you to say this?"

In the past, Ellie kept her personal life out of the office, but she was always direct and open with Robert about business. This situation, however, concerned both aspects of her life, and she had decided that she wasn't going to confide in him. She recalled all too well Jason's reaction to the news of her Amish background. The thought of exposing the Kings to the possible ridicule of Robert and the other people in the firm whom he would doubtless tell made her sick to her stomach. Besides, she thought, nowhere did it say she had to bare her soul to leave a job.

Of course, Robert was right to be shocked. The Ellie he knew wouldn't have quit her job in a million years. Except, her life had been turned upside down, so she wasn't that Ellie anymore.

What truly surprised her was that, once she finally resolved to take this step, she found that she felt more awake, more energized than she had in years. When she received a reply from Leah and Isaac King to her letter suggesting she move closer to them, there was no turning back. They wrote that they would be happy to have her living nearby if that was what she wanted. They even supplied her with contact information for people who could direct her to a local real estate agent. Once that permission was granted, if she had any doubts left at all, they were gone.

Still, she had to find a graceful way to leave the company that had been everything to her for nearly a decade. It was hard to picture extricating herself from the place to which she had been so devoted, day in and day out, year after year.

"Try to understand. I'm thirty. I've done nothing but P.R. my entire working life. I need to breathe a bit. Think about whether this is what I want to do for the next thirty years."

"That's the most ridiculous thing I've ever heard." His usual expression of controlled neutrality was fading into displeasure. "No one has the luxury of that anymore. You're a vice president here! You want to stop and smell the roses? To *think* about whether you want this fantastic job—which, by the way, you've had to fight tooth and nail for."

"I want to get out of the business, do something else."

"You're going out on your own, aren't you? Starting your own shop." His eyes blazed in anger at the idea. "Don't even think about taking our clients with you. I'll have you in court before you can say 'contract violation.'"

She tried not to show how shocked she was that the conversation had gotten so ugly so fast. After the years, and all the nights and weekends, she had put in working side by side with this man, she hadn't expected him to turn on her like this. Anger rose in her. No matter what, she didn't deserve such treatment.

Her own voice grew quieter in response. "I'm not going on my own. I have no interest in taking the company's clients anywhere."

"Well, let me in on what secret skills you've got stashed away up here"—he tapped his head—"that you're going to use to support yourself."

The insults were getting personal now. She had said all she was willing to say, so she stood up. "I'll always be grateful to you for everything."

"I don't get it. This place has been your life."

That's exactly the problem, she thought.

For an instant, she had an overwhelming urge to take it back, to tell him that she was kidding, that she had no intention of resigning. No, she couldn't go back to the way things were, as if nothing had happened. That part of her life was over.

"Please try to understand that things change and people change," she said. "That's all."

He got up as well, buttoning his suit jacket. "And I hope you'll understand that I'm going to call Security to escort you out of the building. With so little information, I have no choice but to assume the worst." He went to his desk and reached for the phone, turning his back to her as he spoke into the receiver. "Jim, get on over to Ellie Lawrence's office right away. She's leaving for good, immediately, so bring a carton for her stuff . . ."

She was stunned. Just like that, he reduced their years together and her dedication to a cardboard box for photographs and a few personal items. No doubt he considered letting her go back to her desk to be a gesture of kindness.

"Good-bye, Robert."

She shut the door behind her, not waiting to hear if he answered or not. She strode quickly to her office, grabbed her purse and iPhone from the desk, and hurried out without packing up anything else. She wasn't about to endure the humiliation of collecting memorabilia with a security guard looking over her shoulder.

As the elevator descended, her mind went blank. She stared up at the lighted numbers indicating the passing floors, waiting for her heart to stop its wild beating. Emerging into the huge, cool lobby, she hastened out onto the street. She had no idea where she was going, but she turned right and started walking at a rapid pace, thinking of nothing except stopping when the lights were red. Then, as if a switch had been clicked on, it hit her. She had done it. Quit her job. Quit this life. It was over.

A smile crept across her face. She was free. Soaring free, running-and-shouting-down-the-street free. Whatever might come, she was young and healthy, and could handle it. She figured she had enough savings to carry her through the next six months. Besides, she wasn't alone in the world. She had not one, but two, families on which to rely. The idea made her laugh out loud, eliciting stares from a teenage couple hurrying by. A new life was ahead of her, and she couldn't wait to get to it.

Chapter 23

It was another overcast and humid September day, the third one that week. Katie had recently started school, but as soon as she returned home each day, she and her grandmother would get back to work in the garden.

Rachel spotted them in one of the far rows. They didn't see her until she was nearly upon them. Katie smiled up at her, and Rachel put a hand on her daughter's shoulder.

"School went well today?"

Katie nodded.

"Good. Would you make meadow tea for everyone while I help out here? I put some mint on the counter."

If she was surprised to be sent away from the job at hand, Katie didn't say anything. She hurried off to do as her mother asked.

Leah looked at her expectantly, knowing there must be a

reason Rachel had interrupted their work and requested her daughter to leave.

Rachel kneeled down, replacing her daughter by reaching for the closest cabbage. "I wanted to tell you that I'm going to New York, and I'm taking Katie. I'm not sure how long we'll stay, but I'll arrange for some kind of schooling for her."

Leah shut her eyes, as if the news had overwhelmed her. When she opened them, her gaze was hard. "This is wrong. You would take Katie to live among the English? Why? So she can learn their ways and never come back?"

"That's not why I'm doing it. She and I both need to spend time with the Lawrences there. Not to learn their ways. To learn about ourselves."

"There is nothing to learn." Leah's lips were set in a thin line.

"That's not true and you know it!"

Leah's eyes blazed. "You do not talk to me that way. Such disrespect!"

Rachel knew her mother was right, and softened her tone. "You think it's a good idea for Ellie to move here. It should be a good idea for me to go there, then."

"No! It is completely different. It doesn't matter where Ellie lives, New York, here, anywhere in the world. But for Amish people, it is not the same. You will have no one to care for you, to look after you."

"The Lawrences care for me."

"Yes, you are their daughter by birth, but they don't understand who you have grown to be. They cannot live the way we do. They wouldn't want to. So, soon, they won't know what to do with you, and they will lose interest in you."

Hurt, Rachel words exploded. "You don't know them, so you have no right to say such a thing! You and Ellie can be close, but no one would want me around?"

"It's not the same thing," her mother snapped. "And these people have no place for a child anymore. I know, Katie told me. They have an apartment where they live alone, nothing there for children. Outside, no grass, no trees, just cars and buildings and crowds."

"We will have our own apartment. Ellie's apartment. She offered it to us."

"The two of you will live by yourselves?" Leah shook her head vehemently. "This is a terrible thing! You have no idea how to live in a place like New York City."

"I'm a grown woman!"

Leah picked up the half-filled basket and rose to her feet. "I see now what you will learn in New York. To go against your family. To cause trouble. And, also, to make your child into a bad teenager who will do bad things."

Rachel got up to face her. She wondered why she continued trying to explain her actions to her mother.

"Are you ever coming back?" Leah demanded.

"Yes. At least, I'm planning to come back."

Shock appeared on her mother's face. "You're *planning to*? That is the best you can say? You are talking about throwing away your life."

"No. I don't mean it that way. I just don't know when exactly."

"And the farm? Who will do your work here?"

"Ellie offered to do my share. I realize she can't really do all of it, but she'll do whatever she can. And I can make my quilts in New York, and get them back here for you to sell."

Leah shook her head, as if in disgust at the inadequacy of this explanation.

"You can teach her to bake pies and bread, I'm sure. To do the canning, too. Many things."

"You will not be here to see whether I can teach her or not. You will not care."

"That's not true!" Rachel couldn't control herself any longer. "You'll be very happy with Ellie. Happier than you ever were with me!"

Leah looked as if she had been slapped. She turned and walked away. Of course the trip was a bad idea, Rachel thought; her mother had never considered Rachel's ideas to be worth considering. Even in something as important as this, Leah felt that her daughter, a thirty-year-old mother herself, had no opinion worth considering.

Rachel went to find her father. No matter what her mother might think, in the end, Leah would go along with whatever Isaac King decided. It was the one way to silence her mother on the subject, and Rachel pushed aside the guilty thought that it was wrong of her to use it. Still, her father had to be told she was leaving. And after that conversation with her mother, Rachel decided she would be leaving soon.

She found him, in the process of looking over the calves. She came up beside him, absentmindedly reaching out to straighten one of the food buckets secured to the outside of the stall as she greeted him.

"You're happy that Ellie is moving here, aren't you?"

Isaac knelt down to take a closer look at the bottom of the half-door. "It's what she wants to do. Work here and be with us." He looked up at her and smiled. "More family is good, even if you just discovered them, yes?"

"Even if she's not Amish?"

"She is my child. As you are. I can't say what will happen beyond that."

"So you think it's good that she comes here for a longer time."

"Yes." He pressed on what seemed to be a weak spot in the wood.

She took a deep breath. "So you would understand if I wanted to go be with the Lawrences for a longer time. If Katie and I went to stay with them for a few months?"

Her father took his time standing up, then reached for a rag slung over the stall door and wiped his hands on it. "Is that what you're thinking of doing?"

"Yes."

He waited what seemed to Rachel like an agonizing amount of time before saying more.

"I understand why Ellie would want to get away from the world she lives in, but why would you leave here? What is out there for you?"

"There's nothing out there that I want. But these people—I need to know them better than I do. It hasn't been enough, just the few days. Katie and I both need to spend time there. Our lives here are what's important, but I don't think I can go on as if nothing happened. It feels like I lost who I am."

Her father's eyes darkened. "You know who you are!"

"No, it doesn't seem that way. My life doesn't feel real any-more."

"You mustn't say such a thing."

She was about to answer, but stopped herself. It wouldn't serve any purpose anyway.

"I want to take Katie and stay in Ellie's apartment in New York. I won't disappear."

"Live in New York City alone? You must not!"

"That's just it!" She was losing her composure again. "I must! Nothing makes any sense because I don't know what's real for me. I have no choice. I have to find the connections be-tween me and these people so I can find my place in the world."

Her father stared at her. "You would leave our people?"

"I didn't say that!" Tears stung her eyes. "You always under-stood me so well. Can't you understand that I have to go!"

Her father gazed out over the fields of corn, apparently mulling things over. At last, without looking at her, he nodded. Then he knelt down once more and turned his attention back to the stall door.

She walked away, wondering what new trouble she had just brought to her family. What had seemed a shocking suggestion when Ellie brought it up in the restaurant had come to seem in-evitable. Normal life would be suspended. She had to walk through the door and experience that other life, the one that might have been her life. Of course, this would cause terrible pain for her father, and it broke her heart to hurt him. But she couldn't be dissuaded now that she had made up her mind. She would follow this road to its end. She prayed she would find some answers there.

As she came back toward the house, she saw her grandmother sitting in a rocking chair on the porch outside her own front door. Hannah King had a bowl of strawberries in her lap, and was in the process of hulling them, her gnarled hands working slowly but steadily with a small knife to cut off the green stems. Rachel went over and sat on the step, near her grandmother's feet.

"A special visit?" Hannah smiled. "You have time?"

"No, but let's have a special visit anyway."

They sat quietly for a while.

"Grandma, did you ever have doubts about anything in your life?"

"Of course. But what do you mean 'about anything'?"

"Well . . . like being baptized, let's say."

Hannah gave Rachel a sharp look. "Baptized to become Amish? No, never. Why?"

Rachel regretted bringing up the subject. "No reason."

Her grandmother's tone softened. "Those doubts should be addressed before you are baptized. I never had a single doubt, though. Your grandfather didn't, either. We didn't need time to think about it. We got baptized and married as soon as we could. I have had many blessings, and I did the best I could to be worthy of them."

"I'm sure you always were worthy."

"No. I have many faults. We can only try to live a good life."

"What would you say if I told you I was going to New York

with Katie to stay for a few months? Live near the Lawrences in my own apartment?"

Hannah paused in her task. "I'd ask why you would want to do such a thing."

"To get to know my other family."

Her grandmother was quiet, and went back to concentrating on the strawberries. At last, she spoke. "Did you ask your father about doing this?"

Rachel nodded. "He understands. Or, at least, enough."

"Then you have the answer you need, if that is what you want to do, and he said it is all right with him."

It occurred to Rachel that, as usual, her grandmother was wise. She had immediately grasped that if Rachel had gone so far as to ask her father's permission, then she had already made up her mind to do it. There was no point in adding opinions that might complicate matters further.

She got up to go. "I'm baking blueberry pies later. I'll bring you one."

"Good." Hannah smiled at her. "And, Rachel?"

"Yes?"

"You have a good heart. It knows what to do and what is right."

Rachel wished she could believe it.

Chapter 24

Holding a bag of groceries with one arm, Ellie let herself in the side door, which led directly into the kitchen. There was a wooden table with turned legs and a painted white top to her right, and she dropped the keys there, setting down the heavy bag beside them. She used a chair to prop open the screen door, then went back and forth from the car, carrying in suitcases and boxes. The house came fully furnished down to the dishes and linens, so everything she needed went into the back of her rented SUV.

At last, she finished emptying the car and went inside for the last time, hot and exhausted. As soon as possible, she reminded herself, she had to see about buying a used car. Her decision to rent this particular house was based primarily on its proximity to the King farm, and, fortunately, the charm that had come across online actually did exist. The place was cheerful with good light, and cozy as well, exactly what she wanted.

The two bedrooms weren't big, but she would use one for sleeping, and swap the bed for a desk to have a small office in the other. Her plan was to use her computer only to the extent necessary to find work when the time came. She wasn't giving up her electronics altogether, but she was going to cut back to the bare minimum. Her cell phone was going into the desk drawer. The house had a landline, and she had given the number to members of her family, plus her building superintendent in case of an emergency. She also left it for Rachel, who was due to arrive with Katie at Ellie's apartment today. Anyone who wanted to find Ellie would have to use this phone number; she wouldn't be carrying a phone around anymore. Not such radical steps, she thought, but radical for her. She was thrilled by the prospect.

The whole house appeared clean, but she felt the need to give it an extra going-over. She filled a spray bottle with a mixture of vinegar and water, part of another resolution she had made to abandon chemicals wherever she could; it seemed to fit with the new life she was making.

She was grateful to have a supper invitation from the Kings for tonight. It would be nice to eat with everyone on her first official night in Pennsylvania. She gave a wondering shake of her head. Who would have envisioned this—Ellie Lawrence in a little house in the country? Truly, anything was possible.

By the time she arrived at the King house for supper, she was glad to have a respite from unpacking. She parked her car, recalling how conspicuous she had felt on her initial visits here, driving up to the house when there were only buggies to be seen. By now, though, she understood that the Amish had nothing against cars; they just didn't want to own them. Owning them increased the likelihood that travel away from home would become more common, and the ability easily to travel great distances would change the nature of their communities. She was glad to think that she might make their lives easier if she could give them a lift here and there if they wanted one.

Inside the house, the adults greeted her with hugs and handshakes, and warm words of welcome.

As they ate, Ellie wondered how Rachel and Katie were faring in her apartment on their first day. When she said as much to Leah and Isaac, they gave her tight smiles and changed the subject. Uh-oh, she thought, apparently not everyone here is excited about this arrangement.

After the main meal, Moses got his binoculars and took the children outside for some bird-watching. The remaining adults sat at the table with coffee and apple pie.

"This is absolutely delicious," Ellie said, enjoying the last bite of her slice. It wasn't too long ago, she couldn't help thinking, that she wouldn't have eaten an entire piece of pie if her life depended on it.

"It's from a batch Rachel baked yesterday," Sarah said. "We took the rest to be sold."

Although it was barely perceptible, Ellie saw Leah stiffen at the mention of Rachel.

"You know," Ellie said, changing the focus of their talk, "I wonder if you could teach me how to bake a pie . . . a really good pie, like the ones you make."

"It is not so hard to bake a pie," Hannah said.

"I've had a lot of bad pie in my life, so it can't be that easy." Ellie smiled.

"Later this week I will bake," Leah said. "You can watch."

"Thank you."

"Tomorrow morning, it is back to the cows for you?" asked Amos.

"Of course. I have to admit, I've really come to like the milking."

Daniel stirred sugar into his coffee. "You'll stay here all day?"

"As long as you want me and will put me to work."

Ellie didn't mention that, at some point, she needed to find a paying job as well. She had her savings, but eventually that would run out. While she intended to spend most of her time working on the farm, she would have to figure out an arrangement where she produced some income for herself. So far, she hadn't come up with any ideas, but she wouldn't worry about it now. She would think of something.

For now, she had accomplished her goal. She was living here, right near the Kings, settled into her own place and, tonight, surrounded by this family, which was, mysteriously, her family. She couldn't believe she had made it happen.

As she sat there, the enormity of what she had done began to sink in. She was smiling as she listened to Daniel tell a story about something that had taken place on his construction job that day. Suddenly, she no longer heard his words, and the smile froze on her face. She realized that she had left everything and everyone familiar to her, in order to sit in this farmhouse with no idea what the future held.

Seeing the women get up to clear the dessert dishes snapped her back to the present. Grateful to have something to do, she joined them. For the first time, she felt as if she belonged. As if she was contributing. It would be all right.

Later, back at her house, she found a set of pale yellow sheets and a lightweight blanket in the small linen closet. She made up the bed, regretting she hadn't done it before supper, certain she would be asleep within seconds of crawling in.

It was almost nine-thirty. She set her alarm to go off in the morning at four-thirty. The drive to the farm was only a few minutes, so she could make it there by five for the milking. To her surprise, when she finally got into bed, she felt wide awake. Part of it, she thought, was that she was in a strange place, a house for which she was now responsible. She had never lived in a house, never lived anywhere but in an apartment. There was no superintendent to call. It was time to learn how to *do* things, not just manage them. She liked the idea. The Kings were competent at so many things, a huge range of skills Ellie had never thought to learn. It was as if a new universe was opening up to her, with new things to try. She was excited to get started, starting with tomorrow's tending to the cows. *I can't believe I'm lying here awake*, she thought. *I'll be useless tomorrow.* She closed her eyes and was instantly fast asleep.

Chapter 25

"This one is for the top lock." Nina Lawrence stood off to one side as she inserted the key so Rachel could see what she was doing. "You turn it to the left. Then this other key unlocks the bottom."

Rachel doubted she would remember which key was which when she was on her own, but she wasn't about to voice that doubt. Eventually, she would figure it out, just as she would have to figure out everything else about living in Ellie's apartment.

Nina pushed open the door to reveal a small foyer with a table in it. Beyond that, Rachel saw a living room in shades of beige and white. Carrying her suitcase, Katie went in behind Nina, looking around in bewilderment.

"We're going to stay here?" she asked her grandmother. "It's for us?"

"Yes, sweetheart. It will be your own home right here in New York."

"It's so . . ." Katie struggled to find the right word.

Ellie's apartment wasn't like her parents', Rachel noted, with their many antiques and overstuffed sofas and chairs. It was elegant in a different way. Simple furniture in light-colored fabrics, a few paintings, no clutter. She wanted to breathe a sigh of relief, knowing there was less to worry about breaking during their stay. Borrowing Ellie's home was a huge responsibility, and she wanted to keep it in perfect condition.

"You can put your things in the bedroom if you like," Nina said. "I'll leave the books here on the coffee table."

She put down a shopping bag she had brought with her containing several maps of the city and travel books covering everything from New York's history to tourist attractions to walking tours. Rachel and Katie went into the bedroom, and set their suitcases down next to a wall lined with pocket doors.

"You two get comfortable." At the sound of Nina's voice, they went out to the living room. "Gil and I will be back in a couple of hours, let's say six o'clock." She took Rachel's hands in hers. "You'll be all right here by yourself? You're sure you won't let me stay? I can help you unpack."

"No, please go ahead. We should get used to it. Having our own home here will be fun." She looked at her daughter, hoping she sounded brighter than she felt. "Right?"

"Oh, yes!" It was apparent to Rachel that Katie was also doing her best to be upbeat.

"You have my phone number if you need me. I put milk and

juice and some other food in the fridge, but you should make a list of what you want. We can go to the grocery store together, and I'll show you around."

Nina opened a small drawer in a low desk by the window and put a white envelope inside it. "Here's where we'll keep the money for you to use. Start with this three hundred dollars, and we'll replenish it as we go."

Rachel started to protest, but Nina stopped her with a raised hand. "We've been over this, honey. It's settled. You can't live here and spend your own money. You have to allow us to do this. That's it."

She gave Rachel a quick kiss on the cheek, then went over to do the same to Katie before going out, shutting the door behind her.

"Now we're really and truly on our own," Rachel said.

If the idea of moving to New York had made her nervous, actually doing it this morning turned out to be far more frightening. She had never encountered most of what constituted a normal day for people living in this city, and she had no idea how she was going to contend with an endless parade of new situations. As far as Katie went, she could only pray she hadn't made a mistake in bringing her here. This would change her, in ways they probably couldn't foresee, but Rachel hoped the good would outweigh any possible bad.

Still, however scared she might be, whatever difficulties she might encounter, this was what she needed to do. Besides, the Lawrences were clearly eager to help her every step of the way, so she wasn't alone. There was no point in being afraid. She gave a little nod of resolve.

"Okay, then," she announced. "Let's move in!"

It didn't take long for them to unpack. When Nina and Gil rang the doorbell at six that evening, Rachel and Katie were sitting side by side on the sofa, looking through the maps Nina left for them.

"How's my wonderful granddaughter?" Gil asked, giving Katie a hug.

She seemed only too glad to hug him back. Rachel wondered if she associated this grandfather with her grandfather at home. Katie had always loved spending time with Isaac, taking long walks with him, stopping to kneel down and identify a plant or insect. Did she compare the two men?

The four of them went back to the Lawrences' apartment, Nina saying she wanted them to relax inside and not have to deal with any more people that day. Rachel was grateful. She was pleased to reenter the familiar peace of their home. Gil excused himself to call a patient, and Nina served Rachel a glass of sparkling water, telling her to relax while she finished putting supper on the table.

"See," said Nina with a smile, "I called it supper, like an old pro."

Rachel laughed.

"Come, Katie, my love, please help me in the kitchen."

The two of them left Rachel alone. Sipping at her water, she wandered over to the bookcase, tilting her head to read the book titles. Some of them revealed little to her about their subject, but others made it clear they were about art, history, travel, science. *So many books,* she thought, reaching out to touch the thick spine on one.

"Do you like to read?"

Rachel whirled around at the sound of Gil's voice, her face flushing as if she had been caught stealing.

"I'm sorry, I didn't mean to startle you." Smiling, he took a seat on the sofa. "Is there any particular subject that interests you?"

"I don't have much time for reading. We read aloud to the little ones, but there's a lot to do on the farm."

He nodded. "Well, if you had the time, what kinds of things would you want to read about?"

"I . . . I don't know. Anything, I guess."

He seemed to give this thought. "What was your favorite subject in school?"

She smiled. "That was a very long time ago. Let me think. I liked reading stories. But I liked everything."

"Did you graduate from high school?"

"No, not high school. I graduated from our Amish school. We go through the eighth grade. That is how we do it. We learn what we need to, and then we're done."

"I didn't know that. I'm sorry, again, that I'm so ignorant of the way you live."

It dawned on her that, without her chores, she would have a lot more free time now. "I might have a chance to read while we're here."

"If there's anything here you'd like to take, please say so. Any book we have is yours."

She glanced around, abashed. "I would have no idea what to pick. Could you recommend something to me?"

"It would be my pleasure." He went over to the bookshelves

and ran a finger along the books, considering his choices. "This is good, animals in Africa, beautiful photography. Katie would enjoy that, too. Now, we need a novel . . ."

When he was done, he set down a stack of six books on the coffee table.

"Take them back with you, and browse through at your leisure. See if anything appeals to you. We'll take it from there."

"Thank you so much." Rachel put out a hand to touch the glossy cover of the book on top. Suddenly, she couldn't wait to get back to Ellie's apartment to start reading.

Katie appeared. "Grandma said to ask if you would please come in now to eat."

Grandma. Up until now, Katie had been calling her Nina, and Rachel wondered who had initiated the change. She considered whether or not it bothered her. No, she decided. That's what Nina was to Katie, her grandmother. It made sense. They were here to forge relationships, and this was part of it. She herself wouldn't be making the switch to Mom and Dad, which seemed to be going too far for her. No, this was a good step for Katie. Rachel smiled.

"Tell Grandma we'll be right there."

Chapter 26

Ellie held the smaller container of horseradish with one hand and the apples with the other, leaning slightly to one side to resist the bucket's weight as she followed Leah outside and across the street to the vegetable stand. Saturdays were the busiest selling days, so both Annie and her thirteen-year-old son, Zeke, were working in the shade of the white wooden structure, moving among the shelves. Along with their neighbors, Ellie had discovered that the customers tended to be tourists who usually drove past the sign, then came to an abrupt halt as they realized what they had seen. They would back up for the chance to buy fresh food, and maybe converse with the Amish.

"Good morning." She extended the bucket of apples questioningly, then set it down on the shelf to which Annie pointed.

Leah and Annie got busy rearranging the display of lettuces, spinach, and onions to fit in the new additions. Any time she came by the stand, Ellie found herself entranced by the variety of colors and textures, fruits and vegetables in one area, flowers in glass jars and Laura's candy and noodles in another. She was amazed by the craftsmanship of the toys whittled by Judah and Annie's eldest son, William, only fourteen. It had been a surprise for her to recognize Rachel's hand-quilted place mats and table runners, but Annie explained that Rachel always kept a supply on hand, and had stockpiled extras before she left for New York. A couple of days ago, Ellie had taken a close-up photograph of the stand, and planned to blow it up and frame it for her kitchen wall. It was an amateur effort, but the result made her feel happy. She made sure to ask Annie's permission before she took the shot, even though she had no intention of capturing anyone Amish in it.

"How are you, Zeke?" she asked Annie's son, who was holding a bushel basket of zucchini for his mother while she continued to arrange the vegetables.

"Fine, Ellie. It's a good day today."

She smiled. She loved talking to the King children, every one of them polite and enthusiastic. She couldn't help thinking that it was the startling contrast between them and the people she had typically spent her days with before coming here that made such an impression on her. The utter pleasure of not trying to analyze anyone's underlying motives was a sensation almost like muscular relaxation, as if she could go mentally limp and still feel completely safe. She didn't have to protect her flank, keep her enemies close, or outmaneuver the opposition—all the military analogies of business she had come to despise.

The next day was Sunday, when the community went to worship services, as they did every other week. That meant no work would be done other than what was absolutely necessary, like milking the cows and feeding all the animals. Ellie hadn't requested to go to worship, nor had anyone suggested it to her, and she was getting the idea that outsiders were not typically invited. Last week, when there was no church service, the family had gone to visit friends, but Ellie stayed home, not wanting to intrude. So far, she wasn't sure if the Kings had told anyone about her relationship to them, but she doubted it would stay a secret very long, if it even still was. Either way, her presence would create all sorts of distractions during a get-together with their friends, and she was happy to read and catch up on some paperwork left over from her move. She had even baked a dozen biscuits, wanting to practice some of the new recipes Leah had been teaching her. They weren't the best biscuits she had ever tasted, she decided, but they weren't the worst either, which she took to be an excellent sign. She didn't know if she had it in her to be a good baker, but she was certainly going to try.

In the morning, Ellie was back to milk the cows, but immediately afterward, she returned to her house to shower and change. She didn't want to say anything to the Kings yet about her plan to get a job until she had something definite to report. Getting into her car, a seven-year-old used Ford that Isaac helped her find, she followed her local map until Carson's restaurant came into view. She pulled into a parking spot, glad to see the Waitress Wanted sign still in the window. Two days before, she had remembered the sign, although she wasn't sure how or why. She must have noticed it out of the corner of her eye the day she told Rachel that she was moving here. Waitressing might be the perfect job for now; she could do it in the evenings, so it wouldn't interfere with working on the farm. It wasn't glamorous or high-paying, that was for sure, but she would be busy, and when the day was done, she wouldn't bring work problems home with her, as she had done for years.

Smoothing down the front of her shirt, she went inside. An older woman at the register smiled. "May I help you?"

"I'd like to apply for the waitress job."

She pointed. "You need to talk to Carson."

So there was an actual Carson, Ellie thought. She could see a man in a plaid shirt with the sleeves rolled up, seated at a table at the farthest end of the room. His head was down, and he was looking through papers, a cup of coffee at his elbow.

"Thanks."

She made her way between tables, about half of them occupied by customers, and stopped in front of him. He had dark brown hair on the long side, extending below his shirt collar in back. She would have thought he could sense her presence, but he didn't look up.

"Hello. I'm Ellie Lawrence and I wanted to talk to you about the waitress job. Is it still available?"

He kept his eyes on his task, flipping through pages with columns of numbers on them. "Yes, it is. You have experience waitressing?"

He could at least look at me, she thought. "Well, not exactly."

"What does that mean?" He still hadn't raised his head.

She was getting annoyed. There was no reason to treat her so rudely. "No, I haven't been a waitress. No."

"So why do you think you qualify?"

Fuming, she snapped at him. "Because I was a vice president at a corporate New York public relations firm, so I know how to work hard. And I can be trained."

At last, his head came up. He was, she saw, in his late thirties, younger than she had expected. His face was somewhat rugged, and he had large, hazel eyes that looked intently into hers.

"Well, that certainly got my attention," he said. "I don't get too many corporate VPs applying to wait tables here."

"It shouldn't have taken that to get your attention, you know," she retorted.

"You're right. I'm sorry." He sat up straighter. "I've had a lot of applicants, but none of them have worked out, so I suppose I'm not jumping up anymore when someone comes in. And I was caught up in these numbers, but that's no excuse."

She shook her head. "Not the way to do business. Not that you asked."

"Please." He rose halfway, shaking her hand and gesturing to the chair across the table from him. "We'll do a proper interview. I'm Carson Holt. I own this place, plus two others."

He signaled to the waitress, the girl with spiky hair who had taken care of Ellie and Rachel.

"Something to eat or drink?" he asked Ellie as she approached.

"Thank you. Coffee would be great."

He asked the girl to bring them both hot coffee, then leaned back in his chair and stretched his long, blue-jeaned legs sideways so they extended out past the table. He gave Ellie a questioning look. "So. May I ask what made you wish to change careers from vice president to waitress?"

She hesitated. This man was attractive, and she didn't want to deal with that. She had no interest in starting anything romantic with anyone at the moment. She looked directly at him again, and he smiled. Was that actually a dimple on one cheek?

She coughed to give herself a chance to concentrate on the matter at hand again. "It was time to leave. I recently moved here, so I'm looking for work. I do a lot of work on my family's farm, but I need something else. Nights, Sundays maybe. That would allow me to do both."

"You grew up on a farm around here?"

"No."

He looked confused. "I'm sorry, you said you work on your family's farm . . ."

"Oh." She smiled. "It's a long story. But I grew up in New York City."

"What did you say your name was?"

She repeated it.

"Okay, then, Ellie, why don't we give this a try and see what happens. You want to shadow Lisa here today? You can see the brunch situation. Mondays we're closed, but you can help on Tuesday night. We'll see how that goes. Is today okay?"

"Today is fine. What's the salary?"

"Minimum wage plus tips." He looked amused. "I'm guessing you might have made a little more in your old job."

"Yes, but here, I'm hoping I don't have to sell my soul to collect my paycheck."

His eyebrows went up in surprise. "I think that's a manageable goal."

She smiled and extended her hand. "Great. Then we have a deal."

Chapter 27

Katie came through the doorway from the bedroom. "Is this all right?"

Rachel, wrapping up the zucchini bread she had just finished baking, leaned to the right so she could see through the kitchen's open doorway. She tried not to show any emotion at the sight of her daughter with her hair down in long braids, dressed in English clothes. Nina had helped them shop for the skirt and blouse the day before, but Rachel hadn't seen the pieces on together, her daughter's *kapp* off. Nor had Katie put the clothes on at home yesterday, instead leaving them in the shopping bag overnight. Perhaps, Rachel thought, her child was as stunned as she by the idea of wearing them, and a little afraid to go near them again. The white cotton blouse and blue flowered skirt were both modest. Still, the effect shocked her. She had never seen her child wearing anything but Amish clothing.

It had never been her intention to dress Katie in English clothes. What prompted the change were the accumulated effects of a couple of weeks in New York, watching what Katie had to endure because of her Amish garments. It wasn't just the pointing and whispering on the street. When they went into stores, the salespeople spoke slowly and loudly to her, as if she were deaf or incapable of understanding English, not that shouting would have helped anyway. Strangers often treated her as if she were a doll, kneeling down and commenting on how adorable she was, touching, without asking permission, her sleeve, and, incredibly, her hair, and firing questions at her. If Katie was going to interact here, she would have to blend in. Her clothes was the obvious place to start.

"I wonder what the kids at school will say on Monday." Katie went back into the bedroom. Emerging from the kitchen, Rachel could see her examining herself from different angles in the mirrors lining the closet doors.

Indeed, Rachel thought. With the help of Nina and Gil, Katie had been enrolled in a small private school, with only ten children in each grade. They explained that every child there worked at his or her own pace, so if Katie was ahead or behind in different subjects, it wouldn't matter. Rachel had agonized over whether or not to homeschool her, but decided this would give her an opportunity to meet other children. The two of them couldn't stay in the apartment all day, and she needed to be with people besides her mother and grandparents. So far, it was working out well. The school term had only begun a few weeks earlier, so Katie hadn't missed much. She had already brought a little girl named Jessica back to the apartment to play one afternoon after school. Jessica was stunned to find they didn't watch the television that was there or even own a computer, but Katie distracted her with puzzles and board games, and she seemed to have a good time in the end. Jessica's mother picked her up at five o'clock, and her effort to make casual conversation while stealing glances at Rachel's clothes were almost comical. Rachel didn't mind. She was glad that her daughter seemed to be settling in. Katie knew she wouldn't be allowed to play at anyone else's house—that was too big a risk for Rachel to take—but she was welcome to bring anyone over at any time. It wasn't a big group to select from, with only five girls in her grade, yet she appeared to be happy. That was all Rachel cared about. When they first got to New York, Katie had wet the bed three nights running, which had worried Rachel. But that seemed to have stopped. The new English clothes would play down the differences between Katie and the other children even more. Rachel herself wouldn't exchange her clothing for English clothes. As a member of the Amish church, she wasn't allowed to. Katie was a child, not even baptized, not yet a full church member. Therefore, she wasn't breaking any rules.

"Are you ready to go?" Rachel picked up her purse and two sweaters, one for her and one for her daughter. It was sunny outside at the moment, but the October afternoon could quickly grow cold.

Clearly self-conscious in her outfit, Katie followed her mother into the hallway, ringing for the elevator while Rachel locked the apartment door behind them. Today, they were having lunch with Nina and Gil, plus Blaine and Louis Lawrence,

Rachel's grandparents and Katie's great-grandparents. This was the third time they had gotten together with the older Lawrences, and Rachel was developing affection for her newly acquired grandparents. She liked their quiet dignity. They treated Rachel and Katie as if they were family members with nothing unusual about them. She wished the same could be said for all the other people they had met lately; a number of them were ill at ease around them, or awkwardly waited for Rachel to make conversation, as if afraid they would say something wrong. She understood their nervousness, but it was exhausting to set other people at ease all the time. She herself was growing overwhelmed with trying to make a good impression, meeting more people in a few weeks than she had met in ten years at home, and learning what seemed like hundreds of new things every day. At least Katie was responding well to the stimulation; she had developed a fascination with the city, studying the street maps and reading about the landmarks.

By now, Katie was more advanced than Rachel in knowing what buses they had to take to reach their destinations. Today, though, they had only to walk about five blocks. As they stopped at the corner to wait for the light, Rachel realized she had left the piece of paper with the restaurant's address back in the apartment. She recalled that they had to make a turn, but she wasn't sure if it was left or right. She told Katie, and they retraced their steps to Ellie's building.

They waited for the elevator. When its doors opened, a man in his early twenties rushed out, dressed in a gray suit, preoccupied with checking his pockets. Rachel and Katie stepped inside the elevator and faced front. Katie pressed the button for

Ellie's floor, and the man turned back, hurrying into the elevator, muttering under his breath.

"Forgot my phone," he explained in annoyance, repeatedly pressing the button to his floor, as if that would somehow get him there sooner.

They waited for the doors to close. An elderly woman with a cane entered the lobby from outside, slowly and painfully making her way toward them.

"Oh, man, no way," he murmured.

Katie was reaching for the button to hold the elevator doors open, when he leaned across her and held down the Door Close button. She looked at him with wide eyes as the doors closed and they began to ascend.

He noticed her unhappy surprise. "I gotta get to work. She'll catch it when it comes back down," he explained curtly.

Rachel and Katie stood immobile, afraid to speak. The elevator stopped on the third floor, and he got off, leaving the two of them staring at each other in horror.

"She was an old woman, like Grandma Hannah," Katie said, her voice low as if he might be able to hear her. "Who would do such a thing as that?"

"I don't know. I can't understand that." The elevator stopped, and they got out.

"He was so *mean*." Katie was growing upset. "Are there a lot of mean people here like that man?"

Rachel put a hand on her shoulder. "There are mean people just as there are nice people. We have met so many nice, good people, let's remember that. Okay?"

They walked down the hall toward the apartment. Who

would treat their neighbors that way, Rachel wondered. It had been puzzling enough to ride the elevator with other residents of the building and learn that the most they could hope for was a slight smile or possibly a brief hello. No one seemed to want to converse at all. They were busy sipping at tall thermoses of coffee, texting on cell phones, or staring straight ahead, lost in thought. But this was even worse, and that man had thought nothing of it. What was this place, this world outside her community?

She and Katie put the incident out of their minds as they arrived for their lunch, receiving hugs and kisses all around. Rachel was pleased that no one made too much of a fuss over Katie's new clothes, although she could see Nina looking Katie up and down with approval when she wasn't watching. Nina caught Rachel's eye and smiled. The two of them frequently discussed how to make this experience a good one for Katie, and Rachel knew how much it meant to her to see the little girl doing such a good job handling so many changes.

"So, my little caterpillar, how are you today?" Blaine Lawrence had taken to calling Katie by the names of insects or flowers, which invariably made her laugh. The restaurant was crowded and noisy, so she had to speak more loudly than usual. "I brought you something." She reached into her purse and took out a gold-colored box. "Chocolates. We never talked about whether you like chocolate, but I thought I would take a chance."

"I love chocolate!" Katie grinned. "Thank you."

"Perhaps I'll hold that," Rachel said, taking it from Blaine. "A treat later, right?"

"Of course," Louis put in. "You want to be able to enjoy a big lunch first."

"We eat a lot, but we don't work a lot," Rachel noted.

"This is like a vacation," Gil said. "Plenty of time to work."

"Would you like to go work out at a gym?" Nina asked. "I'd be happy to buy a membership for you."

Rachel must have looked startled, because Nina hastily corrected herself. "I don't know what I was thinking. That's ridiculous."

"What do you do at a gym?" Katie asked.

Nina turned to her, speaking up to be heard above the din. "You keep your body healthy. Exercise on the machines, or take classes."

Katie smiled at the notion. "You pay for that? Why would you? Working keeps your body healthy."

There was a pause as the adults considered how to answer. Rachel jumped in.

"Not everybody does physical work, work that involves their body. So they want to be sure their bodies don't get rusty."

"Oh." Katie still looked confused.

"You're completely right, Katie," Louis said. "Hard work is the best way to keep your body healthy."

"That's right, Daffodil. It's all this sitting around we do that's so bad," said Blaine. "If I could still run around, you and I would do the things you've told me you do at home. Camping, walking in the countryside, playing kickball. Sounds wonderful."

"It is," Katie said. "Right now, it's apple cider time, too. I love the cider we make every fall from our apples." She sighed.

They ordered lunch and chatted about the experiences

Katie and Rachel were having so far. Rachel was amazed at how comfortable the two of them had become with these people. It was more than she would ever have expected, or could have hoped. The world in which they lived was frightening in so many ways, but they made it so much easier than it could have been, always ready to meet Rachel and Katie, explain things, take care of things. They might not live in the same house, but they did provide a support system. Different from the Amish, she thought, incredibly different, but still based on love and loyalty.

As lunch progressed, she noticed that Katie was growing quieter, as if the effort to be heard above the other noisy diners was too much for her. When they were done, they all decided to go for a walk. They adopted a slow pace to accommodate Blaine, who was using a cane. She insisted the walk would do her good. Katie and Rachel followed behind the others. Turning on to a main avenue, they found the streets much more crowded. It seemed as if they were going one way, while everyone else was coming toward them. She put a protective hand on Katie's shoulder, and noticed how stiffly her daughter was holding herself. It dawned on her that she hadn't said a single word in quite a while. Rachel glanced down to find Katie looking unhappy.

"What is it?" she asked, leaning over to speak quietly.

At that moment, a large woman carrying several shopping bags passed by. The shopping bags banged into Katie, knocking her off balance so that she fell against her mother. The woman kept on going.

Katie regained her footing, then burst into tears.

"Are you hurt?" Rachel asked, kneeling down and putting an arm around her child. "Tell me."

"Make it all stop!" Sobbing now, Katie buried her face on Rachel's shoulder. In between sobs, she could barely get out the words. "Please make it stop!"

Rachel stood and called out. "Nina!"

All the others stopped and looked back at her.

"Katie's not feeling well. I'm going to take her back."

Nina started toward them in concern.

Rachel waved her off. "Just a headache. Please excuse us. We'll talk later."

"Are you sure we can't help?" Louis asked.

She smiled to reassure them. "We'll be fine when I can get her home."

Katie tugged at her mother's sleeve in excitement. "Are we really going home? To the farm?"

Rachel looked at her daughter, her wet eyes shining behind a hopeful smile. Her heart sank.

She glanced over at the concerned faces watching Katie, and repeated that they would be fine and she would call them later. Then, she ushered Katie in the opposite direction, off the crowded avenue to a quieter side street.

Rachel put her hands on Katie's shoulders. "Do you want to go back? To the farm?"

Katie looked down and didn't respond.

"We will, you know. If you are unhappy here, it is no good to stay. The only reason we are here is to get to know our other family better. But if this is too much for us, then we should leave. It's not like home, and it's hard, I know."

"But you want to be here, don't you?" Katie asked in a small voice.

"I only want to be here if we both want to. If you say we should go, we will pack up and get on our way."

Katie seemed to relax at her mother's words. "If I ask to go, then we will?"

Rachel nodded.

The little girl thought about it. "We don't need to go yet." She put her arms around her mother's neck and hugged her. "Thank you. But, Mama . . . ?"

"Yes?"

"When is Christmas?"

"About two months from now."

"Can we go home for Christmas? I don't want to miss Christmas at home."

Rachel smiled. "Me neither. Absolutely. I promise. By Christmas, we'll be home."

Chapter 28

Ellie ambled along the side of the road, pausing now and then to widen the berth between herself and the occasional passing car. Sometimes the drivers waved to her, and she waved back. In the past few weeks, she had taken to walking from her house to the farm whenever she could, leaving her car at home. She still drove in the mornings for the milking, though; the sky was dark and she didn't want to be late.

As she approached the Kings' house, she paused to wave at William and Zeke, Judah and Annie's older children, manning the roadside stand across the street. They were doing a brisk business this month in apples and potatoes, but for the moment there were no customers.

She went over to the door leading into Sarah's section of the house, and let herself in. They were planning to bake apple pies this afternoon. Sarah was already getting started, laying out pie pans on the kitchen table. She greeted Ellie, and gestured to an apron slung over a chair. "Ready to work?"

Ellie made a quick count of pans. "Twelve pies?"

Sarah nodded. Ellie put on the apron and went to the sink to wash her hands. Secretly, she was thrilled with her advancing abilities with pies and breads. It was amazing, she thought, that she had never been attracted to a hobby that involved using her hands to create something tangible. Lately, she had also begun spending time with Isaac when he made repairs around the farm, trying to learn from him. Making something out of nothing or visibly improving something gave her tremendous satisfaction. Of course, previously, she hadn't made time for any hobbies at all. Happily, things were different now.

She would never have imagined that her life could undergo such a transformation. It was almost shocking to her how quickly and happily she had thrown off the mantle of pressured executive. Every day, she learned something new. It felt as if what she was doing now was exactly what she should be doing. Yet, in a million years she wouldn't have been drawn to such a life. What did that say about what she had been doing with her life up until this point?

The time passed quickly, until she suddenly realized she had to get ready for work. On Saturdays and three weekday nights, she waitressed at Carson's from five to closing. Sarah wrapped up a pie for her to take home and said she would see Ellie in the morning.

She got to the road and saw Annie leaving her own house in

a small, open wagon. She turned it onto the main road and pulled lightly on the reins, causing the horse to stop in front of Ellie.

"On your way home?"

Ellie nodded.

"I'm going that way. Would you like to ride with me?"

"Thank you. That would be great."

Ellie climbed up, pleasantly surprised by Annie's offer. She still wasn't sure what Judah's wife thought of her, but she was glad the two of them would have time alone.

Annie gave a quick click of her tongue, and the horse moved forward. "Do you hear from Rachel?"

"No, I don't. From what my parents have told me, she and Katie are doing very well." Ellie herself had wondered what communication Rachel had with Leah and Isaac, but she didn't feel it was her place to ask.

"I hear they eat in a lot of restaurants, and it is very expensive."

Ellie smiled. "That's true. New Yorkers do eat in a lot of restaurants. I know I did. And, yes, it can be crazily expensive."

Annie frowned. "What is that teaching Katie?"

"Hmmm." Ellie tried to sound as noncommittal as she could, casting about in her mind for a change in subject. "You know, I was wondering—how late into the year do you keep the stand open? Through November, or are the tourists gone by then?"

Annie launched into a discussion of available crops and the seasonal rhythms of tourist crowds, which carried them until she pulled the wagon up in front of Ellie's house. She cast an appraising eye over it. Most of the other women in the King family had been inside, but so far there had been no occasion for Annie to come over.

"Please, won't you come in?" Ellie asked.

Annie followed her in as far as the kitchen, her eyes assessing the scrubbed appliances and uncluttered, clean surfaces. Ellie always kept the room clean, but she was glad that she had taken a few extra minutes with it that morning.

"Would you like to see the rest of the house?"

"No, that's fine." Annie put a hand on the doorknob. "Very nice." She pointed with her free hand. "Lemon juice will take those stains out of your cutting board."

Ellie fought off a powerful urge to laugh. *You just couldn't resist, could you?* Aloud, she said, "I'll definitely try that. Thank you so much for taking me home."

She was rewarded with one of the first genuine smiles Annie had ever directed to her. "I enjoyed our talk."

"Well, well," Ellie muttered to herself when her guest was gone. "Do I detect a thaw in the ice floe?"

She took a quick shower and changed her clothes, then drove to the restaurant, making it with two minutes to spare. At the front, she greeted Harriet, the older woman who worked the register and had directed Ellie when she came in to interview for the job. She hurried through the rows of tables toward the swinging doors that led to the kitchen, waving to Suki, the other waitress working this shift. The heat of the kitchen hit her squarely in the face as she tied on her black half-apron, and felt in the pockets to make sure her pen and pad of checks were there.

"Ellie, hey, baby!" Anita was the one female among the three cooks who worked there, rotating shifts to divide up lunches and dinners. Married with two grown children, she had worked in restaurant kitchens for nearly twenty years. She had a great sense of humor, but wouldn't dream of putting up with any nonsense from anyone when it came to the job. Ellie thought she was terrific.

"Hey, Anita!" Ellie called back, racing away.

Out of the corner of her eye, she saw Carson standing by a table, talking with a couple seated there. Old friends, no doubt, judging by the way they were laughing. He knew a lot of the people who ate here, possibly because this was one of three restaurants he owned. It was also the smallest and most informal, and tended to have a number of regulars. All three of his places were known for serving good food with a healthy bent, a little lighter on the butter and sugar, but still satisfying, nearly everything made on-site or purchased locally.

He ran his hand through his thick hair. Ellie gave an inward sigh at the sight. She had an enormous crush on him, but he showed no interest in her. Besides, she was still in the dark about his personal circumstances, not to mention that he was her boss. Opening that can of worms, she had decided, would be a mistake. But she couldn't help her thoughts, and she thought he was undeniably attractive.

It was a hectic night. Cleaning up a table in the rear around nine o'clock, she glanced up to see Carson backing out of the kitchen as he pushed open a swinging door with one foot, in the middle of a conversation.

" . . . stop there. Then gotta get home to the little woman

and the kiddies," he said, raising a hand in farewell. "See you tomorrow, lunch shift, right?"

Ellie could hear Anita respond, but couldn't make out the words. Not that she was listening. Now she had her answer to the most important question about Carson. He was married. And had children as well. Disappointment welled up inside her. It didn't matter how she felt, though; that was the end of that. She should have guessed he wouldn't be single. His wife was doubtless gorgeous and perfect, the light of his life.

"G'night, Ellie." From the other side of a row of tables, he passed her on his way and smiled.

"Right," she forced herself to answer. "Good night."

He was probably going to check on another of his restaurants before he went home. The door closed behind him. Married, she thought. Just as well. She hadn't had a successful romantic relationship for a long time; there was no reason to think she would break her pattern now. Worse, when things went bad, she would probably wind up having to quit. For the moment, this was a perfect job, allowing her time to do everything she wanted at home and with the Kings. Things were going so well, she told herself; now wasn't the time to jeopardize her good fortune. Still, she allowed herself another sigh, this one of regret.

In the course of the next few weeks, Ellie settled into a routine, starting off her days by milking the cows with the King men, then having breakfast with the family, and joining in on whatever chores were scheduled for that day. Little by little, her shifts were increased at the restaurant, so she was waitressing most nights, and would leave before supper to get changed for work. She tried to stay as far away from Carson as she could, but it was impossible for her not to notice that he was spending more time engaging her in conversation. He had started asking her opinions about how things were going when he wasn't around to observe, how the rest of the waitstaff was doing, whether the dining room was running as smoothly as it could be. She answered him as best she could, but tried to keep it brief, fearful that if she looked at him for too long, her expression would give away how she felt.

Still, she was completely unprepared when he caught up with her in the back one evening around ten o'clock and asked if she'd like to go somewhere to get a cup of coffee after the restaurant closed.

"Let's have something cooked by someone else," he added. "No business. Just personal."

She stared at him, shocked and angry.

"Are you joking?" she demanded. "You think I'd go for that?"

He looked confused. "Go for what? A cup of coffee? Well, yes, actually, I believe you like coffee. I mean, I've seen you drink it . . ."

"Very funny," she snapped. "This is how you're wooing me to be your girlfriend on the side? Forget it."

"Whoa, hold on now. Who said anything about girlfriend, much less 'on the side'? It's not a lifelong commitment, just coffee."

"You'll probably fire me for saying this, but you've got a lot of nerve. I'm not interested in having my married boss hit on me."

"Married?" He was clearly bewildered. "Excuse me, but the last time I looked I was not married."

"Don't lie, please—just don't insult me like that."

He put a hand on her arm, and she glared down at it. "What are we talking about?" he asked. "If you don't want to go out with me, that's fine, I understand. But please don't accuse me of lying about being married. That's pretty ridiculous."

"I *heard* you. I heard you talking about your wife and children."

"Now I have children, too. I've been awfully busy."

"Stop acting like I'm crazy. I heard you talking to Anita a couple of weeks ago. You told her you were going home to your wife. You said you had to get home to the little woman and the kiddies. I was right out there and I heard it."

He shook his head in confusion. "No way. When did you say this happened?"

"I told you, about two weeks ago."

A realization came to him, and an enormous smile spread across his face.

It infuriated her. "What's so funny?"

"Oh, Ellie." He began to laugh. "I said the little woman and the *kittens*. My cat had kittens two weeks ago. She's the little woman, you know, new mother and all."

She stared at him, speechless. Uncharacteristically, a bright red blush spread up from her neck. She could feel her cheeks grow hot with embarrassment.

"Oh," was all she could whisper.

He threw back his head for a good, loud laugh.

"No wife? Not even a girlfriend?"

"Nope. I don't do stuff like that, cheat on people I supposedly love."

"Okay, okay, so I'm a fool and a lunatic both."

"No, you're not." He smiled at her. "We'll just put it in the category of great stories to tell our kids. More importantly, does this mean you'll have coffee with me? Or perhaps you'd rather meet the kittens. I'm still in the process of locating homes for them."

As her humiliation began to recede, she realized that this was what she had been hoping for. He was, in fact, single. Even better, he was interested in spending time with her. "Coffee will be just fine. See you at closing."

He was still smiling as he left. For her part, Ellie smiled for the rest of her shift.

Carson was delayed by a problem at the other restaurant that night, so they changed their coffee appointment to a dinner date the following night, when Ellie wasn't scheduled to work. He picked her up at home. As they got into his car, he paused before turning on the ignition to pull out his cell phone and show her a picture of himself surrounded by kittens.

"Took it this morning, just for you."

"You'll never let me live that down," she said as he drove away from the house.

"Probably not," he grinned. "Do you like Italian food? I have this place in mind. Rarely get a chance to go there, but it's great."

Over salad and pasta, they quickly dispensed with talking about work and moved on to their personal stories. Ellie wasn't sure how much she could confide in him, so she started with the facts of her life up until the time she learned about the existence of the Kings.

"I'm confused. It seems to me you said you worked on your family farm."

She was surprised he remembered that comment. "I'll explain later. First, we trade. You tell me something about yourself."

"I was born in Virginia, but my parents died in a car accident when I was eight. I got shipped off to my only relatives, my dad's parents in Boston. Very rich, very cold people. They never approved of my dad marrying some poor girl from Fairfax, and they certainly weren't pleased to be saddled with his noisy little boy. Who might bring over other noisy little boys to ruin their rugs and antiques. I didn't see them much. Guess I grew up as kind of a loner."

"That's your idea of 'not much to tell'?" Ellie asked. "That's quite a story."

He shrugged. "I went to college on the West Coast, which was fine by my grandparents. They paid my tuition, but made it clear they expected me to pay it back. After I graduated, my only contact with them was those checks I sent the first of every month. The problem was, paying back that debt meant I got stuck in a bunch of jobs I hated because I needed the money."

"Where are your grandparents today? Still alive?"

"No, they died within a year of each other, about ten years ago. We hadn't spoken in a long time. They left pretty much everything to their charities, but for some strange reason, they left me fifty thousand dollars. It couldn't have been more un-expected, I can tell you that."

Ellie nodded, reaching for a piece of bread. "I'll bet."

"The thing was, I always had this idea in the back of my mind that I wanted to open a restaurant. But I didn't have the capital. Now, suddenly here it was. I was living in Philadelphia at the time, making a good living, so it was a tough decision to take the leap. I mean, did the world need another failed restau-rant? But I had really come to hate what I was doing.

"Anyway, jumping into this business was a now or never kind of thing. I found a good spot out here, and rented a place right next to it. That first year nearly killed me, and I almost went under a couple of times. But the second year was better, and by the third, I had enough to think about another place."

"You're good at what you do, anyone can see that."

He twirled spaghetti onto his fork as he considered his reply. "I loved the business even more than I expected to. So that makes it worth the ridiculous amount of work it is. I guess I'll keep opening places as long as they keep succeeding, and I can manage to keep my life from being swallowed up altogether. This new place may be the tipping point, though."

Ellie considered this. He had discussed a lot with her about the fourth restaurant he was planning to open just after Thanksgiving. It would be larger than Carson's, but more in-formal. "You're a workhorse."

He smiled. "Exactly."

"You still live near your first restaurant?"

"I finally got around to buying my own place. Although it's

kind of a waste of space for just me and the cat. Plus my dog, Marcus. He's my buddy. A brown Lab."

"It's interesting that a self-described loner would love the restaurant business, which is all about dealing with people."

"I guess." He picked up his wineglass.

"If you'll allow me to indulge, I'm wondering if it lets you create the home you never had. You give people a warm welcome, instead of all that cold, proper silence."

"Wow, that's some heavy psychoanalyzing." He laughed, but she noticed he didn't contradict her.

From that point, she had no doubt she could confide the rest of her situation to him. Little by little, she laid it out. He was intrigued by the situation, but it was his immediate understanding of her confused emotions that made an impression on her. Maybe it was feeling so alienated from his only living relatives that allowed him to understand. Plus, having lived among the Amish people for so long, the idea of making jokes, as Jason had, would never have occurred to him. Even if he hadn't been so familiar with them, Ellie could see he wouldn't think that way, and that made her admire him all the more.

"How have these people taken to you?" he asked.

As she started going over her relationships with the various members of the family, Ellie was astonished to realize how much affection she felt for each one of them. So slowly it had been almost imperceptible, they had taken her into their circle, without fanfare but also without reservation. She could appear unexpectedly in any of their homes and find a warm welcome. They asked for her help in the same casual way they asked each other, which told her she was no longer considered a guest or outsider.

"They're amazing people. It's as if they've allowed me to join them in a different world. And I love it there."

Carson took her hand across the table, and Ellie curved her fingers around his in response. "Such a strange tale, your coming here. I'm so happy you did."

She looked into his eyes. *Not as happy as I am*, she thought.

Chapter 29

�֎

The evenings that Ellie worked were becoming progressively more hectic as Carson started spending the bulk of his time at the location for his new restaurant. The cashier, cooks, and other waitresses seemed to gravitate toward Ellie when they had questions or problems. Somehow, they trusted her advice and treated her as the de facto manager, although she hadn't tried to assume such a position. She was glad to help, anyway; compared to what she had done in the past, this was pretty straightforward problem solving, and it gave her satisfaction to see a problem solved or averted. Carson told her word had gotten back to him that she was performing duties above and beyond her waitress duties, and he added a generous bonus to her paycheck. She stared at the check, recalling the large numbers on her former bonus checks, and had to laugh when she realized how much more she appreciated the genuine gratitude behind this far smaller amount than the indifference behind those far larger ones.

Ellie was also enjoying the camaraderie of the staff at the restaurant. Aside from Anita, she had also become fond of Lisa, the twenty-year-old waitress who had waited on her the first time she'd come into the restaurant, and whom she had shadowed on her first day working there. Lisa could be moody, but her cheerful nature more than made up for the times she preferred to retreat into herself. Ellie noticed that she missed a few days of work here and there without much explanation, and wondered if it had to do with the girl's mood swings, or possibly some more serious form of depression. Otherwise, though, she was always ready to joke and have some fun.

She was surprised to leave after a shift one night and find Lisa leaning against Ellie's car in the parking lot. When the girl turned her face to Ellie, she saw by the glow of the streetlights that Lisa was crying.

"What's wrong?" Ellie immediately put a comforting hand on Lisa's arm.

Lisa rubbed her wet eyes, further smearing her dark eye makeup. "I'm really sorry, I shouldn't be bothering you with this."

"With what? Are you okay?"

Lisa let out a small sob. Ellie rummaged around in her purse until she came up with a small package of tissues.

"Here." She extended the tissues and Lisa took one. "Now please tell me what's going on."

"It's my mom. She's been really sick, and I've been using the money from this job to pay for her medicine. We don't have insurance. The medicine is for her kidneys, and it's really expensive."

"Oh, honey, I'm so sorry." Ellie felt terrible, hearing that she had been keeping such a burden to herself all these weeks.

"But now . . . I don't know what we'll do." Lisa looked away.

"Why? What's happened?"

"Carson fired me. He said I'd missed three days of work in the past month, and that was three days too many. He pointed a finger at the door and said, 'Out.'"

"Carson actually said that?"

Lisa nodded, miserable.

Ellie couldn't imagine him being so brusque with an employee, much less Lisa, who had worked for him for a couple of years, and with whom he typically joked around. Then she recalled the first time she had met him, when she had applied for the waitress job, and he so rudely kept his head buried in his notes; he hadn't bothered to look up at her until she mentioned that she was an executive. Maybe there was a much harder side to him than she knew. She certainly wouldn't have seen it lately, though, even if it did exist; things had been going so well between them since their dinner date.

"Anyway," Lisa said, wiping her eyes one last time, "I don't have my car anymore. Couldn't make the payments. Would you mind terribly giving me a ride home? It's just a couple of miles that way."

She pointed down the road, in the opposite direction from where Ellie was headed to get home.

"Of course."

They got into her car and drove what turned out to be some ten miles. Lisa confided in Ellie along the way about how long her mother had been sick, and how difficult it had been to care for her without assistance or any money other than what she made as a waitress.

"This new batch of medicine costs three hundred dollars, and now I don't know what I'm going to do." She sighed.

"Can I help you out?" Ellie asked.

"Oh, no," Lisa said at once. "I wouldn't take money from you. I couldn't. You've been so great to me, and who knows when I could pay you back."

"It's okay, really," Ellie said.

"Absolutely not," Lisa said in a firm tone. "But thank you anyway." She pointed. "Make a left here, and then a right. I'm the last place on the left."

The street where Lisa lived was crowded with run-down houses. As soon as Ellie pulled up to the curb, Lisa jumped out and turned back to speak to her through the window.

"Thanks for the ride."

She was gone into the darkness. As Ellie turned her car around, the headlights revealed a car parked on the tiny front lawn, and what seemed to be some cinderblocks and tires, but not much else. Grim, Ellie thought. As she drove, she felt progressively worse about Lisa and her situation. The family obviously had very little, and this young girl was burdened with supporting a sick parent all by herself. No wonder she had dark days.

As she approached Carson's again, she saw a light on inside, and decided to stop at the restaurant instead of bypassing it to continue home. She knew Carson had been planning to come by at the very end of the night to collect the receipts, and he was obviously there right now.

Sure enough, when she knocked loudly on the door, he emerged from the back to let her in.

"Hey, what are you doing here?" he asked, obviously pleased to see her.

"I was on my way home, but I took a little detour to drop Lisa off at her house."

"Lisa?" He frowned. "Was she still here? She should have been gone hours ago."

"I don't know about that, but she said you fired her."

His smile faded. "Yes. Yes, I did fire her."

"Wow, Carson, I was surprised. The kid told me she's the one supporting her mother, who's sick."

He didn't say anything.

"I mean, did you really tell her 'three days of not showing up is three days too many, so out' or something like that? Why would you be so harsh with a nice kid like her?"

His eyes turned cold. "I don't believe what I do with my other employees is your business, frankly."

Ellie bristled. "Wait a minute. We're all kind of close. They talk to me, and I care about them. It's one of the benefits of working here. And you've seemed to not mind my getting a little more involved in how things are done here. So why are you suddenly the big, bad boss?"

His words were angry. "You're a smart woman and you know a lot of things, Ellie. But you don't know everything, and that includes when to stay out of things that aren't your concern."

"Whoa." She took a step back. "I don't know where that came from."

"It's pretty obvious. If I want to fire someone, I will do it without asking your permission. And I don't expect to have to justify my decisions to you. Are we clear?"

She spoke in a clipped tone. "Crystal clear, I assure you."

"Good." He suddenly seemed impatient to get back to whatever he had been doing. "Was there anything else you wanted?"

"No, not a thing." She turned to go. "Thank you for your time."

"You're welcome." He was already walking down the row of tables toward the back.

Ellie yanked open the restaurant door and returned to her car. She was furious at Carson, and she wondered if she could have a relationship with somebody who was so cold when push came to shove. She remembered how Robert Clark had spoken to her when she quit her job in New York. It hadn't felt good, having to take that verbal lashing from someone she liked and respected. She could imagine how Lisa must have felt, not to mention her financial problems on top of it.

So Carson Holt wasn't any different from all the other selfish businessmen she encountered: interested and appreciative when it served his needs, indifferent to everyone else when the situation was no longer beneficial to him. She was so disappointed in having misjudged him, she wanted to cry.

It was a long, unhappy night for Ellie. In the morning, she left the farm after breakfast, and drove straight to the bank, where she withdrew three hundred dollars. Regardless of what Lisa had said, she was going to help, at least to get the girl over the hump of buying this one batch of medicine. It didn't take her long to return to Lisa's house, which looked even sadder in the daylight, in dire need of a paint job, with a dirty, plaid sofa on the sagging porch.

She parked and went to the front door, knocking a few times. There was silence from within. She knocked again, more loudly this time.

"Hang on, I'm coming." Lisa opened the door, wearing jeans and a faded black T-shirt. She looked exhausted, yet unsurprised to see Ellie standing there at eight o'clock in the morning. "Hey, there," she said, running a hand through her short, black hair.

"Listen," Ellie said, "I know you told me you wouldn't, but you have to let me help you. I brought you the money you needed. I insist that you take it."

Lisa smiled broadly, suddenly animated. "Oh, you're the best!" She put out her hand for the cash. "Can I take your car to the drugstore? I'll be right back."

"Oh." Ellie hadn't been prepared for that. "Well, why don't I drive you?"

"No, that's fine. You just wait here." Lisa took the car keys from her hand and rushed off. "Be right back in five."

Ellie turned to watch her yank open the car door and get in, tearing out of the driveway and down the road. She frowned.

Turning back to the front door, she pushed it open slightly with her finger and peered inside. The room was a mess, dishes, clothes, overflowing ashtrays everywhere. The air was stale. Where was Lisa's mother? In one of the bedrooms, no doubt. She didn't want to disturb a sick woman, so she entered as quietly as she could, glancing around to see if there was a place to sit down. She moved some old comic books and papers off a chair and took a seat. Well, she thought, looking around, twenty-year-olds could be unbelievably messy, although this seemed a bit over the top, even for them.

When a young man appeared in a doorway, Ellie almost jumped. Dressed in dirty jeans and a faded flannel shirt, he put one arm up to rest it against the doorjamb. Ellie judged him to be in his early twenties. He was looking her up and down.

"And you would be . . . ?" he asked in mild amusement.

"I'm Ellie Lawrence. I work with Lisa. Waitressing."

"Ah, yes, a friend of Lisa's." He was grinning. "Lisa seemed to go off in quite a hurry."

"She had to go to the drugstore."

He laughed. "You don't say."

Ellie was growing distinctly uncomfortable. "Yes," she said in a cooler tone, "for her mother's medicine."

He burst out laughing. "You don't look stupid, lady. But you are."

A cold feeling was creeping up Ellie's back. She was suddenly piecing it together. The mood swings, the tale of woe, the sudden excited reaction when Lisa saw the money.

"And who would you be?" she asked the young man, still smirking at her.

"Lisa's brother. Pleased to meet you." He extended a hand without moving. Ellie ignored it. "You don't look like most of the people Lisa gets to, shall we say, help her."

"Lisa went to buy drugs, didn't she?" Ellie asked. "Not medicine for her mother, but drugs for herself."

He tilted his head. "Our mother's been dead for about, oh, three years now. She doesn't have much need for medicine anymore."

"Right." Ellie nodded, wondering if she was perhaps the easiest victim that Lisa—or anyone else in the world, for that matter—had ever conned. She sighed. "Will Lisa be bringing back my car?"

"Oh, sure. She knows better than to mess with that kind of charge, stealing cars. But it might be a few hours."

Ellie took this in.

"Carson finally cut her loose, eh? I wondered just how far she could push him. Now we know."

Ellie looked at him, startled. "Do you have a phone? I think I'd like to call for a ride."

When the taxi arrived, she asked the driver to take her to one of Carson's other restaurants, where she knew he was spending the morning. On the way, she tried to figure out what she was going to say to him. She hadn't made any headway by the time she arrived, so she hastened to go in before she could lose her nerve. The restaurant was still closed this early in the day, but the front door was unlocked.

She saw surprise flicker in his eyes when she unexpectedly appeared. Then he quickly turned away, back to a discussion with the cashier. Ellie waited quietly until he was done. He nodded politely to acknowledge her, then started to move away.

"Carson, please." She put out a hand to stop him. "I need to talk to you. To apologize."

"No need," he said in a curt voice.

"Please, at least let me explain. I know now, I get it."

He looked at her.

"Lisa and drugs. I understand."

"Come on." He led her to a table.

"I owe you a huge apology. You were absolutely right. I shouldn't have stuck my two cents in where they didn't belong when I didn't know the facts."

His eyes bored into hers. "You need to understand, Ellie. Lisa's mother was a good friend of mine, one of my chefs. When she died of kidney failure three years ago, I wanted to help her kids in whatever way I could. I never knew Lisa was into drugs. Maybe she didn't start until after her mother died. I don't know. I gave them money that first year, and then, when she turned eighteen, I hired her to work. Her brother has some job, and he seems able to make some kind of a living. But she hasn't been able to keep it together. I paid for her rehab three times."

"Oh," Ellie groaned. "This is way worse than I guessed."

He nodded. "I put up with the missed days and the minor stuff. But last month, I saw she was stealing money. I can't keep her off the drugs, and she doesn't seem to want to get off them herself. So there's not much else I can do. I had to let her go."

"Of course. This is so terrible . . ."

"What made it even more so was how fast you were to think the worst of me." He leaned back in his seat. "I didn't see that coming."

I should have seen it coming, Ellie thought. *I've been so confused, I can't tell the nice guys from the rotten ones anymore. Here*

I thought I was coming to this girl's rescue when all I did was cause trouble, make Carson justifiably angry with me, and manage to throw away three hundred dollars as a bonus.

Carson smiled at her. "You look so miserable, I actually feel bad for you. Even though you really had no business saying what you did to me." He reached for her hand. "Why didn't you trust me to do the right thing? You know I care about everybody who works at my places."

"I know, I know. I'm humiliated and embarrassed and really sorry."

"Wow, okay, not so much groveling required. A simple, 'Hey, Carson, I think you're actually okay' will suffice. Besides, I ask your opinion on lots of things when it's appropriate. This just wasn't one of those times."

"Hey, Carson?"

"Yes?"

"I think you're actually okay."

He grinned, rose up halfway and leaned across the table to kiss her. It was an odd moment for a first kiss, she thought, but she would gladly take it.

Chapter 30

Rachel finished writing the address and capped the black marker. When she and Katie returned from their trip, she would mail the carton home to her mother. It contained half a dozen quilt tops, which Leah and the other women would complete before taking them to be sold. Sometimes Rachel had to stay up late at night to sew, but she was determined to send back more quilt tops than she usually produced to compensate for missing out on so much other work on the farm.

"First thing Monday morning, I'll walk this over to the post office," she said. Katie was reading on the sofa, and didn't respond. The intercom from downstairs buzzed, startling Rachel, as usual, with its shrillness. That would be Nick. She went over to press the button and tell him they were on their way down. Katie jumped up to put on the fleece jacket Nina had bought her for the colder weather.

"Let's go." She grabbed the wheeled suitcase they were sharing.

Seeing Nick was always a welcome adventure to Katie, and the fact that he would be driving them up to Providence for an entire weekend was a special treat. Uncle Nick worked all week, but he made time on a Saturday or Sunday to visit the two of them, or take Katie somewhere fun in the city. He introduced her to the top of the Empire State Building, the carousel in Central Park, and the busy streets of SoHo.

Rachel was delighted when she received a phone call from A.J. asking if she and Katie would come to Providence to visit her and Steve one weekend. Up until that point, she and her newfound sister had talked on the telephone a few times, but they had little to say to each other, and the conversation was stilted. A.J. must have been bothered by that as well, and decided the time had come to do something about it. This was exactly the reason Rachel wanted to come here in the first place: to get to know her new family. Still, she would have been unlikely to make this trip without Nick, and Katie was thrilled about a weekend with her new aunt and uncles.

Rachel retrieved her black cape and bonnet from the closet as Katie zipped up the fleece jacket.

Wheeling the suitcase, Katie walked ahead to hold the lobby door open for her mother. They emerged into a cold November afternoon, the sky already dark. Nick was standing by his car. He came to take their bag and get a hug from Katie before they settled in and headed toward I-95 for the three-hour drive. On the way, Nick regaled them with humorous stories about his colleagues at the news website where he worked, and they shared with him what they had done during the week. It was a pleasant trip and Katie seemed almost disappointed when they pulled up in front of a gray house on a small suburban street.

"Everybody out," he announced, honking the car horn several times before coming around to Rachel's side of the car to help her out.

The noise summoned A.J. and Steve to the door. There were handshakes and hugs, and they all sat in the living room while Steve fed more wood to the fire. The house, Rachel saw, was small and cluttered, but pleasant. The numerous bookshelves reminded her of Nina and Gil's apartment. Unlike their neat shelves, though, these were so packed that many books were shoved in sideways, and others formed piles on the floor just in front of the shelves. After some discussion about the drive, A.J. led them into a tiny dining room for a dinner of roast chicken and butternut squash.

"This is a big treat for us," A.J. said to Rachel and Katie as she filled water glasses for everyone. "Along with you two, we get Nick. I don't think you've ever been here to our house, have you?" She looked at him.

"Never. I like it, though. This gave me a good excuse to visit."

Steve directed his comment to Nick. "I'm guessing the women want to be by themselves tomorrow, so you and I should figure out something to do."

Nick paused. "Actually, I was hoping tomorrow Katie would

go exploring with me." He turned toward her in the seat next to his. "What do you say? You want to hang with me and Uncle Steve?"

"Oh, yes." She bobbed her head with enthusiasm.

"That's great!" Steve said in surprise. "We'll have an outing, the three of us."

A.J. spoke to Rachel. "I figured I could show you around Brown, and however much of Providence you want to see."

"Wonderful."

They lingered over dinner, everyone contributing bits and pieces about themselves to the conversation in an effort to get to know one another better. By the time they got up from the table, it was nearly eleven. A.J. made up the couch in the living room for Nick, and showed Rachel the extra bedroom she and Katie would share.

In the morning, Steve served them all pancakes, juice, and coffee before he, Nick, and Katie took off in his car.

"At last," A.J. said, finishing up the coffee in her cup, "it's quiet. Just you and me." She smiled. "I didn't mean it the way it sounded. But I am glad to have some time alone with you."

Rachel was washing the dishes. She glanced over her shoulder and smiled back.

"Oh, leave those dishes," A.J. said, with a wave of her hand. "I'll get them later. I want you to sit down and talk with me."

Rachel did as she was asked. "It's very nice of you to have us," she said as she took a seat.

"No, it isn't, and please don't be so formal with me. I need to get to know my sister, but it's so difficult to make it down to New York while I have school. And even if I could, I'd have to fight everybody else there for your time. Now I have you all to myself. My older sister."

"I have to keep reminding myself of that. I am your older sister, aren't I?"

"But without the benefits of being one. You never got to boss me around or yell at me, or any of that fun stuff Ellie got to do."

Rachel laughed. "I can't imagine doing that to you."

"You say that now. You wouldn't if you had known me as a kid."

Rachel's tone was wistful. "I wish I had. It's funny, though. You seem older than I am, because you're so experienced in the world."

"That's just in my world. In your world, I would seem like a bumbling fool."

"Not at all."

"Should we walk?" A.J. took a down jacket off a hook on the wall. She watched Rachel don her cape and black bonnet. "Will you be warm enough? It's pretty cold today."

"Absolutely."

The two of them stepped out into a sunny but frigid day. As they walked, A.J. paused to explain different things about the university and the buildings. When they grew hungry, they stopped at a small restaurant on Thayer Street for some lunch. Afterward, A.J. took Rachel into the Brown bookstore. They wandered downstairs where the course books were sold, and Rachel meandered among them, transfixed by the variety and sheer number of different subjects, some of which fascinated her, many of which she had never heard of. She picked up some of the spiral-bound notebooks, running her hand along the shiny covers, picturing herself carrying one as she walked along the street.

Eventually, they made their way to the school's central green, where they sat on the wide stone steps of one of the buildings, watching students crisscrossing the green, talking, texting, hurrying, lost in thought. Rachel envisioned the class-rooms surrounding them, where professors lectured and students took notes. She felt an ache that she pushed away before she could examine it too closely.

"How long has this school been here?" she asked.

"About two hundred and fifty years, give or take."

"So many students have passed through. It's such a beautiful place, all these brick buildings and old trees." She sighed.

"Do you wish you had gone to college?" A.J. asked.

"It wasn't a choice."

"I understand . . . but I'm just asking if you ever wish you had. Even if you couldn't."

Rachel hesitated. "Can I tell you a secret?"

A.J. nodded.

"When I was seventeen, I lived away from home for a bit. During that time, I studied. I worked, but at night, I studied books I wasn't supposed to be studying. And I really liked that. But it's not okay to do that once you join the church."

They were both quiet.

"That's really something," A.J. finally said. "It's hard for me to imagine you having to study in secret."

"We learn everything we need to know in our schools. But past eighth grade—it's not what we do."

"What about now, when you're older? Would it be okay?"

Rachel shook her head. "Oh, no. Besides, there's too much work to be done. There's no time for that. And there's no point to it."

A.J. seemed to consider this but didn't pursue the subject. "I'm freezing," she said, rubbing her gloved hands together. "How about some hot chocolate in the Blue Room." She pointed to a large building at the far end of the green.

They went inside to a large room with booths, tables, and chairs. While A.J. went to get their drinks, Rachel found an empty table. Some of the students were watching her, but she was far more interested in watching them. So many nationalities and accents all around her. She caught a glimpse of a stack of books on a nearby table; the one on top had a long title she couldn't quite make out, something about Latin America. At a booth, she saw a girl about to open a large textbook with the words Organic Chemistry on the cover.

"You can study anything you want here, anything at all," she observed as A.J. joined her with two cups of steaming hot chocolate.

"Not anything, but almost."

"You study education, don't you?"

"Basically."

"Gee, I—"

She was interrupted by the ringing of A.J.'s cell phone. A.J. took it out of her jacket pocket and looked to see who was calling.

"Sorry." She held up a finger. "One second. It's Nick." She pressed a button and held the phone to her ear. "Hi."

As she listened, her face grew solemn, then she drew a quick breath. "Ohhh . . .," she moaned. She listened some more. "Right. We'll meet you back there."

She clicked off the phone and looked over at Rachel. "Nick just got a call from our parents. Gram died."

"Blaine? Oh, no," Rachel cried. "But we just saw her two days ago. She wasn't sick."

"She had a heart attack." A.J.'s eyes were filling with tears. "We're all driving to New York. So we should get back to my house."

Here she had just discovered this lovely woman, Rachel thought, her very own grandmother, and now she was gone. Time was so fleeting, with so much going on in her life now. Suddenly, she felt a longing to see her parents.

But which set of parents? she asked herself. The answer, she realized, was both.

Chapter 31

The Wayward Café wasn't due to open for another week, so finishing touches were still being applied to the interior. As Carson and Ellie walked the space, they discussed the plans, from what should go where to how the traffic should flow.

When Carson asked her opinion about opening for breakfast, she hesitated. "You know, I'm just giving you my personal feelings, not anything based on actual information."

He smoothed her hair, more as an excuse to get closer to her than because it was necessary. "I'm not expecting you to speak as a professional. But I value what you so casually call your feelings about this stuff. You're always dead-on."

"All right, buddy, you're asking, just remember that."

They continued to walk, debating and tossing ideas back and forth. Ellie was thoroughly enjoying herself and the old surge of excitement she got from confronting a business challenge. It was one of the benefits of dating Carson, the way he included her in his plans; he had been casually asking for her suggestions before they started going out, but, once the incident over Lisa's firing had been sorted out, they had grown even more open to discussing the business. She loved having the fun of coming up with ideas without any of the responsibility for implementing them.

She and Carson had rarely been apart since the night they made up after fighting about Lisa. Never had Ellie imagined that it could be so easy to slip into the life of another person, and have him slip into hers. Nothing with Carson was difficult. His easygoing way reinforced the calm she found among the Kings. Sometimes, she had told A.J. on the phone, she was so relaxed she was afraid she might slip into a coma. Her sister had roared with laughter at the idea of, as she put it, "uptight Ellie finally letting it all hang loose." She had no idea where they might be going as a couple, but at the moment she was savoring the joys of being with him. A week ago, she had taken him to dinner at the farm, where he had been a big hit with the Kings. After the meal, he, Isaac, and Amos had disappeared for two hours. Turned out they'd been in the barn, discussing the horses and next spring's crops. Even Leah had given her stamp of approval with a simple, "Seems like a nice man."

Between spending time with him, working at the farm, and waitressing, Ellie was physically exhausted. But she had never felt better or happier.

As they were leaving the restaurant site, Carson's cell phone rang. He stopped outside the car to talk, so Ellie got into the passenger seat to wait for him. She was surprised when he appeared right outside her window and made the inaccurate but universally understood motion for her to roll it down. She laughed, gesturing to indicate the car was off so the button wouldn't work, but then she noticed his expression, and stopped laughing. Opening the door, she started to get out.

"What's wrong? Who was it?" she asked.

"Harriet. Your mother tracked you down to the restaurant."

"Leah called?" Ellie was alarmed. Leah stayed away from using a telephone unless it was an emergency.

"Not Leah. Your mother in New York."

It surprised her how quickly she had jumped to the wrong conclusion, but she didn't dwell on it. "Why did she call the restaurant? She can reach me on my phone at home."

He took her hand. "She wanted to get the message to you right away." He paused. "I'm sorry, but your grandmother died."

She stared at him. "My gra–Gram died?"

"The message was your grandmother in New York. Would that be her?"

"Oh, no, not Gram." With a soft wail, she sank back down onto the car's seat.

"You were close to her?"

"I adored her. Oh . . ." She shut her eyes. "My poor grandfather."

"Your mother also said to tell you the funeral will be tomorrow."

Her eyes were wet with tears. "I'll grab some stuff and get on the road. Would you drop me at my place now?"

"Of course."

He hurried around to the driver's side. Ellie swung her legs inside the car. She should get word to the Kings. At the moment, though, the Kings didn't seem very important. What was important was that she hadn't seen her grandmother in months, and now she would never have another chance.

He backed the car out of its parking space. "Ellie, would you like me to go with you to New York?"

She considered the offer. "No. Thank you, but I think it would be best if I went alone."

"Okay, if you're sure. Let me know if you change your mind."

She looked over at him. He was opening his new restaurant in a week, not to mention running three others, but he was willing to drop everything to go to her grandmother's funeral, hours away. She knew then that she could fall deeply in love with this man.

Ellie drove from Pennsylvania directly to her parents' apartment, and slept there rather than displace Rachel from her apartment. It had been a good decision, enabling them to catch up on what had been going on. A.J. and Steve had driven down from Providence and were also sleeping there. The night before, Ellie and her sister stayed up until well after three o'clock in the morning, talking about their grandmother and their childhoods with her. Then A.J. wanted to hear all about Ellie's Amish family.

Once the service got under way the next day. Ellie's other thoughts were forgotten as she listened to the stories and memories about her grandmother. She watched her grandfather, impeccably dressed as always, but appearing somehow diminished in his seat, looking almost as if he were unaware of where he was. She wondered how or if he would recover from this.

When it was over, the Lawrences were joined by some two

dozen people at their apartment. Nina kept busy making sure everyone had food and drinks from the buffet in the dining room. Gil and Aunt Lillian remained by their father's side. If possible, Ellie was even more saddened that day by her aunt's demeanor. Her usual sharp-tongued cracks and imperial presence were nowhere in evidence. Instead, she said virtually nothing, wearing a conservative black dress and enormous sunglasses, which she kept on throughout the entire day. When Ellie went to give her a hug, the only comment her aunt made was, "Thank you, darling." The sight of a stricken Aunt Lillian broke Ellie's heart all over again.

From her perch on the sofa, Ellie watched Nick talking with Katie. Their easy familiarity made it clear they had an affectionate relationship. Rachel, too, clearing away dirty dishes and glasses, was obviously comfortable with their parents, as well as with Nick and A.J. Given how comfortable she herself now was with the Kings, Ellie reflected, it shouldn't strike her as strange that Rachel had developed bonds with the family here. She didn't feel the same stab of jealousy she used to experience when she encountered signs of Rachel's closeness with her relatives, but she nonetheless still felt unsettled.

Glancing over, she noticed her grandfather was momentarily by himself, and hurried over to his side. "Can I do anything for you?" she asked.

"No, sweetheart." The sorrow in his voice made her wince. "But I appreciate your asking."

She tried to keep the tears from welling up again. "You know, Gramp, you two had the best marriage in the world. I always envied you, and wanted to have one just like yours."

"It was wonderful. She was everything to me. But don't envy other people's marriages, my dear. It wasn't always easy. Not for me, and certainly not for her, I'm sure."

"I guess not. But you sure made it look like it was."

"We definitely had our tough times. All marriages do."

"How did you get through them?"

He thought for a moment. "I suppose we were both committed from the beginning, and we never deviated from that. Neither of us was going to walk out no matter what. We put our hearts and souls into it, you could say, no holding back. And, somehow, we muddled through."

"You more than 'muddled,' Gramp."

He gave her a sad smile. "Yes, we did."

She kissed his cheek. "I love you."

He patted her arm absently as he turned away, distracted by his grief.

So much love translated into so much loss, she thought. Carson appeared in her mind's eye. What struck her was the pain she suddenly felt at the idea that she might not see him again, might lose him. No man had ever evoked that feeling in her, a cold fear at the idea of his being taken away from her.

"Hello, Ellie."

She turned to find Rachel behind her.

"I'm so sorry about your grandmother." The words came out a bit stiffly, but Ellie could see that they were heartfelt.

"She was your grandmother, too."

Rachel looked down. "You may find this hard to believe, but I was actually starting to feel like she really was."

Ellie thought about Hannah and Amos, working outside

with them, talking in the evenings. "No, I don't find it hard to believe. Not at all."

"She was so good to me and to Katie. You were fortunate to have all those years with her." Suddenly, as she heard her own words, Rachel's face seemed to freeze.

Ellie could see her instant regret, the significance of what she'd said painfully clear to them both. They stood there in awkward silence.

"How is everything in the apartment?" Ellie finally asked.

"Great," Rachel quickly answered. "Thank you. We're so grateful to you for letting us stay there."

"And how do you like living in New York?"

Rachel considered the question. "It's very good and very bad, both. Exciting and too much at the same time."

Katie must have seen her mother talking to Ellie, and taken that as a sign that it might be all right to approach. "Hello," she said in a small voice, as if she still weren't sure it was okay.

Ellie bent down to give her a hug. "I'm so glad to see you!"

"I'm sorry about your grandma," she said.

"Thank you, honey. I'm happy you got to spend some time with her, even though it wasn't enough."

Katie nodded. "She was nice. I really liked her."

"Me, too." Ellie gave her a regretful smile. "But you've also gotten to spend time with everyone else here. I hope they've been nice, too."

Katie brightened. "Oh, so nice! Uncle Nick takes me all over the place. Grandma and Grandpa do, too." She lowered her voice conspiratorially. "They let me get ice cream all the time."

Grandma and Grandpa. Ellie smiled. It was hard to keep up with all the new allegiances that were forming.

"So they tell me that you're in school here. How do you like it?"

A slight hesitation. "It's okay, I guess."

Ellie scrutinized her face a little more closely. The lukewarm endorsement wasn't quite what she had been expecting from Katie, normally so enthusiastic. Before she could inquire further, Rachel spoke.

"Come, Katie, let's go see what we can do in the kitchen."

Ellie watched Rachel lead her daughter away, wondering what might be going on. So many surprises on this visit.

The biggest surprise from her point of view was the intensity of her reaction to coming back to New York and her family. She hadn't realized how much she had missed her parents, how thrilled she was to see Nick and A.J. On top of that, just walking the city streets reminded her how invigorating it was to live here. She felt an excitement, a sense of anticipation that she used to take for granted, but had apparently lain dormant in her since she left.

"How's my girl?" Nina came over and leaned in for a private conversation. "It's so wonderful to have you and A.J. both staying here at the same time. I mean, it is for a horrible reason . . ."

Ellie took her mother's hand. "It's so good to see you, Mom."

"I've missed having you around, angel. Being able to talk to you. Who would have dreamed you, of all people, would wind up with that one phone—not even an answering machine!"

"I promise to call more often."

Nina looked surprised. "Wow—that was easy. I wasn't even trying to make you feel guilty."

"No, I want to. I've missed you."

Ellie was already starting to regret her plan to leave the following day. She gave her head a slight shake, confused by her own thoughts. She wondered if it was actually possible that, for the rest of her life, she would always feel torn about where she belonged.

Chapter 32

�֍

Rachel opened the oven door and removed the pie, setting it on a cooling rack on the kitchen counter and laying the pot holders in a neat row beside it. She and Katie were going over to Nick's apartment later to have dinner with him and the woman he was dating. They had met Winnie the previous week at Thanksgiving dinner. Spending Thanksgiving without her family in Pennsylvania had been difficult, but Rachel consoled her child—and herself—with the promise that they would make it back for Christmas. In the meantime, they got to experience a big family holiday with a host of newly acquired family.

That evening, Nick had raved about Rachel's pecan pie, part of what Nina served for dessert, so she promised to make another one just for him. That conversation turned into an invitation for tonight. Before leaving for school in the morning,

Katie, excited to be going there tonight, reminded her mother twice not to forget to make the pie.

Rachel had timed the baking so she would be done in time to turn off the oven before going to pick up Katie from school. She bundled up against the chill and darkness, and went out, glad the walk was a short one. Backpack slung over a shoulder, Katie was one of the first children to come through the school's double doors. As she drew closer, Rachel could see that she was crying.

"Katie, what is it?" she asked in alarm.

Katie shook her head and started walking, obviously not wanting anyone to see her cry. She hurried ahead of her bewildered mother, barely making it into their lobby before she started to sob.

"Oh, Mama," she wailed, burying her face in her mother's cape.

Rachel hustled her upstairs and into the apartment. "Now, sit down and tell me what's going on," she said, locking the door behind them, and slipping off her cape and bonnet.

The little girl was crying so hard, she could barely speak. Rachel led her to the sofa, and enveloped her in her arms, murmuring soothing sounds. At last, Katie's breathing became more regular.

"Okay." She wiped her eyes with one sleeve. "I'm going to tell you."

"Well, of course," Rachel said in surprise. "Why wouldn't you?"

"I don't want to bother you with this."

"With what? You could never bother me."

Katie sniffled as she gathered her thoughts. "You know things haven't been that great at school lately. With the kids, I mean."

Rachel nodded. Over the past several weeks, Katie was finding herself alone at school more and more. The children in her grade, even though there were so few, had been forming alliances, and Katie didn't understand how these social situations worked or what she was supposed to do about them. She was the only child without a cell phone or computer, which meant she was never part of the conversations outside school, never included in the gossip. That was fine with Katie, who had no interest in gossip, yet it apparently marked her as an outsider, or as she put it—evidently mimicking a term she had learned from her schoolmates—a loser, despite the school's insistence that it did everything possible to prevent such hurtful situations. Her Amish background, now linked with this absence of everyday technology, suddenly no longer struck the children as interesting but as distinctly weird. Recently, Katie had realized that even Jessie, whom she thought of as a close friend, had been declining offers to play, not because she was busy as she claimed, but because she no longer wanted to be associated with Katie.

"I did something that maybe wasn't good. Smart, I mean." Katie took a ragged breath. "I guess I thought if I told Jessie something special, you know, something private, it would make her like me again. The kids like to share secrets, and I figured that could be a good thing for me to do."

"Okay. What secret did you share with her?"

Katie averted her mother's eyes. "I-I told her that I some-times wet the bed." Her lower lip started to quiver again. "That seemed like a good secret to tell. Not so terrible, but really private."

"It's not a big deal," Rachel reassured her.

The tears spilled over. "*Yes, it is!* Jessica told everybody. She put it on her computer. All the kids thought it was so funny, that I was like a baby. They teased me all day. Not even just the fifth graders! The fourth and sixth graders, too! They all knew!"

She began to sob again, burying her face in her hands.

"No, sweetheart, don't." Rachel reached for her, but Katie jerked away, inconsolable.

Rachel wanted to cry herself, though it would never do to let Katie see that. Watching her child in pain this way was more than she could bear. And it was all her fault. She had brought this upon Katie by insisting they come here. She was the one who had enrolled her in that awful school. The great adventure they were going to have among the English! What had she been thinking? Back at home, Katie would have been in school with children she knew and had grown up with, sur-rounded by members of their community who loved and cared about her. Instead, her own mother had sent her to be among strangers—people who not only didn't care about her, but treated her with cruelty.

"Tomorrow, I will go to that school and tell them you won't be coming back. I'll tell them exactly why. We'll study to-gether, here, from now on. You don't ever have to see those children again."

536   ※   Cynthia Keller

Still crying, Katie ran into the bedroom and shut the door, locking it behind her. Rachel, shocked, stared at the closed door. She had never seen her child do anything like that before. She rarely cried to begin with, but, if she did, she explained what was bothering her, they talked it through together, and the storm blew over. This was something else entirely.

Katie refused to come out of the bedroom all evening. Rachel called Nick and made their excuses, claiming an oncoming cold. She alternated between trying to convince Katie to come out and ordering her to, neither of which did any good. Until this point in her life, Katie had never even questioned an instruction or request by her mother; open defiance was unheard of for her. Consumed by guilt and furious at herself for setting off this chain of events, Rachel sat up on the couch for much of the night until she eventually fell into a restless sleep.

When she awoke, it was still dark, but she glanced at the wall clock in the kitchen to see it was nearly five A.M. With relief, she saw the bedroom door standing open at last.

"Katie?" she called, hurrying into the room. "We really need to talk about this."

By the moonlight that slipped in through the curtains, Rachel could see Katie's quilt thrown back to reveal only pillows atop the white sheets. She called her daughter's name again. Silence. There was no one in the bedroom.

Refusing to acknowledge what she already sensed, she went over to the bathroom. Even if Katie had been in there, she would have heard her mother calling. Still, she threw open the door. The room was empty. Rachel's heart started to beat faster. She called Katie's name several times more, her panic growing as she received no response. Crossing the bedroom, she yanked open the closet door. Katie's new clothes seemed to be there. Then she noticed what was missing: their suitcase and all her daughter's Amish clothing.

Rachel ran to the apartment door. The chain lock was unlatched. No one had come in since they had returned from Katie's school the day before. Which meant that, sometime while Rachel was sleeping, Katie had gone out.

Her stomach heaved with fear. She grabbed the phone, her fingers trembling so badly she misdialed and had to start again. *Come on, come on,* she told herself. Gil answered on the third ring, his voice thick with sleep.

"Hello?"

"It's Rachel. Oh, Gil, please help me . . ."

He was instantly awake. "Rachel? What is it?"

"Katie's gone. She's not here."

"What do you mean, gone?"

"I was asleep, and she left. Sometime during the night. I don't know if she went with someone or by herself. But she's not here, in the apartment!"

She could hear Nina's sleepy voice in the background. "What is it, Gil?"

"Rachel, stay right there," he commanded. "I'm going to call the police."

"Yes, the police," she repeated, thinking she might faint.

"Could she really have gone off on her own?" he asked. "Where would she go? Did she have any money?"

Rachel hadn't thought of that. She yanked open the desk drawer where she kept the cash that the Lawrences replenished regularly for everyday expenses. There was usually around two hundred dollars there. The drawer was empty.

"She took the money from here. Oh, Gil, what was she going to with it?"

"Don't worry, we'll find her. Just sit tight and we'll be right over."

"Please hurry." She hung up the phone and broke down completely, her body shaking as she wept in pure terror.

Chapter 33

"... and when I came back in, there was Noodle on top of the table, finishing off the loaf of bread I had just put out for dinner and the stick of butter next to it." Sarah shook her head in amusement as Ellie and Laura laughed. The three were cleaning up in Sarah's kitchen, having just finished making an enormous pot of beef stew and another one of chicken and rice soup. Fragrant heat filled the kitchen.

"If we like butter with our bread, why shouldn't he?" Laura asked. "He just didn't bother to spread it."

Ellie was still smiling as she hung the dish towel on a hook. The camaraderie she had developed with these two women was a source of great pleasure to her, but also one of amazement. Initially, they had been polite and friendly, but that had developed into a warmth and good humor that she now cherished. Being with them had become so remarkably easy. The three of them smiled at the same things—and with the same smile.

While the two women had once seemed like strangers on a distant shore, they now felt to her like actual sisters. And this town had started to feel like home.

Ellie said her good-byes and drove down the road, planning to stop at home to shower and run a few errands before going to work the lunch shift. As she was unlocking her front door, she could hear the phone ringing inside. She rushed to answer it.

"Hello?"

"Ellie! Oh, thank goodness, you're there! It's Rachel."

Ellie could hear something frantic in the other woman's voice. "Rachel? Are you all right?"

"It's Katie. She ran away."

Ellie caught her breath.

"She left the apartment sometime during the night. I was asleep. I don't know where she went."

Ellie sank down into a chair. "Oh, no!"

"The police are looking for her. Gil and Nina are helping me. And Nick. Everyone. But I've been wondering if there's a small chance she somehow tried to go back to the farm. I don't know how she could do it, but maybe she got on a bus or train by herself."

Ellie listened with mounting horror. Somehow, she felt complicit in this situation. Having them stay in her apartment, and for such a long time, had been her idea. Apparently, it had led to something terrible enough to push this most innocent of children to defy everything she had been taught. Ellie couldn't imagine the girl making her way alone through the streets in the dark, buying a bus or train ticket. Not only could she have been in danger, traveling by herself at night, but the sweet, naïve child who had left here would have never done that. Something must have changed in Katie. Or hardened her. Ellie was sickened by the thought that her actions somehow brought this about.

Rachel started to cry on the other end of the line. The sound galvanized Ellie.

"I'll go look for her. You'll be at the apartment if I have to reach you?"

"Yes," Rachel got out.

"Fine. I'm on my way right now."

Ellie hung up and raced out, back into her car. She tried to think where she should go first. As she drove, she scanned the road, hoping against hope she would see Katie making her way back to the farm. If anything happened to her, Ellie knew she could never forgive herself. Afraid panic would overtake her, she gripped the wheel more tightly.

"Take it easy and think!" she commanded herself.

The bus station first. That was how she got to New York and back in the past, so that would be the likely way she would return this time. But where was the bus station around here?

Nearly passing a gas station, she whipped the wheel to the right, hard, and pulled in, stopping right by the glass door leading to the inside food mart. She left the driver's-side door open, running in to ask the attendant where someone coming from New York City would get off a bus.

He thought for a moment. "Lancaster would be best, I guess."

Calling out a thank-you, she ran back to her car and headed toward Lancaster. It seemed to take an eternity, but when she got there, she stopped at another gas station to get directions and sped over, her brakes screeching as she parked the car and ran toward the building. She yanked open the door and practically burst inside.

Over in a corner, Katie sat in a plastic chair, her head down, her suitcase on the ground beside her. Ellie thought her heart would burst out of her chest.

"Katie!" She flew across the room.

The little girl looked up. The expression on her face was both relieved and afraid.

"Ellie?" she asked hesitantly.

"Oh, sweetheart." Ellie gathered the child in her arms. "You're actually here. How did you get here? Does anyone else know you're here? Did you call your mother?"

She shook her head. "I—"

"Never mind." Ellie stood up. "We have to find a pay phone." Holding Katie's hand, she half dragged her to a window, asking where they could find a telephone, only to be informed there weren't any public phones there.

"Miss, would you like to use mine?" A middle-aged man had seen how upset Ellie was at the news, and extended his cell phone to her.

"Oh, thank you so much!" Grateful, Ellie pressed the numbers to her apartment in New York. Rachel picked up on the first ring.

"I've got her, Rachel, she's okay," Ellie said.

"She's there, at home? And she's safe?" Rachel's voice broke as she started to cry with relief. "Oh, Ellie, you don't know. . . . I was so afraid."

"You don't need to be afraid anymore. She's fine. She took a bus."

Rachel's voice made it clear how stunned she was, even though she had suggested the idea earlier. "I can't believe it. I taught her how to get around the streets in case she got lost. She was better at it than I was. But that she understood enough to do something like this . . ."

"She's fine, so you don't have to worry. She's home, safe and sound."

"I'll be on the next bus."

"Fine. I'll tell everyone."

The idea of her other family members gave Rachel pause. "Yes, everyone," she finally echoed. "Good-bye."

Ellie disconnected the call and gave the phone back to its rightful owner with her thanks. She turned to look at Katie, who was clearly exhausted and upset.

This was the worst of the Kings' fears realized, Ellie thought. Right now, though, they had to be told what had happened. She knew they wouldn't blame her outright, but she would always feel responsible for this mess. She had brought the outside world into their community, and this was the result.

She put a gentle hand on Katie's shoulder. "Have you been sitting here long?"

"I didn't know what to do. I got here, but then . . ." she trailed off.

"It's okay, it doesn't matter. What's important is that you're here and you're in one piece. Now let's get back to your grandparents' house."

Filled with dread, Ellie led her back to the car and started out for the farm. When they arrived, she took Katie by the hand and opened the kitchen door.

Sarah, Laura, and Leah were all there. They turned at the sound of the door.

Sarah, standing closest to it, saw their visitors first. "Katie! I didn't know you were coming home."

Katie's expression didn't suggest she was happy to be home. It was such an uncharacteristic expression, all three women looked at her with concern.

"Where's your mother?" Laura asked.

Her eyes on her shoes, Katie said something too quietly for them to hear.

"What was that?" Sarah asked.

Ellie realized distress must have been evident on her own face, as the women looked at her and she saw they immediately knew something was wrong.

"I drove Katie home from the bus station," Ellie said, wondering how best to explain the situation.

"What do you mean? Where is Rachel?" Sarah asked.

"She isn't here." Ellie realized she wasn't going to come up with any good way to break this news. "Katie left New York City last night without telling her mother. Somehow, she got to a bus station and rode here all by herself."

Laura's hand flew to her mouth.

"No!" Sarah gasped aloud.

Sarah came around to bend over slightly in front of Katie, who looked into her aunt's eyes. "Your mother didn't know you left or where you were going?"

Katie shook her head.

"You just disappeared."

"Rachel called to tell me she was missing. I just spoke to her again, and she knows Katie's home. She'll be on the next bus back," Ellie informed them.

"What did she say?" Sarah wanted to know, as if trying to comprehend.

"That Katie ran away, and the police had been looking for her. She cried with happiness that Katie was here and okay."

"It is no thanks to her that Katie is okay." Leah had said nothing so far, and the icy tone she used now was one Ellie had never heard from her. "She put her child in harm's way, and now is thankful that nothing happened? I warned her about going to that city!"

Ellie wanted desperately to ask Katie what made her do something so drastic to get back to the farm, but she knew it wasn't her place to do so. She also understood her presence was unwarranted and probably unwanted at this point. No one spoke or looked over as she let herself out.

Ellie had planned to eat supper at Sarah's that evening, but decided it would be best if she stayed away. She didn't want to be an interfering presence in the family's crisis. Even though she had come to feel like a true member of the family—as much as a non-Amish person could be—she knew this was a time to remember that she was, in fact, still an outsider and always would be.

Carson was working late, and she was off that night, so it wasn't until she got hungry much later at night that she fixed herself a sandwich, and sat down alone at her table to eat. As she bit into it, she was startled by the sharp buzz of her doorbell. She was hard-pressed to guess who would be visiting her so late on a cold December night. Before opening the door, she asked who it was. She was shocked to hear the reply.

"It's Rachel."

She stood outside, one of Ellie's small suitcases on the ground beside her, looking cold and utterly dejected.

"Come on in." Ellie grabbed the suitcase and waved her in from the frigid air.

"I'm sorry," Rachel said, stepping inside, "I had to borrow one of your bags because Katie took—"

Ellie made a dismissive gesture to indicate the suitcase wasn't important. "Please, let me make you some tea." She glanced outside as she pulled the front door shut, but didn't see a taxi or buggy pulling away. "How did you get here?"

"I walked."

"From the bus station?" Ellie went to fill the teakettle with water.

"I took a taxi from the bus to my house. But my parents won't let me in. So I walked here."

Ellie stopped what she was doing and stared at her guest. "What do you mean, your parents won't let you in?"

"My mother doesn't want me to see Katie. She says I knew it was the wrong thing to do, to take her there, but I did it anyway. For selfish reasons. She said I shouldn't ever be allowed to see Katie." Rachel was fighting back tears.

"Oh, my," Ellie whispered. This was even worse than she had feared. "What about your father?"

"He wouldn't come to the door."

"I'm so sorry." Ellie came over and sank down in a chair next to Rachel. "You'll sleep here, of course."

Rachel managed a small smile. "Thank you."

Ellie's heart broke for both Rachel and her child. "Do you know why Katie ran away?"

"It was a lot of things, but I know what finally made her leave."

She told the story, then sat back, misery on her face.

"Tomorrow, we'll sort everything out," Ellie said, getting up and reaching for the suitcase with Rachel's things. "Now it's time for you to sleep. Luckily, I never got around to moving the bed out of my second bedroom here, so you have your own room for as long as you need it."

"Thank you again."

Ellie couldn't bear the sadness in Rachel's eyes. "It will be all right," she whispered, more to reassure herself. "We'll make it be all right."

In the morning, Ellie bundled up against the cold and left without seeing Rachel, only the closed door to her room. At the barn, Isaac, Moses, and Judah offered subdued greetings. They were usually quiet, but today there was near-silence as they all worked. By now, Ellie was adept enough to do her part without instruction or supervision. When she finished, she told them she wouldn't be staying for breakfast, receiving nods in return. It hadn't been an angry silence, she reflected as she drove home, but a sad one. There was trouble, and one family member's trouble was everyone's.

Ellie walked into her still-dark house to find Rachel sitting at the kitchen table, fully dressed, drinking a cup of tea.

"May I turn on a light?" Ellie asked.

Rachel nodded, so she flicked on the overhead light but adjusted the dimmer to keep it low. She sat down across from Rachel.

"Did you get any sleep?"

Rachel set down her teacup. "Here's the problem," she said, as if they were in the middle of a conversation. "I shouldn't have brought Katie with me to New York, although I can't see how I could have left her behind. But I should have. I was the one who needed to go there, not her. It *was* selfish, and being selfish is a terrible thing. But could I really *not* spend time with my family when I had this chance? Or not have her get to know them?"

"I might not be the one to ask. Look at what I did—I forced you and everyone else to let me meet you all. I didn't even try to find out whether you wanted that or whether it would be a good thing for everyone else involved. I forced my way in. I even moved down here, just like that!"

"Are you sorry you did?"

"No, oh, no. It's been one of the best decisions I ever made. But now I have to ask myself, at what cost to you? I pushed you to take my apartment, and from that, everything else followed."

Rachel's eyes widened. "Don't think that! You can't! It's not true." She sighed. "Once we both got the letter, it all had to happen the way it did. Even if you hadn't come here, and I had gone on pretending nothing had changed, sooner or later I would have wanted to meet my other family. You made the first move, so I got to pretend I didn't want any part of it. But I was lying to myself."

"Wow." Ellie got up to make herself a cup of coffee as she considered Rachel's surprising admission. "So now what do we do?"

"I realized some things on my bus ride, some things I wasn't quite ready to face. Until this forced me." She closed her eyes momentarily as if it was too difficult to look at Ellie while she confessed. "There is something about me that's not Amish, that must be from the part of me that's a Lawrence daughter. I want to learn."

"Learn? Learn what?"

"I want to study. Gil gave me books to read, and we would talk about them. I loved that so much. At night, if I wasn't working on a quilt, I sat up with some book he lent me, and I was completely happy. Some days, while Katie was at school, I went to the public library just to sit there and read. Then, when I saw those students at A.J.'s school . . ."

"But how? You've already gone through school here."

Rachel bit her lip. "I don't know how. But I have to."

Ellie stalled for time, slowly pouring milk into her coffee cup before returning to the table. She was at a loss for words, but Rachel didn't wait for her to say anything else.

"I know it's not acceptable for me to go on. But I need to find a way. Now I see that this has been what's missing for me. I love delving into things, getting to the heart of issues I'd never even heard of before. I want to go to school. Or I'll teach myself, I don't care. But I need to learn."

"But what about—"

Rachel held up a hand. "There are so many questions. I don't have any answers yet. I know only two things. I'm Amish, and I always want to be Amish. Maybe if Jacob had lived, I would have gone on very happily just that way. But now I know a second thing, too. I need my life to be a little bigger, a little broader."

They sat in silence.

Rachel finally broke it. "May I ask you for a favor?"

"Of course."

"Would you tell Katie I'm not angry or upset with her? She may be worrying about that. Tell her I'm very sorry about what she went through, and I'm just happy she's okay."

"Oh, yes, right away." She jumped up. "I'll go now."

Rachel's voice was quiet. "Thank you, Ellie."

When she pulled the car up to the King house, she saw Katie, wearing her shawl and bonnet, heading toward the horse barn. She called the little girl's name. It was still dark, but Katie recognized her voice and came toward the car. Leaving the headlights on, Ellie got out and put an arm around her.

"Your mother is at my house."

Katie's face grew anxious. "Is she okay?"

"She's fine. She wanted me to tell you something."

As Ellie relayed the message, she saw Katie's worried expression relax a bit.

"I didn't mean to cause so much trouble," she said. "I just wanted to get away from everything. The other children. And the big buildings, and no space. I loved it so much at first. Then it was all so—I couldn't think straight. But I shouldn't have done such a thing to my mother and everybody. Are Grandma and Grandpa in New York mad at me?"

Ellie quickly reassured her that no one was mad at her, just glad she was safe.

"I've made a mess of everything."

"Sweetheart, no!" Ellie put an arm around Katie and brought her close. The little girl didn't protest, but leaned into her. "If there's a mess, I promise you had nothing to do with it." She put her hand under Katie's chin and lifted her face up so she was looking directly at her. "You don't want to be running away again, though, right? Giving a whole bunch of people heart attacks!" She smiled to try to lighten the impact of her words. "But you've been the greatest kid, and I know that for a fact. Grandma and Grandpa loved you so much. Everyone did—Nick and A.J., everyone. You made a lot of people very happy."

Katie shook her head. "Not my mother. When can I see her?"

Ellie had no idea how to answer, so she took a step back, rubbing her gloved hands together. "Listen, it's too cold to stand around out here. You're off to the barn, right? I'm going inside, and I'll see you later, okay?"

"Okay."

Ellie made her way to the house, not sure what to expect. By now, the family would have finished breakfast, so they would probably be scattered, doing their various chores. Instead, she opened the door to see Leah, Isaac, Hannah, and Amos sitting at the kitchen table, coffee cups before them, solemn expressions on their faces. Fearful of how they would react to her, she stuck just her head in.

"May I come in?"

Isaac answered first. "Yes, of course."

Ellie joined them and waited to see what they wanted—or were willing—to say to her.

"Coffee for you?" Hannah asked.

"No, thank you, nothing."

"They tell me Rachel is with you," Amos said. "Is she all right?"

"Yes. She's very upset, but she's all right."

"We are very upset as well," Isaac said. "This turned out badly."

"I can only apologize with all my heart for the part I played in bringing this situation to all of you."

"But we don't think you played a part in this," Isaac said. "I don't know why you have such an idea. It was Rachel's decision to go to New York. You had nothing to do with it."

"But if I hadn't come here . . ."

Leah spoke for the first time. "Ellie, you don't understand. You are part of our family. You came here and brought us many good things. We are very happy that you now live here. It would have been terrible to find out we had a daughter, and never know her. Rachel is like the other side of a coin. The two of you are forever connected, but not together. What she does about the situation is her part of it. It has nothing to do with you."

"That's very gracious of you."

"Not gracious. It is just the way it is. Like what you do is not because of anything she does."

"It is such a situation to be in," Isaac said, "to find out you have new parents."

Ellie saw an opening to plead Rachel's case. "Because everyone wants to know their parents, and needs their parents, no matter who or where they are."

"Yes, of course," Hannah said.

"I'm lucky. I have four parents to love. I want to be with all of them, and I'm not even a child." She paused. "By the way, I saw Katie outside. She asked me when she could see her mother. I didn't know what to tell her. So I hope you'll tell me what you want done as we go forward."

Pain was evident in Isaac's eyes. "We will."

Ellie got up. She hadn't been subtle, and from the tilt of her head, she saw that Leah understood exactly what she was doing. Ellie knew she had overstepped her bounds, and she hoped they wouldn't be upset with her for it. But she had come to love all these people, and she would do anything if it would help resolve the fissure that was threatening to tear them apart.

"I'll go help tend to the horses," she said.

Isaac suddenly looked exhausted, and Ellie wished she could go over and hug him. "I'll come outside soon. We still have much to talk about here."

Ellie only hoped their talk would end up with all the broken parts—and hearts—being put back together.

Chapter 34

�֎

"Hi." Ellie, her nose red from the cold, came in and greeted Rachel, who was scrambling eggs to go along with a platter of pancakes. Seeing the enormous breakfast, Ellie laughed. "The two of us are going to eat this?"

Rachel looked a bit sheepish. "It's habit, I guess. I tried to cut down, but when you're used to cooking for so many, it's hard. I did it a lot in New York, too, but I froze the leftovers. We could freeze the pancakes, right?"

"I suppose. Anyway, it looks great." Ellie retrieved a bottle of syrup and poured two glasses of orange juice.

"So, please tell me what you saw."

The two of them sat down and helped themselves to food as Ellie spoke. She had just returned from the morning chores at the farm, and knew that after her second sleepless night in Ellie's house, Rachel had been waiting anxiously for her report.

"It seemed better than yesterday. Less tension in the air."

Ellie took a large bite of pancake. "So do you know what you're going to do when you go over there?"

"I have to see what happens. Maybe they won't want to talk to me."

"But you're going to talk to them about school, right?"

"I guess."

Ellie's tone turned stern. "Rachel, you have to! You have to try, at least. If it can't be done, that's one thing. But do you want to give up without even finding out if it's possible?"

Rachel gave her head an unhappy shake.

"There's got to be some way. This is such an unusual situation—can't you get some leeway here?"

"I don't want to do anything to my family that's going to cause them more pain."

Ellie finished her eggs, considering Rachel's words. "You know, it's really not for me to tell you what to do. Coming from my background, I can't help but encourage you. But that's not fair because it's not your background. Maybe I'm pushing you, and I shouldn't sow seeds of dissatisfaction. I apologize."

Her food only half eaten, Rachel pushed her plate away. "No, I appreciate your support. It was simpler before I found out the truth about me, about *us*."

Ellie took several plates to the sink and turned on the water. "I wonder what would have happened if we'd found out when we were younger. Like, say fifteen years old. Maybe I would have become Amish. It might have been possible when I was that age."

Rachel deposited the rest of the dirty dishes on the counter. "That was around the time I actually did experiment with living like the English. I might have spent more time away from here than I did. Still, now that I see what it means to come home, I think in the end I probably would have returned anyway."

"And maybe I wouldn't have appreciated the things here that I can appreciate now. We'll never know what either one of us would have done, eh?" Ellie smiled.

The telephone rang. Hurriedly drying her hands, Ellie picked up the receiver. Rachel heard her mention Carson's name, and a brief conversation followed.

She hung up and turned to Rachel. "One of the waitresses at the new café called in sick. They need me to do the lunch shift. But I'm going over now to help get ready."

"Oh."

Ellie looked concerned. "I wanted to go to the house with you. You'll go, right?"

"Of course I will. I didn't know you wanted to come with me."

"Moral support." Ellie gave her a quick hug.

Three hours later, however, Rachel was still in Ellie's house, dreading the confrontation with her family. But she knew if she waited much longer, Katie would get home from school. Her daughter had been through enough without being exposed to whatever unpleasantness might result from her appearance there; it was that thought that finally forced her to put on her shawl and bonnet.

The day was overcast and bitingly cold. Head down against the wind, she made her way along the road. When she reached the Kings' farm, she walked toward the barn, where she figured she was most likely to find her father. Entering the building, she recognized the warmth and smells from what felt like a long time ago. She saw Isaac at once, moving around among the cows. When he emerged into the wide middle aisle, he looked in her direction and stopped.

"Hello," she called, hoping her voice didn't shake.

"Rachel." He took a few steps in her direction.

Her relief was so great, she practically ran toward him.

"It's a long time since you've been at home," he said.

"Yes."

"I've missed you very much, you and Katie."

Fighting against tears, she nodded. "I've missed you, too."

"Many things happened there in New York City."

It wasn't a question, but she knew he was waiting for an explanation.

"It wasn't good for Katie, I see that now. But there was a lot of good in it."

He didn't say anything.

"You understood, didn't you—that I had to go?"

"I did."

"You were right, of course; it's easier for Ellie to live here than for me to live there. She can continue to be who she was before. Too much there is wrong for us." She paused. "But those people are my family, too."

"Yes, little one, they are."

He hadn't called her by that nickname in many years, and hearing it made her want to cry all over again.

"They're good people. They were so kind to us. And . . .

they taught me some things about myself that I needed to know."

"What things are those?"

She took a deep breath. "I want to go back to school. To study again."

She saw the stunned look on her father's face, but couldn't stop the words from pouring out of her. "It's always been what I wanted. I just didn't realize. You never knew, but when I was a teenager, living away from here, I took some high school courses. It wasn't allowed, so I never told you. But now I've seen all the learning going on everywhere around me, and I want to be one of those people. Those people who learn."

Isaac rubbed the back of his neck as he considered the significance of what she was saying. "You want to go back to school? You know this is not how we do things. Besides, there isn't any place for you to go. You would need to go to high school, but you are a grown woman."

"There are things you can study through the mail. Or get a home course. Oh, I don't know what's involved, but you don't have to go to a physical school."

He looked at her for a few moments. "This is something you have always wanted?"

"I think so, yes. But I didn't understand it. I was so busy with Jacob and then Katie . . . But when I read books in New York, it was like I found a place that belonged to me. Or a place where I belonged. My life had an empty spot in it, and I finally saw that."

He sighed. "I don't understand this. But I guess for you it is different."

"Tell me what to do," she whispered.

He thought. "There's only one answer. We must speak with the bishop. He'll decide what can or cannot be done, and how we are to do it." He smiled at her. "You know he is always wise, and very fair. I'm sure he will have the answer."

She nodded. The bishop for their church district was the one who would decide what came next. All such major decisions about what was permissible or not were made by him. She had always respected him, and she hoped he would find a way to help her now.

"Have you seen your mother?" Isaac asked.

"I wasn't sure she was willing to see me."

"Go to her."

Rachel looked at her father with love, and he smiled before turning back to his work.

She didn't have to go far to locate her mother. Coming around the corner of the house, she found Leah King standing in the doorway, waiting for her. As usual, she missed nothing.

"Good morning." Rachel stopped in front of her.

"I'm ironing. Come with me."

Leah turned and went back to work without waiting to see if her daughter followed. For a moment, Rachel reveled in being back amid the comforting sight and smells of the family kitchen.

Leah still hadn't spoken, and Rachel was unsure how to break the silence. She mustered her courage as best she could, then went to stand near the ironing board.

"I know you're disappointed," she finally got out.

Shaking her head, Leah looked at her. "That was yesterday.

I'm not today. And I'm very sorry for my anger. Being wrong that way is as bad as doing something wrong."

"You're not angry?" Rachel knew her mother meant exactly what she said, but she found it hard to believe.

Leah set down the iron. "I'm just a person. I have many weaknesses, as we all do. But forgiveness is so important . . . I'm very sad and ashamed about my anger. I hope you can forgive *me*."

"Don't say that! There's nothing for me to forgive."

Rachel was surprised when her mother took her by the hand and led her to the sofa to sit down.

"It's time to speak of some things I never thought I would speak of," Leah began. "The truth is that I was always harder on you than I was on the other children."

"Harder?"

"I was more strict. I didn't allow you to do what I allowed them to do. You may not have realized it, but it was so."

"But why?"

Leah looked down as she folded her hands in her lap. "Because I worried the most about you."

"I don't understand."

"You were the most like me. And I tried to change that about you."

Stunned, Rachel didn't know what to say. Her mother's eyes rose to meet Rachel's as she continued.

"I was a girl like you. I had a lot of questions and doubts. I wanted to do and see all the time. When I was a teenager I had my own times when I thought about leaving for good to go into the English world."

"Not you." Rachel couldn't believe what she was hearing, the words contradicting everything she thought she knew about her mother.

"Yes. It was very hard for me. Then, when I married your father and I left my family to come live here, it was hard in other ways. But we had our children, and our life has been a good, busy one. I found contentment in our ways, and any doubts I ever had disappeared."

Rachel could only nod.

"I know this must shock you. But you need to understand that I knew what you were going through. I was very afraid that you might actually leave us, first when you were around seventeen, and then, after Jacob . . . Now, you find a different family who would take you in, to live in the English world if you want to go. I've been so worried that I didn't do a good enough job, and you would take this chance and go."

Rachel spoke softly. "I always thought you didn't have the same feelings for me as you did for the others. Because I caused you so much trouble."

Leah was clearly shocked. "That's not true! I felt for every child the same. But I feared for you because you were so much like me. The others are more like your father."

"All these years, I thought . . ." Rachel shook her head in amazement. "The crazy part is that it turns out I'm not even your daughter."

"Don't say that. You are. I didn't give birth to you, but you are."

"But you were worried because I was so much like you." Rachel started to laugh. "You realize how confusing this is?"

A smile spread across Leah's face, and she began to laugh as well.

"Grandma, we can start—" Katie came into the room at that moment. When she saw her mother, she bolted across the room and threw her arms around her. "Here you are!"

Rachel hadn't realized she'd been at the house long enough for Katie to get back from school. She was grateful beyond words that her daughter had come in to find her mother and grandmother laughing together; it so easily could have been otherwise. "Yes, my Katie, here I am. And so are you, I'm thankful to see."

"I'm sorry. I'm so sorry."

"Shhh . . ." Rachel rocked her child. "It's over now. Everything is fine."

"So, now you will come home," Leah said in a satisfied tone.

Rachel considered how to answer. She looked up from Katie to her mother. "We have much more to talk about, you and I. Tonight, yes?"

Leah leaned back with a small sigh that indicated she understood the situation was far from resolved. "Tonight, Rachel." She shook her head, but with a small smile. "Yes."

For the first time since she had returned from New York, Rachel felt a glimmer of genuine hope. Somehow, she felt, she would find a way to put everything together: her life here, her child, her wish to study. This was where she would find her peace, even if it would have to be forged in an unusual way. It would be all right; she knew it.

What surprised her was that the first person she wanted to share this knowledge with was Ellie.

Chapter 35

Ellie peered out the living room window. Snow blanketed the ground outside, sparkling in the sun, and the air was crisp and clear. Their company was due any minute.

Carson came up behind her. "You're watching for your parents? You're as excited as a little kid."

"I can't help it," she said, turning to smile at him. "Having my family meet everybody here—I can't wait to see it."

"Not nervous, are you?"

"A little, I guess. Although I don't know why. By the way, did I tell you how handsome you look in your jacket and tie?"

"You did, but please feel free to tell me as often as you like. The least I can do after being invited. If I didn't pull out a jacket for Christmas, when would I?"

She caught sight of two cars approaching from far down the road. "Hey, there they are."

"They're outside?" Having finished lighting the candles

along the table, Laura was now attending to the ones in the windows.

Ellie nodded. The room was already buzzing with people and activity. Everyone in the King family was in attendance for Christmas dinner, although at the moment the children were out back, alternating between making snowmen and throwing snowballs. All the women from Hannah down to Katie were busy in the kitchen putting the finishing touches on what Ellie knew would be a true feast. She had brought along a basket with nearly fifty biscuits, glad she had mastered the baking of at least one thing that would be useful at this meal. Earlier in the week, the children had made and sent out Christmas cards, mostly to their non-Amish family acquaintances, with Katie including A.J. and Steve, plus her many relatives in New York. For today, they had contributed their handmade decorations of angels and stars to hang around the room. This, Ellie now understood, was the type of decorating typically done in an Amish home for Christmas; no trees or Santa Claus, just a simple celebration to recall the purpose of the day.

Taking in the smells of cooking food and the simplicity of the room, she almost sighed aloud with pleasure. From working in a world filled with artifice, she had magically come to be celebrating Christmas in this place of spiritual peace and truthfulness.

The two cars pulled up just outside the door. Ellie and Carson went out to greet everyone. Her parents and grandfather had driven up together, followed by Nick in a separate car with his girlfriend, Winnie, plus A.J. and Steve. Typically, Christmas was a two-day holiday for the Amish, and the Kings would be having their big holiday dinner on the following day, December 26, but this was the only day Ellie's family could come, so it was agreed. In fact, Ellie knew the Kings would have another get-together tomorrow for their Amish friends. Today, though, was just for the two families to meet.

The visitors were laden with shopping bags full of gifts. After consulting with Ellie about what would be appropriate, the Lawrences had brought food for the adults: several boxes of chocolates, five pounds each of pistachios and cashew nuts, two cheesecakes and a huge box of assorted pastries, plus enough of what had been Katie's favorite ice cream in New York so everyone could have some. For the children, they had art supplies, bats and balls, a skateboard for each family, and board games. Katie got a pair of ice skates, which Ellie had told her parents she needed.

Nina and Gil were overjoyed to see Ellie, both of them remarking how happy and healthy she looked. There were introductions all around for Carson, and Ellie got to meet Winnie, with whom Nick was apparently getting serious.

"You're brave to come here with him today," Ellie whispered to her.

Winnie was a petite brunette with a wide smile. "I'm thrilled to be asked."

Ellie went over to her mother, and the two of them watched as Nick's date moved to stand beside him. She linked her hand through his arm, and he immediately drew her into the conversation he was having with Carson.

"What do you think?" Ellie whispered.

"She's lovely, and good to him," Nina whispered back. "He seems crazy about her. I hope this is the one that sticks."

"That would be great."

"What about Carson?" Nina nodded in his direction. "How do you feel about him?"

Ellie couldn't help grinning as she watched him. "I wouldn't believe I could feel this way about anybody if I hadn't seen it with my own eyes."

Nina smiled at her. "Or felt it with your own heart."

They were interrupted by the appearance of Rachel in the doorway, calling out welcomes and urging everyone inside. The noise level rose as the children chose that minute to come inside through a side door. With happy cries, the Lawrences hugged Rachel and Katie, exclaiming how much they had missed them. There was a brief interlude of some confusion as, all over the room, coats were shed and hung on hooks or deposited in a bedroom, and boots pulled off.

Ellie and Rachel wound up standing next to each other at the moment their mothers finally came face-to-face. They watched as Nina Lawrence and Leah King stopped and looked at each other. There was a silent exchange of emotion and recognition for what the other had gone through, what they had lost and now gained. Then, without a word, they embraced as if they were long-lost sisters themselves.

"Total strangers, yet look. I wasn't expecting that," Ellie murmured to Rachel.

"No, but I guess it makes sense." Rachel moved to assist with the food now being taken to the fully extended table. Over her shoulder, she added, "This is their life story, too, isn't it?"

Ellie had never thought of it that way. Both mothers had lived through stories they would never have expected. That Ellie had moved to Pennsylvania had drastically changed Nina Lawrence's world. Of course, for now, it was Leah King who had made the biggest accommodation. Her daughter was living in Ellie's house and taking an accelerated study program for a high school equivalency diploma. That had been the most difficult adjustment for all the Kings. Fortunately for Rachel, the bishop felt that the extraordinary circumstances allowed for this most unusual arrangement. Katie continued to live at the farm with her grandparents. During the week, Rachel took classes, studied, and visited whenever she could manage. On the weekends, Rachel returned to the farm to sleep there and be with her daughter. It had been the supreme sacrifice for Rachel, being parted from her child for much of the week, but she wanted her to be brought up Amish, with all that entailed. She felt that living on the farm was the best thing for Katie, and that made the sacrifice worth it.

Ellie watched Gil Lawrence shake hands with Isaac. She could guess that he was wondering how she viewed this man, her new father, with his unfamiliar beard and haircut. She recalled how odd Isaac had appeared to her the first time she met him, and how absolutely normal all the Amish men's appearances struck her now. His patience and kindness had won her over, changing skepticism into respect and, finally, into love.

There was Katie, hugging her great-grandfather Louis, as

Hannah and Amos looked on. Nina and A.J. had already infil-trated the kitchen crowd, helping the other women take enor-mous platters of food to the table. Steve was engaged in conversation with Judah, Lonnie, and Daniel. Various children were summoned over to be introduced to the visitors; Ellie ob-served them making their customary cheerful greetings. She saw Moses, Nick, and Carson off in a corner looking at some papers, intent on their conversation. Just like that, she thought, everybody had found a spot.

"It is time to sit down now." Leah had to raise her voice to be heard above the din.

Following the Kings' lead, everyone found a place, men on one side of the table, women on the other. Ellie looked out over what appeared to be a sea of food. In the center were an enormous turkey and ham, surrounded by three kinds of pota-toes, at least five vegetables that she could see, various salads, buttered noodles, her biscuits and two types of bread. She knew there was practically this much food to follow for dessert.

Isaac announced they would have a silent prayer, and then the conversation grew loud once more as plates were passed, glasses filled, children settled in. The crowd ate and talked. Ellie, sitting next to A.J., told her sister that Carson had asked her to manage the four restaurants, and she had agreed.

"A promotion for you?" asked A.J. "With attendant salary increase?"

"Of course. Carson can't do it alone anymore, and he wants to build an organization that doesn't have to rely on him run-ning out in the middle of the night to deal with every little cri-sis."

"So you'll be in charge of things." A.J. raised one eyebrow. "Working your way back up the corporate ladder?"

Ellie laughed. "Not much of a corporate ladder in this case. If I suddenly notice I'm on one, I'll be sure to have you come catch me when I jump off."

Despite her teasing, A.J. was happy enough to hear Ellie's news that she passed it on to Nina, who immediately told Gil, and it went around the table until all the adults had heard about it.

Then Isaac indicated he wanted to speak, and everyone fell silent.

He smiled, looking around at his guests. "We welcome you to our home on this most important day. We have all experienced something together that very few families have or ever will. It is something we share, something that binds us all. At first, here, in my family, we were not sure what would happen. Two children, grown-ups, yes, but never living in the right house. We were afraid that we could have only one of them. We didn't understand what that would mean."

Ellie saw from their expressions that Isaac's words hit home with her parents. So many people had been affected, she thought, by the act of one person long ago.

"But," he went on, "it turns out that we can have both children. And so can you. Our children have two families. People they will care for, who will care for them in return. We are grateful. This is truly a gift for Christmas."

There were words of assent from those seated around the table.

Ellie observed her families, so many differences among the

members, worlds apart. Yet they were united by their good will in resolving a situation that could have torn them apart.

She had finally come to understand that she didn't have to choose. She could stay here, enjoying a way of life she had come to treasure and recognize as closest to her true nature. And she could go to New York to get a jolt of the special excitement she had grown up with, to relish the speed and noise before coming back. No one had to choose one set of siblings over another; they were all precious to her, Nick and A.J. more so now than ever. Like Rachel, she was a combination of all the traits and influences that surrounded her at this table today.

She caught Carson's eye from across the table. He looked at her lovingly, a smile on his face. Then, he gave her a quick wink. She grinned, and turned to hear what A.J. was saying to her. Rachel came up behind them with a refilled pitcher of water, and leaned over to put it in the center of the table, resting her hand on Ellie's shoulder. Ellie looked up at her and they locked eyes, registering without words their gratitude at having come so far from the mistrust and fearfulness of their early meetings to this moment.

The two of them had spent so much time, alone and together, pondering the meaning of what had happened, Ellie thought. Maybe identity was more fluid than she had ever realized. It could encompass all the feelings of belonging they had each come to know in both their worlds. As for the unanswerable question of what their proper destinies were meant to be, she knew that from then on, she would believe this was it, that they were both blessed to have two families.

No one could say where the two of them would end up.

Their stories were very different from what they had been before, but far from over. Yet, with all the disruption and overwhelming changes, they both had found a peace that had eluded them their entire lives. Until now. They might live within two worlds, but they had the best of both.

Read on for an excerpt from

An Amish Gift

BY

CYNTHIA KELLER

PUBLISHED BY BALLANTINE BOOKS

"What do you say, Scout? You want to stop for something to eat?"

Jennie Davis swiveled around as far as she could manage in the front passenger seat to direct her question to the black mutt with white paws and intelligent-looking black eyes, wedged in between the two teenagers in the back of the Honda.

Thirteen-year-old Willa rolled her eyes. "Mom, why do you always do that? Do you actually expect Scout to answer you?"

Jennie smiled at her daughter. "What makes you think he doesn't?"

Tim, her fifteen-year-old son, spoke with exaggerated bewilderment. "Now why would we think that? Maybe because that would make you the first person in history to have a conversation with a dog?"

Shep Davis glanced over at his wife. "After Scout has expressed his preference, could I get a vote? I'd like to stop for some coffee."

Jennie rested her hand on her husband's arm. "You know what? Even if Scout says no, we're stopping for your coffee."

He smiled. "Wow. I'm honored."

Jennie smiled back. "On the day Scout drives for seven hours, he can decide when to stop, too."

"She actually is insane." Tim looked down at the dog by his side. "Don't you think so?"

Scout only crossed his two front paws on the seat and rested his head on them.

Jennie nodded, satisfied. "You didn't think he would talk against me, did you?"

Willa smacked her hand to her forehead in a theatrical show of exasperation.

"Hey, more cows." Shep gestured in the direction of a small herd, tails swishing as they stood patiently in the hot August sun.

"It'd be nice to have our own cows," Willa said.

Jennie swung around in her seat again. "Honey, we're not going to have room for that. Not that we'd know how to take care of a cow, anyway. But, remember, this isn't a farm—it's a regular house. With a lot of farms around the area."

Jennie figured she was safe in making this limited assertion, but she hesitated to say anything more. They had seen only an old photograph of the house, taken from across the road. Online maps revealed it wasn't large, but they knew it contained at least three bedrooms, which was one more bedroom than they'd ever had before.

"Even with just one cow, we could have our own milk." Willa was getting excited by the idea. "It'd be all natural and stuff."

Tim groaned. "Listen to this. Wilma, do you know how hard it is to take care of a cow? You getting up in the middle of the night to milk it?"

"Don't call me Wilma!" She had always hated her brother's nickname for her. "And, don't worry, nobody expects you to get up to milk it. Hard work is definitely not for you."

"No, you're going to do it, right? The person who's afraid of her own shadow, just going to take charge of that two million pound animal."

"Will you two stop?" Shep asked in annoyance.

Jennie was pleased to see an opportunity for distraction. "Look, there's a place for coffee."

"Can I get some?" Willa asked.

"We've gone over this," Shep said to her. "No coffee at your age. The end."

"You can get something else, though," Jennie threw in. As long as it's not too expensive, she silently added. It was hard to know how long they would have to make their money last, and it was little enough to begin with.

After arming themselves with coffee and soda, they continued on the last leg of the trip, another forty-five minutes to the heart of Lancaster County. Jennie and Shep commented on the beauty of the countryside, admiring the wide-open fields dotted by clapboard houses and storybook-perfect farms. The children were far more intrigued by the occasional horses and buggies they passed, staring at the Amish men and women sitting in the open wagons. Willa waved at them, and was sometimes rewarded with a return wave from a woman or a man in a straw hat.

"That is beyond . . ." Tim's words were lost as he rolled down the window to stick his head out and get a better view of a man and a boy in a closed buggy.

"Stop gawking," Shep said. "They're people, not exhibits for your amusement."

Tim settled back into his seat. "If they didn't expect people to gawk, they wouldn't go out like that."

Shep glanced at his wife, who was consulting a map. "I can't believe what I'm hearing." He looked in the rearview mirror at his son. "I'm ashamed that you would say such a thing."

"Naturally," Tim snapped back. "When are you not ashamed of me?"

Jennie interrupted. "According to this, we should be coming up to our street soon. But I don't know whether we go right or left."

No one said anything in the few minutes it took to get to the next intersection.

"This is it," Jennie said. "There's the street sign, that little one."

"Okay, we'll try this way first." Shep made a wide turn to minimize any disturbance to the contents of the U-Haul trailer attached to their car. He drove slowly down the narrow road so they could check the mailboxes.

Their daughter, Willa, spotted it first.

"I think that says two-twenty-five. See?" The thirteen-year-old pointed, keeping her other arm securely wrapped around Scout.

The numbers were partially worn away from the old mailbox attached to a tilting wooden post. Shep pulled into the driveway, drove a few yards, then stopped so they could get a broad view of the house. He turned off the ignition. The four of them stared at the sight before them in dismayed silence. It was a small saltbox half hidden behind long-untended bushes.

A fresh beginning, Jennie reminded herself. This will be a fresh beginning. Inwardly, she groaned. They could deal with the overgrown front yard, but the driveway desperately needed repaving, and the house's paint was visibly peeling. She spotted a number of broken shutters at several windows; some were missing altogether. The whole thing was just sad-looking, she couldn't help thinking. Nor did it bode well for what they might find inside.

Her son was first to break the silence, his tone threatening. "This better not be the place."

Jennie tried to keep her voice cheerful. "It's the place all right."

Her husband glanced over at her. "We passed all those big, open fields. I kind of hoped . . ."

She put a hand on his. "I know."

Tim interrupted. "We left Lawrence for this?"

"Mom?" Willa's voice was tremulous. "Mom, is this for real?"

"Come on, kids." Jennie turned to them a final time. "It's not so bad. I know it's not what you probably dreamed of, but we'll fix it up."

"What we 'dreamed of'?" Tim snorted. "This place is a dump."

"But it's our dump. All ours, free and clear."

"Not sure what kind of person would pay for this," her husband muttered under his breath.

"Shep, that's not really helpful." Jennie spoke softly but forcefully to her husband. "We need to have a good attitude."

"In front of the children, you mean?" Tim turned to his sister. "Yes, by all means, let's delude the children. It's not as if they're smart enough to see for themselves that this is even worse than Lawrence."

"That's enough out of you," Shep snapped at him.

Jennie watched her husband get out of the car and slam the door. He was shaking his head, whether about the house or his son, she wasn't sure.

"Mom, Tim is right. This is way worse than our house," Willa pointed out in alarm.

True, Jennie thought, but she only smiled. "Nonsense. This place is ours, and our old place wasn't. We can make it into anything we want." She opened her car door. "And we'll make it wonderful."

Getting out to stand where the children couldn't see her, she let her smile fall away. Finding out four months ago that Shep was inheriting a house had felt like winning the lottery. It meant they could leave their half of the cramped two-family house they had been renting for nearly ten years and move into a place that was theirs alone. Even more incredible, it was completely paid off. It came to them courtesy of a cousin of Shep's mother whom no one had even known about. His mother had been dead for some twenty-five years, but apparently this cousin, Bert Howland, had been a close playmate of hers when they were children. His wife had died long ago, and he had no other living heirs, so he named Shep as the sole beneficiary of both his home and the bicycle shop he had apparently operated for over thirty years.

They had been astounded by this act of generosity from someone who may have been a family member but was a total stranger to them. It had even come at the perfect moment, with Shep having just lost his most recent job, and the two of them coming to the end of what little savings they had. It wasn't an easy move to make, but there wasn't anything holding them in Lawrence, the small Massachusetts town where they had both grown up. There were few jobs to be had there, and it had gotten grimmer with every passing year. Yet they had never considered leaving, certainly not to go to a strange part of the country where they didn't know a soul. The children were in shock about being dragged off to Lancaster County, which might as well have been the moon as far as they were concerned; characteristically, Tim was furious, Willa quietly miserable. Still, that was all beside the point. By some miracle, they had been given a reprieve from financial calamity through a place to live and a business handed to them with no strings attached.

The heat of the afternoon was oppressive. Jennie gazed at the large damaged patches on the roof of the house, wishing she could still feel the same gratitude toward this mysterious relative that she had felt earlier. At the moment, though, what she felt was dread as she contemplated the work ahead of them. Thank goodness she and Shep could do most of the physical labor themselves; he was a magician at fixing things, and she would help. Still, they couldn't afford to buy the materials they would need. More important, he had a new business to run, and she had to presume that it would demand most of his time and energy.

Well, she thought, they would simply find a way through this. Somehow, it would work out.

Scout bounded out of the car, thrilled to be released from his confinement. He gave a few joyful barks then raced over to follow Shep, tail wagging, as Willa came to join her.

"Let's see what it's like inside," Jennie said. She bent over to peer at Tim who was still in the backseat, his arms folded, his expression enraged. "You going to stay in there all day? I'd have thought you spent enough hours in the car today."

"I'd rather live here than there."

She sighed. "Okay, you've made your point. Now come on out."

Making no effort to hide his annoyance, he threw open the door and emerged. Tall and broad-shouldered, he looked remarkably like his father, with the same sandy-colored hair and hazel eyes. The only thing missing was the dimple on Shep's left cheek, which, to Jennie, made her husband only that much more handsome when he smiled. Willa, in contrast, resembled Jennie, both of them with brown eyes and long brown hair usually tied back in a low ponytail.

Tim leaned back against the car, hands shoved in his jean pockets, refusing to look anywhere but the ground.

"Fine, be that way," Jennie said in resignation, turning away and gesturing to her daughter to follow.

Her husband was already at the side of the house, frowning as he knelt to inspect the foundation. Jennie reached for the screen door, pleasantly surprised to find it appeared relatively new. That was one less thing they had to worry about, she thought. She would be grateful for small favors.

Inside the narrow front hall, she wasn't at all surprised to see a covering of dust practically everywhere. At best, no one would have been here to clean since Bert Howland had died, although, judging from the entryway's appearance, she guessed it had actually been a lot longer than six weeks. She took a quick tour of the cramped downstairs. Kitchen, half-bathroom, living room, dining room—all small, all apparently unchanged in decades. Dark, heavy wooden furniture did nothing to make the tiny rooms seem any larger. The living room had a rug with areas almost completely worn through in spots. She guessed that the old rocking chair next to a small table and black gooseneck lamp was where the house's inhabitant had spent much of his time; it held a flattened, faded seat cushion, and a thin pillow with a grimy gray pillowcase offered minimal back support. A coffee cup rested on the table. She leaned forward just far enough to look in, relieved to see it had a dried coffee stain on the bottom but was otherwise empty. In the kitchen, she found outdated appliances, rust on the stove and sink faucets, the refrigerator's door handle broken. Everything looked grimy.

Scout came bounding into the room, his tail wagging at the sight of her.

"So, what do you think?" she asked the dog, kneeling down to scratch behind his ears. "Could have been worse, you know. Way worse."

Hearing Willa's footsteps coming down the narrow staircase, she called out.

"In here, honey."

Her daughter appeared in the doorway, looking pale. "I checked out the bedrooms."

Jennie stood. "And?"

"They're, like, the size of shoeboxes. I mean, I'm not even kidding. There are two that are a joke, and I don't think anybody's been in them for about a hundred years. There's a third one, the big one, if you want to call it that, but don't bother. That's where he must have slept." She wrinkled her nose in distaste. "The bed has this nasty brown bedspread. I'm not touching it."

Her words reminded Jennie of what was missing here. She walked around a dividing wall that stuck partway out into the kitchen. Hidden behind the wall was a small mudroom area leading to the back door, crammed with old boots and work shoes, shovels, rakes, tools, and a large garbage can. With relief, she noted the washer and dryer beneath precarious piles of newspapers. She prayed they worked.

They both recognized the sound of Tim's footsteps, and listened as he apparently paused to peer into the rooms clustered close to the staircase. When he joined them in the kitchen, Jennie saw the familiar look in his eyes that said he was about to let his temper get the better of him. It was the expression that typically set his father off, which always resulted in the two of them fighting long and loud. She, however, chose to ignore it whenever possible. She held up a hand as if to stop him.

"Don't, Tim, just don't. There's nothing you can say that we don't know."

"Can we go back home, please?" He made no effort to hide the fury behind his words. "Like, right now."

"You know there's no 'back home' to go to. This is home."

CYNTHIA KELLER lives in Connecticut
with her husband and two children.